I0649874

His Alpha, Her Prince

Book Six of The Brother Series

C. Hazlewood

C HAZLEWOOD AUTHOR LLC

To my pain in the ass husband.

Contents

1

BUTTERFLY

Rosie

"Rose, your dad is going to kill you," Sophia hissed, staring at the outline of a tattoo on my shoulder in dismay. "What the hell are you thinking?"

"Calm your tits. Jeez. I'm an adult now. He can't tell me what to do anymore." I said, but knew it wasn't true. The only time my dad, Alpha Parker Snider of the Crystal Moon Pack, ever blew up was when I pushed his buttons. Even mom couldn't piss him off as well as I could.

Getting a tattoo, marring my skin permanently when he already told me no, was one of the things that would undoubtably set him off. Big time set him off. I was going to have to throw a fit back to get him off my case, but it would be worth it.

I've wanted a tattoo for over a year now, since the last time I saw *him*. Taegan. He had just gotten a full sleeve before coming with my cousins for a visit to Miami from their pack in Canada. An intricately designed tattoo, a swirling mosaic of ethereal pictures and complicated shapes, covered the thick muscles in his arm. There was something otherworldly about all the images. It made my mouth water with the desire, wanting to trace the delicate artwork with my tongue, something I hoped I could do soon.

Taegan Kissinger, the Alpha heir to Blue Cliff Pack, had been my crush for almost my entire life. He told me years ago, when we were still little kids, that he knew we wouldn't be mates, but I was still clinging to that hope that when I saw him tonight at my 18th birthday party, there would be sparks between us.

There had to be. I've been drawn to him since I was a toddler. He even promised me when we were still in elementary school that he would make me his mate.

"I can't believe you are getting this because of some guy," Sophia huffed. "What are you going to do tonight if he isn't your mate?"

"Quit being negative," I gave her the side-eye as the human tattoo artist came back from the backroom. We couldn't be talking about mates and werewolf shit in front of him.

"Ready to get this butterfly going on your beautiful skin?" the tattoo dude grinned, flirting with me once again.

"I'm ready for your magic touch." I fluttered my eyelashes, flirting right back. He was giving me a huge discount, and I planned on milking him for as long as I could.

Sophia, my best friend, cringed before huffing dramatically, watching the guy glide the needle over my skin. I barely felt it. My pain tolerance was pretty high.

I was so excited to see it finished. When I was checking out Taegan's sleeve, I found several tiny but intricate purple butterflies mixed in with the art. I was getting a blue butterfly on my shoulder; the same color blue as his eyes.

His eyes, his build, his kissable lips and powerful jaw. Every single thing about him was perfect. When the goddess created Taegan, she went all out. He had everything I wanted in a mate.

Yes, we were both Alpha heirs, and yes, Miami and Canada were so far from each other, but I know we can make it work.

I mean, he has tons of younger sisters that could take his place as Alpha. Aly, his sister just a few years younger than him, was biting at the bit to prove herself.

If we were mates, which I'm sure we are, I know I can convince him to move down here with me. Dad would move the moon if mom wanted him to. Mates do anything to make each other happy.

The tattoo took almost four hours, which was cutting it close. I needed to be home soon to get ready. Mom wouldn't care if I was late, but Aunt Simone would. She and Aunt Lilly, both not really my aunts by blood, just honorary aunts since they were both my mom's best friends, were the ones dressing me up like a fucking doll. I was more like mom. I would rather attend the party in shorts and a tank top. Even my bikini would be preferable to a dress.

Tonight was special, though. I actually wanted to dress up for once. Taegan would be there with my cousin, Calum, and the prissy little fairy prince, Rian, who I couldn't fucking stand. But I was fucking thrilled to see Taegan, but I could go without seeing the fairy prince.

Rian tagged along with Taegan and my cousin most of the time, but he was so stuck on himself that I would avoid him like the disease he was if it wasn't for Taegan.

"In *my* kingdom, ladies don't fight. It's so uncivilized," "In *my* kingdom, a woman could never rule so easily."

I always imagine his voice in one of those whiny, accented voices that remind me of old-money, trust fund brats. "*My* papa drives a Rolls Royce and eats caviar harvested only from albino sturgeon with his 1947 Chateau Cheval Blanc." He irritated the crap out of me.

If he wasn't being a douche canoe about me being the alpha heir and a woman, he was using his pretty boy looks to get the attention of every she-wolf in my pack. It's fucking annoying. Seeing the way some girls just throw themselves at "the prince" makes me want to punch him and them in the fucking mouths. I'd love to knock a few teeth out of his perfect smile that he flashes to all the ladies.

"Lady-getter 9000" is what Reese, my brother, calls Rian's smile. Rian just has to grin and girls start offering him their panties, hearts, or even their souls.

Fuck that. Who wants a guy just for his smile? I prefer men like Taegan, who are all muscle, have a strong and handsome face, and exude Alpha perfection.

Rian was technically Taegan's uncle, or step-uncle, since Taegan's grandpa found a second-chance mate who just happened to be a fairy princess. Rian's mother is the sister of the current Northern Fairy Kingdom's ruler, making Rian a prince. Taegan and Rian are about the same age, but Taegan was just so much more mature. Rian is an annoying stuck-up prince and Taegan is like my white knight, with piercing blue eyes and an aura that makes me quiver.

The only thing I feel when I look at Rian is repulsion.

"Hey, is that fairy prince coming with your cousin to your party tonight? Brinley just asked me," Sophia looked up from her phone as the tattoo dude walked to the front to answer a phone call. I checked out my shoulder in the mirror, and thankfully, it looked like he was almost done.

I rolled my eyes. Even hearing his name annoyed me. "Yep."

Sophia laughed at my expression. "Still don't like him?"

"What's not to like?" I grumbled. "The fact that he thinks women shouldn't lead, or that he likes to hook up with all my friends every time he visits?"

"Kissing Julia one time in the pool doesn't count as hooking up with all your friends, Rose. She kinda pushed herself on him, too."

"Whatever," I grumbled, lying back down when the guy started walking back. "Calum told me he was going back to *where he came from* soon, anyway." Where he came from, meaning the fairy kingdom run by his uncle. Rian was eligible to inherit the throne, and since he found most of pack life to be barbaric, he had already told his mother and Alpha Max, Taegan's grandfather, that he wanted to return to his land where things are easier for a stuck-up fairy prince like him.

Calum also told me that Taegan was trying to talk him out of it. I say, let the brat go. If he doesn't like werewolf life, why force him to stay? It's not like he has a mate keeping him in a pack. If he wants to leave, let him. It will be easier and more enjoyable for me to hang out with Taegan if Rian goes back to Alfheimr, the fae realm.

"Alright. All done," the tattoo artist stated, rubbing some kind of ointment all over my skin. He placed a covering over it that looked a lot like saran wrap. "Keep it moisturized. Apply this cream I'm gonna give you twice a day after gently washing it with mild soap and water. Only keep it covered tonight. Remove this in the morning. If you have any trouble, come back and let me know." He grinned crookedly, flicking his tongue over his lip piercing. "You should come back just to see me, anyway. I would love to work my magic hands on other parts of your body." He eyed me suggestively, his eyes raking down and back up my body.

"Oh, gawd," Sophia rolled her eyes and walked away, making me chuckle.

I paid the dude with a dismissive chuckle, then headed out, too.

Now that I had my first tattoo, I was excited to see what Taegan thought about it. I couldn't wait until tonight.

∗∗∗

Rian

The instant the plane landed in the Miami airport, I felt the moisture in the air. It made my skin tingle with rejuvenation. Being half siren along with half fairy, I always enjoy these trips down to the southern tip of the United States. The ocean surrounded Florida, and even the air was rich in water. Water is life for sirens.

"I hope you guys enjoyed your flight," the flight attendant winked at us, mainly Taegan, as we get off the plane.

Calum snickered, and I just laughed. We were both used to Taegan getting all of the attention. He rarely responded to any of it, and it was humorous to watch the women who approached him get shot down.

Speaking of which....

"What time is your dear cousin's party?" I asked Calum as we navigated the busy airport, ignoring the looks of admiration from all around.

Three supernatural men with supernatural looks always garner attention when we are out in the human world. Blue Cliff was so small compared to Miami that I tried to enjoy the gawking and praise while I could down here.

Back home, I was a weak fairy prince that no one was much impressed with. Here, I live like a king. I get asked if I'm a model or actor frequently, and all the she-wolves in the pack here don't mind that I'm not bulky or terrifying like my hulking nephew. They aren't so traditional here. Crystal Moon is a far more diverse pack, with many fae, vampires, witches, and humans than Blue Cliff Pack. My mother and I are the only two fae members of the pack, and technically, I'm not even a member of the pack. I have no real ties to it besides my mother's mating to their former Alpha.

If it wasn't for Taegan and Calum, I would have gone mad at Blue Cliff years ago. The other males in the pack had found me to be annoying or a nuisance since I was younger. I'm the far younger stepbrother to the current Alpha, but don't have a position myself in the pack. I've been dealing with harassment for a long time.

If my mother had mated with someone here in Miami, I think it would have been easier for me. I wouldn't be so determined to go back to live with my uncle in Alfheimr.

But things didn't work out that way. I have no ties to Miami, no matter how much I like it here.

"It starts at seven. I think we have time to eat and take a nap before we have to go."

"You just ate on the plane!" Taegan shoved his cousin roughly.

I took a step back, knowing how this would end.

Just as I predicted, Calum shoved Taegan back, and then Taegan attempted to put Calum in a chokehold.

I stood there with my arms folded, tapping my foot until the two of them were done. I learned long ago to not get between two fighting wolves, even these two.

Wolves, I thought to myself, shaking my head.

Taegan always won. He had more than just a mere wolf inside of him. His Lycan counterpart was too proud to let him lose.

That was probably why Rosie, Crystal Moon's alpha heir, was so set on Taegan being hers. I get so much attention from the she-wolves in this pack, thanks to her claim on Taegan. She lets everyone know Taegan is off limits, threatening bodily harm to any girl that goes near him. Calum is Calum. He doesn't leave himself open to she-wolves to flirt with, since he is set on holding out for his mate. That just leaves me. Whenever we visit, I am swarmed with the ladies' attention.

I liked it when I was younger, but it has gotten tedious over the years.

One of Rosie's friends forced a kiss from me a few years back while we were barbecuing with her friends. The look Rosie gave me, like I was complete garbage, left a bad taste in my mouth for a long time.

I tried to smooth things over with her, but I ramble when I'm nervous... and she makes me really nervous. I just annoyed her more, though that was never my intention.

Having her mad at me, and being the object of her scorn, makes my chest hurt, making my mouth taste like acid. I know she loves Taegan, and if it weren't for him, she wouldn't tolerate me at all.

That's a painful thought; one I don't want to linger on for too long.

The human world is hard. I just have this vacation to get through, then I can start planning my return to the fairy kingdom.

2

— · —

UNEXPECTED MATE

Rosie

"It's so badass," mom snickered while checking out the already healed tattoo showing on my shoulder. Werewolf healing made it heal right away. It was on full display in the fitted mermaid party dress that looked more like a prom dress Aunt Sim had commissioned for me. A new fairy tailor she has been raving about made it. "Your dad know about it yet?"

I could tell by mom's smile she already knew the answer to that question.

"I'm an adult now." I crossed my arms stubbornly. "What is he going to do?"

"Pout a lot. Don't worry, baby girl. I got your dad taken care of. He can't hold you to a standard he didn't even hold himself to."

"He did get a tattoo when he was still sixteen. Right?" Aunt Sim chortled. "What was it again? A snake?"

"Worse. A snake coiled around a wolf's paw. He thought it was badass," mom choked.

"Is that what that thing on dad's upper arm is supposed to be?" I gaped. I always asked him but he told me it was "*a mistake*". I thought it was a ball of yarn.

"Yep. Grandpa Jared told him he couldn't get one because they were tacky."

"He sure showed him," Aunt Sim chuckled. "Did it hurt?" she ran her fingers over the blue butterfly gracing my skin.

"Nope. Barely felt it," I grinned.

"Of course you didn't," mom rolled her eyes. "You didn't even flinch when we got our belly buttons pierced."

Neither did mom. We both really have a high threshold for pain.

"You look gorgeous, hun," Aunt Sim finished the last of my curls in my hair. "You'll be turning heads for sure. Who knows? Maybe you will find your mate from one of the visiting packs."

I smiled coyly, running my fingers through my hair to loosen the curls. "There is only one visiting pack official I'm interested in being mates with." I've never kept my crush on Taegan a secret. He didn't either when we were young kids.

That changed over time, but he still keeps up a healthy friendship with me.

He usually visits Miami a couple of times a year. He and Callum went to work on their pack's mining plots in Alaska with Phoebe, their pack's future Beta. She had just graduated from college the spring before last and all their parents wanted them to work to run part of the business together for a year as a test run for taking over the pack soon.

Because of that, I hadn't seen Taegan in over a year, and my excitement was almost bubbling out of me now.

He might think we aren't mates, but I didn't want to let my hopes die just yet.

"Rosie, honey," Mom pushed the hair around my face behind my ears. "He already said you weren't mates. Don't get upset when you see it for yourself."

"Mom," I pushed her hands away. "I wasn't eighteen yet. I still could be."

She shook her head. "Your dad knew I was his mate the moment he turned eighteen. Even before that, there was a connection there. It was blurry for us, because of, uh, just the shit going on with our parents, but it was still there. The stronger your wolf genes, the earlier you just know, Rosie. Taegan *knows* you're not his mate."

"But I feel a pull!" I tried to argue. "I do!" Ever since I got my wolf, whenever they visit, I just felt this unsettled feeling in me. It's like my body just knew my mate was near.

No, I didn't feel tingles and sparks, but I wasn't eighteen yet. Taegan might not think we are mates. Fine. I'm still not ready to admit we are not. After tonight, I will know for sure. After tonight, if it's not him... then I will give up.

Maybe....

Okay, I will. But not until I know for sure it's not him.

"Just don't be too disappointed, baby," Mom rubbed my back.

I gave her a dry smile, not wanting to be pacified.

"Why would she be disappointed? You look hot as hell and you're eighteen now. Your mom and I can be your wingmen at the club later tonight." Aunt Sim bumped me with her hip. "Being single in Miami is nothing to be disappointed about."

"Is that right, my love?" A smooth voice purred from the open doorway of my parents' bedroom. Uncle Vincent was leaning against the frame with a sultry smile on his face.

Mom rolled her eyes, but I sighed along with Aunt Sim looking at him.

Thank fuck he wasn't really my uncle, because I get sinful thoughts sometimes. I didn't know anyone unmated who didn't. His unyielding devotion to Aunt Simone on top of his raw sexuality was hard not to find attractive.

He may not be my real uncle, just like Simone isn't my real aunt, but it looks like we will all be a real family soon. Even now, my brother Reese is probably off with their daughter, Karina, making out in some deserted room or closet. They were both so sure they were mates, even though they had about a year and a half left before they could confirm it.

Aunt Sim strutted over to his side, and he practically whisked her off her feet. He was no doubt taking her somewhere to prove to her that being single was not preferable. Not when she was mated to him.

Going to his nightclub filled with sexy vampires just like him didn't sound half bad. I could go for a vampire seeing him and Aunt Sim together. Uncle Vince worships everything about my Aunt Simone. Everything. He uses his sexy vampire mojo to keep her spoiled and endlessly happy.

Seeing a mated couple outside of the normal pairing of two wolves has always intrigued me. Not just because of Simone and Vincent, but because of all the other inter-racial couples in our pack. Even our Betas are a gay wolf/vampire couple.

It's always amazed me to see that the mate bond isn't bound by race or any other limits. Love is love, and if two souls are a perfect match, that's all that matters.

When we finished getting ready, Mom took my arm and walked me downstairs to greet the guests. The party already started, but mom and Aunt Sim, who was still busy with her mate, both said it was better to be late to your own party than early.

Mom had me greet several officials from other packs, other alpha children eyeing me appraisingly, and young single men, no doubt sent to find out if the single female alpha heir of the Crystal Moon Pack might hopefully be their mate. There were lots of looks of disappointment so far.

After a while of playing my part as the alpha heir, welcoming the visiting guests to my party, Dad caught sight of us. His eyes light up with pride. That was until he took me in for a hug and saw the tattoo on my shoulder.

I prepared myself for his wrath, but mom was true to her word and told him to shut up before he could say anything. She mind linked something to him that made his tense jaw loosen and the fire in his eyes cool in no time. A hungry expression replaced the anger as his eyes raked down her body; I don't want to imagine what Mom told him.

"You're not off the hook," he muttered in my ear when mom flitted away to hug Melody, a fae friend of hers. "We will be speaking about this at training in the morning. In excruciating detail."

"Come on, Dad. It's pretty. Isn't it?" I turned so he could see it better.

"Hmph," he grunted, but he still ran his fingers over the design. "You are too much like your mom sometimes."

"Really? Mom always says I'm too much like you," I smiled sweetly, wrapping my arms around my dad's waist.

"Yeah, yeah," dad caved, hugging me back and kissing the top of my head. "You're still doing suicides until you pass out tomorrow."

"That might take a while," I smirked. "I can outlast you, I'm sure."

"Are you trying to make your punishment a competition?" He laughed. "So, so, so much like your mother."

"That's why you love me so much," I said. "I'm your favorite."

"My favorite daughter," he countered with a lazy grin, and I knew I was in the clear. "That's also why I know you are going to be a good Alpha for the pack one day."

"Because I'm like mom?"

"Because you got the best of both of us." He held my face in his large hands. "Happy birthday, my fierce little girl. Even with a tattoo, you will always be my baby girl." He tenderly pressed his lips to my forehead before rubbing his nose with mine.

I knew dad couldn't be too mad for too long.

Grandpa Tommy interrupted our moment with a glint in his eye. He made a show out of spinning me around in his arms to wish me a happy birthday.

Grandma Elena, after forcing her mate to put me back on the ground, gave me a peck on the cheek, then walked to where my mom and Melody were standing talking with some of the Lunas from other packs.

All our family members passed me around, giving me many of the same birthday greetings. After slipping away from Grandpa Jared and his questioning about colleges, I finally joined my friends hanging out around the dining hall near the punch bowl. Someone spiked it, I was sure. The guys were snickering too much while mixing it with the spoon.

"You survived!" Sophia laughed. "I saw your dad checking out your tattoo."

I shrugged complacently. "What can he do? Like I said, I'm an adult now."

"Yeah, you are," Lenny, a future warrior I graduated with, winked at me.

I flipped him off. I didn't date or even flirt with guys in my pack. That was something both my parents were always sure to instill in me, especially as the future alpha. It's disrespectful to their future mates and I should never give my pack members any reason not to trust me.

"I want to see your tattoo," Brinley gushed, turning me around so my back faces her. "How pretty! The detailing is amazing. It almost looks real."

"Thanks. I went to the artist the Meyers brothers go to."

"No wonder," Brinley sighed. "Those two are way too hot to be old business men."

"They're not any older than my parents," I laughed. "They are also mated, so watch it."

"Lucky woman," Brinley eyed Mitch and Mark Meyers with their mate, Hadley, from across the room. The men were trying to keep their twin girls under control while Hadley talked to Lilly, her sister-in-law. The Meyers brothers were actually triplets, but Matt, the other brother, came from his own egg and Mark and Mitch are identical twins. Matt was the Gamma of the pack, and the other brothers worked under Hadley at the resort they own on Miami beach.

The resort was where Taegan, Callum, and Rian were staying. Taegan always insisted on staying there for some reason.

Probably because of stupid Rian. His prissy ass probably would rather stay in a resort on the beach than here in the packhouse. We don't have room service or turn down the beds.

I was tempted to run over and ask Hadley if she knew when Taegan would get there. They landed in Miami earlier today. I felt it. That familiar pull that warned me they were close.

That feeling I always get was one reason I couldn't believe just yet that Taegan wasn't my mate.

Taegan was strong. He had the strongest alpha genes you could get, and he had other powers on top of that. That had to be why I could always feel it when he and his family were here. There can't be any other explanation other than him being my mate.

Right?

"They're here," Brinley squealed, staring at the entrance to the dining hall.

All the girls around me were squealing and buzzing, and most of the guys were groaning in disappointment.

They don't build men down here like they do in Blue Cliff. At least not any that looked like my cousin, Callum, and Taegan. Both of them were massive, with perfect muscles, powerful bodies, and auras that would make weaker werewolves tremble.

Wow. Even Rian had filled in a lot since I last saw him.

Like, a lot, a lot. His shoulders were much broader and his face wasn't as pretty as it once was. His jaw was more defined and his muscles were pretty impressive, too. Almost as massive as Callum's, though still fairly smaller than Taegan's.

Taegan was unmatched in that department.

I tried to remain calm, trying to look as mature as I could, as I started making my way to them, giving Sophia a knowing grin before I walked away from my friends.

I was about halfway to them when this overwhelming scent overtook me. It was like the sweet smell of the beach in the early morning. Like brine and sunshine with a hint of tropical flowers enveloping me in a warm embrace.

My eyes went dark, searching for the source as the telling words leave my lips in an ever-soft whisper. "Mate."

The scent was coming from them. The three men that just walked in. My heart skipped inside my chest, thinking all my hope has come to fruition, but as Taegan and Callum stopped to talk to my dad, letting Rian walk ahead of them, I realized it was not Taegan at all.

Rian stopped short, and was also staring at me with wide eyes, their hazel hue boring into my face. He was taking me in with amazement and something else shining in those eyes. Something I hadn't seen in him before. It was not a proper or prim expression. It was tameless and possessive.

The desire to go to him was so strong that I almost gave in. My body and the beast within me were demanding I claim him. Every cell in my body screamed that this man was mine.

Before my body could move on its own, a woman's voice sounded from behind me.

"Rian!" Julie squealed, running up to him and latching her arms around his neck. "It's been so long! Why didn't you call me?"

A deep, low growl vibrates in my chest, just low enough for Julia to miss it, it seemed, but I could tell it didn't go unnoticed by Rian.

Rian looked flustered, his wide eyes moving between her and me. He kept opening his mouth to say something, then closed it, like a damned fish or some shit.

That was when the reality of this situation hit me.

Taegan was not my mate. He was right all along.

Rian was. Rian, the fairy fucking prince, was my mate. Not only was he not a fucking werewolf and the prince of a fairy kingdom, he was set to return to his own realm soon.

And he had one of my friends that he had already hooked up with hanging on him like he belonged to her.

This wasn't right. This wasn't how it should be.

Everything about this was wrong. My head was trying to reason this out, but my heart and the bond were almost demanding me to tear apart my friend to claim a guy I never even liked.

What the hell was I supposed to do?

What else could I do? After a last glare and a deep snarl of bitterness, I turned around and walked away, grabbing Sophia and heading outside to get some fresh air so I could think without his scent tormenting me.

3

His Shadow

Rian

Ten minutes earlier....

"Tonight's the big night," Taegan rubbed his hands together as we stopped at a red light. He was smiling with that knowing grin, like he had some big secret he was just waiting for someone to ask him about. "Are you excited?" he slapped the top center of my back right between my shoulder blades, making me grunt.

"Why would I be excited?" I snapped. "You are the one who made me come. I don't know what I'm doing here." I was content staying back in the resort, but Taegan forced me to get ready for the Alpha she-wolf's birthday party.

I didn't need to be here. I agreed to come, but once at the resort, I was quickly invited to lounge along the pool in a cabana with some visiting college girls, and that sounded much more appealing than this destined-to-be-awkward party.

The girls wanted the three of us, but Callum gruffly said "no thanks," and Taegan lied, saying he was taken, leaving only me. I had absolutely no reason to refuse, but Taegan had to pipe up with a "He's taken too," then pulled me along with him.

Now I was sitting in the passenger seat of the Audi convertible Taegan borrowed from the resort owners, feeling pretty sour about going to a party for a girl that didn't even like me. I was averse to see that offended look on her face that she got whenever she saw me. It hurt in my chest every time.

At least her friends seemed to like me. A little too much, at least among the girls. It put me in an awkward place. Taegan and Callum were always insistent not mess around with women in your own pack, and they extend that rule to the pack in Miami. I'm not a true member of the pack, so you would think I wouldn't be held to that standard, but Taegan insists I follow that rule as well.

Last time we were there, when one of Rosie's friends nearly shoved her tongue down my throat at a pool party, Taegan scolded me quite harshly for some time afterward. He apologized later, saying he just didn't want me to get myself in a situation where I might get hurt later, but that just hurt my pride even more.

It's hard growing up with him as my "nephew". He's a year younger than me, but he acts much older. He always has. His power as a witch and the only one with a Lycan counterpart in the world is no joke. He is this all-powerful being, and I feel insignificant in his shadow.

I love him, but he is one of the main reasons I want to be back in my realm. I love my mother. I love my stepfather, Max, as well as all my nieces and extended family, and I love Taegan fiercely, but my fierce love is miniscule when compared to him.

It's suffocating.

I stayed quiet the rest of the way to the Crystal Moon pack house. Callum was cackling away, eating a party-sized bag of Doritos in the back seat, laughing at Taegan's windblown hair as we drove over the bridge. Callum always had long, messy curls, and my hair was too short to easily be messed up. Taegan's carefully tamed and gelled down blonde locks were sticking straight up. He looked like he just ran into a door and his hair stuck in place.

When we pulled into the packhouse lot, Taegan chose not to use the valet and just parked in a spot in the back, staring at himself in the rearview mirror to tame his hair again.

"That's what you get for leaving the top down, dipshit. I told you not to," Callum snorted, emptying the rest of the bag of chips by dumping it into his mouth.

"We're in fucking Miami. Why drive a convertible with the top up?" Taegan retorted.

"Look at your hair," I muttered while attempting to wipe the smile off my face. "That's why."

When he was happy enough with his still slightly windblown hair, we got the gifts we brought from the trunk. I didn't know what the two got her, but Axel, my much older Alpha stepbrother, helped me to pick out a necklace that Rosie could wear in both wolf form and human form. It was made of platinum and the length was enough to accommodate her neck size when she shifts. Bailey got Axel one for his birthday a few years ago and he hasn't taken it off since.

I found a butterfly pendant to put on it. A blue topaz stone made up the butterfly's body and the wings are an intricate pattern of platinum metal on either side. She seemed enraptured with the butterflies on Taegan's tattoo the last time we were here, and when I saw the design, it made me think of her.

It was pricey, but something drove me to buy it. It was like a nagging feeling in the back of my head that I needed to get it for her. I even infused a bit of my magic into the stone, using my siren abilities to cast a protection spell on the jewel.

She was to be the Alpha. I'm sure she could use the added protection if she's anything like her reckless mother. My stepfather dislikes Rosie's mother because of her recklessness, but I think she's rather fun. Dad just can't stand anyone who is more crude and headstrong than he is, except for my mother.

The thought of any harm coming to Rosie made my chest feel tight and uncomfortable, almost like it does at the thought of her disliking me. It's unsettling, and I wish I knew where the irritating feeling stemmed from.

Many people don't like me. I'm a fairy prince living in the rough wilderness among nothing but testosterone-filled werewolves. I have no desire to work in the lumber or mining fields and spend my time lounging with my nieces and family instead of training like the male members of the pack. I get a lot of dislike for many reasons. I never cared much before. I don't know why I care so much about this one girl thousands of miles away not liking me. I also don't know why I went out of my way to buy her an expensive gift and infuse it with my magic if she doesn't like me. It was just something I had to do, even without knowing the reason.

Now that we were here, that feeling was stronger than ever before in my chest, and I just wish Taegan would have let me stay back at the resort with the group of women that actually wanted to be around me. If Rosie scoffs or dislikes my gift, I don't know how I will react.

I do know. It will hurt, but it will solidify my resolve to go back to Alfheimr, where I belong.

We were a bit late for the party, which was in full swing when we walked in. Right away, Taegan was greeted by nearly everyone. He is always sought after at these types of events. The visiting Alphas from other packs always seem eager to introduce him to their unmated daughters, no doubt hoping he might be their mate. He always refuses politely, and this time is no different. He waves away a lot of the attention and heads straight for Alpha Parker, Rosie's dad.

Alpha Parker used not to like Taegan much, but since Taegan stated he wasn't Rosie's mate, the two of them get along much better. Alpha Parker is just fiercely protective of his daughter. I can understand that. I even appreciate it. I enjoy knowing she is being treasured and protected. Again, I can't quite explain why I feel this way, but I do.

Callum joined Taegan in greeting the birthday girl's dad. I chose to walk ahead of the two, not in the mood for forced pleasantries quite yet. I was still fighting that uncomfortable feeling in my chest. It wasn't just in my chest now. My entire body was buzzing, this air of anticipation around me. It was like my body was a live wire, waiting for something to connect to. An electric current was traveling through my blood. All my senses came alive with this feeling, and I couldn't understand what was wrong with me until my eyes land on her.

Rosie.

She was more beautiful than ever before. An elegant fabric was wrapped tightly around her fit body. The shimmering design was magnificent, but paled in comparison to her. She had more flare to her hips and a more womanly shape than when I last saw her. She was stunning.

Everything about her was stunning. Her eyes, her lips, even the bridge of her nose and the way her mouth almost formed a plump heart shape. I found it all enticing. I couldn't take my eyes off her. It seemed like every single one of her features was hand carved by angels, with only my preferences in mind. Even the way her eyebrows pull down, I found beautiful.

She was mine. I could feel it. The buzzing in my body was reaching out for her, like lightning ready to strike. She was what the feeling inside me was trying to connect to.

I wanted her. Every fiber of my being wanted this girl, but before I could move to claim her, someone cut into my path, interrupting my desirous thoughts with an aggravating squeal.

"Rian!" The impertinent girl from the pool party last time I was here wrapped her arms around my neck. She said something more, but I could hardly hear her through the violent ringing in my ears. The electricity inside me was revolting from her touch.

I wanted to push her away, but before I could, a deep, low growl caused me to freeze. Rosie was glaring at me with so much anger, I didn't know what to do.

This was her friend. Do I push her away harshly, or was Rosie going to handle this? I didn't want this rude girl on me. Rosie had to see that. What should I do?

I wanted to beckon her for help, but she just snarled and turned away, pulling her friend along with her as she headed out through a door at the back of the room.

That was it? Is she just going to walk away?

"Get. Off," I sneered through gritted teeth, jarring my head back to remove the girl's hands without having to touch her. I couldn't take the revolting touch of her hands on my skin a moment longer.

At my words, everything around me seemed to have come to a halt. I glared at the girl whose name I didn't even remember. I could not keep the disgust off my face or the revulsion out of my voice.

"Whoever you are, do not think you can touch me freely. It disgusts me. Pathetic." I was way harsher than necessary, but the energy buzzing inside me was loathsome, wanting retaliation. It was seeking revenge, blaming this girl for Rosie's scorn.

"Rian," Taegan was beside me, gripping my arm. I could feel his magic latching onto mine, siphoning the negative energy from me. I didn't even realize the anger in me was causing my magic to flare, burning in my hands and through my body.

The girl in front of me was shaking in fear. Good. She will think twice before touching me again.

Taegan led me away, continuing to siphon my magic as we went. I was still reeling over what had just happened. It felt like my world was coming into focus, only to crumble apart a few moments later. Everything in me was moving towards her, pulling me in her direction like she was my reason for even breathing. It felt like my heart was beating just for her. Her departure set everything inside me ablaze, burning me up, and I yearned to renew and repair what was broken. My mind is so muddled between rage and regret, I can't quite make right of anything just yet.

When Taegan and I are alone in a hallway, somewhere towards the back of the pack house, he turns to face me, his expression somber.

"What happened?" he demanded. Not ask. He demands. The Lycan in him asked nothing. He demanded answers.

"I don't know," I gritted my teeth. "But I need to fix it."

I tried to push past him to head back toward the direction we had come from, so I could find Rosie, but he stopped me with a firm hand on my shoulder.

"Fix what? What happened, Rian? Did Rosie reject you?"

My eyes opened wide at his question. Reject me? Why would she?....

"She's my mate..." I felt stunned again, and then something dawned on me. My brows pulled downward with suspicion. "You.... you knew?"

His lips pressed tightly together, and I knew his answer before he even said it. That was why he wanted me to come so desperately tonight. It was why he always demanded I come to Miami with him, and why he was so angry when Rosie's friend kissed me last time.

"How long? How long have you known?"

I felt I already knew.

He didn't have the decency to look guilty. "For a while."

Now my anger was flaring towards him. My hands were glowing again as my blood boiled. "And you didn't think to tell me?!"

"I couldn't," Taegan raked a hand down his face. "I'm not allowed to disclose things I know to mortals. You know that."

"SHE HATES ME!" I snapped. "She.... she hates me," I repeated. "And she wanted you. It's always you."

I have a mate; a werewolf mate. A woman so perfect and beautiful, but she doesn't want me. She never wanted me, even now, after feeling the pull we have for each other.

She wanted the man whose shadow I have lived in my entire life here on earth.

My magic continued to ravage my body, anger still coursing through me. I was just so.... So pissed at Taegan. I'm pissed at myself.

"She isn't in love with me, Rian. She's not. She just liked the idea of me."

"And the idea of me repulses her." So much so that it took a single touch from her friend to cause her to turn away from our bond.

"I'll talk to her," Taegan said.

"Don't bother," I scoffed. "You've done enough."

I never thought there would come a day when the fierce love I held for my nephew would turn into fierce disdain. It may not even be his fault, but right then, that's all I could see. His fault in all this.

The promises he told Rosie when they were young children were well known to everyone. Before the incident that brought me back to my mother, when he gained his Lycan and traveled through the moon goddess's realm, he was dead set on being Rosie's mate. He told her they would be mates. He planted the idea in her head, and then he left me in the dark.

He may have insisted since that time they would not be mates, but he still kept me in the dark, and it almost felt like he was still stringing her along. Why else was he coming to Miami so often? I don't understand what he was doing all these years. Was he coming here and dragging me along so much for my benefit? It didn't help.

If I can't convince Rosie to not let the connection between us go, I don't know I can keep the connections I have with earth anymore. I don't know if my heart could take anymore of a life living in this man's shadow. If I can't step into the light of her world, then my time here is done. I'll go back to Alfheimr and leave this world behind for good.

4

---•---

PAST REGRETS

Rosie

"What's wrong?" Sophia asked in a frenzied huff as I threw myself down on a cushioned lounge chair by the pool.

I just dragged her out here with no explanation and didn't know where to even explain. I didn't know if I could yet. I was too pissed.

I threw my head back and covered my eyes with my arms so I could focus on my breathing, calming my rage enough not to run back inside and rip Julia's face off. I wanted to break both her arms and tear her lips right off of her, knowing they had once touched his.

"Fuck!" I roared. What the hell do I do? Do I even have a right to be mad at her, or *him*, for that matter?

It's not Taegan. It was never Taegan. It was Rian. The guy I've always shown only disdain for, and the one most of my friends are all over every time he's here.

Was that why it always bugged me? Fuck, this was a complete mess.

I thought I hated him for being a womanizing prince, but maybe it wasn't that. Maybe I just hated him giving all his attention to my friends and not me.

There was no way I could hold that against him. I was so stubbornly set on being with Taegan that I didn't take any time to consider why Rian bugged me the way he did.

The fucking mate bond was strong. Too strong. I don't even remember the reasons I was so infatuated with Taegan. Nothing about him could come into focus in my head.

Only one thing took root in my thoughts. Rian. His hooded hazel eyes and perfect face. His jaw looked so sexy; masculine and sharp. His entire body was more masculine and rigid. He didn't look like a pampered prince today. He looked like a fucking man.

A very sexy man. One that never had issues gaining admirers in the past. Girls probably flock to him even more now.

Then, the image of Rian with Julia hanging off his neck came into focus at the forefront of my mind. I couldn't dislodge it, no matter how much I try.

And I just left her with him. Just like that. Her lips would be on his in no time. Any woman wouldn't miss the opportunity to kiss his perfect lips if they could.

I started rubbing my chest. The ache of that thought was making it throb. If she or anyone else kissed him, or worse, I would feel it. He's my mate. I'll feel it if he is with someone else.

What the hell am I supposed to do?

Do I tell him: "*Hey. I know I've been a bitch to you for the past decade, but since we're mates, your lips and body can't touch anyone but me.*" Yeah. If I said that to him and he laughs in my face, I don't know what I would do. It would crush me.

I kicked my feet against the chair, spiraling into grief. I wished I had dragged Julia out here with me, so I at least know she's not trying to hook up with him again. I might have ended up killing her if I did, but that seems like a viable solution now, anyway.

"Rose, you're scaring me. What the hell is wrong with you?" Sophia pulled off my shoes, sat at the end of the lounge chair and held my feet in her lap.

I lift one of my arms, glaring at her, knowing what she was about to do.

"Tell me," she smirked, her arms locked around my legs, one hand raised to attack.

"Don't," I glared. "I'm not in the fucking mood to be tick- AHH!"

I buckled over, halfway falling off the lounger as her hand started tickling the bottom of my feet. I was thrashing with laughter, so much that it hurt my chest.

"Fine! I'll tell. I'll tell you. Just.... STOP!"

She made a threatening face while lifting her hand, ready to attack again. I couldn't keep myself from smiling at her expression. She was as threatening as a mouse to a lion. But she just knows my weakness. Tickling. The bottom of my feet are the worst. I had better just tell her before she attacks again.

"He's my mate," I blurted out.

Her eyes went wide. "Taegan?! Really?"

"No, crazy. Would I be out here thinking about popping Julia's head like a zit if it was Taegan?"

"Julia?" Her brows pulled down in confusion. "Wait. RIAN'S YOUR MATE?!" The corners of her mouth floated up. She looked far too amused for my liking. "Seriously? The fairy prince you hate?!"

"I don't hate him!" I snapped. I added in a much quieter, tamed tone, "I just don't like the way he is with girls. I didn't know why until now."

"That's not the only reason you said you didn't like him. You said he was a weak, pretty boy that used his good looks and royal pedigree to get by."

"Shut up." I tried to kick her with my foot, but she gripped it tighter and threatened me with her raised hand. Her eyebrows went high on her forehead. She looked comical, but that's why I love her.

"I didn't like him. You're right. That's... that's not the same now."

I thought he just used his title and family connections to get by. That's what I told myself, at least. I don't want to voice that now, but growing up, it was the truth. It irritated me seeing him taking it easy and spending all his time when he was here flirting with my friends while I was working my ass off. Now, I realize I was probably just pissed about the flirting part and kept creating more excuses to hate him on top of that, since him being a flirt wasn't really a logical reason.

Now that I was thinking about it, now that I knew he was my mate, I liked the idea of him not being a warrior or a fighter. Both of my parents are warriors, and I know it stresses my dad out quite a bit.

I liked the idea of having a mate that wasn't an alpha wolf as well. Everything that was brought up as an issue of being mated to another alpha wolf seemed to just fall into place when I thought about Rian being my partner.

There is still one major issue, though.

He was a fairy prince. He was also about to return to his own realm. The fairy realm was somewhere I could not go. No one besides the fae can. Even if I could leave my pack behind, which I can't, I couldn't chase after him, back to his own kingdom.

Callum said that Rian was dead set on going back. Did I even have the right to stop him? After how I treated him the last several years, do I have any right to ask him to stay?

I wouldn't if I were him. I would reject myself.

He's a fae. The bond won't be the same for him as it is for me. For me, it's all consuming. For him.....

I didn't know, but I bet it was something that could easily be ignored. That's why he didn't come after me. He just looked confused. He didn't even push Julia away.

Fuck, this was so frustrating.

"Why did I have to be such a bitch?!" I threw my arms over my face again, slamming my head back against the cushion.

"That's like asking a fish why it swims," Sophia snorted.

"You whore," I growled, trying to kick her again, but she struck before I even pulled my foot away, tickling me violently while pinning my legs beneath her weight.

"I'm a what?!" she demanded, not letting up, even though I was screaming for relief, begging her to stop. "I couldn't hear you. What am I?"

"You're..... You're a..... A NICE LADY! NOW STOP!"

My top half was halfway on the ground, flailing as I laughed uncontrollably.

"I *am* a nice lady." Sophia finally stopped, dropping my legs from beneath her weight onto the ground with the rest of me. "Remember that. This *nice lady* is the only one who can put you on your ass."

I laughed as she helped me up, but my heart still felt heavy. She must know, because she pulled me into a fierce hug.

"It's going to be okay, Rose. If you want, I can go and pop Julia's head like a pimple for you. I don't mind. *I'm* not going to be alpha."

I laughed at the image of Sophia trying to be mean to anyone. Her go-to move was a tickle attack.

"It's okay. I really can't blame her."

"That doesn't mean you don't want to kill her," Sophia smirked.

I shrugged, unable to deny it.

"Want to head back in?" She asked me. "Or do you want to sneak away from your own party? Want me to kidnap you and take you to get a froyo or another tattoo to piss your dad off with?"

"No," I grinned. "Thank you, though."

After getting my shoes on and Sophia helping me to look less of a mess, since she was the one who practically dropped me on the ground, we headed back in. She stayed by my side, gripping my hand in support.

She knew I didn't want to accidentally hurt one of my friends in a possessive rage if they started in on Rian, so she led me away from the dining hall to the adults who were still lingering in the foyer and front rooms.

I saw Callum in the distance inside of another room farther away, glued to Aunt Sim as usual, but I didn't see Rian or Taegan anywhere. There was an awkward tension in the air, too.

I tried not to create a scene. I tried to keep my agitation in check until I got outside. Did people still notice what was happening? My nerves started getting the best of me. Not knowing what happened to Rian after I left was eating at my gut. I didn't see Julia anywhere either.

Sophia could tell that I was searching for them. She pulled me in closer to whisper in my ear. "Brinley just mind linked that Julia's parents took her home. I guess your prince told her off and scared her pretty badly."

A deep sense of satisfaction rested in my chest. I was about to go crazy thinking Rian and Julia snuck off somewhere together. It felt good to hear that he pushed her away, even though it was after I left.

I still didn't know where he went, though. I was nervous about finding out, but I needed to know.

Reese and Katrina came down the stairs hand in hand, trying to sneak by unnoticed. Kat's lips were swollen and looking a little rough, and Reese had a smug look on his face. I could just guess what they had been doing.

I stopped Reese as he tried to get through to the dining room.

"Hey. Are you just getting here now?"

He shrugged. "Who wants to know? Did mom ask where I was?"

"No. It's not a mystery what you were up to." I winked at Kat, who blushed deeply. She was so cute, especially when she got flustered. "I was wondering if you knew what was going on? If you knew where-"

"Taegan went?" Reese tried to finish my sentence with a wise-ass smirk.

"What? No. Not Taegan. Rian. I was wondering where Rian was."

For a moment my brain went *Taegan who?* since I was so worried about Rian.

"Lady getter 9000? I haven't seen him. Why? Did he piss you off over something stupid again?"

I growl low in my chest, making my younger brother laugh.

"What? You get pissed at him for the stupidest things every time they're here. Doesn't she?" He looked at Kat for confirmation.

The corner of her mouth lifted up, but she just shrugged. I could still tell she was in agreement with Reese.

"Seriously, Rose. Leave the guy alone. The way you get overly sensitive about what he's up to makes me think that you actually like him and not his boy-wonder nephew."

Sophia snorted a laugh, trying to contain it. I sent her a warning look, but she just stifled more laughter.

"What?" Reese looked between my disgruntled expression and Sophia's amused face. Kat's eyes went wide after a few seconds, then she pulled Reese down to whisper something in his ear. He mirrored her surprise and then looked back at me. "No. No way. Is he....?"

"Go away," I growled, turning away from the twerp. "You're no help."

"Fucking hell, this is priceless," Reese called after me. "Congrats, sis!"

I flipped him off, while inwardly hoping Vincent catches him and Kat before they sneak in to mingle with the rest of the high schoolers and try to act like they were there the entire time.

Sophia and I searched for Rian in a few more rooms while I tried to dodge conversation with everyone as much as possible. I probably seemed rude, but I didn't care at the moment. I needed to find him. It was eating away at me, not knowing where he was.

I finally found Taegan talking to Mitch and Mark Meyers back in the dining room, but Rian wasn't with him. He was not with Callum either, who was still standing with Aunt Simone.

Sophia's eyes kept lingering on Callum the closer we get to them. Callum must have felt her gaze, because he looked up with a perplexed expression. I was about to just go ask him where Rian might be, but then the powerful scent of the sun and sea overwhelmed me again, like it had before. Rian was close. I could feel it.

I turned around, searching the larger foyer of the packhouse, and my eyes instantly connected to his. It was like there was this new radar inside of me, and the second he got close, my whole body just wanted to gravitate towards him.

His eyes were intense, strained in the corners. His mouth was set in a grim frown, and my anxiety started to set in.

He must have realized by now that we were mates. I was sure he figured that part out. He might have pushed Julia away, but he didn't seem happy to see me again. He looked brooding, or maybe he was mad about the whole situation. I didn't know.

It was my own fault. I didn't know how to make this right or how to apologize for how aggressively bitter I had always been towards him.

"Wow," Sophia whispered softly. "I thought maybe the bond would override every-thing, but he doesn't look happy. I'm sorry, Rose. We can still get out of here if you want."

"No," I shook my head softly. "I don't want to run away."

5

FEARS

My heart was beating uncontrollably. From the pull of the bond or fear of rejection, I did not know. My entire life was hanging in the balance, and the only one who was aware was him.

What should I do?

Rian's gaze flickered at someone behind me, then a worried expression crossed his handsome face. I reluctantly turned to see my dad headed towards me.

"There you are. Are you ready, Rose?" Dad asked.

Ready? Ready for what? Does he know?

I looked back towards Rian, not able to keep my gaze away for long. But when I turned my head back, he was gone. He was no longer standing there. I didn't even feel him in the room any longer.

Was that his answer? Did he not want this? Would he rather disappear than just face me?

Could I blame him?

"Rose?" Dad grabbed my shoulder, giving it a gentle squeeze. "Did you not hear me?"

"What?" I stared back at him.

"Are you ready?" He repeated. "For me to announce you?"

Oh. I had forgotten in all the drama happening what the point of this party was. It was also the day that I was being officially announced as the next Alpha.

Sophia reached for my hand, giving me a subtle nod before slipping away.

"I'll find him," she mind linked, going in the direction I just saw Rian before he disappeared.

What did she plan on finding him for? What was she going to do? Tickle him to death until he decides to accept me? I doubt he will just hand her his feet like I did.

It felt like a lost cause. It was killing me, making my insides feel like they were turning and twisting painfully.

He was a prince. One that I have never been kind to. Why would he accept me? He only wants to go back to his kingdom; to his realm. Did I have any right to stop him?

I swallowed down my agony as best I could and pasted on a smile that I did not feel for my dad.

He was a prince, and I am an alpha. I have a duty to my pack, and I couldn't let my sorrow show. Not yet. Today was not about me. It was about the future of my pack. If I couldn't keep my composure, I was not the only one who would be worried or feel like their world was ending. I didn't need my pack to lose confidence in me as I am being announced.

Not today.

"Let him go, Soph. If he doesn't want me, it's better to face a rejection later."

"But.... Rosie. I don't think that's it. He won't reject you. You at least need to talk to him."

"Not now," I groaned painfully. *"Please. Just.... Let me get through tonight. I will talk to him after tonight."*

Sophia sighed in frustration. *"Fine."* I could tell she was anything but fine with my decision, but was letting it go.

"Thank you."

I just needed to focus on this next ten minutes with dad, then I could slip back into my despair.

Dad pulled me to the center of the foyer, walking with me hand in hand halfway up the grand stairs. We stood and waited a few seconds for everyone to quiet down, all eyes turning towards us.

Mom met us on the stairs, reaching out to hold my hand. She gave me a strange look. I knew she could tell something was wrong.

I shook my head subtly, hoping she wouldn't pull me away to ask what the matter was. I couldn't tell her yet. She might drag Rian over here and force him to accept me whether he wanted to or not.

Thankfully, she just narrowed her eyes, then turned to look at the crowd of people as my dad started to speak. She was letting it go. For now.

"On behalf of Crystal Moon, I would like to thank all of you for coming to celebrate my beautiful daughter's eighteenth birthday with us this evening." Dad smiled brightly, wrapping an arm around my shoulder. His proud stare barely helped to ease the failure I felt inside.

"Rosie Elaine. I remember the day that you were born. It seems like just yesterday your mother was demanding all the pickles in the packhouse, refusing to sit still or rest. I should have known the child she was carrying then would be such a strong-willed warrior now. You went on many missions to defend your pack, even while you were in the womb.

"Now, with your mother's fierceness, and my good looks," he grinned, while mom growled and everyone else laughed, "and with all the qualities of a great Alpha, I am proud to finally announce you as my heir. You, my beautiful, fiery, tenacious daughter, will make a great Alpha to all of us one day. I know you will only grow and strengthen in your abilities and wisdom as you get older. I am so proud to declare you the next Alpha of the Crystal Moon Pack."

Dad kissed my head, then took a step back as everyone below us applauded.

Now, it was my turn to give a speech, but my head was in a thousand other places. No. Not a thousand other places. It's only with Rian, but seeing as I didn't know where he was, I couldn't say where exactly my head was either.

Mom squeezed my hand, and when I looked at her, I saw the strength in her eyes. It was the strength she passed on to me.

"*You got this,*" she whispered in my head.

I took a deep breath, then lifted my lips into a smile that felt so wrong compared to what I was really feeling on the inside.

"Thank you, dad." I turned my smile towards him. "Thank you for always being an example of what an Alpha should be. With you as a father, I learned from the best, and I am really grateful for all the lessons you have taught me. Thank you for the trust you are giving me now. I know the pack is the most important thing to an Alpha, putting our members' well-being above all else. Even yourself. I am thankful for your belief in me, and I promise to show the same dedication as Alpha one day as you have shown for the past two decades. You are everything I hope to one day be, and for that, thank you. Thank you for being not only the best dad, but the best Alpha as well."

"Butt kisser," mom whispered softly, so only dad and I could hear as the rest of the crowd clapped once again.

"You're still in trouble for the tattoo," Dad whispered in my ear as he hugged me, but I could tell he was teasing.

I could barely even hold my smile anymore. Even with his and mom's jokes, my world still felt like it was crashing down.

Then, I felt him. I could feel his eyes on me again. It was burning me. His stare seared my soul.

When I looked back towards the crowd, there he was, right by the door. He held my eyes in a hypnotic stare for what felt like hours, though it was only seconds. Then he turned and left, taking my heart and my hope of happiness with him.

It was what I expected. He didn't want the bitchy girl who treated him like shit for the last several years. I need to face the facts. He was going to reject me. It was only a matter of time.

I had no one to blame but myself.

***

Rian

I couldn't do it. I couldn't face her.

She was looking for me. I could sense it. Some invisible force was pushing me towards her, my heart beating at the sound of her name. "*Ros-ie, Ros-ie, Ros-ie.*" It was hammering her name into my chest. My entire entity was under her spell.

If I had seen her anger or scorn in her beautiful features, I might have been able to brave talking to her. I wanted to speak with her. I wanted to tell her I could be every bit of a catch as my nephew.

If it was her temper I was going to face, I would have faced it. I had seen her anger plenty of times before. I didn't recognize the look on her face, though. The sorrow and sadness in her eyes scared me more than her anger ever could.

The only reasons I could think of that she could be sad or mournful were unfavorable to me. I didn't want any scenario that came to my head.

"Hey! Hey, Rian!" A blonde girl chases me as I walked fast towards the car in the parking lot where I planned on calling an Uber. It was the girl I would see with Rosie most often. I didn't remember her name, but she seemed to know mine. "Where are you going?!"

Her shoes clicked on the concrete as she ran over to me.

"I'm sorry?" I frowned at her. If this was another one of Rosie's friends coming to try to kiss me and make even more of a mess of my chances at convincing Rosie to accept me, I wanted no part.

"Where are you going? Rosie... Rosie was looking for you."

I grimaced. Surely she wanted to get the rejection over with so she could go back to pine over Taegan. No way was I going to let that happen.

"I'm heading back to the resort. Something came up," I lied.

The blonde girl gave me a disapproving look. "You're running away."

My breath caught. She knew. I almost wished she had been there to try to kiss me like the other girl. That would give me an excuse to walk away from this question.

"Come on." She stomped her foot, whining like she knew me well enough to command me to do what she wanted. It would be amusing under normal circumstances. "Don't run away. Talk to her."

"I can't," I managed to say. "Not... not tonight." Not on her birthday.

Shit. I still had her present.

I pulled the box out of my pocket, the blonde girl watching me curiously, looking like she still wanted to argue.

Before she could, I thrust the wrapped box towards her. "Can.... can you give this to her for me?"

The girl pursed her lips to the side of her face. "I think you should give it to her yourself."

I dropped my outstretched arm, then looked down at the gift. My thumb traced over the tape that was keeping the wrapping in place. I wanted to see Rosie's expression when she opened it. Even before seeing her tonight, back when I first picked it out, I wanted to see her reaction to my gift. I was hoping she would treasure it in some way.

Now, I was not sure if she would even accept it.

"Tomorrow," the blonde girl said. "She will be at the cove tomorrow. I'll make sure. Meet us there and you can give it to her then. You two can.... talk. You both need to talk."

I smiled weakly. "Okay."

She sighed, placing her hand over her forehead like she had a headache. "Stupid Julia. If it wasn't for her....."

"If it wasn't for her, what?" What would have happened if that horrible girl from earlier hadn't interrupted?

Would Rosie have rejected me then, in front of everyone?

Or would she have gotten carried away with the bond? Would she have claimed me before she had time to think?

"Just.... Be there tomorrow, Rian. Don't run away from my friend for too long."

The girl gave me a reassuring smile before turning and heading back inside.

It felt like she was telling me it would be okay with that smile. The only way it would be okay is if Rosie accepted me. Was that what she was saying? Was that what she was hinting at?

The cove? Where could that be?

I would have to ask Callum later.

The present felt heavy in my hands, even though it was as light as it could be earlier. The weight of the burden of giving it to her myself now, possibly facing the worst situation I could ever face, was heavy. It weighed down on my very soul.

Could I convince Rosie that I was not inferior to the man she really wanted? Could I show her that I can be equally good for her?

I haven't even been able to convince myself of that very thing. How do I convince her?

***

"Are you sure you don't mind coming with me?" I asked Callum the next day.

My explanation of the party and my subsequent Uber ride surprised him. He had no idea. It seems Taegan was the only one who knew I was Rosie's mate.

I asked Callum about the cove, telling him about Rosie's friend asking me to meet them there. He volunteered to come with me. He seemed really eager to go, too.

"I need to go too, bro. I wouldn't miss it."

"Why?" I looked at him weirdly as he sprayed Taegan's cologne on his neck and wrists. He never wears cologne. He looked more eager than me. Even his hair was styled today. He was wearing something other than workout attire, too.

He shrugged, but had an anxious face. "I just need to see something."

"What?" I probed. He was usually uninterested in this kind of thing. He normally would rather stay here at the resort or with his aunt when we came to Miami, only tagging along with Taegan and me when Taegan forced him.

"I think I felt something," he frowned. "I'd rather confirm it now than let her..... Nevermind. I just need to go."

I wanted to press him for more, but it was his business. If he wanted to tell me, he would.

Taegan and I still weren't talking. I knew he didn't think my situation was his fault, and it might not be... But I was still upset. I still wanted to hit him whenever I saw him.

Who wouldn't be mad in my shoes? The girl that was supposed to be mine has been in love with him for years. Instead of staying away from her, he came back here every chance he could to lead her on some more.

Right now, he was out with the Meyers brothers and their twins, doing who knows what, while Callum and I got ready.

The cove was apparently a party boat hub, where all the teenagers from the pack tied off their parents' boats and barges to one another so they could party and have fun with other supernaturals. This wasn't the kind of place Taegan would condone us going.

Screw him. I was not going for the party. I was going to see Rosie and convince her to give me a chance.

I pocketed the present in my swim trunks, then walked out of the hotel room with Callum, hoping that somehow I could show her that she needed me, just like I now know I needed her as I need oxygen to breathe or water to drink.

I needed her. Her name was now ingrained in my soul.

6

— ❖ —

COUSINS

Rosie

"Stupid," I groaned, looking at my reflection in the mirror. "Fucking fuck, fuck, I look so fucking stupid." I tore the wrap cover-up over my swimsuit off and threw it on the fucking bed.

I tried to wear something more girly, something not so basic and athletic. Most of my swimsuits and bikinis were just plain, made for comfort more than anything. My grandma Mary bought me the one I was wearing two summers ago, and I just tried it on for the first time today, hoping it would help me look more feminine and less tomboyish.

It just looked fucking stupid on me.

I was not a ruffles and floral print kind of girl, no matter how hard I tried to be. It was a fucking tankini on top of that, with a frilly matching wrap to wear around your waist. On the wrack it looked like something a princess might wear, but it just looked fucking stupid on my body. I had too much muscle in my stomach and arms to pull it off. They designed it for women with softer figures. Not girls like me.

No wonder Rian ran away from the party last night. I was a bitch and, on top of that, I didn't have a girly bone in my fucking body. I was no match for a fairy royal. I was no fucking match for a prince.

I stripped out of the offending, pastel-colored, flower print ugliness and tossed both pieces into the trash bin. I kept the thing on the off chance that Grandma Mary might one day ask me to wear it, but she's been living with Lady Delilah for the past year, no longer interested much in her family. I hadn't seen her since she moved in full-time with the vampire leader and if I do see her again, I doubt she would care about my swimwear. Lady Delilah was all she cared about now.

Grandpa Jared gave up trying to bring her back to her humanity. He moved back into the packhouse to be closer to us and just visits her once or twice a month when Lady Delilah calls to tell him she was having a more human day.

Lady Delilah sired my grandma seventeen years ago to save her life. Grandpa Jared knew that one day she would care more for the vampire leader than him. He accepted the loss of what he once had with his mate. I felt sorry for him, but he claimed being our grandpa fulfilled him, so he's fine now.

He was not fine. Even mom said so. He's essentially lost two mates, not just one. Yes, Grandma Mary was still alive, but she was just a vampire's puppet now. She wasn't always so devoted solely to Lady Delilah, but now that's her sole purpose in life. Pleasing her master.

Maybe my pity towards Grandpa Jared also contributed to me keeping the ugly swimsuit. It was one of Grandma Mary's last humanly and grandma-y acts towards me.

I'll just make sure to give him a huge hug as an apology later, even if I don't tell him why. I was not keeping the swimsuit and I'm not trying to wear ruffles ever again. Fuck that.

I groaned, cursing loudly, and started digging through my drawers until I found my favorite bikini. Just a basic black one I got at the athletic outlet store last summer. It wasn't cute or pretty, but it was comfortable and the bottoms didn't rise up when I swam.

I was about to put it on when mom just barged into my room while I was still completely naked.

"Mom!" I groaned, hurrying to cover my lower half.

"Oh, please. I have a vagina too. It's nothing I haven't seen."

"Still!" I glared at her. Mom was a little too comfortable with nudity. "You could have knocked."

"I wiped your ass, little girl. Nice tan line, by the way."

"Thanks," I grunted, pulling on the swim bottoms before fastening the top. "Do you need something, or do you just want to watch me change and make me feel as uncomfortable as possible?"

"As much as I love making my children feel uncomfortable, I wanted to know who you're cussing out." She quirked a brow. Sitting on my bed, she lifted the wrap for the bathing suit I had just tossed and made a face at it. "Ew. You still have this?"

I shrugged. "Grandma gave it to me."

"Yes, well, she gave me a Santa figurine riding a unicorn one Christmas. Guess where that ended up?"

"In dad's office," I rolled my eyes. "Are you saying you want me to give the swim suit to dad to wear?"

"The one your dad puts up in his office is the one she got him. They were meant to be a matching set. Mine got tossed in the fucking trash. But I like the idea of your dad in a flower print. Go ahead and try giving it to him."

"Should I?" I took the wrap from her and tossed it with the rest of the horrible outfit. "Ruffles aren't his thing, either."

"I guess they're not. Not really anyone's thing," Mom chuckled. "So, was it the toddler-looking swimwear that offended you or were you cursing at someone else? You've been in a funk since last night at your party."

I bit my lip as I searched for a pair of shorts to put on over the swim bottoms. Mom asked me last night what was wrong, but I was able to put off telling her. I acted like I was just tired and went to bed early, despite her and Aunt Sim trying to get me to go out with them to Uncle Vincent's night club.

She was not going to let it go now. Mom never just let shit go.

"I'm just trying to get ready to go out with Sophia tonight, mom."

"You're going out with Sophia, so you thought you'd try wearing something that was going to just piss you off? I don't buy it. What's up?"

"Mom," I groaned.

"Rosie…" She narrowed her eyes at me. "Is this because Taegan isn't your mate?"

"What?" I snapped, taken back for a moment. "No!"

I haven't even thought about Taegan once.

"No? You've been adamant that he's your mate for years. You're telling me you just don't care now? It's okay if you're disappointed, baby. Anyone would understand. Bailey called me this morning to ask me how you were doing."

"Mom, it's really not that. Seriously." I felt a bit embarrassed now at hearing that Taegan's mom called my mom to see how I took the news. Everyone was waiting for me to be disappointed.

Mom eyed me warily as I grabbed a tank top and pull it on. "Then what's going on?"

"It's noth-"

"You tell me it's nothing one more time and I'll get your dad up here to make this a family affair. He can get you to talk and wear the floral takini at the same time. Two birds." She shrugged. "One stone. Your choice."

She wasn't going to let this go. "Fine," I huffed. "Don't freak out on me, though."

"Why would I freak out?" She glared at me accusingly.

"Mom....."

"I'm not promising anything but bodily harm if you don't tell me now," she growled. "No way I'm letting you not tell me after saying that."

My goddess, she was fucking persistent.

"Fine! I.... I found my mate."

"What?!" Mom sat up straighter on the bed, a broad grin spreading on her face. "Who?! Do I know him?"

"Maybe," I grumbled.

She gave me a confused look. "Why don't you look happy? Who is it? Do I need to kick someone's ass?"

"No, mom." I rolled my eyes. I feel like kicking my own ass. "I just.... I just wasn't that nice to him for a long time, is all. He.... He is probably going to reject me."

"Oh, baby," Mom patted the bed, giving me a look, daring me not to sit by her. Forceful comfort was a thing in this home. You want to be left alone to wallow in self-pity? Too fucking bad. Mom was going to love on you until you feel better whether or not you want her too.

I plopped down in a huff and she wrapped her arms around me, resting her head on my shoulder.

"Who is it?"

I groaned internally. I was not telling her. No matter what. She really might beat him up to get him to accept me. She was that kind of mom.

"Not telling you."

Mom sighed. "You're so stubborn. Just like your father."

I scoffed. "He said I got it from you."

"The fuck he did," she grumbled. "I'm not stubborn. I'm just always right."

I rolled my eyes, laughing softly.

"So, did he feel the bond, too? Is he younger or older?"

"Older," I answered honestly. "I think he did. He... he avoided me after the bond clicked into place. He left the party early and everything."

"Someone who left your party early, huh?" Mom mused. "Maybe he just needed to leave early? He doesn't have a chosen mate or kids, does he?"

"No," I shook my head. "He's.... He's not mated." I'm 99.9% sure he doesn't have kids either. I'm sure Callum would have mentioned that if he did.

"Oh, good." Mom let out a breath. "Not that you couldn't make it work with a single dad, but you give off evil step-mom vibes."

"What the hell?" I jerked away from her while she laughed.

"I'm just kidding. Kind of. So, is he going to be where you and Sophia are going tonight? Is that why you tried to wear that ugly thing?" She pointed at the swimsuit.

"Yeah. I.... I wanted to look more girly."

"Oh, sweetie. That swim suit is just juvenile, not girly. If you want to look girly, get out of this sports bra and tank outfit and put on a real bikini and a dress over it."

"This isn't a sports bra. It's a bathing suit."

"Sweetie." Mom gave me a reprimanding look. "It's a fucking sports bra. Not even a flattering one. Wear the white bikini Sim got you. You can borrow a sundress from me."

I groaned at the idea of wearing a dress. I was willing to try the wrap, but a dress sounded constricting for where we were going.

"Up!" mom smacked my thigh. "Get the white bikini on. I'll be right back. You don't need to look girly to attract your mate. You just need to look hot, and then the bond will take care of the rest."

***

Rian

"Do you see her?" I asked Callum. He was busy looking at the dozens of boats and barges tied together, looking for a place to tie us off to.

"Chill, man. I need to dock this thing, then I can help you find her."

"Just tie it off there." I pointed to a random barge.

"No! I don't want to get blocked in. This isn't really my scene and I want to be able to get out fast."

Looking around, I could see what he meant. Callum didn't like loud parties or drinking. He'd rather be home on a Saturday night lounging on the couch while eating a whole pizza and a two liter of some sugary toxic beverage by himself.

Too bad, because this party actually looked fun. The atmosphere was vibrating with magic. The hue of fae essence was lighting the air. Even the barges were connected with magic. The sun was just starting to set, lighting the scene with an ethereal glow. Music was echoing in the trees on the land close by, shaking the Spanish moss and leaves to make them appear like they were dancing along.

There were all teenage supernatural races in attendance, including sirens dancing beneath the surface of the water. My throat itched from my gills with the desire to dive in and join them.

My mom was a fae royal princess, and my real father was a siren knight. He was not a good man, and was killed by my uncle to save my mother, but I still carry his siren blood. Living where we do, I haven't had many opportunities to explore my siren heritage, but my body was throbbing with the desire to shift into my fins and join in on the swirling trance of scaled bodies under the sea.

"There," Callum pointed to one boat on the far edge of the cluster. "That's the Alpha's boat. I bet that's Rosie's."

I looked at where he was pointing, seeing the large speed boat. Rosie wasn't on it. My heart dropped in my chest from the disappointment.

But she was here. If her boat was here, that meant she was here, too.

I started frantically looking around again, searching for the stunning Alpha that I couldn't even muster up the confidence to talk to yesterday. My hand instinctively went to my pocket to feel for the necklace.

I was still looking around, much to Callum's annoyance, as he tied off the boat with barely and help from me. Then, at the first level of one of the barges at the center of the cluster, I saw her. She was absolutely glowing. Beautiful. Beyond a doubt, she was the most beautiful girl I had ever laid eyes on.

She was in a group of friends, the one from yesterday that followed me into the parking lot right beside her. Both of them had red cups in their hands. Her friend was fancied in a sundress, but she has nothing on Rosie. No one did.

Rosie's face and hair were all natural today, no makeup or a pinned-up updo. Her skin glowed in the ethereal lights. I had never seen her in a dress like this before. She was usually in athletic gear. The dress was short, cutting off at the top of her thighs, flared out a bit at her sensual hips. Her back was bare except for a single blue butterfly tattoo, the dress tying around her neck. Straps to a bikini were sticking out teasingly, making her smooth skin look more enticing. The ivory shade made her tan glow even more.

She was breathtaking.

"Wow," Callum breathed out beside me.

Vile rose in my throat, and anger flared in my chest. Was he gawking at his own cousin? But then his next words left me stunned instead.

"I knew it," he grinned. "She's my mate."

7

INTERRUPTED

"Who?!" I demanded. He better not be talking about his dang cousin. I have never fought a wolf, but I suddenly felt strong enough to take him on.

"Her." Callum pointed to the girl next to Rosie. The one who followed me out into the parking lot to invite me here. "The pretty one."

I smiled and huffed out a laugh. "Good, because the gorgeous one is mine."

Callum snorted. For the first time, he didn't look reluctant to join a party. We leaped between boats and barges to get to our mates, both of us with different kinds of determination.

Callum was a Gamma, and a monster of a warrior. He would have no trouble securing his mate. Though, from the curious look on her face when she caught sight of us, I suspected she had yet to turn eighteen. Her eyes showed she was attracted to Callum, but I didn't see the frenzied obsession I saw for a moment in Rosie's eyes yesterday. She was not sniffing the air or anything. Just watching Callum as he moved closer to her. She didn't even notice me.

"What's her name?" Callum asked.

"How should I know? She's your cousin's friend."

"She's your mate's friend. I thought you said you talked to her yesterday."

"I did, but her name didn't come up. If you actually socialized outside of your warrior training, you might know her name. Don't blame me."

He growled in annoyance, making me laugh again.

When I looked back at the women, Rosie was looking our way. She eyed me questioningly. Her brows pulled into a conflicting, almost sad expression, which took the smile right off my face.

What was she sad about? Was she.... Was she really going to reject me? Was this a lost cause?

No. I could show her I could be a suitable partner to her. I could prove that even though I had no wolf blood, I could still be a match for a strong alpha wolf like her.

I hoped.

Damn it. I wished I could just tell what she was thinking. I wished I knew what words to say to win her over. My blood felt like it was running backward under her gaze. Her beautiful, beautiful gaze.

The necklace felt heavy in my pocket. The meaning of me giving it to her was different now. I didn't just want my magic infused in the pendant to protect her. I wanted her to give me a chance to prove I could protect her, too. All my magic, all of me, I wanted to be devoted to her.

"Hi," I heard Callum say in his deepest voice, trying to sound alluring to his mate, no doubt. "Do you know who I am?"

Rosie broke her gaze from me to look over at her cousin speaking to her friend. After a few more seconds of letting my eyes linger on her beautiful features, trying hard not to stare at her entirely in her very sexy attire, I did the same. I turned to watch her friend blush, staring up at the smoldering Gamma.

She nodded softly. "Gamma Callum. You're Rose's cousin."

"Just Callum to you." Callum ran a finger down her cheek. "Mate." His voice was gravelly, full of possession.

The girl gasped, her eyes going wide. She was definitely not of age yet, but the connection between them was clear. Even without her fully feeling the bond, she was shivering from his touch.

Rosie growled deep in her chest. "You have got to be fucking kidding me." She then turned those powerful and fiery eyes on me. "We need to talk. NOW."

Without waiting for me to respond, she grabbed my hand and hauled me away from the others. The electricity I felt where her hand gripped mine was like nothing I'd ever felt before. I made the most embarrassing sound in the back of my throat that I hoped she didn't hear over the noise of the party.

As we weaved through the people, Rosie dragging me to the farthest barge, we got plenty of curious and concerned looks. Rosie just ignored them. I noticed the girl that pissed me off yesterday, the one who had forced a kiss on me before. She was wearing a very scanty bikini, but wrapped a bright pink towel around her body when I glared at her stare. She quickly hung her head, then hurried away from us. Whether she feared me or

Rosie, I didn't know, and I didn't care. I was just happy she was leaving. I didn't want her interruption again.

Wait. Maybe Rosie pulling me away to talk to me alone wasn't a good thing. She growled when she heard her cousin was mated with her friend. I got excited at the moment as she grabbed my hand, but maybe this wasn't going to go well for me. I got lost in the feeling of her hand in mine, but she didn't react at all. No shivers like her friend.

"Wait. Rosie," I panicked, pulling against her hold. She gripped my hand tighter, looking back for a brief second with a hard expression. "Um, where... where are we going?"

"To talk," she Said curtly. "I can't even be fucking happy for my friend until I get our shit sorted out."

Sorted out? I gulped nervously, my panic making my heart race.

"Rosie," I tugged against her hand. "Wait. Are you going to...." I couldn't bring myself to finish that sentence. Are you going to reject me?

She stopped, then slowly turned to look back at me. Our eyes were locked for what felt like forever but, at the same time, no time at all. The entire world around us disappeared. It was just us. I couldn't even hear the music over the pounding of my heart.

A heartbreaking expression crossed Rosie's face, making my heart hammer in my chest even harder and my mouth to go dry. "Am I going to what? What are you so scared of? Do you hate me that much?"

"What?" Me hate her? She was the one that hated me. I thought she did, anyway. Was this not going to be a rejection?

Before I could find the right words to ask, a terrible scream echoed from the other end of the party, resonating in the darkest corner near a boat tied to the barge with the fewest people. I got an ominous feeling. The energy stirring around it was dark. Demonic.

Rosie snapped into action in a second, letting go of my hand and sprinting for the boat with a determined look on her face. She lept over the water and gaps between the different water vessels. I was close on her heels, running on instinct, just chasing her.

When we got to the boat, blood was all around the deck, along with a single pink towel.

After a split second, I realized it was that girl's towel. It was the one she wrapped around herself before walking away with fear in her eyes.

"Julie," Rosie gasped, touching the blood and sniffing its scent. Callum was soon beside me, smelling strongly of Rosie's friend.

He was all business now as he looked at the blood and around the boat for some sign of what had happened. It was the three of us, but others were crowding around to see what happened.

I felt it now. The dark energy in the air was thick and familiar. It was similar to the magic inside me, only feral. It was the magic and aura of a siren.

Leaning over the side of the boat, I felt the magic already deep in the water, still lingering near the boat. With a flick of my wrist, I pushed a strong pulse of my light energy into the depths, watching through my magic as it traveled like a sonar illuminating the surrounding water.

There he was, eyes black as coal and scales glimmering in the light of my magic, reflecting their sharp edges.

He wasn't just a siren, but the worst of the species. More demon than fae energy inside. The result of demons and sirens intermingling in the past. His blackened eyes and blackened razor scales were a tell-all sign.

The girl, Julie, was unconscious but still alive. I could see the pulsing of her blood in her neck. Deep claw marks broke her flesh, her blood like ribbons streaming around her in the water from the wounds. She would drown soon with the creature's claws still embedded in her legs as he dragged her behind him tauntingly.

"Julie!" Rosie screamed, making the thing turn to snarl menacingly back, his face threatening as he showed his razor-sharp teeth. Rosie moved to dive in, but I blocked her way, pushing her back to her cousin, then dove into the water myself before she tries again.

I couldn't let her get hurt. This wasn't a normal merman like what she must be used to. He was dangerous, likely trying to lure more of them into the water. That was why he hadn't swum that far. With her being a werewolf, even an Alpha, she would be no match for him. Like a lion trying to fight a shark.

As for me, I was not a mere siren or just a fae. I was the son of a fairy princess and the highest order of siren knights. Instantly, my body shifted, transforming into my siren form. My tail and fins replaced my legs, causing my shorts to fall to the rocky bottom. My gills emerged, and I sucked in a much needed breath before swimming full force towards the demonic siren.

His coal eyes widened in surprise as he darted off. He likely thought I was just a fae when I used my magic. He now knew. He could sense my energy now that I was in the same waters as him. I saw genuine fear outline his face before he gripped the girl's leg tighter and sprinted through the water, leaving a trail of bubbles and a current behind.

Pushing my magic forward, my eyes glowed, my scaled hands pushed forward through the water to send out a stupefying pulse. He narrowly dodged it, changing course and pushing harder. Before I could try again, a black vortex opened before him, sucking him and the girl in like a whirlwind before funneling closed, preventing me from following.

That was a portal. The energy was powerful. Too strong. No simple siren could make a portal to my realm like that. Not even one with demon blood.

He wasn't working alone. He couldn't have been. I would have felt that level of power traveling out of him. It would have moved the water differently and sucked the life force from nearby. That was how demon energy worked.

That portal came from the other side. Someone in Alfheimr pulled him there.

I scanned the ocean water around, searching for some sign that someone else might be watching. A third party to act as a scout. I tried to feel for another's aura, but the only sources I felt were back towards the party. Even the regular sirens who had been dancing in the water in the sensual serenade had stayed back in the crowd, where it was safer.

Shit. I wasn't able to save Rosie's friend. I wasn't able to do anything but chase him away.

8

NEW FEELINGS

Rosie

"Rose, stop!" Callum locked his arms around my stomach and shoulders as Rian dove into the water. He was still wearing his clothes, but looked determined as his magic glowed around him.

A deep growl ripped out of me, unable to watch my mate face the monster that looked like the spawn of King Trident and Satan himself. I had never seen Rian fight. He couldn't face a demon-looking thing like that. I couldn't lose him. All the fear I felt for Julia when I heard her screams and saw her being dragged away by the sea monster was nothing compared to the drive I felt now to protect my mate.

I was not letting my cousin stop me. Slipping my legs between Callum's, I hooked my foot around his calves, then threw my head back. His nose making a sickening crack, causing him to trip backward and let me go as he groaned, clutched at his face.

Looking over the side of the railing, I was about to dive in to fight for Rian, but was caught off guard by the beautiful creature beneath the water's surface. I had never seen Rian in his siren form. I thought he would look similar to any of the other mermen in the cove, but he was anything but. He looked regal, his power glowing in each one of his shimmering silver scales, like an angel in the water.

He was magnificent. I was so stunned by his image I forgot what it was he was doing in the first place. That was, until a surge of magic pushed from his glowing palms, the blast shooting towards the dark creature who stole my friend.

The creature looked scared of Rian, swimming towards a black abyss in the water that didn't belong there. It swam right through it, dragging Julia with it before the blackness swirled quickly until it was closed, preventing Rian from chasing him further.

I selfishly breathed a sigh of relief, then guilt hit me. I was relieved my mate didn't get hurt... but my friend was still taken, and might be dead for all I knew. I was so fucking selfish. No wonder Rian didn't want to be alone with me. I didn't even feel worthy of being an alpha at that moment, let alone his mate.

But, hell or high water, I was not giving up either. Not without a fight.

Rian swam around the spot where the black vortex disappeared. He was looking exasperated before he turned back to swim towards the boat slowly, scanning his surroundings as he went.

"Everyone, stay put. No one leaves!" Callum yelled, recovered from my assault. "Rose, we need to make sure no one leaves. They need to stay here and stay together until reinforcements get here."

I heard my cousin, but I made sure Rian was closer to the boat before I looked back to acknowledge what he had said. Looking from Callum to everyone else in the crowd, there were many scared faces, but I also saw many of my warriors ready to step up.

"Keep them on the barges. Two warriors at each end. Callum, can you get a few to patrol around the cove close by? Use my dad's boat. I'll mind link him now to call the council." I looked around until I saw a fairy girl I knew well from school. "Elida, can you call Melody so she sends someone sooner?"

"I already alerted Lady Melody, Alpha. She is coming now."

Melody was the fae representative on the council for supernaturals here in Miami. She was a long-time friend of my mom's.

As the warriors started to move into action, directing the party-goers to the main barges that are well lit, I sent a mind link to dad, letting him know what just happened. He was on his way before the link even closed.

Callum moved quickly, grabbing a few of the volunteers to get on my boat and another speed boat that someone else volunteered to patrol the waters. He stopped to check Sophia, making sure she was fine and giving her a brief but sweet kiss. It made my heart pang, seeing how quickly they accepted one another. Even though Sophia wouldn't be eighteen until late this summer.

Water splashing behind me caused me to turn back around, watching as Rian tossed his sopping wet shorts onto the deck, then pulling himself up. He still had his fins and tail, so I went to help him, but then he shifted back before his feet landed gracefully on the hard surface. He was completely naked. I stopped and looked away, embarrassed. I almost grabbed a hand full of... him.

"Can't even look at me?" I heard him whisper under his breath, scoffing slightly.

Was he joking? Did he want me to look at him naked? I would. I was all for it.

Well, I'd seen men naked at training, but that felt different from having my mate naked right beside me. I never lusted after one of them like I was doing now. My body and mind were on a whole other wavelength, leaving me mortified.

The pull on the bond and the Alpha blood in me was demanding I claim him. The adrenaline of what had just happened made my blood rush, fanning the flames inside me. The fear I felt when I thought he was diving into danger was suffocating, and being near him was like finally getting air.

If I lost him before having the chance to really know him, to make him mine, I don't know what I would have done. How I would have carried on.

Seeing his magic and the power he held in the water was like nothing I had ever seen. That monster swam as hard as it could to get away from him. It was eye-opening. He was always reserved on land, looking like the life of the party more than a fighter, but in the water, he was like the ruler of the sea, his royalty shining through. Pride welled up in me for being gifted him as my mate.

Shyness gripped me now. I'd never felt shy like this before. The pull of the bond and the desire in me had me frozen again, not knowing what to do. I wanted to help him up, but with him naked, I didn't know if I could just approach him the way Callum did to Sophia. I wanted to, but shyness was not something I was familiar with. I didn't know how to stifle it down.

I'd never touched a naked man before if I wasn't kicking his ass while we sparred between wolf and human forms. But that was training. Was Rian teasing me now, or was he disappointed I wouldn't look at him?

Chancing a glance, I saw him pulling up his shorts, fumbling with something in his pockets with a disgruntled face before looking up through his lashes at me. "I'll find her," he stated.

I was confused for a moment. Who? His shorts? I think I would prefer it if he lost those again.

"Your friend. I'll find her. I promise I will."

Shit. I had almost forgotten about Julia again in my desire for my mate. My pack member had just been stolen from the party, her blood still all over the boat's deck, and I was daydreaming about Rian without shorts. She could be dead, and I'm just here lusting after my unclaimed mate.

"You.... You don't have to promise that." I forced my voice, trying to get past the shy feelings now that he had his shorts on and was no longer naked. He shouldn't have to make that promise. She was my responsibility. Not his. I didn't want to burden him more than I had.

"I do. I will get her back, Rosie. I can do it. I can portal to the fae realm, unlike most fairies. I'm of royal blood."

His insistence made my throat go dry. The jealousy I felt yesterday at the party when Julia wrapped her arms around him came back. I quickly tried to shake that feeling away. She was just fucking kidnapped.

My selfishness was unchecked today. I was growing so disappointed in myself.

"Thank you," I said meekly. "I would appreciate your help."

What else could I say? Don't help me because I'm a selfish bitch and I'm jealous? You're mine and not hers?

I was looking down at the blood, trying to focus on that to keep my jealousy in check. I was an alpha and had an unclaimed mate before me. Jealousy was unfamiliar. This kind of jealousy, anyway. This uncontrollable drive to overpower any thoughts he might have of any other woman and fill his mind only with me. I wanted to sink my teeth into his nape, feeling the sparks directly again, like I did earlier when I was on a mission to talk to him and grabbed his hand.

Julia's blood was all around my feet, and it was the only thing keeping me from my selfish desires.

"Rosie," Rian reached out, touching my hand so softly, causing me to gasp and look up. The sparks were so strong, so overpowering. "I'm sorry."

Why? "Why are you sorry?" Because you would rather have my friend than me?

No. He told her off at my party yesterday. Everyone said he made it clear he didn't want Julia near him.

So what was he sorry for?

His eyes bore into mine, hypnotizing. I could see the magic he possessed moving in his beautiful irises, like the galaxies dancing around each other.

His soft touch grew tighter, the sparks now shooting up my arm. "I'm sorry I couldn't save your friend. I will help you, Rosie. I will help you in every way I can. I can prove myself to you."

"Prove yourself?" His words caught me by surprise.

He looked nervous now, shifting on his feet and looking around anxiously before his beautiful eyes met mine again.

"Don't reject me. Please. Just….let me prove that I can be every bit as worthy of a mate as the one you always wanted."

"Rian," I said his name like a plea, chancing a step forward. "No. You never have to prove yourself to me. I was the one…. I just-" I couldn't think of the right words to say. Should I apologize for being a bitch? Do I confess that I wanted to prove myself to *him*? I fucking put ruffles on to try to be somewhat of the woman I thought he would want to be with, but now he was saying he wanted to prove himself to me?

No. It was not right.

His brows pulled down, his gaze heavy, trying to decipher what I could not find the words to say.

"I am not going to reject you," I whispered.

His eyes widened in surprise. Then, the magic in them danced even stronger than before. "Really?" The corner of his lips quirked up.

"Really," I smiled softly in return. "Tonight, I wanted to convince you to accept me."

9

FLIRTY MERMAIDS

My dad and mom showing up deterred us from talking much more. Even though it was all I wanted to do, it wasn't the time. Not when one of our own, one of my friends at that, was just brutally kidnapped from the party.

Our eyes remained on one another often, watching each other as I worked beside my dad and he spoke with Melody and the mermaids that remained in the cove. When he got too close to one of the beautiful mermaids floating in the water, while she was gazing up at him like he was made of gold and diamonds, a fierce growl resounded out of me, causing everyone to turn and stare.

"Rosie?" Dad furrowed his brows, wondering what the hell was up with me. Mom just followed my gaze before I moved it away from Rian, then smirked, knowing exactly why I was growling.

Shit. She was going to harass the crap out of me later. I could see the wheels turning in her head already.

Fuck, that was embarrassing. I couldn't help myself. Even during this shit and the investigation starting up, I couldn't stop worrying about my mate. My mate, who I barely got the chance to clear the air with or talk to, since we both admitted we would not reject one another. Seeing the mermaid openly flirting enraged me like nothing I had felt before.

Well, besides Julia, but since she was the one taken tonight, I couldn't really find it in me to want her hurt the way I want to hurt tuna-fish-Barbie.

"Sorry," I muttered to my dad. "I'm just pissed," I said vaguely, hoping he assumed I was pissed about Julia missing and not a damned fin-flipper fluttering her wet eyelashes at Rian. I mean, I was pissed about Julia too, but since I couldn't yet murder the siren who took her, the mermaid floating a few feet away from my mate would make a decent substitute for an ass kicking.

Dad patted my back soothingly. "I know, sweetie. We will find your friend." When he turned back to Trevor, his Beta, and they started to talk about pack politics and what it would take to get Queen Aisling to allow for us to send a team into Alfheimr, I took another hesitant look at Rian.

Rian was watching me intently, now standing on the other side of Melody, having her talk to the mermaid instead of him. The mermaid was still stealing glances at Rian, but his eyes were only for me. The longer we stared at one another, the stronger the pull was to join him. Not just join him, but touch him, hug him, kiss him.... And so much more.

I just wanted to bury my face in his nape and inhale his intoxicating scent, like the sweet, briny sea and endless sunshine.

"Your dad is going to catch on if you don't stop staring," my mom surprised me, bumping her hip against mine. "Not that he could do anything, but you know how protective your dad can get. Irrational, I know, but most parents are when it comes to their kids."

I made a face, not sure I wanted dad to know until I had a real chance to talk to Rian. More needed to be said than just 'I'm not going to reject you'. There were still other issues we needed to make clear and sort out, like him wanting to go back to be a prince in his fairy kingdom, and me being the next alpha of my pack. That would make him my Luna if he accepted me.

"I take it the two of you still haven't talked?" She raised an eyebrow.

I looked over at my dad to make sure he was still too engrossed in his conversation with Beta Trevor to overhear us before I answered her.

"We established we aren't rejecting one another. That's about it."

"That's a start!" She said encouragingly. "Just walk over there and bite him. In front of everyone. Little mermaid and her school of hussies would back right the fuck off then, and he would be yours forever. Problem solved."

"Mom," I groaned, not appreciating my mother's irrational advice. She was the queen of jumping the gun. "I'm not taking his choice from him."

"What fucking choice? Look at him. He can't keep those dreamy eyes of his off you." She bit her lip and moaned. "Is it weird that I'm excited to hear about what that magic touch of his can do to you?"

"Mom!" I snapped. "It's more than fucking weird."

"What?! Thyra has told me stories. Did you know she can jerk off her brute of a mate without even touching him? She makes him fall to his knees and just has her way with him, only using her magic."

"Oh my goddess, mom. Stop!" That's my future mother-in-law and Alpha Max she was talking about. I knew for a fucking fact Alpha Max would be shitting bricks and blowing smoke out of his nose if he knew how my mom was talking about him and any aspect of his sex life.

Plus, I was her damn daughter. Even if she wasn't my mom, it would be weird to talk about this kind of shit. I hadn't even jerked someone off before. I didn't want to hear about my mate's mother doing it to his step-dad.

"What are you two talking about?" Dad suddenly asked.

"Nothing!" I blurted out, making my mom stifle her laughter.

Dad narrowed an eye, tilting his face while scrutinizing us.

"Girl talk," mom murmured with a hand over her mouth.

"Girl talk, huh?" he repeated, not believing her. Mom and I were not girly women. She never stopped 'girl talk' on dad's behalf. She had no filter, so her saying girl talk was more suspicious than anything. "What kind of girl talk?"

Rian chose that moment to approach us. The hair on the back of my neck tickled me with excitement when his scent came closer and closer. My excitement was mixed with anxiety since dad still didn't know. The pull I had towards Rian was magnified the closer he came. It didn't lessen even when he was standing right next to me. My mom was eyeing us with amusement. I barely registered Melody while trying so hard to hide my inner frenzy in front of my dad.

It was not a very Alpha thing to do to lose your cool because of your mate. Especially at a time like this.

Peeking up at Rian, he looked as handsome as ever, but there was still a trace of anxiety outlining his features. Was he nervous about being in front of my dad, too?

"Alpha Snider, sir," Rian bowed his head in a very fairy-like manner, looking every bit the prince he was. "We have spoken to the sirens present."

"None of these children knew the fiend who abducted one of your own," Melody informed us. "None actually saw the creature until Prince Rian illuminated the waters."

"Was this creature not a siren?" Dad asked.

"I believe he was more of the demonic race than a simple siren, Alpha," Rian filled in.

"It's strange that the being would capture a she-wolf and not one of the mer-people that were easier to apprehend in the water," mom mused. She was looking around at the other werewolf teenagers still lingering on their boats and the barges, waiting to be released back to the mainland.

"He was taunting us with the she-wolf. He didn't swim off until I dove in and shifted." Rian said.

"Why would he do that?" I stared up at him.

Rian held my gaze for a few moments, making my face feel hot before he answered. "I'm not sure. Maybe he was trying to get more of your warriors in the water."

Dad looked between Rian and me, narrowing his eyes, and it took mom coughing for me to pull my eyes away from Rian's.

"Everything okay between you two?" Dad asked.

Fuck. The fucking mate bond and the pull it had on me, along with the unyielding attraction I felt for this sexy, sweet-smelling man, made it impossible for me to hide my inner desires, even in front of my dad.

While I took a few seconds to wrack my brain, trying to come up with some excuse as to why I was so enamored with the fairy prince beside me, Rian was the one to speak up.

"She is my mate, sir," Rian admitted boldly. He left me, Melody, and even my mom, stunned. Mom was wearing an impressed smile while gaping at him.

"What?" Dad looked at me for confirmation.

I cringed under his scrutiny, but nodded just enough for him to catch it, not wanting to deny Rian at all. Even if it meant my dad might end up going all protective dad on him.

Dad huffed, pressing his lips tightly together while looking between the two of us. His thoughts were unreadable.

Rian surprised me further by reaching out and grabbing my hand. The sparks shot up my arm from his touch, calming me instantly, but also making me feel giddy and anything but calm in a way that is hard to describe. I was calm in the way that my thoughts weren't conflicting about hiding the fact he was my mate from my dad, but I was frantic to claim him as my own.

That didn't go unnoticed by dad. He grunted, then nodded to himself.

"Good for you," he sighed, then placed a tense smile on his face. "Actually, great for you, Rian Kissinger. We will be having a lengthy discussion later about why this is so great for you, among other things."

Oh my goddess, I was going to kill my dad...

"I'm happy for you, sweetie." His face softened when he looked at me. "As long as you're happy?"

He left the question hanging in the air, making me wonder what all he was thinking even more. Did he have something against Rian? Mom was even staring at dad like she was trying to figure out the meaning of his words.

I nodded tentatively, not sure what dad was probing for.

Dad sighed, looking back at Beta Trevor, who was watching with an amused look on his face. Melody looked stunned still. A fairy prince mated to an Alpha was probably a big deal in his world, and he just boldly proclaimed it for all to hear.

For all to hear....

I looked back at the water, seeing the mermaid from earlier and her friends with disappointed looks on their faces. He said that loud enough for them to hear, too.

I felt like the queen of the fucking world. He was obviously nervous about being in front of my dad, but he boldly claimed me as his mate because of my sensitivity to the mermaids being flirty with him earlier.

Fuck, I wanted him more than ever before.

I squeezed his hand, grateful and proud. Watching him from the corner of my eye, I saw a small smile hinting at his perfect lips.

"I'm happy," I told my dad, more confident than ever. "I really couldn't be happier than I am right now."

10

SHADOWED CAVERNS

*T*he infernal siren hauled the unconscious body of the werewolf girl up to the shore of the cavernous bay on the ocean outskirts of Alfheimr. His breath was coming out in desperate gasps, the extra weight he hauled slowing him down now that he was on dry land. He hadn't been directly struck by the prince's magic, but the power behind the blast had seared his gills, making it hard to breathe under the water. He panted, trying to suck in much needed air now that he was on the land of Alfheimr once again.

Slowly, his dim, inky scales faded away, absorbing back into his body as his legs appeared in place of his fins and tail. His fangs, like little needles in his mouth, thickened to a more human form as he took this human shape.

Movement in the shadows caught his eye. Sinister glowing purple eyes followed his movements from the darkest, dampest corner of the cave. He had to crane his neck back to stare at it. The giant figure had a lithe body, helping it to hide more than would normally be possible outside of the water.

The creature looked furious now, making the demonic siren take a few unsteady steps back nervously.

"So you failed?" the croaking voice accused venomously before the giant creature's body shrunk down into that of a humanoid figure. A very tall humanoid figure.

With plenty of bulk, he would rival the greatest of warriors of any tribe in any world. His figure as a human was one of the many reasons he thought he could accomplish this task in one day. One look at his purple eyes and all his greatest desires would just fall into place. It took someone of the highest caliber to overcome him.

He was still a giant, even in this form, but much more manageable on land. In the water, his natural size was easy to maneuver with the help of buoyancy, but on land his massive weight made moving a task. Human form was best.

If his plan had gone as it should have, he would be spending much more time on land soon, anyway. Gravity was something he would have to get used to in the future.

"There was an unexpected hiccup, my master. The lowly mortal sirens were not the only sea creatures in attendance tonight."

Slarkrethel walked out of the shadows, letting the light from the cracks in the cave filtering in the moonlight illuminate his scarred but gravely handsome face.

He bore a face that had driven many women to temptation, which was why he was left scarred and outcast in the first place. Only one man was powerful enough to expel Slarkrethel from his rightful place, and after that person accomplished what they set out to do, Slarkrethel remained stuck in the shadows ever since.

"What, pray tell, would prevent you from accomplishing the simple task you were given?"

"There was a royal there," Grynrus stated, throwing an accusing hand towards the she-wolf bleeding and unconscious on the shore. "A fae royal. He had the blood of sirens too."

This perked Slarkrethel's ears. "A siren royal?"

"I do not know, my master. I just felt the power of his magic." He showed his still damaged neck and the trace of the prince's magic burned on his scaled skin. "The essence was not of normal pedigree. He was superior to my abilities, I am afraid to admit. I thought that it would be better for me to return with a token than not at all."

Slarkrethel hissed, not in agreement. He wanted one thing. It was something he had wanted for so long, waiting for the moment he could gain this as his own.

Again, a royal had ruined everything.

That just made Slarkrethel want it even more.

He leaned over the girl's broken and sleeping body, studying her more intently. This one could prove useful, after all. Maybe it was not a total waste bringing this she-wolf here.

"The alpha is aware that she has come over to our world?" Slarkrethel lifted an inky brow.

"If the fae royal hadn't dived in, the alpha would have herself."

A wicked smile spread on Slarkrethel's face. "Good. Good. It is not a total waste then."

He walked to a shallow pool, waving his hand above the still water, using his magic to project an image from the other side. There they were. The werewolf Alphas were discussing what they believed to be a simple attack on their territory. Little did they know that it was so much more. This was predestined for quite some time. Nothing would change the monster's mind.

Slarkrethel guided a hand over the surface, stroking the image in a wanting caress.

"I am coming for you, young one. You will soon be mine."

11

— · —

WAITING

Rosie

That was a fucking mess. All the tingles and feel-goods I felt about Rian were gone now that I was alone with my family back at the packhouse. I groaned to myself, leaning back in one of my dad's office chairs and watching my mom and Grandpa argue. They had been going on for way too long now.

"There is nothing we can do," Grandpa Jared said.

"There has to be something," mom argued. "She's one of ours! She's still a child!"

"Hun," dad rubbed her back. "You heard Melody, the same as the rest of us. They're sending knights to find and extract her."

"But it's *our* job. She's one. Of. Us." My mom stressed every word, not getting her point through to anyone.

"She's in the fairy realm, Carli," Grandpa reiterated once again. "None of us can enter the fairy realm without a royal escort. Queen Aisling has already been gracious enough to send her own men-"

"And women," mom growled.

Grandpa nodded, "and women. Queen Aisling has sent her own men and women to save the child. We wouldn't even know where to start looking for her. There is absolutely nothing we can do. All we can do now is wait."

Mom snarled, looking ready to take the full force of her rage out on grandpa. Dad grabbed her around the waist to anchor her in place, while grandpa just looked used to the reaction from her.

After the initial investigation at the cove was finished, Melody reported all her findings to her queen. Now, mom, dad, grandpa, Beta Trevor and myself were sitting and standing around dad's office, trying to figure out what to tell Julia's parents, who were waiting for news in the conference room.

I was with mom. I wanted to do something, but like grandpa said over and over again, our hands were tied.

"Fine," mom growled, shoving away from my dad while glaring at grandpa. "You be the one to tell that child's mother and father that all anyone can fucking do is wait. I'm going to raise hell in the fucking council until someone lets me through."

Mom turned and left, slamming the door behind her.

"Fucking hell," dad muttered, pinching the bridge of his nose.

"She already raised hell," Beta Trevor mumbled.

"That's what she does," dad sighed. "If she can't do anything productive, she's just going to raise hell."

"Someone should," I murmured, crossing my arms over my chest. "Mom's right. Julia is ours. We should be the ones to save her."

Dad gave me a look of sympathy. "Sweetie. I know she's your friend but-"

"But nothing! Even if she wasn't my friend, I'd still think the same. Hell, she had her fucking tongue down my mate's throat before, and tried to do it again just yesterday. I still want to be the one to go in and get her back from whoever it is that took her, then fillet him like a fucking fish."

Beta Trevor looked uncomfortable between me and my father. "Um, I think I'll go and talk to the family now. You guys should talk this out yourselves."

"There's nothing to talk about. We can't do anything but wait," Grandpa said again.

I growled, not liking his answer any more than my mom did.

"Fine," I pushed myself up from my chair.

"Where are you going, Rose?"

I glared at my dad and grandpa. "To not talk somewhere else." I don't think I can sit around and do nothing either.

I was about halfway down the hall when my dad came walking up behind me.

"Wait. Rose. I think there is more that we need to discuss here."

I glared back at him. "I don't think that it's the right fucking time for that."

"Rose," he gave me one of his looks. "Watch it."

I sighed. I knew what he wanted to talk about. He tried to order Rian away when we got back to the packhouse, though his command didn't work since Rian was not only not a werewolf, but he was fae royalty. Dad couldn't command Rian any more than he could command Queen Aisling or even Thyra, Rian's mother. Rian did agree to head back to the hotel for now, even though he didn't have to. Dad, for whatever reason, was being extremely hostile towards Rian, hiding behind his passive-aggressive tendencies and comments. Rian had been too forgiving of my dad's actions, and even left without an argument, which just pissed me off more.

I haven't gotten a fucking second alone to talk to my mate. I sure as hell didn't want to talk about him now with my dad, while I was already pissed.

"My mate is not your concern."

"Everything about you is my concern. You're my daughter."

"Dad." I stopped to turn my full frustrated rage on him. "Not now. I'm not talking about him with you."

He looked offended. "You talked about him with your mother."

"Mom figured it out herself!" I snapped, though the bathing suit ordeal helped me to open up more than I wanted to. If I were to tell dad I thought Rian was going to reject me, dad would have killed him. Or he would have tried to, at least. After seeing Rian in the water, I was starting to think I'd underestimated his abilities all these years.

"Why won't you talk to me too?" Dad pouted.

"Because you were a jerk to him!"

Dad recoiled, like I just slapped him. I sighed heavily, then rested my hand on his.

"I haven't even had a chance to talk to him yet. We just established we're mates. Nothing else. Shit kinda hit the fan before we could say much more. Let me at least talk to him before I talk to you." I opened my eyes wide, playing at his heartstrings. "Please, daddy?"

It worked. The pout disappeared and a loving smile replaces it. "Okay, baby." He kissed my forehead.

I was still upset about everything, but he was my dad. It was not his fault that we couldn't get into Alfheimr or that Julia was taken. Even if he was being a jerk to Rian, he was doing it out of love. If I kept pushing back, it will just cause Rian more problems with my dad. I didn't want that.

Dad went back to his office to deal with things there while I started pacing around the bottom floor of the packhouse. All my frantic, anxious thoughts were zipping around inside my head. As I was doing another lap around the great room, his scent wafted into the open space, making my eyes dilate and my heart to beat heavily in my chest.

"Rosie," his voice made me turn. Rian was standing in the wide doorway, freshly showered and in different clothes than before. He was gripping a box in his hand, a rectangular box that looked a lot like something you would find at a jewelry store.

"Rian," I whispered his name, feeling tingles inside of me from his stare. "I thought you went back to the hotel?"

Stupid. Why did I say that? It sounded like I didn't want to see him, when I really just couldn't think of anything else to say.

"I did," he told me, taking a few steps closer. He was making the tingles inside me intensify. "I came right back. I needed to take care of a few things first." He nervously locked his jaw, looking vulnerable and shy suddenly. "I wanted to finish our talk, but I didn't want to do it smelling like a sour fish."

I laughed softly. "You smell nothing like fish. Ever. You always have an amazing smell." As if to prove my point, I took a deep breath, savoring his scent lingering around me.

His lady-killer smile made my knees feel like jelly. He really was far too good looking.

Unlike him, I had yet to shower. I was still wearing my white bikini and the sweaty sundress I borrowed from mom. I probably stunk. I probably looked like a complete mess. I usually wouldn't have cared, but I was self-conscious around him.

"I could probably use a shower." I looked down and pulled on my dress.

"No," Rian smiled. "You look beautiful."

Sincerity vibrated in every word, and I could feel that he meant it.

I bit my lips, fighting a smile, looking up at him through my lashes like one of those damned mermaids had earlier. He was staring at me with that expression that made my whole body feel weak, something I was not used to feeling. Ever.

12

I Can Help

It was hard to meet his gaze, and I couldn't think of a decent reply. I was not used to the flattery. So, I started looking for some way to change the subject.

"What's that?" I asked, looking from his molten eyes to the box in his hand.

He looked down, turning it over and over again in his hands. "It's, uh, your birthday present," he murmured, closing the distance between us and holding it out to me, looking nervous. "I didn't get the chance to give it to you last night."

My face flushed, and I hesitantly took the box from his hands. Our fingers barely brushed against one another, but it was just enough to make me gasp from the shooting sparks that traveled up my arm. Just like when he held my hand in front of my dad, back at the cove.

My eyes jerked up to meet his as his eyes did the same. I could tell my touch affected him as much as he affected me. He looked stunned.

"Wow," he whispered so softly, rubbing his fingers together like he was savoring the brief touch and the sparks it caused. He then looked embarrassed, his lips pressing together and the fainting hint of pink tinging his cheeks.

I cradled the box in my hand, loving the warmth I felt on it from Rian gripping it for so long. Slowly, I opened the lid, and then gasped. The most beautiful butterfly pendant was in the middle of the jewelry box. It had a blue stone in the center that almost seemed alive with its gentle glow and molten center. There was a long chain necklace coiled around it.

"This is beautiful," I whispered, my fingers tracing over the smooth stone. I felt a subtle spark from the necklace, almost like I was touching Rian directly.

"I enchanted the blue topaz. It contains my magic," Rian told me when I looked at him in question, catching real movement inside the jewel.

"Your magic? What kind of magic?"

"Protection magic," he shrugged, rubbing the back of his head. "Not because I think you need protecting. It's just a precaution. I didn't like the idea of you ever getting hurt. You are to be the alpha of your pack after all."

He had this last night, before he knew we were mates? Does that mean he wanted to protect me before I was anything to him, even while I was acting like a jerk?

"I am," I nodded hesitantly. "Does.... Does that bother you at all?"

His smile stretched once again. "Not in the least. I think you're going to make an amazing alpha, Rosie."

"Really?" I grinned. "You really don't mind that I'm going to be Alpha?"

"Of course I don't. Why would I?"

That was one of the things I was most worried about. Especially since he was a fairy prince. The life of werewolf leadership, especially as Alpha, was nothing glamorous.

"You're a fairy prince," I murmured, too nervous to meet his eyes. I stared at the pendent and the magic moving in the stone as I spoke. "A prince and an Alpha being mates are like two entirely different worlds colliding."

He shrugged. "My mother is mated to an Alpha."

"Well, yeah, but I thought you wanted to return to your own world."

"Ah," Rian nodded, understanding finally setting in. "I did want to return to Alfheimr. But that was before."

"Before what?" I chanced to look up at him.

"Before I had a reason to stay in this world," he said, unwavering.

My face heated again, the meaning of his words like a weight being lifted off me. He wanted me. He really wanted me.

"Here," he whispered, lifting the necklace from the box in my hands, uncoiling the chain and lifting it in the air. "May I?"

I nodded, still feeling all kinds of butterflies inside me, matching the necklace. He gently set it around my throat so it hung low on my chest. His fingers lingered an extra second against my skin, making my breath catch.

"You now have two butterflies adorning your beautiful skin," Rian murmured, staring down at the chain and pendant with pride.

"Two?" I asked, my brain stunned by his proximity and his touch.

He lifted his hand, and I thought he was about to hug me, but his fingers brush the bare skin on my shoulder instead. The most embarrassing noise escaped me, something between a whimper and a moan.

"Here," his voice was deep and smooth like velvet. "You have a butterfly here, too."

"Oh," I managed to exhale, my eyes locked with his. Our faces were just inches away from one another. The pull was so intense that I was fighting myself to keep from attacking him right there. His lips were so perfect and looked so soft. His sweet ocean scent was like a drug with every lung full of air I took.

"Rosie," he whispered my name, almost like a plea.

I couldn't even blink. I was lost in his trance.

"Yes?"

"You want me too, right? It's not just me?" His voice sounded so desperate. "Oh, please tell me I'm right."

"I want you," I confessed, feeling more bold than ever before. "You're my mate."

His strangled breathing fanned over my lips as our faces slowly moved closer and closer together.

Just a hair more. Half a second was all we needed, so I could finally taste his lips to see if they were as sweet as he smelled.

"Rosie!" someone wailed, making me jerk back. Reality was crashing around me as I blinked away the effects of the trance I had been in.

I looked behind a stunned Rian to see Julia's parents coming in from the foyer. Her mother was in tears and her father had a grim look on his face.

Guilt washed over me as Julia's parents pleaded for me to do something to save their daughter. I guess my grandpa and dad had just spoken to them, and they felt the same as my mother and I did. It felt like the pack had resolved to do nothing as we left it in the hands of the fairy knights.

Apologizing and comforting them with my alpha aura was all that I could do. I was not yet the Alpha. There was nothing I could change. I didn't even have the authority to speak with the council yet on my pack's behalf and plead our case.

I understood why the queen didn't allow us to travel to Alfheimr ourselves. Time and magic work differently there. We could go in and come out decades later in our time, though it could only be days to them. It would take someone gifted to navigate us through the realm. Someone with the ability to bring us back out of the realm in our time. It would take strong magic and only royals have that ability. Queen Aisling, in all her sovereignty, can not give us her devoted time to search for a she-wolf that might already be dead.

Logic told me that, but my heart still wished there was something I could do to help Julia's parents either get their daughter back, or find closure. We still didn't know who took her or why she was taken.

After Julia's parents left, I felt a heavy weight on me once again. I was lost in my own world, relishing my time with my mate when they were getting the news that there was nothing we could do but wait.

"Are you okay?" Rian asked. He waited nearby, leaning against a wall as I spoke and comforted Julia's parents as much as I could.

"No," I muttered, with my arms crossed over my chest, still staring at the foyer where her parents had just left. "I hate that there is nothing that I can do to help."

Rian was quiet for a moment, but I could feel his presence getting closer and closer to my back. I didn't dare turn round. I didn't want to get lost in the moment again when Julia might not even be alive. I should have been focused on that, but all I could think about was kissing Rian.

"What if I can help?" Rian said so quietly, it took my mind a moment to register what he said.

I whipped around, staring up at him with furrowed brows. "Queen Aisling already said we couldn't enter the fairy realm."

"Ah, but she is not the only royal you have at your disposal," he reminded me.

I scowled, then tilted my head to the side as I thought. "Can you go against your queen?"

"She's not my queen," he shrugged. "My ruler in Alfheimr is my uncle, and I am one of his princes, with full authority of his crown. I can enter and leave without any problems."

Knots began to form in my belly. As much as I wanted to save Julia, I didn't want to part with Rian as he went in my place.

"Would you go alone?" I asked, holding my breath for his answer.

"You would go with me," he caressed my cheek. "You are her alpha, after all."

13

INTERFERENCE

Rian

When I returned to the packhouse, I didn't think I would be offering something so risky. I didn't think I would be risking something so dangerous. I didn't intend to offer to take Rosie to Alfheimr, where non-faes were not normally not allowed.

After telling Rosie I could take her to save her friend, she went to pack for the journey, agreeing to meet me in the morning in the resort lobby. I asked her to keep it between us for now, so I could only hope she didn't let it slip between now and morning to anyone.

My mom was banished from Alfheimr for doing what I was about to do. She smuggled beings into the fairy realm for decades before she and my real father were caught by my uncle. My father was executed on the spot, and my mom was exiled from the realm for a long period, separated from me.

You would think after the punishment my mom received, I would know better than to do this. Not only did I freely offer this to Rosie, I offered with a smile on my face, like all would be well. I led her to believe that, since I am a prince, it would be okay.

All may very well not be okay. If I was caught, it could be devastating to my magic and my abilities. My uncle may have been forgiving towards my mother, but she was forced to do what she did. She was forced to commit those crimes. I willingly offered to smuggle Rosie through to the other side and was making her think it was okay when it wasn't.

I needed to ensure we were okay and everything was done perfectly. Without detection. We couldn't get caught. I wanted to help her. I wanted to make her happy. I just didn't want to put her and her pack on rocky ground with the queen I was unfamiliar with, who had already refused them entry to Alfheimr.

There was so much to do to prepare. I needed to arrange a location, one that would not trigger any wards to signal the fairy knights that resided in this city. I needed to research where to portal into. I couldn't take Rosie to the fairy courts, but I hadn't been anywhere else. At least, not enough times to picture the places and know where to open the portal on the other side.

I raced back to the resort, and was now giving the car keys to the valet. I was so deep in thought that I forgot to take my ticket and the runner had to chase me inside to give it to me. I was going to have to get in touch with my mother and nonchalantly bring up discreet places to portal back into our realm that would not trigger my uncle's or any other royal's guard. I needed to figure out the best way to bring it up without criminalizing her, too.

Once I got all that sorted out, had other worries. I didn't even know where in Alfheimr to begin looking for Rosie's friend. Alfheimr was as vast as this world, and there were many places unexplored. So many possibilities for someone to be hiding with a young she-wolf. I could try to track her vitality, but she might no longer be alive. That was a siren who drinks blood. He could have taken the girl to feed on. He could be doing any number of things, and it would be too hard to track him down without anything to go on.

As I was walking through the lobby, deep in thought, a hand came down hard on my shoulder, startling me.

"Where have you been?" Taegan asked in a leveled voice. His face was unreadable, but I got the sense that he was not at his happiest right now.

I jerked my shoulder out of his grip. Even though things seemed to be working out for me and Rosie, I was still upset with him for keeping his secrets, leading on my mate even though he knew she was mine. He had yet to tell me why he always came to Miami. If not for her, I just couldn't figure it out.

Though, since the party yesterday, he had given the packhouse and Rosie a wide breadth. I guess I should be grateful for that in some small way. She seemed more than willing to give me a chance, thank her goddess. If she rejected me, I know I would have blamed Taegan and never been able to come back to this world again.

"Unhand me." I didn't answer his question, just continued on my way towards the elevator.

"Rian," he growled low in his chest, following me into the metal box. He was definitely upset about something, but I would not cater to his superiority. I owed him no explanation.

"Rian," he muttered under his breath, staring ahead while the elevator closed. "I know what it is you are planning."

My heart stopped. There was no way he knew. No way. I just told Rosie I would take her not thirty minutes ago, and I asked her to keep it between us. He couldn't know. I chose just to ignore him.

Taegan sighed. "You can't take Rosie to Alfheimr. You know you can't. You're worried about that right this second, Rian. I can tell."

My mouth hung open in disbelief. "How? How could you know that?" Did Rosie call him after I left? I want to ask, but I'm scared too.

"I just know." He looked away from me so I couldn't see his face.

Fucking hell. Did Rosie really tell him? Was that why I could feel apprehension and anxiety rolling off him? I was feeling so elated that things were looking good for me and her. Now, if she was calling him to tell him about our discussion, even though I asked her not to, I was not sure how to react.

"Rosie didn't say anything to me. Quit thinking too much. We are just friends, and she didn't tell me a thing. I haven't even talked to her since her party yesterday."

"Then how do you know?" I wanted to growl the way he often does, but my voice just sounded condescending instead.

"I have my ways," Taegan growled, causing me to roll my eyes and almost throw my arms up in frustration.

"Of course you do," I snapped, marching out of the elevator doors to my room.

To my annoyance, Taegan followed behind me, using his foot to prevent me from slamming the door in his face. He pushed his way inside, and I just let him. No use fighting the brute. His magic was stronger than mine, and his physical abilities were unmatched.

"I'm serious, Rian. It's not safe. Not to mention, her family could get in trouble if you're caught."

"We won't get caught," I argued. "Even if we did, I am a prince of the realm. I have the authority to bring her over as my mate."

"Maybe to the courts, but not to find and kill sea monsters in the abyss. You don't even know what you are walking in to."

"So tell me, since you seem to know everything, anyway. Tell me where her friend is and I'll go retrieve her myself and Rosie will never have to leave the safety of the packhouse."

His lips pushed together in a tight line.

"What? Don't you know? Or does the great Taegan Kissinger not have the answers for once?"

"Rian. Seriously, man. You are being unreasonable."

"Am I?" I scoffed. "What's unreasonable is my younger *nephew* trying to control my every action." I shook my head, sitting on the bed. "She's accepting me, Taegan. She said she wasn't going to reject me. I'm not risking her hating me by going back on my word. She wants to go save her friend, and I'm taking her to do that very thing. The worst that will happen if we are caught is that I will be exiled like my mother was. Only, I don't mind being exiled with her. Living here in the human world might finally be tolerable with her by my side. So, if you are done being an ever controlling ass, I would like for you to leave. I have plenty to prepare for and don't need you here trying to upstage me at every turn."

Taegan looked ready to argue more, but after a few tense seconds of awkward silence, he turned to leave without saying another word.

14

— · —

THE CALL

Rosie

What to pack, what to pack, what to pack? What the hell do you pack for a journey to a new realm? I wished I could ask my mom, or maybe even my grandma Elena, since she works the closest to the fae queen, but Rian asked me not to mention this to anyone.

The fact that he asked me to keep this a secret should probably make me nervous, but I was strangely excited instead. I didn't really want to tell anyone, anyway. Dad might ban me from going, and mom would probably try to come along.

This was a classic ask forgiveness and not permission situation. When we save Julia, though, I doubt I'll have to say sorry to anyone. I wouldn't feel sorry. Not if I could help her come home safely.

I grabbed a duffel and began to load it up with my travel essentials. The more I packed, the more it looked like I'm just packing for a slumber party. A slumber party with my mate. I packed a couple of pairs of underwear, the nicer ones I had, and socks, jeans, a shirt, my toothbrush and hairbrush. I even packed the weapons available in my room. I only had a few daggers and a canister of silver spray, but that would have to do. I couldn't get any more without alerting Gamma Matt, and he would tell my dad straight away.

That was it for the slumber party essentials, weapons and all. I briefly thought about packing sexy pajamas, but decided against it. This was a rescue mission, not a honeymoon. I hadn't even claimed and marked him yet.

We were going to the fae realm, though. I wished I had a nice dress or something to bring with me, but I had to borrow my sundress from mom. I really didn't have any of my own. I eyed my party dress from my birthday for a few minutes, ridiculously debating bringing it or not. It was too over the top. Thyra wears boho dresses and skirts a lot, so I doubted the formal shiny gown would fit in. My jeans and shirt would have to do.

As I'm dumping a packet of mints and a handful of old suckers I found on my nightstand in the duffel, my phone rang. I smiled, thinking it might be Rian, but then I remembered I hadn't given him my number. Not yet, anyway.

It was Taegan.

What did he want that late at night?

"Hello?" I answered.

"Rose. Hey. I need to talk to you."

"Uh, do you know what time it is, Taegan? I was just about to-"

"I know what you are about to do, Rose, and I'm calling to tell you not to do it. You can't go to Alfheimr."

I suddenly froze. Did Rian tell him? I thought we weren't going to tell anyone. It was Taegan, though. Maybe Rian thought he could help us.

"Uh, I can. Rian is taking me. He said he could-"

"Rian doesn't know shit. You can't go. *You* can not go. If he wants to go, fine, but you need to stay here where it's safe."

I never felt annoyed with Taegan before, but I was feeling it right now. Did he not think I could do this? Did he think I was incapable of saving my friend?

"Sure. Whatever you say," I grumbled, knowing him well enough to know not to argue directly. He would just call my dad.

"I'm serious, Rosie. Let the fae handle this."

"Geez, I got it," I huffed.

"I don't think you do," Taegan groaned. "It's really not safe, Rosie. Please. For me? Stay home?"

I was getting angry, and thinking about telling him to go fuck himself, but before I could, the necklace Rian gave me lit up brightly around my neck. The butterfly pendant felt like it was fluttering against my chest, right beside my heart.

***

Unknown

I snarled furiously, waving my hand above the surface of the water again, and then again. No matter how many times I infused my magic into the pool, the picture I wanted to see would no longer come forward.

Something changed.

For so long, I'd been able to so easily pull up the image of the one who had been persistently invading my dreams, infused in my desires and my thoughts when I was awake. Now, I could not so much as to get a flicker in the pool of that person's face.

This was my addiction. Like a substance I'd become dependent on. I needed to see them. I needed that image to come forward, but no matter what I tried, it wouldn't.

I snarled, letting every ounce of my frustration pour out of my hands as I lifted them in the air, calling down bolts of lightning to rain down around me. The storm that had been brewing overhead, called about by my souring, now infuriated mood, had now burst, the wind and rain heaving down like a weapon around me.

The haunted waters where I resided in may be well hidden, but if I did not calm down soon, the guard of the Meridionali Kingdom would know. A storm of this magnitude would attract the attention of anyone.

"GRYNRUS!" I roared, my lightning striking the water's surface in warning to come quickly. The coward's head popped out above the surface, looking at the chaos brewing around me.

Fine. If he was too dastardly to face a little rain, I would go to him. He would not like it when I caught him, but that just might be the thing to calm my anger. For the moment, anyway. Nothing would calm me until I could see the one who this fool was supposed to fetch, too incompetent to do so.

A shiver raced through my limbs, my giant humanoid body elongating, limbs multiplying, my power surging with the change to my core. Grynrus recoiled, diving back under the surface as I crawled into the water. The storm was calming now that my power was concentrated at my center. It made it easier to hold myself together, being in my true form.

"Coward," I snarled, racing for the retreating fiend, my tentacles wrapping around his fin, pulling him back. "Do you think you stand a chance at evading me?"

"No, my master. I was- I was simply going to check on the wolf. She seems to be waking up."

"Excuses," I croaked. I coiled my body to swim for the caverns where I left the werewolf girl in the care of my underling. I dragged him along with me, my grip unwavering no matter how hard he tried to break free.

Like he said, the girl was just about awake. She was lying on the sandy surface, her head bobbing side to side as she stirred.

I tossed Grynrus to the shore beside her, ignoring his yells of protest. His landing thud startled the girl. Her eyes opened, and frantically look around.

Her eyes landed on Grynrus first, and she looked confused. Then, her eyes swept over to my large, bulbous head surfacing. I delighted in the fear I could smell coming from her before the scream left her lips. I kept my true form, coiling my body up onto the shore as she crawled backward. Her back hit a tree. She had nowhere else to go.

My giant true form was horrifying to most, but powerful. My power grew the more I fed on her fear. Alas, I could not effectively stay in my form and have her cooperate. Not the way I wanted.

This girl knew the one I desired. She knew the one I need. She could tell me all the things I did not know. She could be useful to tame the wild, desirous frustration growing inside of me.

With a quaking frame, shifted back into my humanoid form. She visibly relaxed, but not much. My human form was large and powerful, too. Much more powerful than a lowly she-wolf.

She was appraising me with those fearful eyes. "Wha-what do you want? Where am I?" She braved to speak, giving screaming a break for a moment.

What do I want? I want the most intimate of details about my prize. I want to know everything she knows. I want to make her think I will do her no harm, and my only goal is to be joined with the one I seek. Once I get what I want, once I have all the information that I can get out of her.....

Well....

I have one goal. Once that goal is met, I was sure even my prize would understand me ridding myself of loose ends.

I could see this she-wolf's inner turmoil; trying to decipher my actions, what I am, and where she was. She was looking around in a frenzy, trying to take everything in. Her eyes lingered on Grynrus for a few seconds, still recovering from my angry flare up. Then they move back to me.

Crouched down, I bent over to tuck a few muddy strands of her hair out of her face, painting on the image of kindness, though I felt anything but kind at that moment. I needed the object of my addiction. I need to see her or feel connected to her in some way. I felt totally cut off at the moment, and my panic reached an all-time high after multiple failed attempts to see her face.

Just one story. Just a single tale of her life will hopefully satisfy my hunger for her. Even if it was just temporary. Even the most minute details would be a treat at this point.

"Tell me about your alpha," I hissed, my sea breath spraying in her face.

She cringed away from me. "Al-Alpha Pa-Pa-Parker?" The girl's voice came in a cracked whimper.

"No," I said, a sinister smile forming. "His daughter. Tell me all about the Alpha named Rosie."

15

— • —

TIRED OF LAST

Rian

Taegan, to my relief, never came back. He didn't try to argue with me anymore and when I called mom to see if I could coax information out of her without arousing suspicion, there wasn't any hint of concern about my questioning. Taegan, it seemed, hadn't called back home either.

If he had called mom, she would have portaled down here immediately and prevented me from leaving for Alfheimr with Rosie in a fit. She would have lectured me to no end, forgetting that I am a couple of years into being an adult now. I can drink in the human world, but my mom will still reprimand me like a child if she deems it necessary. She would probably even bring my stepdad, and there was no way he wouldn't have left Alpha Parker out of the loop.

Alpha Parker. The man was probably going to kill me upon our return. Damn it. Just another thing to add to the list of stressors eating away at me.

But, at that moment, it seemed I had nothing to worry about. Nothing but the arrival of my mate.

Now morning, it was just twelve minutes before I was to meet Rosie. There were no signs of anyone coming to stop me as I waited anxiously in the lobby for my mate to arrive. Taegan may be an imperious brat, but at least he hadn't stooped to involving our parents or informing others of my plans to help my mate in the only way I know how.

My mate. I had her. Well, as much as I could without being marked or infusing my mark onto her. She wanted me. She admitted she wanted me, and was letting me get closer to her. Her eyes when I told her that I would do this lit up, and that hopelessness she had been wearing was all but washed away.

From the moment I felt the connection and knew, I felt this unyielding drive to prove my worth to her. She expected greatness from her mate. She expected perfection. I had to be that for Rosie.

She was so distraught after learning that her pack would have no involvement in getting back her friend. She wanted to help, and I provided a way. I couldn't take that from her now.

When I talked with mom, I had to be very careful with my questions. I mentioned wanting to see Loreana, my pegasus, but not wanting to set wards off in Miami to visit my beast.

Miami was a large, diverse city, with many supernatural communities influencing its political makeup. Because of this, there were many places not warded by the fairy knights. They only warded the places their people frequent near their own communities. As long as we went outside the city limits, we should be fine. Mom even told me of a place deep in the nature preserve that was completely neutral territory, with no influence from any races. She said that witches would often use the location for their seances and rituals, and in her dark days she had been to a calling or too there. The witches were trying to call on powerful beings from other realms and worlds for more magical power.

The Miami pack drove the dark witches out from using it right before Rosie was born, so she said it would be a prime location for portaling. It would allow space for Loreana to fly freely on this side of the portal as well. She advised me to keep Loreana out of the city because of a bad dealing with a Pegasus in the past for the southern kingdom.

Mom let me know it would be safe to portal to the pen where the pegasus were kept. It was my uncle's domain, so no knights of the southern Queen would be aware. No one would be aware. Because of my mom's constant visitation with her horse, Nelly, my uncle removed the wards years ago. His men stopped getting notified when my mom was on the other side.

I guess he never thought that I might be the one to do it.

Mom had some pointed questions for me, and I could feel her desire to hear more about why I was at the cove to begin with. Callum must have told his mom about finding his mate. I hadn't told mom about Rosie, but perhaps Callum had indirectly.

I was not ready to tell mom about Rosie. No matter how pointed her own questions had become. I wanted to wait and make sure everything would work out. Mom was meddlesome. She might start conspiring with Rosie's mother to plan a wedding before I even get to being marked.

Sighing, I tried to dislodge some of my more tiring thoughts as I looked around the resort. Rosie would be there any minute.

The resort lobby was still pretty vacant in the early hours of the morning. The sun hadn't even fully risen above the ocean. It was just a distant sliver in the skyline. The water looked still as it could be. The boats in the harbor were just barely rocking with the gentle movement of the ocean.

This was my favorite time of day to swim. Sea life was most vibrant at the early hours of the day, when the sea was steady, and the humans on shore had yet to get out of their beds.

Swimming at these hours is the most beautiful. Those first rays to hit the ocean waters send a kaleidoscope of colors beaming through the ocean currents. It looks like jewels raining down.

I hope to one day have the opportunity to show Rosie that earthly magic lives right in her backyard. She was always so busy training, and with school and working towards becoming the next Alpha. I was sure she never took the time to just see the magic of the world around her. She had never seen the true beauty of the water that had been her neighbor her entire life. I couldn't wait to show her everything. I wanted to share all the reasons I loved her home before I even knew what she was to me.

I was lost in my happy thoughts. All of Rosie and what we could do together once we got back to her world. Smiling to myself, I earned some questioning glances from the baristas that just showed up to open the coffee stand in the lobby. The front desk person, some young woman with a rather unprofessional-looking uniform that wasn't buttoned as far up as it should be, asked me for the third time if she could get me anything.

I saw that same receptionist batting her eyes at Taegan not two days ago. He swiftly asked for the resort owner in an icy voice. Which, in doing so, got the woman to back off. She even attempted to trip and fall against Callum yesterday, but soon regretted it when Callum dodged out of her path of falling and let her land right on her face. Callum barely muttered a "watch it" before walking off.

Since I was the one to help her up after the incident, I guess her attention had now turned towards me. That was how it usually went with the werewolf men living around me. I was usually the last choice, not being as powerful and domineering as Taegan, or as brawny and taciturn as Callum. It was tiring being the least considered all the time.

I refused the receptionist and let her know that I would not need anything in the future either. The last thing I needed was for this woman to be bent over me in her attempt to be seductive when Rosie showed up.

As the receptionist walked back towards her desk with a sour look on her face, her heels clicking on the hard floor, I saw from the corner of my eye a car pulling up out front of the lobby next to the valet. A car I recognized. Taegan got out of the driver's seat, taking me by surprise.

I watched as he came around to the passenger side and opened the door, allowing for Rosie to climb out.

16

—·—

ASS-U-ME

Rosie

Thirty minutes ago....

"You didn't have to come get me. I have a car," I huffed, peeved at Taegan's insistence to meet in person.

After the necklace Rian gave me quit glowing and pulsing strangely around my neck, I told Taegan, "Thanks for your concern," and quickly hung up. The persistent texts came soon after. I finally relented around two in the morning and let him give me a ride.

"We needed to talk," Taegan said gruffly, "and you wouldn't listen."

"The threat to call my dad was very persuasive," I growled.

He laughed dryly. "I'm glad you didn't make me do that. Your dad hates getting calls from me. Always has."

"Yeah, yeah," I huffed. "What's your deal, anyway? Did Rian ask you to help him so I would stay home?"

"Uh, no. Not exactly," Taegan winced, like he could not answer the question.

My heart twinged, thinking that may be the case. Rian wouldn't do that, would he? He promised me I could go with him. He wouldn't take that back.

Or would he?

I was suddenly realizing how little I really knew Rian. While I was acting like a bitch, pining after the jerk sitting next to me, I wrote Rian off for years and never took the chance to get to know him... Maybe he would go back on his word.

No. No, I would not think like that. Assuming shit will only make for more misunderstandings. Grandpa Tommy always says, "to assume is to make an ass out of you and me." He would then follow that with a chart about why his pun was funny, breaking up the word "assume" into "ass", "u", and then "me".

Over-explaining really took the funny out of a joke, but now I was smiling at myself, remembering the chart on the warrior center dry erase board. A donkey drawing contest followed it. The one who could draw a donkey the best would be called the king of the asses for the rest of training, and not have to do laps.

I felt like the king of asses thinking the worst of my mate when he has only tried to help.

"What are you snickering about over there?" Taegan asked with a lifted brow.

"King of asses," I muttered, looking out the window with my chin resting in my hand.

"Are you calling me an ass?" he scoffed.

I smirked, looking over towards him. "Are you *assuming* I am?"

He gave me a questioning look before shaking his head and looking back towards the highway.

"You know, you're a lot less nice as a mated alpha."

"Yeah," I shrugged, sizing him up, "You don't look so *nice* yourself anymore."

"Ouch," Taegan clutched his chest, "You wound me."

"Yeah, well, that's what you get for being an ass."

He chuckled, and the mood felt lighter. We were both less tense.

"So," I pretended to study my nail beds. "What were you so desperate to talk to me about? I'm not going to assume that Rian doesn't want me to go now." I lifted a brow in question.

Taegan pursed his lips, then hesitantly shook his head. "No. His stubborn ass very much still wants you to go."

I smiled to myself. "Good." I wasn't going to stay home. No matter what.

"I don't want you to go, though. So I'm asking you, as a close friend, to stay home. Let him and I do this on our own."

"You?!" I practically screeched. "Why would you go but not me?"

He shrugged, then sighed. "It's not safe for you, Rose. You shouldn't be going at all."

"Oh, but it's safe for you?"

I stared at him in disbelief, but he was still just making that face like he didn't know how to put his thoughts into words.

Sexist jerk.

"Just because I'm a woman?" I scoffed. "You know, I never pegged you to be one to discriminate, but you learn something new every day. I'm going, Taegan. There is nothing you can do to stop me."

He growled softly. "I'm starting to see that," he grumbled.

"See what?"

"That there is nothing I can do." His blue eyes glowed eerily, making me nervous for some reason.

The drive was quiet for the next several minutes until I couldn't take it anymore.

"Why are you so insistent I not go?" I asked again in a less aggressive voice. "I know you well enough to know it's not because I'm a girl, so why? What's making you act like such a, such a-"

"An ass?" Taegan lifted an eyebrow.

I snorted. "Sure. Let's go with the theme of the car ride."

"Ass is the theme we're going for?"

"Why? Do you have a better suggestion?" I resisted, smiling at our banter.

"How about donkeys? I feel like I'm riding with your mom the more you say ass."

I burst out laughing at his suggestion, thinking back to the king of asses contest that was just on my mind.

"No good?" Taegan smiled, lifting his brows in question.

"It's fine. Go ahead and answer the question then, king of the donkeys."

He narrowed his eyes at me. "I'm strangely offended and don't know why."

"I'm not sure why anymore either," I laughed. "Just answer my damn question."

"Fine," he sighed. "I can't really give you an answer, though. I just know that you shouldn't be going."

"Hmm, not good enough."

"I get that, okay." He shook his head. "I'm not going to try to stop you anymore, even though I know I could stop you if I wanted to."

"You could try," I shrugged. "I could take you down if I wanted to."

"Bull shit," he scoffed. "I'm driving the car right now. I could simply detour to Simone and Vincents and let them deal with your stubborn ass."

"Hey, if I can't say ass, you can't either."

That brought a smile to his face. "Goddess, you are maddening."

"I sure am," I batted my eyes mockingly. "You should probably just leave once you drop me off at the hotel. Wouldn't want to be the cause of you going insane."

"I rather come by that naturally," he smiled.

"You're almost there," I muttered, looking back out the window to hide my smiling face.

Taegan chuckled, then sighed again. "Fine. Just promise me one thing."

"What's that?" I turned my head to stare at him.

"Just…. Stay out of the water. Don't go swimming in any oceans or bodies of water while there, okay?"

His eyes did that glowing thing again, and I felt as if this was a serious request.

"Can I still take baths?" I asked like a smart ass.

He smiled. "Sure. baths should be safe."

"But not the ocean?"

"Not the ocean," he confirmed.

I looked back out the window, seeing we were coming to the resort. With a sigh, I said, "Fine. No oceans."

"Thanks," he sounded relieved. "But please bathe."

Taegan parked at the curb for the valet, and I started gathering up my phone and water bottle, putting both in my backpack as he walked around to get the door for me.

I smiled my thanks at him as he took my hand and helped me out of the car. It was low to the ground compared to my car, so I was struggling with my backpack in my lap.

I then sensed him. Rian. I had this alarm inside me that went off whenever he was near, and my eyes always seemed to gravitate right towards him without having to search.

Rian was standing near the entrance of the lobby in front of one of the plush chairs, a backpack resting at his feet. My face lit up, excitement making my heart pound against my rib cage. It felt like the butterfly in the necklace he gave me was fluttering in tune with my heart.

Goddess, the man was so handsome. So much nicer to look at than the ass I just rode with. I couldn't believe I hadn't noticed how good looking he was before.

Well, I noticed, but I noticed for the wrong reasons.

I was seeing him for all the right ones now. I wished it was him I was stuck in the car with this morning, instead of Taegan, who felt like a bossy version of a brother now.

"Hey," I said as we walked into the hotel.

His eyes lingered on my face a bit, studying me. My cheeks felt burning hot under his gaze. Then he scowled, not even answering me, before turning his frown towards Taegan.

"What are you doing? Didn't I tell you to stay out of it yesterday?"

I'm surprised by the brash words he spat at Taegan. I had only ever heard him be kind towards him.

"You won't listen to me, so I don't see why you think I should listen to you," Taegan responded coldly.

I looked back and forth at them with worry.

"Are you two fighting?"

"No," they answered together, then Rian made a face that led me to believe they were both lying.

"Fine, you don't have to listen to me, but I'm not going to sit back and do nothing," Taegan stated with a stoney expression.

"What is that supposed to mean?" Rian snapped.

"It means," Taegan rested a hand on my shoulder, "if you insist on taking Rosie, I'm coming too."

17

JOINING FATE

Rian and Taegan continued to have some weird stare off. They Weren't trying to hide their little tift, though both just claimed they weren't fighting.

Did Rian not know Taegan was coming to get me? I wished I'd asked Rian about it before we left this morning, but I didn't have his number or any other way to communicate with him. I probably should have asked for that last night, but it slipped my mind.

As I was about to ask again what the hell was going on with them, I got a call, my phone buzzing repeatedly in my pocket.

Pulling out my phone, I saw it was my dad. He was probably wondering why I didn't show up for practice. I was curt with him last night when I got back home, mostly because I was trying to hide my plans with Rian, but we did have that argument about Julia. He probably thought I was mad at him or something.

I wouldn't miss practice just because I was mad at him. I'd just try to kick his ass when we split up to spar.

"Um, I think I'm going to go to the bathroom before we head out," I said. Rian tore his eyes away from Taegan to look at me with an unpleasant expression. It irked me. I was excited about seeing him just moments ago, but he was looking at me like I was guilty of something right now.

"Okay," Taegan was the one that answered, faking a smile. His eyes glowed that weird way they do. "Me and the new king of donkeys will be out here."

I pressed my lips together, trying not to laugh at Taegan's continued use of the term. Rian's scowl deepened, his eyebrows pulled down to hood his beautiful eyes.

It was such a different Rian from last night. I didn't know how to take this. I didn't know how to respond to his anger.

So I chose not to. I would to go to the bathroom, give them time to work out whatever crap was going on with them, then hopefully he would be in a better mood and we could be on our way.

As I was walking, my phone buzzed in my hand again, but this time it was a text from my mom.

> MOM| *I can see you are at the resort, you brat.*

I bit my lip, thinking about how to text back. I forgot my mom could track my phone with one of those family location apps. I should have that turned off. I received another text before I could type anything.

> MOM| *Have him put his seal above your lady bits. That's where I would want mine if I were mating a fae.*

Oh, goddess. I was not having a fucking sex talk over text with my mom.

> MOM| *I'll start thinking of hot grandma names. Maybe Ki-Ki. Simone tried to claim it, so help me beat her to the punch.*

> MOM| *I'll take care of your dad and call Hadley to reserve Rian's room for the next week if he hasn't done that already. Have fun. No safe sex. I want to be called Ki-Ki.*

> MOM| *Don't forget the vag seal. He can make that kitten purrrr-rrr....*

Mom then sent me a series of inappropriate emojis to reiterate all this.

Fuck. Well, at least my parents would assume I was off getting my back blown out, and whatever else the rest of my mom's disgusting emojis might mean. They probably wouldn't notice we were missing at all. Everyone would just assume we were mating.

My face got so red thinking about it. When I stared at myself in the mirror after exiting the stall, the color was all down my neck, too. I washed my face with cool water twice before it went away. I was not a blusher. Rian could be pissed at me about something, but I was in the bathroom blushing, thinking dirty thoughts about him.

I stood in the bathroom much longer than necessary after that, just staring at my phone. It didn't feel right to lie to my mom, but at the same time, I knew I needed to do this. I couldn't sit back and do nothing. What if that creature came again? What if whatever sent it sends something worse?.

As I was leaving the bathroom, I finally texted my mom back.

> ME| I love you mom. Thanks

After sending that text, I heard my mate yelling from the lobby.

***

Rian

"What the hell are you doing?" I hissed at Taegan while Rosie excused herself to use the bathroom. He not only invited himself on this trip, he was insulting me in front of my mate. King of donkeys? Was that some fae joke? Was he calling me an ass? Was he trying to just piss me off in every way?

"I told you," he shrugged, placing his hands on his hips. "I'm coming."

"No, you are not," I said through gritted teeth. "You are staying here. It's bad enough I'm taking one non-fae to the other side. I can't take two."

He lifted his eyebrows arrogantly, a smile hinting at his arrogant lips. Arrogant bastard.

"So you are admitting it's *bad* to take Rosie to Alfheimr?"

I narrowed my eyes at him. "You are not going."

"Oh, I'm going," he huffed. "You can try to stop me if you want."

He stood his ground, crossing his arms, looking every bit as imposing as he was trying to appear. Even that imperious beast housed inside his looming body was shining on the surface, his magic making his skin glow a faint blue, just dim enough to not be noticeable by the human eye.

He was challenging me, and I was no match for him.

He knew it. He always knows it.

"Why do you want to go so badly, anyway?" I muttered. There was a slight whine in my voice. I couldn't help it. He was making me feel so helpless.

His aura receded, and his expression changed, looking a bit lost, or maybe worried. He opened his mouth and closed it several times before he finally said something. Something that instantly sent everything inside me into a panic.

"If I can't change fate, I'll join it."

Fate? What fate did he want to change?

Was he.... Did he want my mate? Was that what he was saying?

His eyes went wide, as if he had just realized what he said. "No, not like that. I didn't mean like that, Rian. I don't want to steal your mate or anything. I just want to protect her."

"So you don't think that I'm capable of protecting her myself?"

He pressed his lips together, not willing to answer. His eyes were lighting up, he and his beast communicating. It pissed me off that he never communicated with me. He never communicated with anyone. His word was law. Always.

Not today. Not in front of my mate. Not when I still hadn't proved myself to her.

"Fuck you, Taegan. Just.... Fuck you."

I tried to walk away, towards the bathrooms, so I could maybe get a word in with my mate alone before Taegan imposed on us more than he already had. Before I took two steps in, he gripped my shoulder.

"Rian, wait. It's really not like that, man. If.... If she had just listened to me when I talked to her last night, I could have talked her out of going, then you and I could maybe-"

"Last night?" I repeated, jerking away from him, staring at him with all the disdain I had inside. "You talked to her last night?"

"Well, yeah. I called her and she wouldn't-"

"You called her?" I snapped. Did Rosie tell Taegan after all? "Before or after you talked to me?"

"After," he said. "It was after. She didn't tell me anything, Rian. She wouldn't even talk to me. That's why I showed up to give her a ride this morning. I was trying to talk her out of going. I'm not trying to do anything but help you, man. I'm trying to help you protect your mate."

"I DON'T NEED YOUR HELP!" The baristas and the receptionist all turned to stare. I was too worked up to care. "You always try to do this, Taegan. It's always 'Taegan knows best'. Well, sometimes you don't. You are not helping anyone right now. Expect your own ego. You can't even give me one good fucking reason you don't want Rosie going, other than you don't think it's safe for her, can you?"

His eyes glowed again, him and his Lycan communicating, but he just opened and closed his mouth, no words coming out. He was straining his entire face while thinking of something to say.

"I didn't think so," I snapped, then turned to find my mate.

18

C-Stick

Taegan

I watched with dissatisfaction while Rian raced to find Rosie. It hurt to have him doubt me so much. I seemed to have lost all of his trust. Simply by not being allowed to reveal his future.

That changed nothing. I still could not tell him anything else, besides simply telling him I didn't want Rosie to go. I couldn't even tell him why. It was forbidden. Rieka would strike me down if I started revealing her secrets. No one knew the inner workings of the moon goddess. No one but me.

"*You dolt. Quit trying to tell them,*" Conri grumbled at me. "*Quit meddling where you shouldn't. You know better.*"

"*I do know better. That's why I am meddling. Mind your business.*"

Conri had been against me stepping in since we heard about what happened last night. I knew. I knew what last night's ordeal would lead to. I knew that Rosie would be in danger soon. I couldn't sit back and do nothing. That's not who I am. The hairy idiot living in my head should know that by now.

"*You shouldn't know better. And who are you calling a hairy idiot, idiot? I'm not the one making idiotic decisions right now.*"

"Yeah, yeah," I rolled my eyes, "*Sorry for fucking caring,*" I snapped.

"*This is beyond caring! You are tampering with fate, and you know better. You, out of all people, should know not to mess around with fate.*"

I did know that better than anyone. I knew the consequences of changing fate. I had to live with someone who faced those consequences yammering in my head day in and day out. He told me endlessly for the past twelve hours what tampering with fate would do. Where it could lead me.

Still, that didn't prevent me from trying to change it any less. I know what I saw. I know what will happen if I don't step in.

"You only think you know what you saw. You merely saw one page. One page that your eyes were never meant to see. It is not our job to change things."

I ignored him and continued watching as Rian and Rosie almost collided near the reception desk. That snarky blonde with fake tits made a face like she wanted to snap one of their necks. Probably Rosie's. The woman was a flirt, which surprised me considering Hadley was pretty strict with her female employees flirting while on the job. Mitch had already warned the woman the day of our arrival to knock it off. She wasn't heeding that warning by the look she just sent Rian.

She had better watch out. Rosie would fix her problem real quick. Rian didn't even notice the blonde, his eyes only on Rosie. Rosie sent the woman a death glare, and Blondie quickly looked down at her desk. Rian was already Rosie's property in her mind. Rian just couldn't see that yet. He didn't know the pull the mate bond had on an alpha wolf.

His strained face relaxed as she smoothed his frown away with her fingers. Her touch was slow and tender, but also possessive. She was putting on a show for the receptionist.

How could the jerk think I wanted his mate? This was all I've wanted for him for years.

Rian said something to her, and then Rosie looked up at him through her lashes in that way girls do when they like a guy. It was weird seeing that look on her face. She was not flirty. Not by a long shot. Even with me, she didn't flirt. Even while claiming she still thought we were mates, after I kept telling her we weren't, but she still firmly insisted, she never flirted. Never. She was bossy and domineering, but never flirty.

This was a Rosie only for Rian. Only he could make her act like a girl in love. I wished he could see that so he would quit being wary of me.

Of course, as the guy Rosie has professed her intentions to mate with for over a decade, I couldn't really be the one to tell him that. He gets mad every time I try. Callum might be able to tell him for me. He could just reiterated what I've already said, but Callum doesn't care enough to pay attention to this stuff. If he can't punch it or eat it, it doesn't interest him. He may be Rosie's cousin, but he only notices her fighting skills and the snacks her parents keep in the pantry. Her love interests don't interest him at all.

I guess now he was noticing her best friend, too. The man was staying at the packhouse to be closer to the girl, since she was only seventeen, not old enough to mate and leave with him yet. Dad was going to have to defer our year of training until Rosie's friend graduates. Callum won't leave Miami without her.

Fine by me. I prefer staying here for a year too. Phoebe might be pissed, but her uptight ass could use a vacation, too. I'll call her to join us when we get back from the fae realm.

"*You shouldn't be going to the fae realm to begin with, cunt-stick,*" Conri grumbled again. "*You're sticking your head where it doesn't belong.*"

"*In a true cunt-stick manner,*" I added, earning a growl from my cantankerous counterpart.

"*Keep joking. I know what it's like to receive the goddess's punishment. You learn that lesson the hard way if you want.*"

"*The hard way, huh? Is this another cunt-stick reference?*"

"*Taegan!*" Conri growled, "*Be fucking serious for once in your life.*"

"*I AM BEING SERIOUS!*" I growled back. "*I seriously can't sit back and just let bad things happen to the people I care about. I may be a cunt-stick, whatever the fuck that is, or whatever the hell other name you want to call me, but sitting back and just letting what I saw happen isn't going to work for me. I. AM. Not. That. Guy. So just shut the fuck up and help me, or,*" I growled internally, "*Or....Just shut the fuck up.*"

Conri was blowing smoke from his ugly nostrils, fuming. I knew what the real problem was. He wanted to stay here. With *her*. Even though that might not be as possible as it was before.

Yesterday was a shitty day all the way around. In everything. I was not just going to sit back and wait for shit to change on its own. That's not what I do. I couldn't change what happened with my mate yesterday, but I could change what will happen to Rian's.

"*Piss flap,*" Conri muttered.

"*Shit pouch.*"

"*Cum wipe.*"

"*Fuck nugget.*"

"*I'm going to shave your eyebrows off in your sleep,*" he threatened.

"*I'll shave your nut sack for you so you can finally find that tiny hairy dick you're so proud of.*"

He snarled, but receded back when Rosie and Rian walked towards me. I hurried to put a smile on my face, but Conri took one more swipe at me, making it hard to keep it.

"*Your hair is the color of piss. You smell like piss too.*"

"*Shut the fuck up, you dickless, sasquash bitch.*"

"You first, piss-head."

I let my face slip, a snarl rumbling in my chest. Whether the snarl was from me or Conri, I didn't know, but both Rian and Rosie seemed to notice it.

"You okay?" Rosie asked, earning me a scowl from her mate.

For fuck's sake. Could she and I not even talk now without him being a fucking bed wetter?

"Fine," I replied, trying again to smile. "Just fine."

19

MAMA'S BOY

Rosie

"Yeah, mom... Yeah. Okay... Yes, I miss you bunches, too... To the moon and back... Sure, I'll tell her... Yep... I love you too, mama... Okay. Give them kisses for me too... Okay, bye."

I smiled to myself, pressing my lips together while looking out the window. I was trying so hard not to laugh at Taegan and the way he talked to his mom on the phone. He had to talk to every single one of his sisters, and the conversations were much the same.

"Mama's boy," Rian whispered under his breath. Taegan scoffed, but continued to focus on driving.

Yep. They were still fighting. Well, Rian was fighting, but by what he told me at the resort, I couldn't really fault him for his negative mood. Not towards Taegan, at least. I was just hoping it resolved over time.

"You loved him, Rosie. It's just hard. It's hard seeing the girl that I want to be my everything, my future, get out of a car laughing with the man she has openly loved her entire life."

I understood what he was thinking then, and why he was so pissed that Taegan decided to tag along on this journey, even after Rian told him not to.

The more I thought about it, the more I wished it was just us too, but I knew Taegan made his mind up and would not stay put. For the same reasons that I couldn't stay put. He was an Alpha, and Rian was his family. If he felt his family was in danger, he was going to step in, no matter what.

"How much further until we are there?" I asked, looking at the GPS on my phone, ignoring another text from my mom.

"Five more minutes," both men answered at the same time. Rian rolled his eyes and huffed in annoyance, but Taegan smirked, side-eyeing my mate sitting beside him.

Fuck, this was going to be an awkward trip if these two didn't figure their shit out.

I leaned forward, sliding my hand between the seat to rest on his arm, rubbing it gently. He flinched from the unexpected sparks, then looked at me in the passenger side mirror. His scowl disappeared, replaced with a soft smile.

Moments passed, both of us just staring at one another in the few inches of reflective glass. The bond was tugging between us, the tingles from the small touch making contact so much more than just a mere touch. My entire being proclaimed that he was mine, and I was his in that one touch.

The agitation was all but gone from his eyes, but then Taegan had to go and open his mouth, making Rian scowl once again. "So, Rosie. Where do your parents think you are right now?"

I awkwardly laughed under my breath. "The resort."

"Is your dad going to come hunt you down later? You're skipping all kinds of training right now, aren't you?"

"Nope." I gave Rian's arm one last squeeze, then leaned back on the seat. "Mom is covering for me."

"Your mom knows where you're going?" Rian turned to look at me, his brows pulled down.

"No. Not exactly." I don't know why, but my face started to heat again.

Well, I knew why. The reason was staring right back at me with a confused look on his face. Then there were the series of inappropriate texts I got from my mom.

Taegan started to laugh loudly while parking the car in the middle of an open field with marshes all around. "She thinks you two are getting it on, huh?"

"Taegan!" I growled, slapping his shoulder.

"Oh, you're fucked," Taegan snickered, dodging a second slap from me and patting Rian on the leg.

"Why?" Rian looked even more confused, though there was a hint of pink creeping up his neck.

"You know how most moms plan their daughters' weddings and shit like that when they find *the one*?" Taegan waited until Rian nodded before he continued. "Carli is planning for her grandkids. Plural. She gets baby fever like humans catch colds." Taegan looked at me. "She's probably planning your ovulation calendar and shit right now. She's going to lock the both of you in a room for an entire week every fucking month until you make her a grandbaby."

Rian's eyes went wide. With shock or fear, I did not know. I felt a wave of shame, because Taegan was totally right. Mom said so herself already.

"We're not even mated yet, idiot. Shut up," I hissed at Taegan before getting out of the car. I was too awkward and embarrassed to hear more about making babies when I hadn't even gotten to mark Rian yet. Then I started to think about mom's pussy seal comment, and my face burned even brighter.

Fucking Taegan. If the asshole would just stay home, then maybe I wouldn't be totally lying to my mom about what I was doing over the next few days. Mating was going to be awfully hard to do with the third wheel tagging along, making every conversation more awkward than it needed to be.

The two of them argued in the car for another minute, and I stayed out of it this time. I just checked my phone instead.

> MOM| *Did you come up for air yet?*

> MOM| *How big is he?*

> MOM| *Where did he put his seal?*

She then sent several cat emojis, followed by wildly inappropriate GIFs.

Ignoring every last message, I made sure my GPS was turned off on my phone, then wait for the two men to finish talking so we could get going. I was ready to get my friend back so I could get back home and finally claim my mate.

***

Rian

Babies? Rosie's mom was planning our babies already?

I had only talked with her a few times, so I did not know to expect that from the Luna... But I didn't mind the thought at all.

"Wait," Taegan stopped me when I tried to follow right after Rosie to get out of the car.

I groaned, settling back against the seat. "What, Taegan? What do you want? Are you going to nag again to get Rosie to stay? Because I'm really getting sick of the same argument. If you want to make her stay home, you go argue with her. Not me."

"That's not what I wanted to say," he sighed. He looked out the window at Rosie, who was smirking while looking at her phone. "That would be impossible. She is more stubborn than you."

I didn't enjoy hearing about how well my *nephew* knew *my* mate.

"Thanks for telling me. Are we done?"

"No, no," Taegan smirked back at me. "I'm not trying to piss you off, man. I'm just trying to... trying to help."

"Help me by staying home," I offered.

"Not gonna happen, but nice try. If it's the baby making you think I'll get in the way of, just give me a wink and I'll make myself scarce."

My face flamed. "Okay, we're done." I was not winking at him when I think about to have sex for the first time with Rosie. It was highly inappropriate.

"I kid. I kid." Taegan laughed. "I just want you to know that I am really happy for you. You might not see it, but anyone else can see how fucking crazy that girl is for you already. I want you to know that it's not her I'm tagging along for. It's you."

"Me?" I scoffed. "You don't think I can take care of myself now? In my own realm?"

"No, man," Taegan huffed. "I'm saying I want to help you. I-" His eyes shone with his inner beast for a moment, his mouth gaping like a fish. Then he continued, "I love you too much to let you do this alone is all. That's what I'm trying to say."

I eyed him warily. "You seemed determined to keep Rosie from going this morning and last night."

"I know. I still wish she would stay, but I'm realizing that some things... some things can't be changed. Like either of your minds, for instance," he smirked. "I'm just here to help. Nothing more."

I lifted an eyebrow, studying him.

"You know we're stepping into my world? You won't be the big bad beast and king of the world over there. I will likely be protecting you far more than you me."

"I make one hell of a good-looking damsel in distress," Taegan laughed.

"Yeah right," I laughed. Damn. Maybe this wouldn't be so horrible after all.

Maybe. I still would rather it be just me and Rosie. The help might be nice since we have yet to discover what it is we are up against.

"Ready?" Taegan held out his hand in a peace offering. "You know I got your back?"

With a heavy, exaggerated sigh, I took his offered hand. "I got your back too, mama's boy."

20

ALPHA FLIRT

Rosie

"Do you even know what you're doing?" Taegan growled as Rian paced around the open field, chanting something under his breath.

Rian stopped his pacing to stare at Taegan, who had his arms crossed tightly.

"Maybe we should just call this quits and go home if-"

"Ten minutes. You couldn't even go ten minutes without acting like a jerk."

Taegan shrugged his shoulders, making the muscles flex tightly in his white shirt. "I'm just saying. If making the portal is too hard for you, we can forget this whole thing and think of another way."

"What other way? There is no other way to get to Alfheimr other than a portal, genius."

"Ah, but there are other ways to get a portal. If you and Rosie can just stay here, I can go talk to this fairy queen and handle shit myself. I'll be back before dinner."

"How are *you* going to get Queen Aisling to let us through when my parents can't? You're not even familiar with her."

Taegan gave the most cocky smirk. "I have my ways."

"Please," Rian scoffed. "Not every woman wants to sleep with you. And fae royalty won't take kindly to being seduced if you don't plan on following through."

"I can't follow through. I'm wai-"

"Waiting for your mate." Rian rolled his eyes. "I know. Even if you're not sleeping around, leading girls on for your own personal gain isn't right either."

"You do that?" I made a disgusted face.

"No," Taegan said. At the same time Rian said, "Yes."

"Come on. Even your mom calls you a flirt," Rian muttered, then went back to pacing. "Go stand over there. I need to concentrate, and you're getting on my nerves again."

"I can help if you-"

"*You* are not fae, Taegan. You have no authority to enter Alfheimr, even if you did know how to make a portal, which you don't. Go be a good boy, shut up, and stand by Rosie until I can get the incantation right so this will work. I've never portaled to where we are going by myself, so I need to concentrate to get it right."

"You can't just wave your hand like your mom does and *boom*, we're there?"

"Not if my magic isn't used to being channeled in the direction we are going. Half of us could end up in my uncle's court if I just waved my hand around like you said. If you want me to do that, though, I'd be more than happy to let you go through first."

Taegan narrowed his eyes. "Someone's a bit crabby today."

"That's because someone isn't doing as I asked and getting out of my way." Rian pointed a finger to the side towards me, indicating that Taegan needed to move.

Finally, Taegan stopped being an ass and did what Rian said, coming to lean against the hood of the car beside me.

We watched Rian quietly for a few minutes before I had to ask, "So, you flirt with girls to get what you want?"

Taegan gave me a crooked smile. "Tell me you haven't done the same."

"I honestly don't think I have ever flirted with a girl to get what I want," I laughed dryly.

"You know what I mean," he scoffed. "Like, you don't wink at the fro-yo guy to get extra toppings, or flirt with the smart guy in class to give you answers for homework."

I made an appalled face, about to deny ever doing anything like that, but then the tattoo guy came to mind and I was pretty sure I did just that for a discount. I've flirted a bit with different warriors to get them to switch shifts with me when I had guard duty at night, but made plans with Sophia instead.

"See," Taegan laughed. "Everyone does it."

I looked over at Rian, hands and eyes glowing and green sparks igniting from his fingers. I bit my lip nervously.

"Everybody?" I asked.

Taegan followed my line of sight, then laughed. "Aww, Rosie. Is someone jealous?"

"Shut up," I growled, hitting his shoulder.

He laughed even harder. "Do you really want me to tell you if your sparkling mate ever flirted with a girl before you?"

"No. I want you to do what my sparkling mate told you to do and shut the hell up."

"Wow," Taegan clicked his tongue. "You're crabby too. This is going to be such a fun trip."

"Then stay home," I growled.

"Fat chance, but thanks for asking. Again." Taegan's was quiet for a while, but his eyes were glowing a brilliant blue. His magic, or his beast maybe.

I hadn't really had much of a chance to catch up with him to ask what all the glowing eyes and weird stubbornness were about. I know when we were kids, his eyes would glow a bit when he was talking to the beast he had inside of him. His mom told my mom that he wasn't allowed to tell us much about why he had a beast inside him and why he was not a regular werewolf. We knew that they were descendants of the moon goddess herself, and his mom and sister had the Lycan form when they shifted, too.

Taegan was the only one with a separate beast in his body. It's not him when he shifts. It's his beast taking over. They are two separate entities and only one can be in control at a time. That's what I understand, at least. I may be wrong.

I know Taegan has magic, too. If his eyes were glowing because he was using his magic, I think I would be able to tell. He was probably talking to his beast.

"What's it like?" I asked, studying the blue glow.

"What's what like?" Taegan looked over his shoulder at me, his eyes going back to normal and that cocky smirk back in place. "Being so awesome all the time?" He stretches his arms dramatically over his head, flexing his muscles. "It's not easy, but someone has to do it."

"Jeez. Were you always this annoying?" I huffed playfully.

"Annoyingly awesome? Always," he laughed.

"No, jackass. Annoyingly annoying. And that's not what I was asking. I wanted to know what it's like having someone else living in your head?"

"Oh," Taegan's eyes glowed bright again, and he scowled. "Annoying."

"Annoyingly awesome?" I smirked, lifting a brow.

"Annoyingly annoying. He's hairy and loud."

Taegan's chest rumbled weirdly, like something inside him was trying to snarl. Or he was just really really hungry, but I suspect it was the first possibility. His Lycan didn't like being called annoying, hairy, and loud.

"So you and he don't get along?"

"No. We get along fine. It's just…. We have disagreements sometimes."

His eyes glowed again, and then he growled audibly.

"Are you having a disagreement right now?"

Taegan pressed his lips together. "Maybe."

I didn't know why I was so intrigued about this, but I had so many questions. "What did you do?"

He scoffed. "Why do you assume I'm the one who did something?"

I gave him a 'why do you think' look, and then he sighed, looking away at Rian.

"Conri doesn't think we should go with you guys. But he's just being paranoid. It's going to be fine."

"He doesn't think you should go to Alfheimr?"

"Nope," Taegan smirked at me, "but I'm coming, anyway."

That worried me a little. "Wasn't this beast of yours gifted to you by the moon goddess?"

Taegan shrugged. "Yeah. I guess."

"So, he would know better than you about what she would want. If she doesn't want you to come with us, maybe you shouldn't?"

Taegan stared at me with a critical look on his face. More than a minute passes, and I thought I just pissed him off, but then a slow smile spread on his face.

"If you're just trying to get me out of the way so you can get to your baby making with Rian, I already told him to give me a signal when you want to get it on and I'll make myself scarce."

"You did not!" I gaped, horrified.

"Oh, yes I did. His face did the same thing yours is doing now. Crabby pants turned bright red. Like a crab," he laughed at himself.

"Oh my gosh, just shut up. Let's try the shutting up thing now."

"Quick acting like a shy little virgin," he chuckled under his breath.

My face grew even hotter. I was a shy virgin. By the sudden change in his expression, I could see that he caught on to that.

"Oh, no. Are you really? You're a fucking alpha, Rosie. I thought.... I thought you would have by now...."

"What? Been a whore? Is that what you are, you Alpha flirt?"

"No! But you just.... I mean...."

I started raining blows on his back with my closed fists, just wanting him to drop dead at that point. He was fucking annoying. I felt sorry for his beast now.

Suddenly, a green plane of magic formed in front of us, brighter than the sun, and vibrating with a force of some sensation I couldn't quite describe. It was beautiful and terrifying. Like staring into the sun.

The edges changed, different colors mixing, morphing and bleeding to the center until a picture of a field full of foreign wildflowers and the most majestic beasts I had ever seen came into view.

Horses with wings. Pegasus. It was a field full of Pegasus. Taegan looked unsurprised, but I was stunned by the beauty laid out before me. Rian's laughter pulled my attention from the horses in the beautiful field to look at him.

"My mom said you would be impressed. Come on," he waved his hand for me to join him. "Let me introduce you to Loreana."

Loreana? Who the hell was Loreana?

21

FOLLOW HIM

With the portal looming in front of us, I was nervous about what was to come. Rian's comment about half of us going to a different location came back to me. I really didn't want to lose my head before I had a chance to save Julia's.

Rian tossed over our bags. They seemed to just pass through the plane of magic, like simply being tossed through a doorway. They made a soft thudding sound that caused some of the pegasus to lift their heads from grazing on the grass to stare.

If the bags made it through fine, it was safe. Right?

"You scared?" Taegan chuckled in my ear. "It's okay if you want to back out."

I growled at him, wondering how I ever found the annoying asshole attractive in any sense. He's a nag.

"Are you scared? Need me to hold your hand through it?" I snapped back.

Rian huffed beside me. Crap. Maybe I shouldn't offer to hold Taegan's hand in any capacity. Even if it's just a joke.

Taegan laughed, turned his back on the portal, held his hands out to his side, then fell straight back into it, like he was doing a trust fall or some shit.

I cringed, watching his body move along the surface of the portal. Then, I laughed my ass off when he just fell back, busting his tailbone and head on the flower-covered ground on the other side. Two pegasus that were close by whined and galloped off, one catching a few feet of air with its wings. Taegan hopped up, rubbing his ass and the back of his head while staring at the ground as if it jumped up and slapped him instead of it being his fault for being a show-off.

"Idiot," Rian muttered. "Did he think a cloud was magically going to appear to cushion his fall?"

"What was he trying to do?" I asked, pressing my lips together to keep from laughing any more.

"No idea." Rian was smiling. "Maybe the golden boy thought angels would catch him. It's definitely *not his fault* the ground was there," he snickered.

"Shut up!" Taegan yelled at us, staring at his body print in the broken grass and flowers.

That was the first time I'd seen Rian laughing up close. I couldn't help but to smile along with him, lost in the beautiful movements of his perfect face. That lady-getter smile was truly gorgeous. He'd been so upset all morning. I was selfishly happy Taegan fell on his ass, since it made my mate laugh. Maybe I could push Taegan down whenever I wanted to see Rian laugh again. I was going to be tripping and pushing Taegan down this entire trip, if that is what it took.

"Ready? I can't wait for you to see Loreana."

And just like that, my smile was gone. Who the hell was Loreana, and why was Rian so excited about seeing her? Rian held his hand out to take mine, probably mistaking my frown for nerves. I really just wanted to kick this Loreana off the edge of a cliff.

Still, any reason to make physical contact with my mate was good for me. I laced my fingers with his, the rush of tingles traveling over me with this satisfying pull inside, tugging on our bond. I'd take this man's hand and follow him anywhere.

"Quit eye fucking each other and come on!" Taegan growled, scaring another large black stallion. The enormous beast kicked its hind legs, blowing steam from its nostrils and whining loudly. "Shut up, Philos," Taegan waved his hand at the horse, making it kick the air again.

Was Taegan familiar with the beasts, or did he just make up a name to call one of them?

Rian sighed, shaking his head. He looked at me, making sure I was okay to go. With a small nod of my head as I nervously bit my lip, Rian stepped through the sheen of the portal door, pulling me with him. It was such a strange sensation, like a tickling wave of energy moving through me. Once we were on the other side, everything felt different.

Everything.

The air had an undercurrent of that strange energy in it, filling my lungs with the sensation of every breath. I felt heavier here. There was a force all around that pressed against me, like gravity you could almost touch.

"It's the magic," Rian smiled, watching me wave my free hand through the air. "It's thick here. It's good for the horses, so when they aren't being put to work regularly at the fairy court, this is where they are kept. Feels different, huh?"

"It feels wonderful," I said. I couldn't help the outrageous grin on my face. "It's like I'm being hugged with tingles."

"If you want to be hugged with tingles, fairy boy here could help you out with that anytime," Taegan snickered.

The black beast followed him around as Taegan walked in circles, trying to get away from it. He must have pissed that one off. It was definitely not skittish like the white ones. Taegan got distracted for a second while talking, and the horse bit him right on the ass.

Rian laughed. "You deserved that."

"Did not!" Taegan growled. "Make this thing go away before I turn it into dog food."

"Can't. That's your ride," Rian told him with a smug look, then led me away excitedly. He was still holding my hand. All the while, Taegan cursed at the beast for taking another swipe at him, this time biting his leg.

The further we walked away from the portal door, the smaller the door got. It was closing up. I felt a tinge of excitement and anxiety as the last glimpse of home swirled closed. That was it. I was in Alfheimr with my fairy prince mate, and there was no turning back. Not until we found Julia and took her home.

I suddenly felt like my mother. Headstrong, throwing all caution to the wind. I didn't know if she would be upset or proud of me right now. Dad would be pissed if he knew what I was doing, but with mom, it's always hard to say.

I felt like I was doing the right thing, though. I felt like I was exactly where I was supposed to be, and this was something I had to do. I was nervous, but sure. So, so sure that the hand that I was holding, that was leading me forward, was leading me towards a defining moment in our lives.

Rian slowed his pace when we came upon a beautiful giant white pegasus with a long, flowing mane and tail. Its eyes were like black marbles, rimmed with long white lashes. There wasn't a blemish on the beast. Even her long, folded wings had perfect feathers, un-crimped and not a spec of dirt anywhere. She was magnificent. Majestic.

Rian let go of my hand, then approached the horse, a huge smile on his face. She came right up to him, ducking her head and resting it on his shoulder as if she were giving him a hug. She looked just as happy to see him as he did her.

"This," Rian ran his hands down the side of the beautiful white pegasus, "is Loreana. She's mine. My pegasus."

"Oh," I stared in fascination, my face tinged with embarrassment because of my previous jealousy. I should have known. "She's beautiful, Rian."

His smile stretched, like I was praising him while praising his majestic flying horse. "Come pet her," he said.

I wanted to, but I looked back at Taegan who was threatening the black horse with a stick he found somewhere. He was waving it around like a sword. He threatened to barbeque it over a fire if it didn't leave him alone. The horse swiftly took the stick from him, then charged with its head down right at Taegan, making Taegan yell for help.

Rian laughed. "Loreana is the sweetest girl here. She won't hurt you. I promise. That stallion has been retired from my grandfather. Philos hasn't liked Taegan since Taegan hit puberty for some reason. They'll be fine."

That answered my earlier question. Teagan knew the beast. Actually, if I thought about it, I remembered Aly saying something about having a flying horse once. I thought she was talking about a toy. Maybe the pegasus made frequent visits to Blue Cliff, since I knew Taegan hadn't been to Alfheimr before. Did that mean I'd get to see these magnificent beasts regularly once Rian and I mate? If that's so, I couldn't wait. They really were indescribably glorious.

Rian held his hand out for me to take, and just like that, I was ready to follow him anywhere again. He pulled me in front of him and placed my hand directly on Loreana's mane, holding it while guiding me to run my fingers down her neck. I could feel the heat of his body against my back, his breath tickling my neck, making me gasp so softly I doubted he could hear.

My body was buzzing, pulling at something deep in me. It was such an intimate feeling; him helping me to bravely pet his pegasus. I'd never depended on anyone apart from my parents. The alpha in me wouldn't stand for it. Not unless it was someone stronger than me.

At that moment, I felt entirely dependent on Rian, but instead of feeling weak, I felt even more empowered through him.

"Loreana," he whispered softly. "This is Rosie. My mate."

22

CONNECTION

Unknown

I felt her. I felt her in the place where it all began. I felt her presence in the place where, just over eighteen years ago, she was once promised to me.

Frantically, I jerked the blubbering mess of a girl, the groveling, snot-leaking weeping one who is a tear away from my wrath, to the ground, out of my way.

She had been weeping for some time, begging for her unfortunate parents while leaking small amounts of information I was hungry for between more weeping and my rage-filled outburst. She didn't know a lot, but just enough to not have died by my hand yet.

I'd been watching my Alpha treasure for some time and thought I could handle a she-wolf. This girl was nothing like my promised one. Nothing. My treasure would never blubber on and beg for mercy from a little coaxing. She would smile menacingly in the face of my persuasive ways, her head held high and not shedding a tear for anyone.

That will of hers, that strong dominant will and unyielding drive, is what makes her even more becoming. If not for the restrictions placed on me, I could have fetched her myself. I had to rely on the invalid who brought me the blubbering wench instead.

A surge of prickling heat, like a ghost or spirit tugging on my inner magic made me frantic to see her. These human legs were too slow. Too unforgiving. Their movement was restrictive. I shifted into my true form as I raced to the pools of reflective water, trying once again to force her picture to appear on the plane.

Try as I might, through multiple attempts to conjure up her image, nothing appeared. Something was preventing it. I was sure of it. Something equal to my power was hindering me from breaking through. That magic hindering me may be even stronger....

No. Not possible. Unless....

Royalty. Grynrus mentioned royalty. I waved it off as Meridionali's representative, that hollow queen's kin perhaps, but maybe it was someone else. In all the human years I'd watched, that queen had plenty of relations to my treasure's pack and it was never an issue before. It wasn't even suspected my destined one could have been the target of Grynrus's failed abduction. So what royal would have stepped in and deprived me of my ability to see her?

After one last attempt of waving my magic encased limb over the pool of water and nothing happened, the sensation of her presence left, dread replacing it inside of me.

She was gone. She was there, at the place she was sworn to belong to me, but now she was gone. The phantom of her, the connection to the place her soul first touched mine, just vanished, like she had just stepped through thin air.

Dread filled me, but then a new sensation tugged inside. The connection was stronger than before. Like a magnet close to metal. It caused my bulbous head to lift again from the water, a desperate roar blasting the air around me, creating a thick fog as I channeled all my power and will into one last attempt.

The blubbering wench screamed from the scorching heat of my desperation, but her screams fuel my power further, helping to give it that last push of desperation.

And there she was.

Rosie.

My treasure.

She set her bewitching face in the most alluring smile, her eyes like jewels in the soft sunlight.

My relief only lasted for a moment as the rest of the image came into view. The whole horrid picture of where she was and why the connection suddenly snapped back into place. There was no soft sunlight in her homeland. The sun in her home was scorching and overbearing. It burned the water. It burned the eyes.

The sunlight all around her now was soft... just like the touch of the man standing behind her. Like the look on his face as he inhaled her scent, his nose just inches from her flowing hair. Soft, like the unfamiliar tinge of red on her youthful cheeks. Soft like the brush of her hand in his on the winged beasts of the fairy court.

Those creatures are only for fae royalty. Not the common fairy folk. This man looked to be common in his earthly clothing and human appearance, but his eyes shone with the pure emerald magic of the Septentrional Courts.

He wasn't one of that haughty queen's kin. He was from another branch of the royal-bearing tree entirely. And his next words sent bile to my mouth.

"This is Rosie. My mate."

What was even more sickening was the way she looked at him. She was happy about his claim. She looked.... She had a look like a trifling strumpet, eager for attention as she stared back into his emerald eyes. She wasn't a wench like the one brought here, yet she was smoldering with glee for this royal grunt's affections.

Her eyes drifted down to his mouth, and she licked her plush lips. His eyes followed that movement, and I could no longer watch. My limb struck down on the puddle to destroy the image before it caused me too much pain.

She was mine. Her soul was mine. She was promised to me. ME. I have been waiting for the moment the promise could be fulfilled. Why? Why, why, WHY?!

Why was there another claiming to be her mate? Her mate was my destined role. Not a royal, but me. She was mine. She is mine. She was always mine.

What changed?

That girl. The girl who was blubbering on the other shore where Grynrus was floating near in curious fascination at the blood leaking from her wound on her legs onto the sand.

He could taste her again once I had my answers.

My fluid body moved in her direction, bringing about a strangled scream and another round of persistent sobs from her fear-filled eyes. I only shifted back to my humanoid form when I was a few feet away, ensuring the fear remained. Looming over her broken form, I gripped my hand over the green pus-filled wound on her partially healed leg. The other leg was flailing about as she screamed in pain, making her blood rush out even more.

I could feel Grynrus's expectant excitement at the mess of blood. His filthy mouth was what caused the infection to the first leg, something unheard of in royal lands full of magic and healing. There was no healing out here, and the magic we bear is not the kind used to aid. Not without a price. And this girl has not paid the price for her life yet. Not yet.

If she was lucky, she could have the knowledge I needed to pay that price right now.

"You." I clamped my hand around her mouth, silencing her frenzy. "You know," I stated, not asking. It was not an option to not know this. "You know who that man is. The royal with the emerald magic. The-" I scowled, not wanting to say the words. "The fae who claims he is your alpha heir's mate. Who is he?"

Her bloodshot eyes bulged, her skin turning blue. I realized I was holding her face a bit too tight. I loosened my grip and asked again.

"Do you know who he is?"

She nodded frantically, cringing away from my touch.

"THEN SPEAK!"

The blubbering returned, and I was about to react, until she squeaked out a name.

"Ri-Rian-nn. Rian Ki-Ki-Kissinger. He-he's the fairy pr-prince."

***

Thyra

Something had been bugging me all morning. I just couldn't place what it was. No matter what I did, I couldn't dislodge this feeling deep in my chest.

I was sitting at the breakfast counter, sipping herbal tea as I conjured up all that could be causing my irritation. Nothing. There was nothing I was forgetting.

Maybe it was a different sort of nagging feeling. I had been out of sorts since that late-night phone call with my son. Worry and excitement mixed in a confusing turmoil.

My dear boy. My dear Rian. I was so thrilled to hear from Luna Carli that she suspected our children might be mates. She said after some misunderstanding at her daughter's party, Rosie was worried her mate wouldn't want her. Carli, being her nosy self, deduced it was my son. She was already planning our grandma names and told me to be ready to think of mine.

When Courtney ran in here last night to confirm her cousin's suspicions, and to let me know her sweet Callum had also found his mate, we hugged and danced in a circle, celebrating both our sons finding their fated ones in the Crystal Moon Pack.

Yes, my son would have to move to that balmy furnace of a city, but Miami was much closer and easier to visit than Alfheimr. He will have a place he can finally belong to in this world. The place beside an Alpha.

I know myself that there is no better place to be.

"Mmh, how I would kill to be the rim of that glass right about now." My mate watched me from his recliner. I thought he was watching replays of his silly little ball and stick game, but I guess he was watching me.

The baseball. He teases me when I call it stick ball. Or sports ball. Waste of time ball is what I would like to call it. The channel where they cook food is much less a waste of time than the sports ball channels. I can learn new things from that.

Devices and screens hold this entire generation captive. When we have the girls over, I much rather get them outside doing things than allowing them to sit in front of pointless devices with no purpose other than to waste precious time.

"I have something else you can suck down once you're done with that tea." Max grinned coyly, wiggling his eyebrows to make me laugh. He spread his legs and made himself more comfortable, like there was actually a chance I would agree this early in the morning.

Actually, there was always a chance. A big chance, but not this morning. Not until I figured out where this nagging feeling was stemming from.

"Do you think he needs me?" I asked at random, letting my thoughts leak out.

Max's brows pulled down. "Who? Me? Uh, yeah, right h-"

"Rian," I stressed. "He has just found his mate. She'd never been agreeable towards Rian before. Do you think that's why I'm getting this feeling in my chest right now?" I held my hand over my heart, rubbing my chest. "Do you think he needs me?"

"You think the boy's game is so fucking weak that he needs his mommy to get his mate in bed with him?" Max scoffed. "No, woman. I don't think he needs you. I need you." He pointed both hands towards his crotch. "Right here."

I gave him a disapproving look, but his lap did look mighty enticing. He knew it too. He was rolling his hips in his chair, making his pants strain against his bulge and thick thighs. That cocky look on his face was just as enticing. He had every reason to be cocky.

As I was about to let lust win out over my mother's intuition, Bailey came bursting through the front door, not even bothering to knock.

"Thyra," her eyes met mine, looking frantic with worry. "I've got a feeling."

She had a feeling? Was something bothering her, too? "The boys? Rian? Taegan? Is something the matter?"

"For fuck's sake," Max snapped. "You women coddle the fucking brats way too damn much. Rian's fine. Try coddling me," he added in a grumble.

Bailey just stared at me as I stared at her, and I knew, the same as she, that we were heading down south. I didn't yet know why, but we're heading to Miami.

23

SOARING THROUGH HEAVEN

Rosie

The thrumming was back. The necklace that Rian gave me was pulsing again against my chest, and it was really distracting since I was scared shitless, hanging on for my life, riding on Loreana.

Holy shit, I never thought I would be riding thousands of feet in the air on a flying horse. Dad would shit bricks if he could see me right now. Mom too, for that matter.

One fall. Just one fall and I'm dead. Magical protective butterfly pendent or not, I would not survive a fall like this.

Balking like a chicken blows towards me in the wind, followed by boisterous laughter from Taegan.

"Chicken," he snickered. "Open your eyes!"

"Shut your trap!" I yelled back, not moving a muscle, including my eyelids. When I heard him say, "Whoa," followed by a string of profanities aimed at the horse he was riding, it just caused me to hug tighter to Loreana's neck.

I could feel Loreana tensing underneath me, and knew I should probably loosen my grip, but my body just wouldn't.

Why the hell did I think I would be okay to ride this thing alone? She was extremely sweet, just as Rian promised, but sweet wouldn't save me from a death fall.

When he spoke of the travel arrangements, forcing Taegan on the beast that didn't like him and offering his sweet pegasus to me, I was busy making fun of Taegan's pissy attitude. I forgot to tell Rian I wasn't good at heights. I almost said something as he stored our belongings in some magic storage space he opened up in mid-air with his hands, but I didn't want to come across as a pansy and give Taegan fuel to start dishing out the insults towards me. He was handing them out in abundance because of his anger toward Philos.

I should have just told Rian I couldn't do this. I should have been honest, because I felt like I was about to die from the panic, and then I was really going to die when my panic made me fall.

"Rosie," Rian rode up beside me on the pegasus that was his mother's. My heart leapt with excitement at him being near and then sank deep in my chest with a scream when I relaxed my arm just a bit and felt my butt shift on Loreana's back. "Rosie, she won't let you fall. Jackass up there is giving Philos every reason to buck him off, but he's still seated firmly on his back."

"I don't feel firmly seated," I whimpered. "I don't feel firmly seated at all. I'm going to die."

Rian groaned, then mumbled something that I didn't quite catch. It didn't sound like English. I was focusing on not letting the endless wind knock me to the ground, so I could be hearing shit.

Then, I felt jostling beside me. I opened the corner of my eye, just barely, and caught Rian standing on his horse before leaping over towards me. I screamed, a greater fear than falling ripping through me, causing me to let lean over as if I could catch my mate if he were to fall to his death.

He didn't fall. He fluidly slid up behind me, mounting Loreana with me and gripping my waist so I was molded against him.

"WHAT THE HELL ARE YOU DOING!" I screamed, turning to move my hands up and down his face and chest to make sure he was alright. "Wha-what the hell was that?"

"Shh, Rosie." He wrapped his arms tighter around my torso, cradling my head under his. "I'm sorry. You're okay. I got you. You're not going to fall."

With him holding me so tightly, I could feel how badly I was shaking.

I knew I didn't like heights, but I thought that was just roller coasters and shit like that. I didn't know I would be having a literal panic attack in a situation like this. Fuck, it was embarrassing.

Rian continued to hold me and whispered that I was going to be okay as I turned and buried my face in his chest, trying to believe him and not die of total embarrassment.

"The princess going to make it?" Taegan asked.

He had stopped and circled around, waiting for Rian to take the lead again. I turned my head enough to glare at him, but when I saw how high up we still were, I quickly turned it back into Rian's chest to let the sparks from the bond numb my senses once again.

"I got her. She's fine. Quit being a dick," Rian told him.

"Hey! Snider! I thought you were an Alpha. Alpha's aren't scared of anything."

"The fuck they're not!" I yelled back. "You pissed in your pants when you saw a snake creep up on the training field."

"That was a fucking water moccasin! That's different. It's poisonous."

Rian shook his head. "You're scared of all snakes. Don't act like it's just the ones that are deadly. That's only for humans, anyway. Or are you saying your big bad witchy alpha abilities are no match against a defenseless snake?" Rian said in my defense. "Supernatural or not, heights can always be deadly, so I think your fear is far more irrational than hers."

"Yeah, yeah. I got it. Just hurry up and lead the fucking way before dog chow here starts doing flips in the air again. He's growing impatient. I am too. I have a wedgie like you wouldn't believe."

Rian dipped his head down to look at me. "Are you okay enough to move again?"

His eyes, a mix of different shades of greens and golds, shone brightly down at me. I was too lost in their depth and the complexity of their beauty to remember what I was scared of to begin with. They were like galaxies, rich and abundant with stars and magic.

Rian smiled softly. "I'm riding with you the rest of the way. I promise I will never let you fall."

I nodded slightly, keeping my eyes locked on him until I could bring myself to close them. I didn't want to chance looking down again. Now that I had finally calmed down.

"As long as I don't look, I'm fine," I said as I tightly squeezed my eyes together. "I trust you."

"Good," he husked, then I felt his lips on the top of my head, his hand tucking me back under his chin. "Just hold on tight."

I did as he said, squeezing my arms around his center.

When we moved again, the wind caused me to squeal, but his hold on my body was firm and unmoving. I soon got distracted by the feeling of his firm body, and the rigid way his muscles were pressed up against mine.

Even his back was defined. My fingers started to trace the hard planes and indentions in the lower part of his back. He shivered every time I touched him close to his spine, but he didn't protest. His hand that he kept wrapped around me started rubbing my back, too.

The sparks were unreal. His scent was all around me, intoxicating me with more of that sweet ocean smell than ever before. My nose gravitated towards his neck, and I started taking deep breaths of him. It felt like all of him was seeping into me.

One minute I was terrified, consumed with fear. Now I'm consumed by him.

"Rosie," his body shuddered when my lips caressed the spot where I was most drawn to. The spot that would one day hold my mark. "I-I can't concentrate with you-you doing that."

I chanced a glance up at him. His eyes were twirling with lust, staring down at me. His mouth was parted, his lips so inviting. I licked my lips as I stared at his mouth, then looked back into his eyes. A deep groan left him, then his mouth softly pressed to mine, making everything fade away but us.

"For fuck's sake," Taegan muttered from behind us, but I didn't care. I didn't care who was watching. This is heaven. I was soaring through heaven while kissing his lips.

When his tongue moved into my mouth, I let out a heavy moan. I had never kissed like this before. My body was on fire. Everywhere. It felt like the only thing that could put it out was him. I didn't realize we were getting carried away until Taegan started coughing loudly.

"Dude, I have no fucking idea where we are going. I'm happy for you and shit, but my ass is on fire and I'd like to fucking land soon."

Rian groaned, reluctantly pulling his lips away and resting his forehead against mine.

"I want to land fucking soon, too." He shifted positions on the back on Loreana and I blushed, seeing the bulge in his pants. I could feel it on my hip. He kissed my forehead once, then focused back on directing Loreana on where to go.

The moment was over, but I could still feel the effects everywhere, especially on my lips. I couldn't stop touching them, marveling at the smooth swelling of the skin from the intense kissing.

I wanna kiss him again. I wanna do more than kiss. I want to feel all the magic he had to offer me.

As we started to descend, breaking through the clouds, I asked, "Where are we going?"

"The only place I could think of to start," he told me. "My mother's old cottage on the outskirts of the kingdom."

24

WITCHES AND FAE

When the outlines of triangle-shaped roofs, lined with brightly colored moss and flower-covered vines, came into view in the distance, Loreana and Philos landed in a small clearing in a lush forest outside of the village. Rian explained to me it wouldn't be ideal for the villagers to see the three of us riding in on a couple of the royal family's pegasus. Having two werewolves with him was already a risk. The flight into town on noble steeds would be begging for attention. We were going to land away from civilization and walk the distance between. Rian was going to use his magic and clothes he prepared beforehand to keep us from catching too much attention.

Nelly, Rian's mom's pegasus, had already headed back to the grazing field, and now Rian was whispering to the other two in his native language to go home as well. I was standing there, just watching him sweetly rub both beasts' faces, nestling his face to theirs while listening to his tongue roll in that exotic way when he speaks. It had my body tingling in new ways.

Rian was so gentle. So sweet. So.... Sexy. Fuck, was he sexy. Like, I wanted to join the mile high club in the most inappropriate way about thirty minutes ago, but didn't care because he was too sexy, sexy.

That kiss. I can't stop thinking about it, and every time I do, I end up touching my lips. He was so overwhelming and passionate. I felt like I had no control over my body. I didn't mind not having control, either. I wanted to give him more control, but being thousands of feet in the air, riding on the back of a flying horse and Taegan being Taegan while watching behind us was not the time to do that.

This wasn't the time either, but I was still letting my mind go there while watching him.

"Oh my goddess," Taegan murmured mockingly in my ear, using a faux high-pitched voice. "He's so handsome. I just want to suck on his handsome face all fucking day long. His eyes are handsome. His face is handsome. His toes are-"

"Shut up," I growled.

He chuckled. "Did I get it right? Was that what you were thinking?"

My face flamed. "No," I lied. Well, I wasn't thinking about his toes.

"Bull shit. You look like a fucking girl right now."

"I am a fucking girl," I reminded him.

"I know," he chuckled. "I'm just giving you a hard time. I've just never seen you like this. You're *acting* like a girl for once. It's a good look for you. The alpha persona slips when you're with him."

I grimaced, not really liking that. My Alpha persona couldn't slip. Being an Alpha woman was hard enough. Now that I was thinking about it, I'd been more focused on Rian than on my duty as an alpha since the beginning of this, even when Rian first told me he could bring me to this realm to find my friend. I was more excited about going with him than I was about having a way to save my friend.

It was my duty. My focus should be on bringing Julia back home. Maybe I have been slipping into girl mode a little too much. I'm an alpha, and I was standing there daydreaming about my mate instead of thinking about how I was going to find and save my friend.

The two pegasus took flight, lifting their large wings up in the air and beating them down, sending gushes of powerful wind around them. Their whines of delight echoed through the sky, dancing around one another before lifting above the clouds where they could no longer be seen.

I stared in fascination, but the glum feeling of failure was still weighing on me. I was making this trip about myself. It was not about me and Rian. It was about finding Julia. I needed to remember that and quit acting like a girl, like Taegan pointed out.

"What are you two talking about?" Rian asked, walking towards us with a smile.

I tried to paste on a more business-like smile, ridding all the girlish immature thoughts from showing on my face.

"Princess-pissed-a-lot is fawning like a- Oomph," Taegan buckled over, gripping his stomach after I elbowed him hard in it. "Shit. What the fuck?"

"Nothing. We weren't talking about anything important. Should we go?"

Rian stared at me. Those luminescent, galaxy-like eyes of his seemed to stare right into my soul, and it became so much harder to keep the girlish thoughts out of my head. Why did he have to be so handsome?

Fuck. Now I was thinking about exactly what Taegan accused me of. How do you find this balance as an alpha? How do my parents manage to find a balance between them so they can do what is best for their pack?

But, damn, his lips. My eyes flickered at his lips again, and the feeling of being in his arms thousands of feet in the air came back to me. This wasn't good. I needed to get my head out of the gutter and think back to the mission.

Rian's brows pulled down, then he looked at Taegan for a second and grimaced.

"Yeah. Let's go," Rian said. "It's that way to the village." He pointed towards a cropping of trees.

With his eyes looking elsewhere, I could break out of their spell and hurry away before I embarrassed myself again. Taegan's snickering led me to believe it was already too late for that, but I was going to pretend that I didn't hear him.

The woods were rich with exotic plants and trees. Some emitted glittering displays of glowing light. Some seemed to expel that light into the air around us. It felt like the open field the Pegasus were staying in. The magic must be thick in here, pressing into the trees and releasing into the sky above.

There were a few trees that looked to be dead. Not dead like trees in our world where the roots dried up and they no longer produce leaves. Death in our world still produces life. You could see insects and wildlife take over the decaying trunks to give it life outside of death. These dead trees were devoid of any light, any magic. Not a single creature went near the blackened logs. They felt like black holes of life, sucking the life out of the very air around them.

"What are those?" I asked, pointing to a blackened tree standing to the side of us. The birds in the sky gave it a wide berth, and the sunlight didn't seem to hit it. "There are several trees like that. Why do they feel so ominous?"

"Because they are," Rian said. "Witches from your world like to offer sacrifices to ours in exchange for magic. Skilled witches can find a magic-producing tree like this in the forest and feed off it until they suck all the life from it. They just need to sacrifice something of life in your world to ours for the exchange. The trees are preferable because the witch can tie their life to the tree, so when the tree dies, they die, and vice versa. Witches can live for centuries by doing that. It's restricted now, and my uncle will destroy any trees in his kingdom he feels are being siphoned. See there." He pointed to one felled in the distance. "That's one my uncle had killed, so the witch that was on the other side most likely died as well."

"Are trees the only thing that get siphoned from?" I asked. "I don't really know much about witches. Whenever we have dealings with them, Dad sends the Meyers brothers to deal with it."

Teagan flinched when I mention the Meyers brothers. His teasing attitude turned into a look of dejection, a pensive expression on his face. I wondered why? He was usually really friendly with Mitch and Mark Meyers.

"Witches try to siphon anything they can from our world. Sometimes they mess with the elements, but often the darker witches will find a being on this side willing to make a pact with them in exchange for something else. That's harder to prevent, because it takes a strong species or creature to summon from the other side. Usually it takes entire covens and life sacrifices to call on them."

I've heard nasty stories about covens being found in the marshes and the outskirts of the city, sacrificing children or virgins to demons to get more power. I didn't know you could summon a creature from the fae realm, too.

Mom would get in trouble all the time for trying to handle witches on her own. Dad told me that even when mom was pregnant with me, she went on witch hunts. She abducted Aunt Simone one time to help her, which was stupid, since Aunt Simone doesn't fight. Uncle Casey, Simone's twin, is the Blue Cliff gamma and is a beast, but Simone would have been useless in a fight, even against witches. Uncle Casey can hold his own against witches. He has helped the Meyers brothers at times.

We really don't know much about them. Witches are more secretive than other races. They are not really another race at all, which is probably why. They are usually just humans with a gift to siphon power through other things.

Usually.

There are hybrids like Taegan with a magic-yielding human side, but a powerful supernatural side as well, so they don't have to be as careful. But he doesn't even offer any information about his magic abilities. And I know he doesn't siphon magic in the ways Rian is describing.

"Do you guys have to deal with a lot of witches in Blue Cliff?" I asked. Taegan and Rian exchanged glances, then Taegan lifted his eyebrows. "I mean, besides you. I know you aren't summoning powerful creatures from this world to get a boost. I was just wondering how you know so much, Rian."

"I am Fae royalty," he smirked. "I saw my uncle and the court handle plenty of issues concerning witches while I lived here. If I hadn't been sent back to my mother, I would have had a role in the fairy court as well, so I was taught about such things from a young age."

"He has also been blessed with an amazing family member like me who can wield magic like a boss." Taegan had a cocky grin on his face.

"Steal magic like a boss." Rian rolled his eyes. "You have to siphon from me and mom to get your fix."

"I have other ways," Taegan muttered, staring at the ground.

"I don't want to hear about them," Rian said, making a face.

"What? What other ways?" I was curious, even if Rian wasn't.

Taegan snickered. "That information is too much for your virgin ears."

Oh, fuck, he did not just say that in front of Rian. My face felt like it was about to burst into flames, and I walked ahead, not wanting to see Rian's reaction. Taegan's snickering continued, and I had to walk even faster to not react. I was going to kill him by the end of this trip. I knew it.

I could hear Rian arguing with the jerk, but tried to tune them out. My virginity was not something I wanted brought up in front of my mate.

25

---•---

FAIRY HOME

Rian

"What are you doing?" I asked Taegan, not liking his topic of conversation with Rosie.

He shrugged "Walking right now. I plan on shitting the moment I make it to grandma Thyra's house."

"I mean with her, you asshole. Why do you have to be such a jerk all the time?"

"I'm just teasing her," he chuckled. "She looks cute when she blushes."

My magic flared, reaching out and zipping him in the ass. He yelped, then zapped me back. This continued on back and forth, both of us using our magic to shock the other, cursing under our breath. My zaps stayed strong, but he felt weaker with every burst. He was not home where he could refuel easily using his Lycan and the Lycan's pull on the goddess realm, or even feeding on my mom and myself. Hell knows I was not giving him a lick of magic with the way he imposed so forcefully. His Goddess has no authority here in this realm, either. For once, my magic was stronger than his and he gave in before me.

"Fuck! I give! What the fuck is your problem?"

"Don't make her blush. Don't think she is cute. Don't even talk to her anymore if you're just trying to make her mad. Look at her." I waved my hand in front of us. "She won't even walk with us, you jerk."

Taegan smirked. "She's just shy."

I scowled, "Because you had to make that comment."

"What comment?" He asked with a cheeky grin.

He knew damn well what I was talking about. How the hell did he know that about her, anyway?

I zapped him again, pissed he knew my mate was a virgin, and teased her about it. He was talking shit when he's a virgin himself.

"Stop it, you fish shit! That hurts!"

"You stop! My mate's innocence has nothing to do with you. I wish you would just leave her the hell alone."

He huffed. "Is that why you're so pissed? Shit, man, I've been friends with her longer than I've even known you. Don't be that guy."

"What guy?" I snapped.

"The guy that gets pissy when his girlfriend talks to other men. It's not a good look."

It's not other men that worry me. It's him. Just him. How could he still not get that?

"Would you be fine with another man teasing your mate about being a virgin when you find her?"

His expression turned hostile. "She's eight fucking years old. Who the hell would have the balls to try and-"

He clamped his hand over his mouth as my eyes went wide in shock.

"Eight?! You found your mate and she's-"

"Shut up!" He growled, covering my mouth with his hands.

Rosie turned to look back at us, then grimaced in the most beautiful way. Her perfect brows pulled down, eyeing Taegan's hold on my mouth with confusion. She quickly looked forward and trudged on.

"Fuck," Taegan grunted. "Pretend you didn't hear shit. Got it? Not a fucking word."

"Taegan," I pulled his hands away from my face. "I can't just not hear that. Seriously."

"Try," he growled.

I sighed. That just wasn't possible. Not when he admitted he had found her, but she was eight. Eight. That means he's twelve years older than her. "Does your mom know?"

"No one knows. Well," he scowled. "I guess that's not true anymore." By his tone, I could tell he was not referring to me.

"Did someone else find out?"

"Rian, just fucking drop it," he groaned, running a hand down his face. "Please."

"I can't just fucking drop it if it's bothering you this much. Who found out? I can tell it's not just me." I could see it really bothered him, too. He looked older in his stress. There was anxiety etched across his face. I thought he was being more annoying than usual. This was why. That's what Taegan does. He doesn't let others help. He takes on everything alone and puts up a front that everything is okay.

"Her dads found out, okay? Fucking hell, you're annoying." His eyes glowed. His beast was speaking to him. Arguing with him about something, telling by the expressions he was making.

Dads, meaning plural. We have a gay couple at Blue Cliff with an adopted son, but no daughter. I was wracking my brain to think of any other gay couples we know. The Betas of Rosie's pack had a daughter, but she was older.

As I was running through every possible scenario, I remembered that the resort owners had eight-year-old twins, and those little girls had two dads. The Meyers brothers shared a mate. Not only do they share a mate, but that mate happened to be a seer. The throuple's twin daughters weren't identical, making one a seer and the other a normal werewolf.

I was willing to bet anything that the little girl with vibrant purple eyes, who was always the one most excited to see Taegan when we come to visit, was the eight-year-old girl Taegan was talking about.

Hell, was that why he always insisted on staying at the resort? I thought... I didn't know what I thought, but I never imagined Taegan would have a mate that much younger than him. No wonder he always wanted to come to Miami. It wasn't for Rosie. Just how long has he known?

"How long?"

"How long what, Rian?" He gave an incredulous look.

"How long have you known?"

He pursed his lips, deep in thought. I almost thought that he was not going to answer me, but then he muttered, "A long time. A very long time. Please, just leave it at that."

His eyes continued to glow, and I could see he was having some internal struggle with his Lycan. If it was about his mate, Conri might start getting defensive towards me if I kept up the questions. I had better just leave it alone. For now.

That answered my question of why he was so set on coming to Miami so often. I felt better now that I knew it wasn't for my mate. He still needed to quit talking about her virginity and thinking she was cute when she blushes. Yeah. I was going to be that guy.

***

Rosie

Thyra's cottage was nestled in this story-book village. It was something out of a fairy tale. The streets were lined with various vendors of all different fae races selling all sorts of things I had never seen before. Most were fairy, but there were a great many other races I had never seen.

A woman with the legs of a goat was selling shimmering stones she claimed were blessed by a river goddess for protection. She tried extra hard to call Taegan and Rian over, but neither gave her a glance. I had to work hard not to growl at her staring, possessiveness taking over when she looked at my mate like she could devour him, even licking her lips.

A hairy, burly man with an odd-shaped body and sideburns shaped like leaves was selling tonics and pumices. Rian said he was a forest troll, a species derived from the trees themselves. He claimed they were much friendlier than the mountain trolls, who preferred isolation and could grow as big as boulders.

There was a store close to Thyra's place that sold weapons I had never seen before. Blades of obsidian, bows that were strung with spider webs and shot arrows made of very hard leaves. Rian told us about how the leaves were harvested and then laid out to dry in the sun, getting solid over time so they could be used for various things. Most fae households had cutlery made from those same leaves this shop had made into weapons.

Taegan and I both wanted to look inside the weapon store, but Rian advised against it. The owner was a goblin and goblins had finer hearing than most other species. I guess Taegan and I were being a bit loud in talking about how we would use the weapons we saw in the window display, and were giving ourselves away for not being fae.

Once we got inside, the three of us shed the cloaks Rian prepared for us to wear on our walk through the town. The cloaks shielded our true appearance and hid our scents. To everyone around, we looked like two regular fairy people out for a walk through town. Rian said that his mother's house was a safe place to be ourselves. Because she was a fairy princess in exile, her brother took extra precautions to protect her living arrangements outside of the castle. There were wards up that blocked anyone on the outside from seeing or hearing the things that went on inside.

The cottage was cozy, with a fireplace at its center. The furniture was carved from a gorgeous wood. Even the couches were wood, though they had cushions lining the seats and backs. The fabric looked a bit like a flour sack, but the cushions were a lot softer than they appeared. They were smooth like butter and I sank into them when Rian told me to sit and relax.

He had Taegan follow him to a bathroom, Taegan grumbling about the narrow hall-ways and low ceilings the entire way.

I thought the house looked cute. Tranquil. I could imagine Thyra here knitting one of the woven blankets lying in a basket by the stairs, and sipping herbal tea by the fire. She also looked like the type of woman that would visit that weapons shop and give no regard to the goblin who owned it if he happened to overhear her being a bit improper.

I wondered what Rian's mother would think about him being my mate. My mom was thrilled, but mom would have been happy for me no matter what. Thyra was someone I had never gotten too familiar with. I just heard about her from mom and Taegan's mother.

Rian's step-dad didn't like my mom, and hated the weather in Florida. I probably only met him when I've visited Blue Cliff, and never really interacted with him. Uncle Casey and great-uncle Nate get on Alpha Max's nerves too, and that's who we stay with up north. Maybe Alpha Max just doesn't like anyone from Florida. Was he going to be disappointed that I was his stepson's mate?

"Okay, now that the brat found his home for the next half hour." Rian surprised me out of my thoughts as he came around the corner. "Do you want to help me find something to eat? There may not be much in the pantry, but I brought some canned soup from your world."

I smiled softly. "Is my world not your world too? You've lived there longer than you've lived here."

He shrugged. "Yeah, but this place holds my birthright. It will always be my home."

I didn't know why, but that didn't settle well with me. It made a pit form in my stomach. I knew what he meant. It was like Uncle Casey saying "It's good to be home," when he comes to Miami. I selfishly still wished that he would rather find his home with me.

There I went, putting too much focus on myself and forgetting why we were here to begin with.

"Yeah, I can help. Then we can get to work finding Julia."

26

PHOEBE

The ethereal fog was blooming around the woman's feet, her dark skin taking on a soft glow in the glittering space between consciousness and being awake.

She had been here before. Plenty of times. She usually welcomed these dreams, but this one felt different. This felt ominous, in a sense. It felt like a warning was coming. Building in the woman right now was the aching pulse you get in your chest when you know something foreboding was about to be revealed, changing the course of your future.

Still, she welcomed the dream. The woman felt giddy, despite the prophetic tingles. She welcomed the one who called on her, as she always had.

"My daughter," Reika's voice echoed.

The woman turned in place, searching for the goddess until she finally revealed herself.

The goddess stepped out of the fog in a simmering dress of pure energy and power, rays of golden light bouncing off her dimpled cheeks. Her hair flowed around her, almost touching the ground, like a crowning veil. She was gorgeous and omniscient. She alone held all authority over the creatures of the moon.

"I call, and you never fail to come." Reika smiled warmly, opening her arms as if to embrace the woman.

The woman dropped to her knees, in reverence of her goddess, her savior.

"I am your servant, my goddess. I will always come."

Reika pet the woman's hair, lovingly running her fingers to the side of her face and cradling her cheek to draw the woman's gaze up.

"You are a gift, my child. A gift I praise heaven for. Always."

The woman bathed happily in the goddess's praise, thankful for the opportunity she'd been given to serve such a loving entity.

"I'm sure you can feel the grim intentions behind my calling you." Reika's face saddened. "I am sorry this isn't to be a visit of comfort. Your Alpha, my greatest grandson, is in need of *your help, but he isn't able to call for you himself at this moment in time. He knows not yet that he needs you."*

"Taegan?" The woman furrowed her brows in question. "I had just spoken to him yesterday."

Reika nodded softly. "A lot has changed for my scion in the night. His reactions to these events are to cause a chain reaction that could endanger his and your futures, and also thwart all my efforts to bring back balance in the Crystal Moon Pack. I need you to retrieve him, my child. I need you to go and bring him back before he does something that is irreparable, even to me."

Phoebe

This was going to be a shitshow. I could already tell. I' sat in my corner seat on the pack's private plane, just watching the show already taking place. I should have left earlier, on my own, without the chaotic entourage currently with me.

I knew Luna would figure something was wrong. She gets them too. The dreams. The messages passed directly from the moon goddess. She is the descendant of Reika, and has always had the ability to hear her voice through dreams. She rarely remembers all that was said in those dreams, but she still gets them.

I, on the other hand, always remember. I don't yet have a wolf to help me manage the goddess' blood inside me, because instead of being born with the gift, I devoured it. I had to consume Luna Bailey's blood, then I was essentially born again as a new being, in limbo between the moon and the blood.

I was her's now. The moon goddess's. She told me herself. Taegan has told me. When the brat was half my age, he knew more about what was happening inside my head than I did. It was weird being told about my future from a first-grader when I was half-way through high school. I was thankful, since I was on a pretty destructive path, battling my own shit because of my birth parents. Taegan gave me a place to belong, and if the goddess tells me to go knock some sense into his stubborn ass, I'm going to do it.

The other night, the night before Luna Bailey told me we were going to Florida, I had a visit from Reika in my dream. I didn't expect Luna Bailey to have a similar visit, and for her to remember enough of it to feel the need to go check on her son.

Fucking Taegan. He always has to be a busybody, hurting himself by trying to solve other people's problems. Rian found his mate, which is great, but Taegan is going to mess shit up more than help if he doesn't get his head on. From the cryptic words that were spoken to me, it sounded like Taegan was running from his own problems by trying to solve Rian's. When Reika visited me and asked me to go retrieve him from his stupid mistake, I didn't expect the shit show to be accompanying me.

All of them are here. Taegan's five sisters, Aly, Lauren and Leah, Jade and Jana, Luna Bailey, Alpha Max and Thyra, then the entire Gamma family; Gamma Casey, Courtney, Conner, Casper, Calvin and baby Carter.

The J twins, as I like to call them, are screaming at Alpha Max because he kissed Thyra's lips, which, for whatever reason, he is not allowed to do in their presence. They were both clinging to Thyra and screaming at "gump-y Max" to go away. Alpha Max looked ready to jump off the plane to get away from their crying, but was still trying to calm them down. Bailey was by his side and helping to calm him in his efforts, while Thyra looked amused.

Carter was hanging off Courtney's tit, Courtney not bothering to cover herself at all while she fed him. Normally I wouldn't care, but her mate was staring at her in a disgusting way that made me want to barf.

Calvin had a sharpie and was sitting under a table, unnoticed by any of the other adults, drawing pictures on the legs of the table. He already drew pictures of what I hoped were palm trees on the wall, but the drawings were phallic shaped, and the "leaves" looked almost like a waterfall of some kind instead.

Gamma Casey had his legs splayed out in front of him while he watched Courtney nurse. The oldest twins and Casper had sharpies and were coloring in his tattoos and giving him pretend new ones. That was how Calvin got the sharpie to begin with. He was excluded from the coloring party, so he found somewhere else to color instead.

Aly and Conner were playing some gory video game on the mounted TV, yelling at each other constantly. The two of them were extremely competitive and made everything a life or death battle. Aly cheated and Conner had to tattle on her every other second.

I had a headache already, and we'd only been up on the plane for an hour. We had so much longer to go.

I should have been making this journey alone. I had to wait nearly two days to leave because Bailey and Gamma Casey had to make arrangements for the pack. Alpha Axel was in Alaska at the moment on business, or he would probably be here too.

My moms suggested I wait for everyone else, not wanting me to travel by myself, even though I'm a college graduate who pays her own bills and shit. I should have just done what I wanted and booked a flight the same day to Miami, but even at twenty-nine, I find it hard to tell my moms no.

"Son of a mother duck," Casey growled, finally noticing his second youngest child. "Calvin! Knock that shit off!"

"Look, daddy," he giggled. "I colored the pretty trees you colored on grandpa's car."

I held my hand over my mouth to not laugh out loud. They are penises. The boy just doesn't know it. I bet Gamma Casey called them trees when the younger kids asked what they were. He likes to take window chalk and draw pictures on his father-in-law's car windows.

"Casey," Courtney groaned, shaking her head and staring up at the ceiling. "Go clean those off."

"I didn't do it. He did. Make him clean them-"

"You better get that shit off my plane before I throw you out of this mother fucking-"

"MAX!" Bailey yelled at the same time Courtney yelled, "Uncle Max!" and Thyra yelled, "HONEY!".

"Language!" Half of the kids yelled together, knowing what the next word was going to be out of the three women's mouths.

I sighed, pushing myself up out of the seat and heading to the bathroom to escape the madness for a little while. I hoped Miami was ready for the storm that was about to hit it.

27

— • —

DESIRE TO DISASTER

Sophia

As I ran my fingers through the hair of the sexy future Gamma of Blue Cliff Pack, I could not believe how incredibly lucky I was.

Calum was lying with his head in my lap, napping after bringing me back home to the packhouse after lunch. Dad was off today, at home with mom on the second floor of the packhouse in our apartment, and Rosie's mom was doing something weird with baby clothes on the Alpha floor, so I suggested Calum and I sit in one of the common rooms to talk without dad breathing over our shoulders the entire time, or Luna Carli asking our opinion on nursery colors.

Daddy wasn't too thrilled about me being mated to a ranked wolf of a pack located so far north. He even tried to tell Calum to come back in a year after I graduate and I could feel the mate bond for myself.

I may not be able to feel the mate bond yet, but I definitely felt something powerful towards my best friend's cousin.

Calum had always been Rosie's sexy lumberjack-looking cousin from the north, but he was pretty distant with everyone here. He clung to Mrs. Solace, his aunt, when he wasn't with the warriors and his other aunt, Luna Carli, training. He seemed disinterested in anything but family here. Now, his only interest seemed to be me.

When he called me his mate, and ran his fingers down the side of my face on the barge at the cove, my heart was racing inside of my chest. I had never seen him look at anybody in this way. Rosie used to tease him about probably being mated to a cheeseburger one day, since food was his only love. I'm going to enjoy making her eat those words next time I see her when she gets back from her own little honeymoon with Prince Rian.

"Mmh, you smell good," Calum groaned softly, turning his face and burying his nose in a place that made my face flush. He was half asleep and didn't realize what he had just done.

"Hey, stop it," I squirmed, nudging him so he would move his nose away from my sensitive nerves and wake up. "We're in public."

His eyes fluttered open, and I simpered when his hooded eyes met mine. His eyes moved to my crotch, where his nose was just pressed, then a smug smirk spread across his face.

"It's starting to smell even better now." He had a hungry, predatory look on his face. Gosh, did he have to point out his effect on me?

"Stop it!" I hit his shoulder. He didn't even flinch. He's nothing but muscle, hard and bulking everywhere.

Everywhere.

His personality was as soft as could be. The contrast in his looks and demeanor was one of the most attractive things about him. He looked all hard and gruff, but he's been nothing but sweet to me for the past few days.

"I'm joking," he chuckled in a deep voice that stirred at a place deep inside of me. "Well, not really, but I'll stop teasing you, though you look adorable when you blush like that."

He rolled on his back to stare up at me. His legs were splayed out. One on the floor and one over the arm of the couch. He looked so relaxed and content. I smiled at the tender look in his eyes. A girl can get used to this kind of treatment from a guy. The adoring look like I'm his entire world, and the devotion he has shown since he declared me his.

I've dated my fair share of boys, but never had a guy look at me like this. There was no lust or objective attraction. This was a look full of sincere dedication. Rosie may be the one mated to a prince, but I felt like a princess whenever I was with Calum.

"What are you thinking about?" Calum reached up to trace my chin with his rough fingers. I leaned in to his touch.

"You." I let out a small and quiet burst of giggles, then bit my lip to keep more from spilling out.

"What about me?" His smile widened.

"Just," I let out another burst of giggles, "you."

It was too embarrassing to let him know all the gooey and mushy thoughts running inside of my head.

Calum's smile looked naughty for a split second. Then he lifted his body up, wrapped an arm around my waist, and whipped my body around and under his, pinning me in place in a matter of maybe two seconds. I felt out of breath and completely taken by surprise, but he was still so gentle that I didn't feel any discomfort from the sudden action. He cradled my body the entire time. My hands pressed against his firm chest, and I couldn't help but grope him a little bit. He didn't mind. I wouldn't even think he had noticed if I didn't feel the soft purring against my fingers.

"I'm thinking about you too," he husked, running his nose down my neck. He couldn't mark me yet, but he sure enjoyed lingering over the place on my neck where he one day would.

"Wha-what about me?"

I could feel his grin against my skin. "Just.... You."

"Oh, you think you're funny?" I giggled, then started tickling his sides, making his entire body buck and convulse above me. His uncontrollable laugh was deep and did things to me on the inside. He was thrashing wildly, but somehow was still managing to hold me gently in place, making sure I didn't get hurt in his fit of laughter.

The more his hips started to buck, the more I started to feel a certain part of him grinding against me. Right there. It felt good; the friction making my sensitive area buzz and I couldn't concentrate on tickling him any longer.

He noticed too, and I felt that muscle now getting hard against me. It was straining against his athletic shorts. An all too embarrassing moan escaped me, and he groaned in response, grinding his hips intentionally against me this time.

His kiss was soft and gentle, but I was anything but. I was pulling his body closer to mine, fighting against the steady rhythm of his mouth to cause chaos between us. I was getting carried away, biting his bottom lip, dancing my tongue against his, whimpering and moaning into his mouth. He was steady as a rock, moving with me, but with so much more care and so much more in control. It made me want him even more desperately.

I forgot we were downstairs in an open space, exposed to anyone who would want to walk in. No one was there when we got to the common room, it being a weekday in the mid-afternoon, but anyone could show up and I would be too engrossed with Calum to pay them any attention. My dad could be watching for all I cared. I just wanted him. I wanted to escalate this kissing to do so much more.

Stupid age rule. He had to wait to mark me, but not to have sex. He was too sweet of a guy to have sex with me before then. Last night when we were alone at the Alpha apartment, since Calum was using their spare bedroom to be closer to me, we were getting carried away like we're doing right now. I was practically begging him to take me, but he wouldn't. He wouldn't do it. He helped me get some level of satisfaction, but wouldn't cross that line. Not yet.

Now, I felt like begging again, my legs wrapping around his waist to force him to keep up the torturing friction that was shooting currents of pleasure through my core. He was getting carried away, too. His mouth was no longer controlled. He was as wild as I was, both of us in some competition to drive the other to madness first.

It was a winning game for us both. By the strain in his deep voice and the throbbing between my legs, I we were both just about there.

.... Then the ice bucket got dumped over our heads.

"EWW! GROSS!" A little kid squealed, making both of us freeze. I strained to turn my head to see who was there.

"Oh, ho, ho. What do we have here?" A man asked, standing in the doorway to the room with his arms folded over his chest and a devious grin on his face. He was older, and after my eyes came to focus against the brilliant Florida sunlight blasting through the windows in the foyer, I soon recognized him as Rosie's uncle. One from Canada.

Shit. It was Calum's dad.

"Daddy, I thought you said only you and mama could do that because you need to make more brothers. Is Calum making me another brother?" The little boy asked.

"I want a sister this time!" Another boy, a little older, yelled. "Calum, make me a sister!" He looked around his dad to stare at me. "Oh, she's pretty. She's prettier than the other one you were making sisters with, Calum. The one from your school."

I groaned deep in my chest, not liking that bit of information.

"What the fuck?" Calum growled. He lifted me to straddle his lap, then tucked me beside him when I attempted to wiggle free, embarrassed and a little peeved about the making sisters thing. He was not letting me go. No matter how much I strained against his hold, I couldn't break free. "Why the hell are you guys here?"

His dad pouted his bottom lip, though his eyes were dancing with amusement. "How cold. We came to see you."

"Bull shit. You were excited I was leaving, you douche. What the hell are you-"

"Hey," his dad snapped, "Blue balling is no reason to snap at your father, you little-"

"Knock it off!" A redheaded woman smacked Calum's dad on the back of the head. It was Calum's mom. Aunt Courtney was what she told me to call her one time many years ago, when she visited one summer. She was Luna Carli's cousin. "You're embarrassing the girl. I've put up with enough of your crap for one day. Knock it off."

I wished I could just crawl into a hole. Behind Calum's parents were a whole swarm of people, all from the Blue Cliff Pack, judging by their clothes. Jeans weren't a common thing to wear at this time of year here. They had omegas bringing in piles of luggage, too. A huge old man with an alpha aura was barking orders while two little girls hung over his shoulders.

There were so many people, and I felt so overwhelmed and flustered. I had a very Rosie-like thought of elbowing Calum in the side to get free, then running away to hide somewhere.

"I'm sorry, Sophie. I didn't know they were coming. I don't know what's going on," he whispered to me.

Calum's mom gave me the warmest smile, and I could see where Calum got his tenderness. His mom's smile was very similar to his.

"You must be Sophia," she gushed, coming over to grab my hands and pulling me up into a hug. I was free of Calum, but now at his mom's mercy. "I'm so excited to meet you, sweetie. Call me Courtney."

She squeezed my body so tight that it made me squeak, making my face even more red than it already was.

"My goddess, you are beautiful." She held me at arm's length, looking me up and down. "Whoops. Got a little breast milk on you," she said, then started rubbing a wet spot on my shirt with her thumb, which was dangerously close to my nipple. I looked at her shirt and sure enough, she had a ring of moisture in the middle of one of her breasts. "I probably should have kept my bra on, but it's so hot here. Nursing bras are too thick for this weather."

"Mom!" Calum huffed, pulling me away from her attempts to dry my shirt. "Goddess, you guys are like a fucking disaster." He tried to tuck me behind him, then turned to whisper, "Go get cleaned up. I'll come find you later."

I nodded, then gladly rushed off, murmuring a shy goodbye to his mom and dad as I walked by them and at least ten other people to get out of the room and up the stairs. A vampire woman was the furthest from the group and gave me an apologetic smile as I raced up the stairs.

The chaotic sounds of Calum's parents yelling at him about his disrespect, the old man bellowing about the heat, the omegas trying to sort out luggage with the two other women, and the million children running around in mayhem kept me from looking back.

That went from desire to disaster in a split second. I was so excited to have Calum as my mate, but now I was wondering if I should just hide for the rest of the day, or maybe until my embarrassment goes away. Getting my future mother-in-law's boob milk on me, after his father caught us making out and dry humping one another, and his brothers told me about his making babies with someone else is not how I envisioned meeting my future mate's family.

28

—·—

PREDATORS

Carli

Baby clothes are the cutest. The tiny feet on the onesies are my favorite. Parker was busy out with the fairy knights, investigating the cove and any leads on Rosie's missing friend, and here I was, selfishly chilling in my own daydreams. I had been working day and night for the past three days to help find that girl, and felt like I was just running in circles, getting nowhere. I needed a break. A mental break, or I was going to go insane.

I was grinning to myself, imagining new baby feet in the onesies I'd kept from when Reese and Rosie were babies, when a fucking disaster came storming through my door. No knocking or anything. Just an instant fucking disaster of loud kids and yelling adults.

"You got your tit juice all over my mate in the first five seconds of seeing her, mom! Of course I'm pissed!"

"That tit juice nourished your body for a solid sixteen months, you brat," Courtney snapped. "It's natural. She's a woman. I'm sure she gets that."

"Your mom's tit juice is delicious. I love getting tit juice all over me," Casey commented, like he was helping with whatever argument they were having.

"WILL ALL THREE OF YOU FUCKERS QUIT TALKING ABOUT TIT JUICE!?" Alpha Max bellowed. He had a toddler on his head and another in his arms, both screaming that he was not "Thy-ma" and they wanted "Thy-ma".

"Max, give me the twins. Jade's going to fall."

"No! They need to understand that you're mine and not theirs. I can damn well kiss you anytime I want. And I see your damn smile. You're just making it worse."

The twins started beating harder on Alpha Max's head and chest, screaming in garbled baby talk, something about no kisses and screaming the word "mine" repeatedly.

"Grandpa, Jana's diaper is crooked, and it looks like she pooped." One of the older twins tugged on Alpha Max's flannel shirt.

I didn't know if the man was bright red from his anger or because he was hot. It was sweltering outside today. Not the weather to wear flannel and jeans. Not that we ever have the weather to wear flannel and jeans. This is fucking Miami. Why this family never dresses appropriately, I don't get.

Thyra took the opportunity to rid Alpha Max of one toddler, a triumphant smile on her face. Jana quieted down immediately, her face covered in snot and tears, but her grin matched Thyra's. The other twin was yanking Alpha Max's hair, screaming at the top of her lungs, pissed her sister got their grandma, but she didn't. Maybe she will shit on his head to get him to put her down. If I wasn't so deep in shock, I might suggest it.

"That's enough of that," Bailey, popping in from the hallway, took the screaming toddler and gave her a stern look. Max rubbed his sore head, then looked down to see shit smeared all down his side.

Calum was still arguing with his parents, all while two of his brothers were asking him something about making a sister. The oldest kids were all staring down at their phones, looking unbothered by the whole thing. A vampire woman I knew to be the next Beta of their pack was helping Thyra go through a diaper bag, probably to find a new outfit and diaper for the toddler.

"WHAT THE HELL IS GOING ON?!" I screamed, recovering from the shock of their wild entry. "What the hell are you all doing here?!"

***

Phoebe

My head stopped ringing the moment the Uber driver pulled in front of the packhouse to get me. Even after escaping back down to the lobby, I could hear Aly and Conner somewhere on the first floor, yelling at one another for having chicken legs or some shit. I don't know what they were fighting about this time, but I wanted no part in it. I chose to wait in the hot Florida sun for my ride.

Now, the AC was blowing over my face, and the driver's radio was playing soft jazz music as I closed my eyes to get some rest before being dropped at the resort that Taegan was staying at.

"New to Miami?" the driver asked.

"Nope," I answered, not bothering to open my eyes.

"You look like you're new," he mused.

"Hmm," I mumbled, not caring to carry on with a conversation.

"I can always tell when someone is a tourist or a local. You are a tourist, lady. I can see it. I know these things."

Man, this guy was talkative. Not what I needed right now after the morning I had. I was just not going to open my eyes and let him think I was asleep. Don't open your eyes, Phoebe. Just don't talk and don't open your eyes.

I wasn't planning to, but then I smelled his intentions. The devious, evil flavor of his thoughts began perforating the air. His comments and his aura were sending me red flags. I sniffed the air a few times and then caught the indistinguishable scent of blood.

"Just great," I muttered to myself, letting my eyes fall open to really take the driver in. Fuck. I don't know how this pack handles these kinds of things, but I was not just going to let this guy off. I don't think he meant to let me off, either. I could tell we were driving away from the city, not towards it.

I sat in the backseat, just staring at him, wondering how far I should let this go before dealing with him.

It didn't take him very long to find a dirt road far off the highway to pull onto. I didn't say a word, just watching him in annoyance with my elbow resting on his window. It was a nice car. I think I'll take it with me after we're done out here. Calling another Uber didn't sound appealing any longer.

When he pulled into a marshy swamp, he opened his center console and pulled out a handgun. I rolled my eyes, knowing it wouldn't hurt me. Not unless he had silver bullets in the thing, and I knew he didn't. Judging by the weight, I doubted he had any bullets in it at all.

"If you fight, this will only hurt worse," he looked back at me, waving the heavy metal in his hand like it would scare me.

"Whatever you say, buddy." I rolled my neck, then cracked my fingers, ready to be done with this so I could get to the resort to meet the vampire who was going to help me get in touch with the coven leader here. He would beat me there now, and I hate being late.

I was pretty fucking irritable after that long ass plane ride and trip to the packhouse too. This driver picked the wrong customer to fuck with, but I'm glad he picked me up and not some defenseless human woman.

He gave me an odd look, almost hesitating. He then started to climb back to the backseat, and I just sat patiently, waiting for him to figure his shit out. I knew he'd done this before. I smelled it in the air. I was going to have to remember this location to tell the Alpha here later, because I'm sure there will be other bodies out in that marsh.

He kept his gun trained on me the entire time, and as he tried to crawl over me, he used the muzzle to open my shirt.

"Are you ready?" I asked in a light-hearted voice. His free hand was inches from touching me. His knees pressed into my thighs, his weight trying to keep me in place. I could taste his soured stench of depraved excitement.

"Oh, I'm ready," he snickered.

"Good," I hissed, smiling widely, then enjoying the look of terror on his face as I exposed my fangs. "I'm glad to hear you're ready to die."

His screams lasted about a minute before the gargled sound of him choking on his own blood drowned them out. He tasted disgusting, but, hey, a girl has to eat. Once he was dead and I'd had my fill, I climbed up to the front seat, then climbed out to open the back door to gather what was left of his body. I bet the bastard regretted putting on the child's locks in those first few seconds when he attempted to run away. No escape for him now. Not from death. I tossed him to the edge of the water, smiling when I saw a couple of long, dark green scaly heads floating on the water's surface.

The backseat had a lot of blood on it, and the floorboard, but the front was clean. I just had to change into new clothes from my backpack before I took off towards the highway again, using my phone to get directions to the resort.

I was going to be late, so I called the man I was supposed to meet, Vincent, and asked him to just meet me out front. I really didn't want to deal with figuring out where to park the bloody car, anyway. Not like I could just check it with the valet. That would be a needlessly awkward conversation.

As I pulled to the front of the resort, I looked through the lobby doors for any sign of the vampire friend of Luna Carli's. My eyes stumbled upon two little girls standing with the men I knew to be the resort owners who were talking to another exotic-looking man in the lobby. One of those girls was Taegan's mate. I've known that for years. He attempted to get me to come down several times to meet her, but I always had school or work, and I just hate Miami's heat and the excessive amount of predators.

I must have been staring hard, because both of the girls turned to look at me, and that's when my eyes connected with a pair of gray irises, and my heart began thudding wildly in my chest.

29

Busy Body Moms

Carli

Once the chaos in my home mellowed out, the adults all gathered in my living room and dining room, getting settled for whatever the hell this was. I still didn't know why they were all here, but the mayhem had died down at least. Mostly.

The vampire Beta left soon after I yelled to stop the onslaught of turmoil, excusing herself to visit Lady Delilah. Vincent was supposed to meet her in the city somewhere and Simone was on her way here with Reese and Karina. They were all out fishing together when I called to let her know her brother and our entire families decided to drop by unannounced for a visit.

The younger kids were taken to my parent's house. All but the baby, who I quickly stole from Courtney as compensation for them barging into my house and causing complete and utter chaos. Dad was happy to take the older kids. He had Calvin and Casper hanging off his flexed arms on his way to the stairs, showing off like he always does. Casper is almost as big as he is. He's going to break his back. Not that he cares.

He promised them and Lauren and Leah he would take them to the beach, and Elena was going to put the younger twins of Bailey's down for a nap. Alpha Max looked nervous about seeing all his youngest granddaughters being taken away, but my parents reassured him at least a dozen times they would be fine. Dad and Elena like having younger kids to dote on. They still manage the kids' classes at the warrior center and are pros.

Aly and Conner didn't want to go to the beach, complaining about the sticky humidity, and decided to relax in the game room instead. Or so they said. "You just want to flirt with the she-wolves," Aly teased her cousin as they were walking out the door.

"You were the one checking out those boys outside, you tramp."

"Nuh uh. They were checking me out. You're just butt hurt because girls don't look at you and your chicken legs."

"You are the one with chicken legs," Conner growled.

"No, you are," Aly smirked.

"I bet I can get more girls to give me their numbers with my chicken legs than you can get boys," Conner challenged.

"You're on," Aly giggled, both of them unaware their family heard the whole thing.

Alpha Max growled, attempting to follow after them, but Thyra pulled him back into the room.

"Let them be. You know as well as I do that Conner won't let boys flirt with his cousin."

"Woman, did you not hear what they just fucking said?!"

"Boy's got no game," Casey snickered. "Aly knows that. She's just teasing him. Their battle of the chicken legs will turn into Conner safeguarding Aly's sassy ass."

"Real encouraging, dad," Calum grumbled. "He might have more game if you two weren't so embarrassing all the time."

"Is this about the tit juice again? Jeez. I'd be more worried about your brother telling your mate that you tried to put a sister in another she-wolf if I were you."

Calum's face dropped into a look of horror at Casey's words, then a groan left him. "I didn't try to put a sister in anyone! I kissed a chick one time and you guys just had to walk in. Casper wouldn't even think that shit if you hadn't yelled at me to keep it in my pants. My pants were fucking on!"

"Boy, I've told you all since you could fucking piss standing up not to fuck around with she-wolves in your own fucking pack. No mate wants to deal with that drama," Alpha Max huffed. "It's downright disrespectful."

"It was one kiss!"

"The girl was straddling you, Calum," Casey smirked. "If me and your brothers didn't walk in when we did, they'd have a sister right now."

"I don't think that's how that works," Bailey said softly, staring down at her phone as she repeatedly tried to call someone.

"Your family is crazy," I whispered to Carter. "But you're super cute. You're never going to do anything wrong, are you? Never, ever."

Carter grinned up at me, his single bottom tooth jutting out, making my heart throb. Just think, in several months, I could have one of these of my own again. Well, mine for the most part. I can be the fun Ki-ki. Rosie could be making me my baby right this minute.

I sighed dreamily out loud, hopeful for the possibility.

"Excuse me. Luna Carli." Thyra came to sit down beside me on the couch, avoiding the escalating argument between her mate and the other men.

"Just Carli," I smiled at her. "We're in-laws now." I wanted to skip and jump with excitement. I've done my fair share of that already, but with Thyra here, I'm ready to do it again.

"Carli," she smiled sweetly. "I, uh, was hoping that I could see Rian now. I know he and Rosie are probably, um, busy, like you said, but I just," she pressed her lips together, hesitating. "I get this strange feeling whenever I think about him, and I haven't been able to get in touch with him either. Could you tell me how to find him?"

"Oh, sure. Rosie said they were at the resort." I called Hadley Meyers and had their room paid for on Parker's card, as a small revenge, until the end of next week. It's been three days. I guess it's been long enough to start harassing them again.

"The resort located on Miami Beach?" Thyra asked.

"That's the one," I smiled. "They should be there now if you want me to get a few cars ready to take us over there."

She looked anxious again. "That's kind of you, Carli, but we've been calling the resort too. No one in their rooms was answering, and Max had the front desk send someone up to check on them, and no one came to the door either. The staff said they hadn't seen anyone coming or going in days, and no room service had been ordered to the room. Since Calum was staying here, we were hoping that maybe Rian and Taegan would be here as well."

"No." I shook my head, feeling a bit anxious now. "They haven't been here in days. Is Taegan not answering either?" I looked at Bailey, who was actively listening to us and still holding her phone in her hand.

"Neither of our sons have been reachable," Thyra told me. She and Bailey exchanged another glance, and then she added, "I think Taegan mentioned something to Phoebe, but she wasn't forthcoming with information shared between herself and Taegan. They are very loyal to each other."

As they should be. She's about to be his Beta. I didn't say that to the two women that didn't grow up in our werewolf world. They were just concerned mothers right now.

I wanted to tell both these busybody mamas that their sons were probably fine and not to baby them, but now I was getting worried. Now that I thought about it, Rosie hadn't been texting me back. I figured, or rather hoped, she was just too busy getting it on to look at her phone, but it's been three days. She should have checked her phone at least once during that time.

I moved Carter to my knee, bouncing him as I picked up my phone to search for my daughter's message thread. Not one of my messages sent in the last few days even said it was read.

I pressed the call button, holding the phone to my ear, but all I got was a busy signal. Did her phone die? She should be able to borrow a charger from Rian or even the hotel.

I then called Hadley, pacing the room while freaking out, thinking wild things that just couldn't be true. She wouldn't get kidnapped or hurt. I would have felt that. She just has to be getting it on so much that she hasn't thought about checking her phone. Everyone is like that at first. It's natural when mating for the first time.

"Hello?" Hadley answered on the third ring.

"Hey, it's me. I have a favor to ask you."

"Sure. What's up? Want me to send strawberries and sparkling cider to the lovebirds? I'd send champagne, but the staff is fully aware of how old Rosie is. Your husband made sure of that when he started screaming at our bell boy at the last Christmas fundraiser that she was seventeen and off limits," Hadley giggled.

"No. Not room service. I was actually hoping you or the guys could go up and see if they're there? Taegan too?"

Hadley was silent for a few seconds, then asked, "Taegan is not at the packhouse?"

"No. No one has seen or heard from Taegan or the other two in days, and I guess Rian's stepdad called the front desk and they couldn't get anyone to answer the door."

Hadley was silent again for a few seconds, then she let out a deep sigh. "I'll go up and check, but I should probably tell you, Mitch tried to throw Taegan out of the hotel a few days ago. I thought he was staying there with you."

Taegan was usually always with the Meyers family when he came to Miami. He's had a connection with the younger two of the Meyers triplets since he met them. He's practically part of their family. "Why? What happened?"

"Well, Mitch noticed something, and he didn't like it. He called Mark, and then I had to calm them down, but I suggested to Taegan to give them a few days to process. It's nothing bad. Just, you know, family stuff," Hadley laughed nervously. "I'll go check right away, though, and let you know what I find."

After we hung up, I held my phone in my hand and thought about what Hadley had just said. I wonder what Mitch noticed of Taegan to get them all upset? Should I bring this up with Bailey?

No. Like Hadley said, it's their family business. Taegan is an adult now. If he wants his mom to know something, he will tell her. Plus, I don't have any details to tell her. Telling her Taegan argued with the Meyers brothers would be needless gossip coming from me.

"She said she would go up and check. She'll let me know what she finds." I smiled at the women.

They're both looking at me expectantly, and Bailey had her brows pulled down, thinking hard about something. I wondered if she heard what Hadley said. If she did, she could ask her son about it later herself. That's a relief for me.

I got a text a few minutes later.

> **Hadley|:** *Both rooms are empty, and the maids said the rooms have been untouched for days. I'm sorry.*

I grimaced, then showed Thyra and Bailey the text.

"Where could they be?" Bailey presses her hand to her face, looking lost.

That was it. I went to my family app and searched for Rosie's GPS. She had her current location turned off, but the last pinged address was somewhere very far from the resort. Too far. I squinted at the screen, then realized she was at the nature preserve. The place was unmanaged by any supernatural because it was too wild with gators and other dangerous wildlife, and covered in marshes and swamps. No one but witches use the location, and they use it only for unsavory means. I know. I've been there a few times in the past to ruin their demonic rituals.

I showed my phone to Thyra. "This is the last place Rosie was."

She studied the map, and then gasped. "Loreana. Why didn't I think of that before? Of course."

"Rian's pegasus?" Bailey asked.

Thyra nodded. "He called me so late at night that I was a bit disoriented and tired, but he sounded eager to show Rosie the horses. I actually told him to go to this nature preserve so he would be out of Queen Aisling's jurisdiction here."

"Do you think Taegan could be with him?" Bailey asked.

"I don't know. If he was feeling dejected, then it's a strong possibility."

"Who's dejected?" Alpha Max came to lay his arm around Bailey's shoulders. "You still can't get to him?"

She shook her head softly at her father-in-law, then tucked her head against his chest as he held her carefully, comforting her in a very fatherly manner.

It always amazed me how tender he could be with her and all his granddaughters, but how tough he was with everyone else. Then there was the way he treats Thyra. He's just a plain freak when it comes to his mate. They have their sweet moments, but he treats Thyra more like an equal who he can go toe to toe with and enjoy the battle, whether he wins or loses. He treats Bailey like his own daughter, which I love because I know she has never gotten that anywhere else.

"That brat is fine," he said in his gruff voice. "He's probably just too busy stirring shit up somewhere to answer his phone."

30

DARK STRING

Rosie

"Damn, that was a massive shit," I heard Taegan mutter somewhere down the hall. "Hey! Rian! Do they not have plungers in the fairy world?"

"Are you kidding me?" Rian groaned, freezing while mixing the soup over the old-fashioned stove.

I pressed my lips together to keep from laughing. Getting up from the table where I was told to sit while Rian rifled through his mother's old kitchen to find the things he needed to cook the food he brought, I took the wooden spoon from him he was using to stir so I could take over.

"I'll watch this if you want to go deal with him," I smirked.

He smiled gratefully, resting his hand on mine for a second, just long enough to make the sparks do things to me, and then he sighed and nodded, trudging off down the hall. I heard Taegan yelp, then both men started cursing at one another. They're more like brothers than uncle and nephew. Are they always like this, or is it the stress of why we are here? It amazes me how I once thought Taegan was desirable in any way after hearing him ask for a plunger like that. I could never imagine Rian being that crude.

I continued to stir the pot, listening to their bickering to distract me. I felt restless. The necklace Rian gave me was still throbbing around my neck every half hour or so. It was doing it again, making me feel weirder and weirder each time. It was hard to explain. I felt exposed. Those were things I was not used to feeling. I didn't want to complain to Rian, but wearing this thing was starting to bother me.

While stirring the boiling soup, I absentmindedly lifted the pendant out of my shirt, watching it glow as it thrummed in my hand. It really was beautiful. Delicate and very

feminine. Two things never used to describe me. I wonder why he picked this par-
ticular design. It matched the tattoo on my back, but that tattoo was inspired by his
giant-shit-laying nephew. I really didn't have a thing for butterflies before.

Maybe he just thought it was pretty and thought of me. That thought made me smile,
and I ran my finger over the jewel center. It really was gorgeous. I just wish the magic in it
didn't make me feel so weird.

"Goodness, that idiot is a disaster," Rian said, coming back into the kitchen. "I've never
had to use magic to fix a clogged toilet before. He's got to do it himself from this point.
I'm not his mom, and I'm not dealing with his shit."

I smiled, amused by his agitation. His face lifted into an answering smile while looking
at me, but only for a second. His eyes landed on the necklace in my hand, and his brows
pulled down.

He strode over to me, taking the butterfly pendant in his hand and watching his magic
glow and pulse in the jewel.

"How long has it been doing this?" he asked.

I shrugged slowly, feeling a bit unnerved by the look on his face. "It's been doing it on
and off for a while now. At least since we were at the pegasus field."

"Why didn't you tell me?" His voice sounded more than concerned. He sounded
upset. It took me back a little. My chest tingled, and not from the necklace, but from the
tightening of uncertainty that flooded me from the expression on Rian's face.

"I thought it was just reacting to the magic here," I whispered. "Why? What's wrong?"

Rian didn't answer or even acknowledge that he heard my question. His eyes were
glowing and swirling, his entire body encased in a glimmering radiance. His eyes focused
on the necklace, staring into the jewel as it reacted to him. He grit his teeth. Then the
pendant glowed brighter, the magic inside of it trailing up the chain and sinking into my
body.

I gasped, the strange feeling from before intensifying just as a loud snarl echoed around
us in the kitchen and the feeling disappeared. The snarl wasn't from me, and it wasn't
from Rian. Where did it come from?

The magic died down, the glow on Rian's body fading. He looked livid, his nostrils
flared as he took deep breaths. The necklace was no longer pulsing like before, but the
magic in it felt stronger than ever. The invasive feeling was gone, replaced with a
comforting warmth like the first time I put it on. Sparks were dancing over all my skin,
the bond flaring with the influence of Rian's magic absorbing into me.

"Wh-what was that?" I gasped, taking a step back to calm my racing heart after he dropped the necklace back in place.

Rian's eyes, swirling with fury, slowly dragged up to connect with mine. The anger inside of him made my heart race more. Was he mad at me? Did I do something wrong? I didn't mean to tamper with the magic in the necklace, if that's what he's so mad at. Him not telling me anything, just staring at me with that cold anger, was causing me to want to shrink in on myself.

Fuck, I hated feeling like this. I hated feeling lost and this constant uncertainty. I didn't like the anxiety that came with it. I wanted him to just answer me, but couldn't find it in myself to demand him to answer me like I would anyone else.

"What the hell was that?!" Taegan came rushing in, looking around at the aftereffects of the magic Rian had poured out, then looking with wide eyes between me and Rian.

I shook my head, not knowing what had happened either. My eyes were itching. My throat clogged with some heavy emotion I did not quite understand.

Rian stared at Taegan, some communication passing between them. Taegan's brows knit, but he didn't look surprised. He looks pissed, too.

What the hell just happened!? I wanted to scream. I wanted to demand they tell me what it was they were talking about. I didn't know how to get past the knot in my throat to speak.

Taegan ran a hand down his face, looking far older than he was suddenly. Then he walked towards me as Rian hurried out of the kitchen. I heard the front door open and close a few seconds later.

The soup on the stove was still boiling. My heart was still racing. My mind and my emotions were a jumbled mess, but he was just leaving, without even telling me what had just happened?

Taegan grabbed both sides of my face, forcing me to look at him when my eyes were still trained on where I last saw Rian rushing out the door.

"Hey. Rosie. Look at me," he demanded, then waited until I stopped trying to tear my face away from his hand to stare out the door. "I need to do something. It's going to freak you the fuck out, but I need you to do something for me."

"Wh-what?" I stared back at him, watching as his eyes glowed that cold, icy blue. His hands tingled with magic on my face.

"Remember to breathe," he said, then his brilliant blue glow overwhelmed me, blinding me as a scream ripped out of my clogged throat.

***

Taegan

"You shouldn't be doing this," Conri hissed, though he wasn't doing anything to stop me.

"You heard Rian. If she is tied to someone else, we can see who and how." I already suspect who, but I'm not allowed to say. Not to Rosie or Rian. I can't reveal shit, and it's driving me nuts.

"Or he can just mark her and let her mark him. Then whatever bullshit he heard from whoever he heard it from will be invalid."

Maybe, but this is my friend and my family we're talking about. I don't want to take that chance. While Rian was gone, grabbing the person he needs to help him find who he saw spying on Rosie, the least I could do was check her bonds to put his mind to rest that she could not be tied or mated to someone else.

"Am I her only mate?" was the first thing he asked me. It took me by surprise until he explained, *"That thing, whatever was watching her and sending the protection spell to go into hyper-drive, was powerful and claiming that she was his."*

Something had been watching Rosie, I guess, since we first arrived in the fae realm. The being, whatever it was, pushed back against Rian's magic. He made the entire house shake with the power he expelled to push whatever was watching her away.

I only saw a glimpse of Rosie's future when I was in the goddess' realm. I wasn't supposed to, but I took a peek, and saw something horrible happen to Rosie in the future before she was mated to Rian. It was in the period after she turned eighteen, and I had wanted to confirm she wouldn't be my mate. It was just a glimpse, just a few sentences came to life before my eyes, but they left a lasting impression.

I was never allowed to tell Rian or Rosie they were mates, but I thought bringing them together the moment she turned eighteen would help her avoid what I saw. If she was tied to that thing, mated to it, too, I wouldn't know what to do. I thought it had just taken her or kidnapped her or some shit. I don't think Reika would bring Rian and Rosie together only to have Rosie belong to someone else. Having two mates happens, but I can't believe that it would happen to Rosie and Rian.

It definitely can't be possible between the monster I saw and the girl I grew up with.

"You're meddling with futures, brat. Trust their story and quit trying to rewrite it as you see fit," Conri told me when Rosie passed out in my arms. I laid her on the ground, groaning when I saw she hadn't done as I said and remembered to breathe. I had to coax her to take a breath by blowing in her face. Then, I closed my eyes with my hands pressed to her temples, and continued to use Conri to see Rosie's subconscious, searching through the chaos that was paused inside her head to dig in deep, traveling to her very soul.

"I'm just taking a look. I just need to confirm it for myself."

"If you needed to know these things, Reika would tell you," Conri argued.

"She gave me these abilities for a reason."

"Don't you think if you were supposed to use those abilities here, we wouldn't be cut off from her power now? I can't refuel our magic once you deplete it in this world. Your toilet clogging bullshit and ass zapping your uncle aren't causes to waste the magic you have stored. You have no way to get more magic once this is all gone, and you are expelling too much trying to get to her soul ties."

"Rian can give me fucking magic when I run out. Stop being a baby," I said, digging in deep until I could finally see her inner light encompassing the workings of what harbors her soul.

Everything essential to who Rosie is was encompassed in this intricate orbital brilliance. Her mother and father's influence are at the center, then her closest friends and loved ones. Her family. I'm even engraved here in some small way.

Then there was a brilliant green string of light, extending out towards a glittering mass some ways in the distance. I recognized it instantly to be Rian's connection to her. It was glowing strongly, but there was a painful pulse beating along the string, pulling it tight, then releasing it over and over again. It was like it was being plucked and played, never fully at rest or letting the two ends meet.

The two of them really needed to work on growing closer to one another. They may have been all kissy face in the air, but it's been awkward between them ever since.

"Because you're here," Conri griped. *"I know you're hurt because of what happened with our mate, but that doesn't mean you should bud in on someone else's story. You should have just whined to your mama like you always do, you big titty baby."*

"Shut up," I snapped, moving around Rosie's soul to check every inch of it. *"There's nothing wrong with loving your mom."*

"In your case there is," he growled.

"Your mom was probably a fucking dinosaur. You wouldn't understand."

Conri growled, about to throw another insult my way, but then I saw it. We saw it, making both of us stop bickering, make out what it was. There was a string so dark that I missed it in the light. It was corrupt, greedy, and latched onto Rosie like a leech. Its presence was so overwhelmed by all the good in her life that it could barely be seen, but it was there.

I didn't know if that meant Rosie had two mates, but something definitely latched itself onto her, and there were no signs of it letting her go.

31

DEVILRY

Rian

The jewel in the necklace I gave Rosie glowed brightly as an outside source of magic suppressed its power. Whatever it was, it was powerful enough to override my magic in the stone completely.

It took my full force to push back, clinging to the spell that was cloaking my influence on the stone and peel it away, then push back against the one overcoming it.

When I felt him, my rage flared. Seeing his wicked possessiveness filled me with ire. It wasn't just attached to the stone, suppressing my magic for simple sinister reasons, like to siphon the power I put in there. It was suppressing it to watch Rosie, its demon eyes absorbed in everything about her, obsessing over her like a hunter obsesses over its prey.

No. It was obsessing over her like I've seen countless times growing up in a wolf pack. It's the same look Calum had when he saw Rosie's friend at the party at the cove.

My rage was suddenly fueled by my possessiveness, my magic flaring to new heights. She is my mate. My future. My obsession. Seeing someone else try to overcome me to get to her was not something I would ever tolerate, and he would not be doing it anymore.

"SHE'S MINE! MINE!" the monstrous presence said, snarling viciously while I tried to expel his watchful gaze. "WHO ARE YOU TO TAKE WHAT IS MINE! SHE WAS PROMISED TO ME! MINE! MINE!"

His voice faded into silence when my magic finally overpowered him. I encase all of Rosie with a vein of my power, warding her from anyone being able to spy on her. No one should be able to expel my magic. I should have encased it properly in the first place. When I put the spell on the stone, I didn't know she was my mate. I didn't expect her to ever enter the fairy realm, where fae powers have a stronger influence on those that are not meant to be here. The magic I put there would have been fine if I had never brought her to Alfheimr. Pulling her across that portal made her susceptible to that thing once again.

There was another issue now. When our magic was tangled, fighting for dominance over one another, I felt her in his devilry. I felt a connection between them I could not explain in any other rational way.

Taegan came rushing into the kitchen, demanding to know what was going on.

"Am I her only mate?" was my first question to him. He knew I was her mate. He would know if she had another. He had to know. Taegan always knows. But as I explained what had happened, what I had seen to him, he looked just as confused and upset as me.

"I'll find out," he had told me. "I'll search for her bonds myself."

***

I guess there are some things even Taegan doesn't know, but that didn't help to suppress my anger back in that kitchen, and it's not helping now. I'm still fuming about so many things. I'm angry at myself more than anything else.

That thing I felt, the thing that was watching her, it was powerful. It had magic that was near on par with mine. I gave her the necklace, hoping I could prove my worth to her by keeping her safe. It didn't keep her safe at all. I had failed her. Already. She was under the perverse observation of that monstrous being the moment we set foot in my world.

This is my world. My realm. I should be able to protect her more than any other here, but all I've done is put her in more danger.

Taegan told me not to bring her. Maybe he was right.

No. Leaving her behind didn't feel right either. It still doesn't feel right to even think about doing so. I feel like everything is such a jumbled mess.

We came here to save her friend. Why did it now feel like I need to save her?

I need to know what this thing is that attached itself to Rosie. It wasn't some low-level fae being that I wouldn't have to worry about now that I got rid of it once. It was just as angry and possessive as me. It really believed that Rosie was his.

The magic, though not fairy or siren, felt similar to another magic I know. There is one person I know who will be able to feel the lingering magic around Rosie and be able to identify it, and I was on my way to find her now.

I haven't talked to this girl since I left this world. Not even during the few times I came back with my mom to get things mom was missing from our realm. I never ran into my fae family and friends outside of my uncle the king. Time works differently between these worlds, and there is no telling even how old she might be now.

Many were staring as I pushed through the evening rush of people, all on their way home from whatever profession they do during the day. I didn't bring my cloak to veil my magic. With the anger radiating inside me, the green glow of my eyes and aura, my royal pedigree would be undeniable.

It was too late to go back to get the garment to hide my identity. There really wasn't a point, and with my position being identifiable, people were moving aside quickly upon my approach. No one will know which royal I am, anyway. There are so many in my uncle's court, among all my cousins, aunts and uncles. My adult appearance will not be known to normal citizens.

Plus, just the thought of going back to face Rosie after I failed her made my heart sink. I couldn't even tell her what had happened. "I failed you," isn't something any man wants to ever mutter to their partner. That's what happened. I failed her. I should have noticed sooner that she was being watched. She was being tracked.

Once again, Taegan was the one who came swooping in to fix things while I was on my way to the courts to find the one who can assist me since I could not identify the magic myself.

My uncle's castle grounds are massive, and I could spot the spiraling towers covered in moss and ivy long before I get to the main road. With each block, more of the castle was revealed. It is a glorious place to live, nestled inside a high stone wall that keeps the common folk from the luxury resting inside.

Arrogance is a common trait in all fae beings who call the fairy court home. Seeing my old home after living among the werewolves, I can see the arrogance in its very build. The royals are raised in traditions and pedigree, but my uncle had tried to change things among the royal family and those who served them just in my time there. I wonder how much things have changed. I wonder if I can even get her to help me without paying a hefty price.

Surely she wouldn't ask me too much. Nothing I can not freely give, anyway. She was as arrogant as any other member of the court, but she and I shared many good times. I had hoped we had parted as friends. I can only hope that she felt the same.

"Looking good there, stranger," a woman's voice purred when I got to the outskirts of the palace, about to cross the bridge over the river that leads to the main walkway to the front gates.

I had planned to ignore the flippant statement, but then she added, "Rian Nox Syreni Awender, Prince of the Septentrion." I froze, not having heard that full title associated with my princely name in a long time. "Ah, but I hear that there is a new name to be added to the list. Kissinger, is it? I wonder where one would place your adopted name among all your others?"

Turning to face the woman cloaked in lush green velvet, I tried to make out her face, but it was hidden by the hood. Her long, slender legs, with vine-like shimmering markings similar to tattoos running up and down them, are all that was visible on her body. She was sitting atop the low stone wall of the bridge, her legs stretched out before her, crossed in a sensuous way. She was not alone. Beside her is another woman, also wearing a green velvet cloak. Her hood was up, but she kept her face visible, her red eyes trained on me.

"Hello, Rian," she smirked. "I was just asking my new friend here to help me find you."

The other woman removed her hood with a sultry laugh. My eyes went wide, looking between them in complete shock and amazement. The woman I came to find was with another woman I didn't expect to see.

32

— • —

PITY

Rosie

I came too while lying on the kitchen floor, my head in Taegan's lap. My mind and my body felt sluggish, bogged down like it had been under a tremendous strain.

"What happened?" I muttered, trying to sit up, but dropping back down with a groan, pressing my hands to my head with an extreme case of vertigo.

"Easy, Rosie. You didn't breathe like I told you to," Taegan said in an accusing tone. He was leaning against the wall, legs sprawled out with me between them, looking lazy and comfortable, even though my head just slammed down against his upper thigh like an iron weight.

I growled softly, then pressed my fingers more firmly into my temples when even growling caused my head to pound.

Taegan chuckled. "I know, I know. You handsome, good-looking mother lover should have told me what you were doing if you wanted me to breathe. You took my breath away. That is exactly what you're thinking right now. Right?" He mocked my voice, sounding nothing like me.

"Wrong," I seethed, pushing against his chest with a finger. "You annoying and vain bastard should keep your fucking glittering hands to yourself."

"How rude," he scoffed. "I don't have glittery hands."

I rolled my eyes. "Impertinent jerk."

"Hey," he laughed. "I'm not impertinent. I'm self-aware. I know how breathtaking I am. You don't have to deny it. It's a fact. Your mate can't get jealous of you agreeing with facts."

"It's a fact that you're pissing me off right now," I snapped.

I tried again to lift my head from his lap, but another dizzy spell fell over me. I gave up after one more try, realizing the effort wasn't worth the nauseating dizzy effect it caused. Taegan had a smug look on his face, just staring down and watching me with his blue eyes dancing with amusement.

"You're an ass."

"What?" he laughed. "I didn't say anything."

"You could help me up."

"Eh. I could, but I'm feeling a bit disoriented myself" His smile turned more solemn, less arrogant than before when he admits this.

"Why?" I asked, worrying more about whatever the hell he just did to me. What did he do to me? He just grabbed my face, told me to breathe, then I went under before I could tell him to fuck off. "What happened?"

His smile faltered, his eyes softening with concern. All his body language was telling me that something was wrong.

"What?" I asked again, a bit more forceful. "What did you do?"

His apologetic grin made me more anxious. "I don't know if I can tell you."

"Why?" I demanded. He's pissing me off again. "Whatever you did, you did it to me. Just tell me."

He hesitated, then ran a hand down his face, looking a bit lost. "Something happened before I came into this room, when you were here with Rian. It-it scared the shit out of him. He saw and felt something that was, uh, off, so I told him I would investigate to see if what he felt could be real."

The worry in his voice made it where I almost don't want to ask, but I had to. "What did he feel?" What happened when Rian started using all his crazy magic? What was that snarling I heard?

And....

Why did he just leave without giving me any answers?

Taegan sighed deeply, looking lost for a moment. His eyes were glowing, his inner beast communicating with him.

I lifted my hand, resting it on his face, forcing him to focus back on me. I didn't want him to weigh this with his Lycan. It's not his Lycan's decision to tell me what happened to my body. I'm sick of not being told anything.

"Tell me, Taegan. Someone needs to tell me what is going on." If Rian left without doing so, fine. I bottled that up to cope with it later. But Taegan has been a close friend to me my entire life. I expect him to be honest and tell me the truth. "I don't deserve to be left in the dark."

He rested his hand over mine, then took a deep breath. "No. You don't." His icy blue eyes were warring, flashing between him and his beast. I narrowed mine, daring his beast to keep this from me. "I'm just not sure what to tell you, Rose. What I saw just brought along a new round of questions." His eyes ignited, glowing against my face, then he asked something that threw me off guard. "Do you... do you maybe have another mate?"

Silence spread between us. "What?" I eventually found the voice to ask.

He opened his mouth to say something else, but then we both heard the front door opening. Multiple voices came flooding in. Seconds later, Rian strode into the kitchen.

He stopped, his eyes narrowing, and his expression dark, his stare zeroing in on my hand resting on Teagan's face. Taegan's hand was still resting on mine. I was still lying with my head on Taegan's lap, and Taegan's body folded over mine. It probably looked intimate from anyone else's view, but that's not how it felt. I was simply pleading with my lifelong friend to tell me what was going on while stuck on the ground where he put me.

"You two look quite cozy," Rian commented, crossing his arms over his chest.

I couldn't help but to scoff. Rian left me the second after he used his magic on me. He left me completely clueless. Taegan even said that Rian had told him to find out about something for him. What that something is, I still don't know. Taegan was just about to fill me in before Rian had to walk in to misinterpret us being on the ground. Yeah, I was lying in the man's lap, but only because we were both too disoriented to fucking move.

I was confused, and a bit hurt when Rian left, but now I'm pissed off. I was about to tell him so too, but then two cloaked figures walked up behind him.

One dropped her hood, laughter bubbling out of her soft, angelic face. She has powdery white skin with subtle hues of pink and green framing it along her hairline. Her eyes were enormous, their green irises glowing with her magic. Then her lips, supple and pink, matching her pink lashes and brows, were framing the most radiant smile. I'm straight as an arrow, but her face even had me almost simpering from its beauty.

She's gorgeous. When she moved the rest of her cloak behind her shoulders, I saw it wasn't just her face that's alluring. Her scantily clad body, draped in thin silk cross-crossing along her torso, leaving little to the imagination, accentuated her voluptuous figure.

She rested her delicate chin on Rian's shoulder, staring down at Taegan and me with that sensual grin. When she wrapped her arms around Rian's waist, I almost saw red.

Not almost. I saw red. A snarl ripped out of me, and if it weren't for Taegan, using all his power to push his aura over me, wrapping one of his thick arms around my waist when I hastily sat up, I probably would have lunged at the woman clinging to my mate. My fucking infuriating mate, who had the nerve to look fucking pissed at me and Taegan when he brought some girlfriend back with him.

"These are your friends?" The woman asked, acting oblivious to my brief outburst.

No, bitch. I'm more than that. I'm his fucking mate and I'm about to claw your fucking eyes out. I wanted to scream. Taegan's aura barely contained mine.

Rian said nothing as he continued to stare at us, looking more upset now that Taegan's arm was on my midsection. Hypocrite.

Bull shit. This is all bull shit.

"Rian. Dude," Taegan said in a low warning tone. "What are you doing?"

"What am I doing? What are you doing? I thought we fucking talked about this?" Rian spat back.

"Oh, my. Such colorful words. I usually love a man with a crude mouth, but never expected it from you." The woman poked Rian's nose with her finger.

Another growl left me at her words. If she wanted crude, I'd give her crude.

"Not your friends, then?" The beautiful woman's smile faltered at my hostility, and she turned her chin to stare up at Rian without removing it from his shoulder. I was having thoughts of removing her chin for her. I'll remove her whole fucking jaw from her face soon if she doesn't get it away from my mate. Her jaw. Her hands. Her entire fucking body pressed up against his back. I was thinking of nothing but tearing her to pieces, bit by bit.

He had better tell her to back the hell up. I'm his mate. He needed to tell her that before someone gets hurt.

"No, Parisa. These are not my friends."

My anger dropped, and my heart felt like it was breaking. The anger on Rian's face simmered into regret quickly, but the words already hurt me. They cut me deep.

"Oh, Rian. Come on, man," Taegan mumbled, shaking his head. He looked at my face, then let me go, feeling the tension leave my body as I felt all my fight drain from inside. Taegan rested a hand on my upper back, but I rotated my arm, shaking it off. I still felt dizzy, but I didn't want his support. I didn't want his pity. I didn't want anyone's pity.

Rian was right. I'm not his friend. I was never a friend to him. I gave him no reason to trust me in the past, so why should I be angry at him now? He's my mate, but he's also a fae. He doesn't feel it the way I do. There's no way he does, or his end of the bond would be hurting him as much as mine is tearing at me.

"Hmm." The woman, Parisa I guess, let her perfectly shaped brows drop, then turned back to stare at me. Her eyes shimmered, her magic swirling in them like the dancing sea. The corners of her lips lifted when her green eyes met mine, and I felt like she was pitying me, too.

I couldn't take this.

I forced my body up off the ground, waving Taegan away when he tried to help me as I stagger to my feet. I didn't meet anyone's eyes. I couldn't. I definitely couldn't meet his. If I saw pity there too, it would break me. I felt so lost and weak. This wasn't how a mate should make you feel. Dad and mom never made one another feel weak. I'm an alpha. A fucking Alpha. I'll be damned if I let someone make me feel like this ever again.

There was only one way out of this room, and it was past them. Rian was standing a few feet in front of my only exit with that sensual woman wrapped around him. I kept my head down and held on to the shreds of my pride as I made my way out of this overcrowded room.

"Rosie, I didn't-"

My low growl cut Rian off from finishing whenever it was he was trying to say.

The other cloaked figure just beyond the door let down her hood and reached out to me as I passed, resting her hand on my arm. I recognized her instantly, but never thought I would see her here.

"Take this," Phoebe, Taegan's future beta, told me, unfastening the cloak from her neck and setting it in my arms.

The sympathy on her face did me in. I took the velvet garment and sprinted off and out the door, ignoring Taegan's calls for me to come back. I barely had the cloak on and the hood up over my head when the first tears fell from my burning eyes.

33

MISUNDERSTAND

Taegan

I knew when Rian walked in he would misunderstand. I knew, but I couldn't make my damn body work fast enough to get up off this fucking floor. I pushed all the energy I had recovered into stopping Rosie from tearing into him or the woman he brought with him out of jealousy.

Conri was right. My magic was depleted in my efforts to find out who it was that attached itself to my childhood friend. I looked and looked and looked. I traveled down that blackened string until my magic started to slip and I couldn't go any further.

I was shoved back, snapping like an elastic band being broken when my magic waned, forcing me out. I couldn't even move for the longest time, but having Rosie in my lap helped. Touching her helped, like it once did when we were kids.

I now know why.

Whatever attached itself to her, it's not a leech, feeding on her soul. It's attempting to shroud her soul in its magic, encasing it to make her belong to it. That magic was drip feeding me, helping me to recover.

I wonder how long it's been there. Her entire life? Is that what I felt when we were kids?

I couldn't figure anything out just yet. My entire fucking body felt like I had been running a marathon, or more accurately, running several marathons simultaneously. It just gave out and was numb after the effort I put in.

When Rosie touched my face, the power inside her seeped into me more. Not just the dark magic, but Rian's magic, too. He had tried to ward her from the thing on the other end of that blackened string from invading her space again, blocking any attempts it could make with his royal and superior power.

That power was helping me to recover, along with the black energy leaking inside her. When my hands could move, I held her hand in place, desperate for more. I need to help her. I need to help Rian. I need to save them both from the fate I saw. Rian will not handle losing her. He will permanently come back to this realm and won't set foot in the human world again.

And Rosie....

She's my oldest friend. Aside from family, she was the first connection I made when mom and I came to this life. I've known she wasn't my mate all these years, but I've still kept her close. She really is one of my best friends, and I couldn't live with myself if something happened to her. Not when I knew and could have stopped it.

I didn't want to sit back and watch Rian lose his mate to some dark monster, but it looks like he's doing a good enough job pushing her away himself. He could be pissed at me for touching her. Fine. We could work that shit out between us later. What he was doing now, letting Rosie run away into a world she does not know, while letting some fairy bimbo hang on him was a shit move.

"ROSE!" I yelled again, right before I heard the door slam. I tried to push myself up, but my legs were still numb. The small amount of magic I took from Rosie wasn't enough to replenish me. Conri was sluggish, cut off from the goddess in this realm.

For the first time in my life, I felt powerless. I couldn't even get up off the damned floor.

Phoebe shook her head, then came to give me a hand. I didn't know what she was doing here, and I should ask, but I couldn't quit glaring at Rian, who still had the bimbo attached to his waist. His pissy expression was gone. He looked ashamed and sorrowful, probably because of his own actions. Still, he didn't do anything to stop his mate from running out into this foreign fucking world.

"What the fuck are you doing?" I snarled at him. "Go after her!"

He looked so hurt, but I couldn't understand why.

"You walk in here, grumpy as shit, treating her like fucking crap while she's already disoriented and confused. Now you are just letting some skank hang all over you and not chasing after her? What the fuck is wrong with you?"

"You two were-"

"She fainted!" I yelled. "I fainted, damnit. Trying to do what you asked. Forget the other shit and think about how you just acted. How she perceived it all," I growled. "Fucking think, Rian."

"That is a shit move, Rian," Phoebe said. She was looking at me disapprovingly, but I know she will always have my back. She grabbed my hand, letting me take her vitality. She knows I need it. She always knows. "Lady Parisa may be your cousin, but Rosie doesn't know that. She is misunderstanding this situation as much as you are right now."

Rian's eyes went wide, then he looked down at the skank, Parisa his cousin, I guess, and then looked back at me like he truly did not know how the situation looked to an outsider. I didn't even know these two were related and I'm his fucking family, too. How was Rosie to know?

"We have the same eyes! My uncle took Parisa's mother as a consort. She's my cousin." He told me as if I was the one he needed to explain this too.

"A very affectionate cousin," Phoebe added, eyeing the woman's hold on Rian with raised eyebrows.

Parisa laughed lightly, then let go of Rian as we all stared at where she was still gripping his waist.

"Apologies. The jealousy of the human world is not something the fae folk are accustomed to. I was unaware that my affection for a family member I had long missed would be construed as anything but what it was. Familial affection."

I couldn't help but to scoff. Even Conri was snorting. Her logic was distorted, or she was a manipulative bimbo. Either way, her claim didn't apply to Rian at all. Rian had been nothing but jealous since he discovered Rosie to be his fucking mate. I never did anything to lead her on and I constantly made it known that she was not my mate. I've been trying to push them together for years, even though I could never say anything. If fae folk really are unaccustomed to jealousy, Rian missed that family trait.

"It's the mate bond," Conri muttered. "He was never jealous before. Maybe out of place, but not jealous. It's the mate bond. It changes you. He's going to keep acting out until he claims her and she claims him. "

"That doesn't excuse him from being a whiny asshole," I retorted.

"No, but if you had kept yourself out of this and home from the beginning, LIKE I TOLD YOU TO, they would have grown closer naturally by now."

"I'm trying to help them!" I snapped back at my Lycan.

"You're not helping at all. Take yourself out of everything that has occurred since their arrival in this world. When picturing you out of the way, you can just imagine how much closer those two would have become. They might already be mated now." Conri pulled up the image of Rian and Rosie getting heated while we were all up in the air. They might have fucked on the back of the damned horse if I hadn't interrupted them. That seems unfair to Loreana. Conri continued on. "You even clogged the damn toilet, you punk. I've been telling you and telling you, we aren't supposed to be here."

"But I saw-"

"You don't know what you saw. She is an alpha, the same as you, and she doesn't need you to save her. Whatever she may face, she can overcome it with her own power. She doesn't need you to hold her hand through the trials she faces, and neither does Rian."

Staring at Rian now, I couldn't say that I agreed. Yes, things might have been different for them if I weren't here, but-

"You are trying to take control of someone else's problems because you can't take control of your own," Conri cut into my thought, as well as cutting into my chest with the reminder of the falling out I had with Mitch and Mark because of a mistake. One small, trivial mistake.

"I need to follow her," Rian said. "I-I shouldn't have-. I mean-"

"Go get your mate, Rian," Phoebe told him. "We'll be here."

Rian nodded, then quickly rushed out the door, the sound of it closing loudly vibrating off the walls.

"Well then. He's quite a bit crankier than when he was a child," the fairy skank, Parisa, giggled and threw herself onto one of the kitchen chairs. "When I was asked to accompany this vampire to find him, I never expected to uncover so much turmoil in the process."

She leaned over, letting her boobs spill over the thin fabric that barely contained them, smiling seductively at me.

"Can I let you in on a little secret? I thought that you and that young woman were the.... what does your kind call that word? Mates? I thought you two were mates and my dear cousin was just acting out in some way defensively. I didn't think he would be strapped to your kind in such a foreign way. There has been much talk of his possible return to the courts. Being tied to a shifter of the human world was never mentioned to anyone." Her smile flashed brighter, and her eyes glow. "I can't say I would particularly mind being tied down by one of you myself."

From her flirtatious grin aimed in my direction, I could only assume she was talking about me. No thanks. Never. I would have to be beyond desperate to ever find a woman as brazen as her attractive. She's more to Phoebe's tastes, but even Phoebe looked put off by the woman.

I chose to ignore her, turning to Phoebe instead. "What are you doing here?"

She scoffed. "I'm here to drag your stubborn pasty ass back home."

"My ass is not pasty," I countered. I got a nice fucking tan during my two days in Miami.

"I'd like to see you prove that," Parisa purred, still looking at me like I'm a meal.

Besides making a disgusted face, I kept my focus on Phoebe. "How did you know I was here so quickly? We just left this morning."

A snort escaped her. "This morning? Tae, you've been gone for days. When I left, it had been two days since anyone had heard from you."

My brows pulled down in confusion. "We got here this morning. It's been hours. Not days."

"You're in the fae realm, creamy tush," Parisa giggled. "Time works differently here. It's only been a year and a half since I last saw my cousin, but to him it has been thirteen, close to fourteen years."

I groaned, having forgotten how drastic the time difference was. I talked to my mom before I left, but if it's been days, she was probably so worried by now.

"Mom? Is she the one that sent you?" I asked my beta.

"Uh, no," she chuckled. "But by now, I'm sure she is aware of where you are. Everyone most likely is."

"What?! How?"

She smirked. "Oh, we have so much to talk about, Tae. But first, I wanna ask you," she paused, her smirk remaining but her red eyes glowing with hostility. "Did you know about my mate?"

34

LONELY FRIEND

Rosie

I was too embarrassed to look up for anyone to see the tears running down my face, so I walked staring at the ground, just letting my feet take me wherever they chose, as long as it was away from that scene in that tense and awkward kitchen.

Not his friend. He not only said I wasn't his friend, he didn't say we were anything else. Not mates. Not a couple. Nothing. He said nothing. He just let me go without trying to stop me.

I kept walking until, eventually, I stopped hearing voices around me. I lowered my hood and saw I was all alone near a rustic old stone-built factory of some kind. It looked like one you could find right out of a storybook. There was a water wheel and a large pond with a stream beside the humble building.

I loved a movie called Thumbelina when I was a baby, a movie about a small girl born in a flower who falls in love with a fairy prince. After overcoming many obstacles, she turned into a fairy as well and they had a beautiful wedding near a stone building on the bank of a river that looked similar to this.

I used to watch that movie over and over again. It was the only girly movie I really watched at the time. Or anytime, really, unless Sophia drug me along to watch a chick flick with her. When I was a kid, I would just stare at the screen, enraptured in the perfect fairytale, wishing to one day have my own prince to fly away happily ever after with.

I did get my own damn fairy prince for a mate, but a happily ever after seemed implausible at this point. Stupid jerk, bringing a damn fairy hooker back to his mother's house with him. What was he thinking? He had the nerve to get pissy with me over something that was out of my damn control, all while some hussy was hanging off his damn waist.

Fuck that.

You know what? Thumbelina had to overcome all her shit on her own, finding her prince again after she had defeated toads, moles, creepy insects, and battling the freezing winter all on her own. Maybe I should just go off on my own and find Julia myself. Neither of those idiot guys are helping me. Phoebe was here now, for whatever reason, and besides the fairy skank, I was the only one not from Blue Cliff. I'm the odd one out on my own fucking mission to find my friend. If they don't want to tell me shit, then fine. I'll just figure this shit out on my own. Who needs them?

I sat along the fence bordering the pond, staring at the darkening forest across the way. I could see the magic floating in the air, but without Rian with me, the magic seemed eerie and unwelcoming.

Lifting the necklace from my chest, I stared at the stone, running my fingers over its smooth surface again and again. The magic tingled my skin. It was all comforting and warm.

Why couldn't the guy who gave it to me be the same way!?

I ripped it over my head, raising it above me, and just when I was about to throw it into the water out of anger... I stopped. My hand dangled above me, the sparks traveling through my palm from the butterfly pendant pulsing suddenly, right before I let it go.

Heat built behind my eyes. Fuck, I just stopped crying. I didn't want to cry again. I wanted to fucking punch something... or someone. A certain someone.

I wanted to punch him, but... I wanted to bury my head in his chest and weep my eyes out. I wanted to feel the soothing comfort I felt in him while panicking hundreds of feet in the air. I wanted him to tell me again that he had me in his arms, and that everything will be okay.

I'm an alpha. I have to be strong. I need to be strong. But when I am with Rian, it suddenly feels okay to be weak.

Except for right now. Right now, I felt the wrong kind of weak because of him, and I didn't know what to do about it.

"Stupid fairy prince," I muttered, barely holding back my tears.

"Oh, my," a deep, raspy voice startled me, making me drop my hand, almost dropping the necklace in the water. I looked around, searching for the voice. "I didn't expect to find anyone here at this time of day. I usually have the pond all to myself."

There, coming from the middle of the pond, was a head with dark hair floating along the surface, the black tendrils floating around it, looking like tentacles on the water's surface. His body became more visible as he walked toward the shore.

He was not human, but he looked like one. The magic brimming out of him distinguished him as fae, but he was unlike any of the other beings in this world that I had seen. He was huge. Not just in his body tone, but in his height, and even in his presence. His presence felt heavy and domineering. If I was Sophia, or most other she-wolves, I would start to whimper and call for help if a man like this approached me.

I merely lifted my brow, sucking down all the sorrow I just felt, unwilling to cry in the presence of a powerful creature such as this. I pulled my aura to the surface, but then I remembered that we're supposed to be cloaking our werewolf traits. Instead, I put on my usual mask of poise and confidence, not letting my weakness show.

"I was just sitting here, but if that is an issue, I can leave."

"No, no," the man said. His smile was kind, even on his imposing face. "I'm thrilled to have company for once. Especially the company of a beautiful girl, such as yourself."

I smiled tightly at the compliment, still considering leaving. The man seemed imposing at first, but now that I could clearly see his face, he didn't look malicious. He looked kind and was actually quite good looking, if you like long hair and sharp-angled faces. Like if Fabio and Thanos had a kid. The loincloth around his waist, wet and heavy, did little to hide any of his body. Any of it. My mom would be cat-calling and licking her lips if she were here until Dad ended up carrying her off over his shoulder.

If this man's eyes weren't inky black, his face might even be my type. It seems I have a preference now for the complexity of irises that contain swirling galaxies and moving magic. Even if the man wearing those eyes is a total jerk.

"What is such a lovely woman as yourself doing alone here at the edge of the Caligo Forest?" He leaned against a post, staring up at me with those onyx eyes crinkling in the corners.

"Caligo Forest?" I looked back up at the ominous forest in front of us. "Should I not be here?"

The man shrugged. "Most stay away. That's why even this mill is abandoned. It is not unsafe. Not for you."

The energy coming from the other side of the pond was dark. I wondered what could be so bad in there that all fae kinds stay away from it.

"What's your name, lovely?" The man held out a hand towards me. It was a human gesture, one I did not expect to see.

I raised my brow at the hand. "What's yours?"

"Ah, untrusting, are we?" he laughed. The deep baritone caused me to smile. He seemed so friendly and laid back, not at all put off by my demeanor, which most find to be bitchy. He still kept his hand raised, not discouraged. "I go by Kret."

I hesitantly took his hand. "Rosie."

"Rosie," he husked, giving my hand two firm shakes before releasing it. His hand was warm, and I had this strange sensation come over me while we touched. It was a familiarity of some kind. It was probably just the relief of having a normal greeting with someone here.

His serene smile stretched, and I didn't know why, but I caught myself blushing. There was nothing flirtatious really about the action, or imposing. It was a regular handshake, and my heart leapt at the familiar gesture.

In this foreign place, where I felt so out of place and so out of the loop, it was nice to have something normal happen, as simple as a handshake and a friendly greeting to make me feel not so out of place for a moment.

"Would you like to go for a swim with me, Rosie? The water here is quite warm, and there are hot springs at the bottom. It is good for relaxing and decompressing after a long day."

That actually sounded amazing after the shit time I'd had. Warm waters like what you find at the Florida beaches have that soothing effect on me. That's what Rian's scent reminds me of. The soothing sweet warmth of soaking in the water, in places like the cove where there are tropical flowers, fruit trees bearing ripe fruit, salty air and brine surround you.

I would love to take a swim, but Taegan had asked me one thing before we left, and that was to stay out of the water. I may be pissed right now, but I'm not stupid enough to disregard Taegan's pleas.

"I'm not dressed to swim, as you can see." I waved my hands down my body.

"Ah, you are not. I would suggest doing as I did, just swimming in your undergarments, but I have a feeling that might seem brazen of me, considering we just met. Maybe next time."

I snorted. "Yeah. Maybe next time." This wasn't my world. I doubt there will be a next time.

"I guess I have no choice but to keep you company on shore then."

"No choice? Do you make it a habit of keeping the company of strangers when they stumble upon your pond?"

"Only when they seem down and upset. You seemed as if you could use a friend." His smile was gentle. "Who could leave someone who looks so lost alone, even if they are a stranger?"

"You'd be surprised," I huffed.

He sighed. "You're right. I guess there are plenty of inattentive and negligent beings in all the worlds and realms. I just choose not to be one of them. Empathy and kindness are not hard labors." He nudged my leg. "Even between lonely strangers on their way to becoming friends."

Maybe it was because I was just feeling completely alone, or because I was so down and eager for some escape. I felt at ease all of a sudden, like I could breathe again. My heart didn't feel as heavy, and the easy conversation began between us.

35

— · —

SEARCH AND REGRET

Rian

I was running through the busy village's cobblestone streets, trying to find some trace of my mate.

Taegan was right. I am a fucking moron for the way I acted back there. I was so overcome by my incompetence, thinking endlessly about how I failed her, and Taegan was again the one to come in and take control of what I could not. I was so wrapped in my self-pity that when I walked in the kitchen to find Rosie lying on Taegan's lap, their postures intimate and cozy, all I saw was red.

She has years, most of her life's worth of affection for the man. Bailey has many pictures of the two of them hugging one another, or falling asleep cuddled together. Even as teenagers, until our last visit to Miami, Rosie adamantly sought Taegan's attention while scorning me and pushing me away.

In the mists of my inadequacy, I lashed out in anger, but it wasn't her or even Taegan I was mad at. I was mad at myself. I was trying to claw my way out of Taegan's shadow for her, to show her I could be a fitting mate, but it felt like I took a nosedive right back in.

Then the issue of the misunderstanding with my cousin. No, I didn't think about her misconstrued behavior at all. Quite honestly, my magic was flaring with my anger, and Parisa, being of succubus lineage from her mother's side, was feeding on that negativity. I wanted to bring her with me to examine Rosie because of her succubus powers. She detects magic better than anyone, and can enter the mind or body to trace its origins if need be.

She is overly affectionate because of those abilities, and I just wasn't thinking through the fog of my jealousy. Parisa was helping in her way to prevent me from exploding with rage.

I can see the misunderstanding. It's the same one I came to as I walked into the kitchen and saw them. It's just one misunderstanding after another between Rosie and me.

Are we truly fated to be mated? The mate bond is undeniable, and my desire for her, along with this unwavering devotion that was built up inside of me, is unmistakable. I want her. More than anything. This just seems like an impossible feat for me. The mountain to climb seems much too high, and far too steep.

I scurried between buildings, checking every alleyway and place that would offer any remoteness in the village nearby.

I may not know Rosie well, but I am very familiar with the pride of Alphas. I was raised by one and surrounded by them. If she was hurting, Rosie wouldn't want to show that weakness to anyone. She was likely hiding somewhere, cursing me to high heaven without the watchful eyes of people being around.

It took me nearly an hour, but I eventually found her behind an old mill where trolls used to grind tree bark into dust for healing teas. The mill has been long shut down, the forest behind it now tainted with darker magic, but the building remains. The mill has a large pond with rich vegetation overgrown all around it. I could see the top of the cloak she took from Phoebe coming around the deserted building, and the sparks danced in my chest the closer I got.

I could hear her voice, and thought she was just talking to herself while perched on a wooden fence along the pond, but as I drew near and the vegetation became less obtrusive of my view, I saw a man sitting upon the ground beside her, his feet submerged in the water. His long, dark waving hair hid his face, but I could tell it was a man by the broadness of his shoulders and his massive build.

He would rival Calum, or even Taegan with his size. He may even be bigger. His massive build leaned towards my mate, bumping her swaying leg. Rosie started laughing, the sound somehow piercing my heart, though I found it completely lovely at the same time.

I picked up speed, my possessive jealousy making my magic flare in my chest and glow in my hands and eyes. His back visibly stiffened, probably sensing my approach with my oppressive power raging free.

"The pleasure was all mine," his deep, raspy voice told her, before he dove into the pond, leaving nothing but ripples behind on the surface.

I froze, almost recognizing the voice and the way he said "mine". It sounded similar to the voice from before, the being who was spying on Rosie in my kitchen.

***

Rosie

"A dark merman, you say? Like a demon and merman breed?" Kret asked with an inquisitive look. "Why would you be looking for such a frightening race?"

Kret told me he was a fae race I had never heard of before that was accustomed to the sea, and that he used this pond as a way to cope with the separation when he visited the village.

He told me many stories of his sea adventures, so I broached the question of how to find a creature like the one I saw take Julia. He had been amazingly open and easy to talk to, and even though I'm not going to tell him the whole story, or reveal myself as a werewolf to him, as I've kept my cloak on the entire time, even pulling the hood back up. There was no harm in asking questions in a roundabout way.

I thought carefully before I answered. "I saw one by chance swimming in the sea not too long ago, and he took something from me." I skirted around the truth. "I was just hoping that there might be a village or kingdom out at sea where I could find the one who rules over those creatures to recover what was taken from me."

"And what is it that he took from you?" He smiled. "It must have been something important for you to be searching for this demon merman still. Not a gold coin or a simple piece of jewelry like the one you are holding now?"

I shrugged, trying to remain nonchalant. I couldn't say something like my keys or my cell phone in this world. I wracked my brain trying to think of something.

The necklace Rian gave me was still in my hand, and I started to play with the stone again. The sparks I felt from it made my heart throb.

"My heart," I whispered. "He.... he stole my heart."

It was as good of an excuse as any. Maybe if Kret thinks this wasn't me going to war but it was actually a heartfelt gesture, he would be more willing to give me the information I needed.

"A demonic merman stole your heart?" He laughed. His jaw looked a little tense, but that might be from disbelief.

"It's rude to laugh at lonely strangers," I scoffed, though I was smiling with him.

"You're right," he waved his hand in the air, like he was having trouble stopping. "Good thing we are friends now."

"It's even ruder among friends!" I laughed with him.

"Oh. I'm sorry, treasure. I just didn't expect that." He rubbed his large hand along his jato controlol himself. "He must have been quite the attractive creature to be part demon but still have the ability to steal your heart."

"Yeah, well," I stared at the water, remembering how Rian chased the creature until it disappeared into the portal. "He was beautiful. The power he had in the water..."

The sun here was softer, but it was shining at the right angle to cast a glittering effect on the water's surface. The shimmering effect reminded me of Rian's tail, and his fins. They shimmered brilliantly in the powerful glow of his magic. Then, the way he lifted his body back onto the boat, the water dripped from his toned skin.

"...He was magnificent."

My eyes were dazed while staring at the glimmering water's surface, just thinking about how impressive Rian was the entire night. He even openly claimed me to those mermaids who were being overly flirtatious. I had such confidence in him then. Why couldn't he be that chivalrous when I was stuck on the floor of the kitchen and that fairy hooker started to feel him up? He wouldn't even claim me as his friend in front of her.

"Wow," Kret smirked, making me blush under his amused gaze. "I feel like I have to help you find this demon merman now."

I laughed nervously. "I would appreciate it if you did."

He sighed, remaining quiet and pensive for a moment. Then he leaned over the water, picking up a small stone from just below the surface. He cupped it between his hands, then breathed into them. The air he expelled was a thick black smoky magic, making the air smell a bit of sulfur, but also of sweet flowers. When he pulled his hands away from his face, the stone was black. As black as his eyes, but moving with swirling metallic shimmers. The movements made me think of waves in the ocean.

He extended the stone out to me. I quickly adjusted my hood to put the necklace back on and took the stone from him. His eyes lingered on my necklace for a moment, and then they met mine with a friendly smile.

"I'll see what I can find out about this demon merman who stole your heart. This stone will help me to find you, let's say, this time tomorrow?"

"How?" I held the stone up to the sun, watching the waves glimmer. It looked like a stormy sea. It was quite beautiful. I could feel the magic in it, though it wasn't as strong as the necklace Rian gave me.

"Simply drop it in any body of water and I will seek you out." He stared at my necklace again. "I must warn you, that necklace you wear has a protection spell that will counteract the effects of mine. If you want the stone to work, you need to take the necklace off first."

I touched my necklace tenderly. "Why would a protection spell prevent me from using your tracking stone thing?"

"Well," his smile went crooked. "It protects you from being tracked too. Nothing too concerning, and you only have to take it off until I find you. It will be moments."

The necklace was in my hand the entire time we were sitting there, not around my neck. If Kret wanted to hurt me or meant me any harm, he would have acted on it already. And this was my first lead on finding Julia.

"So I just drop this in the water?" I raised an eyebrow. "I don't have to chant anything or do any strange rituals?"

He grinned at me. "No sacrificial altars. No promise of a first born child. You simply drop the stone in the water. But please," he laughed softly. "No toilets, sinks or bathtubs. Open water only please."

I snorted at the vision of him emerging from the toilet the way he did from the middle of the pond. It looked like a scene from a horror movie until the rest of his body emerged. I was trying not to judge him just based on those two seconds of weirdness. Not being familiar with all these different races of fae beings, I couldn't judge any of them in their natural habitat. I was the outsider and weird one here. Not Kret.

"No toilets?" I smirked teasingly.

"Please no," he laughed, bumping my leg with his shoulder. "You're thinking about it right now, aren't you?"

"Not at all," I laughed through my lie.

He grinned, and then stiffened noticeably, his kind face tensing as his nostrils flare. "It seems I should be off, treasure. I sense someone hostile approaching. I suggest you make your way home as well." His kind smile returned. "I would offer to stay and protect you, but you don't strike me as the type of woman that needs protecting."

In a strange way, that may be the kindest compliment I have received. At least from a man.

"It was a pleasure meeting you, Kret."

"Oh, Rosie." He shifted his body to dive back into the water. "The pleasure was all mine."

I was still smiling, staring at the place he went under, fascinated by the fluid movements. I was feeling like trash when I came here, and he really helped to lift my spirits. A lot.

Suddenly, the hairs on the back of my neck stand on end, and the pull on my bond ignited in my chest. The hostile presence Kret felt must have been him.

"Who the hell was that?" Rian sneered, grabbing my shoulders and pulling me from the edge of the fence, almost making me fall backward.

The sparks did nothing to conceal the contempt I felt coming from him.

"None of your fucking business, ass. Who was that big-titted fairy-time barbie hanging on you? Get off me." I tried to shove him away.

"Do you know who he was?!" He insisted, not letting me go. The sparks were traveling up and down my arms, numbing my fighting spirit and making my eyes burn again. "Did he try to hurt you?"

"No," I seethed, fighting back angry tears. "The only one hurting me is you."

His anger transformed, his eyes widening in shock. I was still trying to pull away from him, and right as I was about to break free, he pulled me towards him, his lips crashing into mine.

I couldn't help the tears that began streaming down my face. My body betrayed me, melting into the kiss. His lips were fevered and desperate, and mine were seeking, seeking some hope that this bond wouldn't fail.

"You're mine," he rasped.

I choked a sob, not believing him. I've communicated more with a stranger in thirty minutes than I have with Rian in the entire time I have known him. That may be exaggerated a little, and everything before yesterday was my fault, but that is how it feels.

"You. Are. Mine." Rian pleaded, brushing the tears from my cheeks with his fingers.

"I don't feel like it," I confessed, our heads resting against one another. "It shouldn't be this hard. This is painful."

36

— • —

MINE

Rian

I panicked. I didn't know what else to do. I don't want to lose her. I don't want to make her run away. I want to bind her to me and have her always by my side. I want to cling to her, forcing her to see only me, love only me, be with only me. I never want another man to have more influence over her than me.

"The only one hurting me is you."

Those words froze my heart. My heart then dropped. I don't want to hurt her. I never wanted to cause her pain, but the glistening tears in her beautiful eyes told me that I had failed. I failed once again to do the most basic of acts to the one I love. I have been failing endlessly from the start.

I love her. I know I do. She's my very soul, but my fear that she will never see me the same way caused me to react badly over and over again. I so desperately want to be in her world, be the main part of it, that I'm the one pushing her further away. I can see that now.

Desperately, I kissed her. I wanted that magic like before from the moment we shared in the air to override all of this, but all I tasted on her lips was my failure as a mate. Her salty kiss stung me, the sweetness no longer there.

I hurt her. I ignorantly hurt my mate, but I know it will never be an option to just let her go. I fear that was what she wanted now. She was just smiling and laughing with a dark being on the outskirts of the Caligo Forest, and moments later, I, her mate, the man that loves her, was causing her to cry once again.

All I seem to do is make her mad or make her cry.

Mine. That word was still echoing in my head, like a ghost haunting my very being.

She was no one else's. She is mine. Even as I tell her that, I am pleading for her to agree with me. I am holding my breath for that guarantee that she truly is mine. Those words that I so desire don't leave her lips.

Instead, her words feel like a rejection.

She doesn't feel like she is mine? This is painful for her?

It was painful for me too, but I couldn't reveal that to her, because it was my own inadequacy that was making it so.

Her sweet breath mixed with mine. The effects of our bond were traveling over my skin, flaring my dying need to make her mine. I needed some reassurance, and I felt like I was searching in the dark. Something needed to change. Some catalyst needed to spark a change in us.

I needed to spark that change. I had to, because I can't lose her.

It's my fear, my inadequacy that is causing me to fuck up again and again. The change needs to start with me.

I will not give up. I will not mess this up any more. She's mine. If she doesn't feel it, then I'll show her. I have to.

Her beautiful face was between my hands, and I was desperately trying to soothe away her tears. I brought my lips to hers, pouring the sincerity of my feelings into the connection, praying she felt it in the sparks.

She kissed me back. Her lips were soft, giving into mine, but the tremor in her body let me know that it's the bond causing her to give into me. She was fighting an internal battle. She was barely holding herself together.

"I'm sorry," I gasped, my guilt making it hard to breathe. "I'm so sorry, Rosie. I'm so, so sorry. I am just so scared of not being enough."

She choked a sob, shaking her head. Her eyes wereblazingg, making a wave of heat travel through me. "Why? Why is this so hard?" She tried to pull away again, but I wouldn't let her. I couldn't. I'm scared of what could happen if I did.

She growled, twisted and turned, but I was steadfast. I hugged her against my chest, refusing to let her go.

"Who was she?" Rosie asked after finally giving up on getting away from me. She sounded like she was losing her fight. Her voice was soft, at the point of breaking. It was shattering me too.

"My cousin," I told her hurriedly, wanting to remedy at least one of my mishaps. "Parisa. She is my cousin. She's blood related. It wasn't what you were thinking. Not at all."

Rosie wiped her eyes with the backs of her hands. "My cousins don't hug me like that," she scoffed.

"Your cousins are much more likely to hug a cheeseburger than any girl," I retorted softly. That made her smile just a little bit. I started to see hope. I just need to explain. There were too many misunderstandings. "Parisa is a succubus. She clings to everyone, but I was...I was upset and she was feeding on that."

Rosie shook her head. "I don't get why! I didn't do anything wrong. You keep getting mad, looking upset, but I didn't do anything." Her confusion was making her beautiful face contort solemnly. "Is it....is it because of the past? Because I-"

"You didn't do anything, Rosie," I rasped, grabbing hold of her lovely face once again. "It's me. It's my inability to-to.... Damn, this is so frustrating. So... so.... embarrassing," I groaned. My thumb was tracing her bottom lip, my eyes beaming into hers. I ironically couldn't find the words to confess to her how much of a coward I am. How lacking I always feel, now more than ever, in light of who she is.

But I need to tell her. I can't let my cowardice cause me to lose her, or hurt her any more than it already has.

"I just want you so much," I whispered in a broken voice. "I'm so scared that you won't want me."

"Rian," she stressed, resting her hands on my chest. "Is it because of my past? Because I treated you so badly before?"

"No," I smiled sadly. It wasn't for that at all. I actually don't mind as much that she didn't pay much attention to me in the past, because she would be so much more aware of how inadequate I am. What was bothering me was that she wanted someone so great, but I felt like a consolation prize. "You just loved him so much. I still feel like I can never compare."

"That's not true." She pressed closer, her hands fisting my shirt. "That is not true. Not at all. The way I thought I felt about him is nothing to how I feel about you now." She made the cutest disgruntled face. She was stretching and hanging by her fists onto my shirt, her frustration being expelled physically in true Alpha fashion. "I almost took your cousin's head off for touching you." Her eyes are searching mine. "I desperately want you, too."

Those words were like a balm to my burning anxieties. My smile unleashed so much tension from inside me and I rested my head on hers. I doubt her desperation could ever match mine, but hearing it from her was still like a gift.

Something was still nagging me. I wanted to ask about that man. I wanted to press her about what they were talking about. Was my jealousy making me hear things earlier when I thought the man's voice sounded similar to the one I heard surrounding Rosie?

"Rian?" Rosie whispered my name while I was still deciding how to ask my questions. "Hmm?"

"In your mother's kitchen.... What was that? What happened?"

That's right. I never told her, and it appears Taegan didn't have time to either.

"That's what I brought my cousin for," I confessed. "Let's go back to the house and I can explain."

***

Slarkrethel

I watched from just beneath the water, almost exploding out of the pond in my true form, when he took her and forcibly kissed her.

That filthy prince. That royal trash was nothing without his pedigree. She doesn't need a pampered prig. She is mine. She always has been. She was promised to me on the altar before her birth. My life was forever tied to hers. He can't take her from me now.

No one can take her from me.

I watched, wishing I could rid her of him, but this being close to the royal courts would prove to be disastrous for me if I did. I was banned from setting foot in royal territory. If I set foot on the land, the King would be aware of my presence right away and within moments, a battalion of knights would appear to rid the land of me once again.

I just put in so much effort. I can't risk her seeing me as the villain. I'm not the villain. I am not at fault for my misfortunes. It was those prude and snobbish royals that degraded so.

Lucky for me, she ended up on the outskirts of the village, upon the waters and forest that possess too much dark energy to be deemed royal land any longer. Being confined to the waters was a risk, but she didn't leave, granting me my first conversation with my treasure. If that prince hadn't interrupted us, I might have even been able to convince her to join me for a swim.

Then she would have been mine. Once again, a royal has taken what was rightfully mine.

There was nothing I could do but watch as he continued defiling her with his lips, then eventually led her off further and further from me. I may not be able to take care of him yet, but to soothe my anger there was another who had equally earned my fury today.

Sinking my body into the bottom of the pond, I secreted my power to create a portal back to my oasis on the sea. There he was, on the sandy shores, feeding once again in my absence.

"GRYNRUS!" I roared, launching my body towards him.

His eyes widened, and he tried to quickly dive back into the water to avoid my wrath, throwing the girl to the ground in the process. He was quickly tripping over her when his legs prematurely shifted into fins.

She didn't do more than groan. He fed more than he should, but that wasn't the reason he had earned my wrath at that moment. This cretin stole her heart?! Even as a lie, that wasn't a thought I could ever entertain.

My tentacles shot out and wrapped around his tail, prods projecting from my suction, digging into his flesh. I coiled around his body, tightening my limbs like a vice and crushing him slowly.

He was lucky, because if I didn't know that my treasure was lying, I would squeeze off Grynrus's head. First, I would crush his bones, every single one of them, letting the hooks of my suckers tear apart his flesh in the process. His blood would stain the beach, running into the sea, and creatures far more primitive than I would feast on what was left.

Right as Grynrus was about to pass out from the strangulation, I loosen my grip. He screamed and groaned, wiggling to free himself. My hooks were embedded inside him already. I ripped them out, then in a rage I roared so loud it sent waves raging in the waters.

This imbecile stole her heart?! Never. Her heart is no one's but mine. Her very soul is mine. She is my treasure. My promised one.

I waited over eighteen of her years for this opportunity. I won't let it be wasted on anyone. Not a moron like Grynrus, and definitely not for a prince.

37

KID SEARCH

Carli

"There it is." Simone pointed to the car she and Vincent loaned to the boys while they visited Miami. Simone actually loaned it to Calum, but Calum has been using Parker's old truck for the past few days and left that car with Taegan. That was a red flag.

Taegan usually borrows cars from the resort. He must have fucked up big time with Mitch and Mark. I wanna know what the big oaf did to warrant them getting so pissed. Taegan is so polite and respectful when he's here, at least with the adults. Does he have some dark secret that I don't know? He's usually everyone's golden boy.

I love him, but I'm glad he didn't end up being Rosie's mate. I couldn't see that working out. Rian is much softer and less complicated. Taegan and Rosie would have been a major power struggle. I can see Rian truly treating Rosie the way she deserves.

Watching the kids interact over the years, I could always tell Rian had a little thing for Rosie. He watched her everywhere she went, but kept silent because of Rosie's insistence that Taegan and her were mates. He reminds me of a male version of Rosie's best friend, Sophia. Soft-spoken but tough when he needs to be. He was always smiling and easy to talk to, even in uncomfortable situations. He was complacent around Taegan, even though Rian was the older one, but I saw him speak up a few times when Taegan was getting a bit too showy with his Lycan counterpart or his magical powers.

Rosie and Taegan wouldn't have ever worked out, but Rosie and Rian will do well together.

I hope she and Rian are working out right now instead of missing like Thyra and Bailey seem to think they are. Fuck, its frustrating not being able to get in contact with her. I can't even mind link her. I'd tried many times. If this leads to nothing, I'm going to have to get Parker involved. I was trying to avoid that on the chance Rian and Rosie were fine and just blocking out the outside world in the heat of their passion.

"Hey, have you heard from Phoebe?" Bailey asked Thyra as I pulled up next to the car. She had been messing with her phone for most of the drive, taking it to her ear and then cursing at it numerous times when it wouldn't connect. I thought she was still trying to contact her son. "I've been texting and trying to call her, but nothing is going through."

"She was with Vincent," Simone said. "Want me to call him?"

"If you could."

Bailey looked exhausted. Thyra was rubbing her back, looking equally worried.

Where the hell have all our kids gone? It's just fucking rude to make everyone worry like this. That had better be fucking lost at this point after causing most of the Blue Cliff family to come down searching for them. I'm bashing heads in when we find them, then putting Rosie and Rian in a room at the packhouse with a lock on the outside as punishment. Like a special baby-making timeout.

The men pulled up in a pack SUV behind us. Simone stayed in the car to talk with her mate while the rest of us went out to look for any sign of our kids.

"What the fuck is this place?" Alpha Max growled, looking wary of the marshes.

Casey grabbed his arms, yelling, "GATOR!" making Alpha Max jump back with a horrified look on his face. When he realized nothing was there, he punched Casey in the arm and started berating him with insults. I've never heard a man use the words "cunt" and "fucker" so many times in one sentence. I was a little impressed.

"Alpha, dad was just fucking with you about the gators here. They're too scared of our scents to come close to us," Calum told him.

"I know that!" Alpha Max hissed, though he was still eying the water with a leery expression.

Reese was pressing his lips together to keep from laughing. He thinks Alpha Max is hilarious. He came along and Karina stayed back at the packhouse to talk to Sophia about Calum. Calum was so worried about the way Sophia ran off that Karina volunteered to help him. Calum is the sweetest and most kind-hearted kid. Karina will attest to that. If Sophia was freaked out by his parents and brother's sudden visit, she can join the club. I've been on edge since they all got here too.

I have a handle on what everyone is doing here now, but now it's the issue of our missing kids. Courtney stayed behind to be at the packhouse in case any information about where they could be came in, but the rest of us are here to start the search.

After looking through the car, we all started yelling for the kids, screaming their names and demanding they come out if they're there. Calum and Reese went to track scents in the area, but there weren't many scents to go by. Their scents were just around the car in the clearing. The clearing is quite big, but the trees around are thick and there are tall patches of cord grass everywhere. Everyone is being thorough.

"You better show your fucking asses you snot-nosed pieces of shit," Alpha Max snarled loudly when just yelling 'Taegan' and 'Rian' weren't working. He's resorting to threats. "I swear, if a fucking swamp monster eats me, I'm taking a bite out of all of you!"

Alpha Max's threats always made me smile, but the longer we searched with no results, the less amusing those threats sounded and the more anxious I became. There wasn't any sign of the kids anywhere.

"Hey," Simone bumped my shoulder as I made my way back into the clearing near the car. "Isn't this that one place?"

"What one place?" I asked, ducking my head to examine the contents of the inside of the car again.

"The place. You know, with the witches."

I looked at her like I had no idea what she was talking about. I've found witches in these marshes so many times, she was going to have to be more specific.

Simone rolled her eyes. "I know it was a long time ago, but it was the only time you dragged me with you to hunt witches. It was when Parker was trying to get you to calm your tits with the missions because you were pregnant."

I gave her another dubious look. Yeah, she was going to have to be more fucking specific. I was a nightmare both times I was pregnant. I hadn't worked through my mommy issues yet and was hurting myself trying to prove my worth.

"Seriously?" Simone shook her head with a smirk. "You forced me to come here with you a long freaking time ago because you heard rumors of a ritual witches were about to perform. They had a truck full of little kids and babies. Like, one of those animal control trucks with kennels on the back."

Now it was starting to ring a bell.

"I was pregnant with Rosie," I muttered. "Yeah, I remember. It made me sick seeing those babies."

That was before Mitch and Mark found out they were Gemini twins, so handling witches was a lot more difficult for our pack. The witches had a fucking alter built where they were preparing to kill the babies to seek more power from a demon. I did end up calling for backup and waiting for Parker to confront the witches that time, and all the kids were saved.

Those witches were creepy as fuck. I remember that explicitly. I think being creepy as fuck is the standard if you stoop so low as to kill children for personal gain, but these witches were, like, brother's grim creepy. The leader even tried to curse Parker or some shit before he killed her. Maybe she was trying to curse all of us there. I don't know.

I just remember her eyes. Right before her throat was torn from her body, she stared right at me, mumbling her cursing words in some foreign language. Her eyes went completely black and she pointed at me right as Parker killed her.

He was vigilant about getting me and Rosie, who was in my belly at the time, checked out by the pack doctors to make sure the witch didn't do any harm to our bodies with her curse. I was completely fine and she was born without a hitch. Parker never had issues and no one else that was there felt any effects. Nothing at all happened to any of us so I had completely put it out of my mind. That kind of shit is common with dark witches. We just let Mitch and Mark handle them now.

"It was right here," Simone skipped to a spot a few feet away from the car. She tapped her foot to indicate what spot she was talking about, even though I remembered now. I thought she was just talking to keep me sane while looking for my missing daughter. "That burning driftwood altar was right here and all the witches were circling around it. Parker and Matt were putting down the witches with your dad's help and the help of a few other warriors. I was right after Elena got the children to safety. We were putting out the blue flames with fire extinguishers while the witches were being unlived, but the fires wouldn't go out no matter what we tried until that last nasty one was dead. You remember her? That raisin-looking one with the yucky eyes who started yelling those weird words at Parker and then at you."

"I remember," I whispered, stepping beside her and looking around at the spot she was talking about. Rosie's scent went from the car to right here, and then it just disappeared. "It was right here," I said absentmindedly, stomping on the ground to see if there were any trap doors or something I was missing.

I then looked up towards the sky. Thyra mentioned flying horses. We learned many years ago from the asshole that stalked Simone that Pegasus horses can go unnoticed in the sky, their magic and ability to go to great heights helping to keep them hidden. I squinted in the harsh sunlight, forcing my eyes to scan every square inch of the sky around me.

"They're not up there," Thyra said, coming alongside us after searching with Bailey in the wooded area. "All our pegasus are accounted for here," she held her hand palm up, letting her magic smoke and glitter into a translucent orb. Then the image of dozens of pegasus horses appeared on its surface. The image moved around until it focused on three specific ones. "These are ours, but I have already checked all of them besides these as well and they are all accounted for, none are missing. There is no trace of their magic in this area either."

"Then what were our kids doing out here?" I asked.

"I don't know, but it wasn't riding the horses."

38

— • —

PATERNAL TENSIONS

Bailey stared at the live image of the pegasus in the magic resting upon Thyra's hand with a forlorn expression, then turned to Simone. "Did your mate say if he was still with Phoebe?"

Simone pressed her lips together and shook her head. "No. He introduced her to Lady Delilah and then had to go with Parker to deal with an issue your son's beta dealt with on her way to the resort."

"What issue?" I asked.

"Well. It seems Phoebe's driver had ill intentions towards her. She killed him and dumped his body in a swamp. Vincent went to make sure the mess was properly dealt with and found the remains of several human girls there, too."

"Oh, no," Thyra pressed her fingers to her lips.

"Is Phoebe okay?" I asked.

"Vincent said she seemed fine." Simone shrugged. "He said she just looked annoyed."

"I imagine she was more than annoyed," Bailey sighed. "That girl has dealt with so much in her life. She is put off by men completely outside of our pack and doesn't tolerate any form of abuse towards women. If it was a serial rapist and murderer, she probably gave him hell."

"Vince did mention the state that he found the man's body in was rather gruesome." She lifted the corner of her lips in a half smile. "He and Parker are heading this way now, by the way."

Bailey nodded, but I could tell she was still bothered about not being able to find her son and now not being able to contact his beta.

"Lady Delilah's court is pretty formal. If you can't get through to Phoebe on her phone, it might be because she turned it off," I told her. She just offered me a sad smile in return.

Thyra was examining the ground now, in the exact spot I was staring at earlier. It's the place where Rosie's scent just disappears. She waved her hands over the ground, then a glowing purple line appeared, lifting into the air and creating a glimmering vertical plane.

Her eyes went wide in horror.

"What?" Bailey pressed up against her side. "What is it?"

We were all looking from the shimmering, translucent purple plane to Thyra, waiting for her to tell us what the fuck she just did.

"I think they went over," she whispered hoarsely.

Over? I was about to ask what the hell she meant when Alpha Max came jogging over with a concerned expression.

"What's wrong?" He placed his hands on either side of Thyra's horrified face. Her eyes focused on his and I could see her crumbling on the inside.

"Rian portaled," she whispered to him.

His brows pulled down. "Where?"

Thyra bit her lip. She looked so broken, so worried. I'm hanging on by a thread. Since Rian can portal, I pray he just made a portal to somewhere tropical or isolated, and he and Rosie are just too selfishly wrapped up in each other to let their mothers know they are both okay.

"Alfheimr," she rasped.

His eyes went wide and Bailey gasped. All hope I had sunk at the mention of the fae realm.

"Is that allowed?" Bailey asked. "Why would he do such a thing?"

"It's not allowed. Not if you are non-fae." Thyra shook her head. "And as far as why.... I don't know. He knows better. This has never happened before. With Rosie, she might be an exception, since she is his mate and his position in the courts. But Taegan...."

Bailey's bottom lip trembled. All of us stood horrified at the reality of what Thyra had just said. If Rian is caught smuggling two alpha werewolves into the fairy realm, it could cause strife between our world and theirs, and put our kids in danger.

"Why would he do that? Why would he put them all at risk like this?" Bailey asked.

I knew why.

"The girl. They went to save the girl that was taken from the party at the cove." That had to be it. Rosie was as pissed as I was that night that we couldn't do anything but wait.

"What do we do?" Bailey asked.

What do we do? When Parker hears about this, he will storm the council with demands to be taken to the fairy realm to bring back our daughter. This could already have disastrous effects on our pack. What can we possibly do?

"Can we go ask Queen Aisling for help to make them come home?" Simone asked softly.

"No," Thyra shook her head. "This offense is too great. I need to speak to my brother before we involve any other royals from other kingdoms. If one of the other rulers finds them first, they may imprison the kids, or worse."

That meant if Parker started raising hell, it could put our daughter more at risk. Damn it, Rosie. Why couldn't she just be off having lots of unprotected sex like a normal mated teenager? This wasn't like her.

To make matters worse, Parker and Vincent found us and were now pulling into the clearing with Calum and Reese running along beside Parker's truck in their wolf forms.

Parker was going to lose it. I was on the verge of losing it. I always thought Rosie was like her dad with these kinds of things, but this was a very 'me' thing she was doing. Running off into a different realm to save a friend is something I would have done at her age.

Well, after all the baby-making sex.

I swear, if she doesn't come back pregnant, I will kill her twice. Please, goddess, just give me a ray of hope that something good will come out of all this.

Most of all, just please let her come back safely. She is still my baby. She is too precious to me to be stuck with the consequences she is about to face. Just bring her back safely. Please.

Parker and Vincent were eyeing our wary crowd suspiciously, sensing the tension. Vincent went to Simone, wrapping her in his arms as she stared up at him. Their eyes let me know she was telling him about everything Thyra had just revealed in a link. Vincent shook his head and held her tight.

"What happened?" Parker asked me. "Vincent said there was shit going on here with you and Rosie and I should probably tag along. What's wrong?" He looked around. "Where's Rose?"

I bit my lip, hesitant to tell him. I needed to tell him, but I knew how he would react.

Instead, I wrapped my arms around his waist and buried my head in his chest, letting a tremor move down my back as the sparks eased some of the tension inside me. I needed to calm myself before I braced myself to calm him.

"Carli, what is it?" he asked, angling his head to stare at my face. "What's wrong?"

"She's not here," I whispered. "Rosie. Rian took her and Taegan to the fairy realm."

His body tensed and I squeezed him tighter, not wanting him to do something irrational out of fear for our daughter.

"What?!" He snarled. "Where the fuck did you say that little bastard took my daughter?!"

"Hey!" Alpha Max yelled. Thyra was holding him similar to how I was holding Parker. "Watch your damn mouth when you speak about my son!"

"Your damn son kidnapped my daughter, you fucking-"

"Stop!" Bailey yelled, the power behind her command so strong that it startled me. All of us instantly closed our mouths and froze. "Fighting isn't going to solve this! No one kidnapped anyone," she narrowed her eyes at Parker. "But Rian and Taegan both knew better," she turned her glare to Alpha Max. "Fighting won't bring any of them back, and the blame lies entirely with them. Quit with the testosterone and help us figure this shit out. I swear." She shook her head. "If us women can talk about this without letting our emotions get the better of us, why can't you men ever do the same?"

Parker's nostrils flared, and Alpha Max's jaw clenched. I stomped on Parker's foot, squeezing his middle, while Bailey continued to glare at her father-in-law and Thyra tried to calm his anger. Slowly, Parker relaxed his body in my hold. I could feel his anger, but it was no longer irrationally aimed at the Alpha who snapped back at him.

"You're right," Parker eventually said. "I'm sorry for my harsh words about your son." I could feel that he didn't one-hundred percent feel that way, but he was slipping back into his job of keeping decorum between alphas. I still breathed a sigh of relief.

Alpha Max nodded gruffly. "He's your fucking son-in-law now. You weren't just accusing my son of stupid shit, you were blaming your daughter's mate. I won't give him to a family that talks shit about him like that."

I could feel Parker's anger rising again. I stomped on his foot again to keep him in check. I didn't want him pissing Rian's parents off and this situation doesn't need any more tension.

"Not the time," I hissed at Parker. "Calm your tits. Please. At least until we get our daughter back."

He grumbled but agrees.

"We want both kids back safely," I told Alpha Max before my mate could say something stupid to him like, "we don't want him anyway" or something similar. Parker's having a hard time treading that line between protective father and hospitable Alpha. I happened to like Rian just fine and I sure as hell was not letting Parker piss off Rian's parents or our daughter by disrespecting her mate. "He's as important to us and our pack as our daughter, Alpha Max. We want all three of our kids back safely."

That seemed to placate him, and his hostile expression dropped.

"How do we get them, though?" Bailey looked at Thyra. "None of us have the authority or means to travel to the fairy realm."

"No one but you, Aunt Thyra," Calum said.

Thyra made a face, looking at first Bailey, and then me. She then turned her face up to stare at her mate, and he was staring down at her with the kindest expression I have ever seen him make.

"What do we do?" Thyra whispered to Max.

"I think you already know, honey." He placed his hand on the side of her face. "I think we're taking a trip to your world."

She bit her lip, then nodded one single time. "I think you're right."

Alpha Max smiled, but then suddenly lifted a finger, wagging it in Thyra's face like he had just remembered something.

"But I'm not riding that fucking glue stick."

39

BOTH OR MATES

Taegan

"Did you know about my mate?" ·

I stared at Phoebe for quite some time, Conri snorting in the back of my head.

"What mate?" I tried to play dumb, but Phoebe's red eyes flared, knowing that I was not telling the truth. "I...I suspected," I mumbled. "I wasn't-..... Wait," something just dawned on me. "How do you know about your mate?"

"How do you think, dumbass?" She flicked my forehead. "I just saw her. I saw both of our mates. When didn't you tell me?"

"Because I couldn't!" I snapped. "Fuck! Seriously. All of you are griping at me about your fucking mates, but you know I can't say shit. You, more than anyone, know that I can't say shit."

She eyed me warily. "So you did know?"

I pressed my lips together, letting the silence answer the question for her.

Phoebe sighed deeply. "Ass. Why didn't you force me to go down there like you did Rian for all these years?"

"Uh, I tried. You refused. Adamantly. You were actually kind of a bitch about it every time I brought it up."

She made a disgruntled face. "The whole fucking state feels like a bowl of sweat soup."

"Yum," I chuckled. "It's not that bad."

"You don't have boobs," she growled.

"I do too," I smirked, flexing my chest together.

"Yeah, you do. You're right," Phoebe laughed. "We should get you a bra."

Phoebe and I argued about my chest size and what bra size I would need. Just stupid shit like we always talk about. She was leaning on my chair, touching me constantly to help me get Conri back to normal. Not in intimate or annoying ways. She rested her hand on my shoulder, teasingly fondled my chest, and held my hand loosely. I could always count on her to do this kind of stuff, fueling me with small touches when I was feeling off. She wasn't attracted to men, so there was never anything to worry about with her.

My magic was really drained, and she knew I was having a hard time without me even saying anything. It's not as much magic and vitality as what Rian could give me, but it should hold me off until he gets back.

"You two are quite entertaining," Parisa grinned, watching us from where she sat at the table. "I take it that you are quite close? I mean, the queen of the night wouldn't have contacted me to help you come over to our realm for someone you weren't close to, I guess, but your closeness is quite remarkable to see."

"I'm his Beta," Phoebe answered, resting her chin on my head. "We're supposed to be close."

"Beta," Parisa tested the word. "Is that wolf talk for wife? Because you both seem like an elderly married couple."

"Ew, no," Phoebe sneered. "Gross."

"Hey! That's rude," I scoffed.

Phoebe looked me up and down. "Even if I did like men, you would never be my type."

"Lies." I folded my arms across my chest. "I'm everyone's type."

"I bet you are," Parisa gave me a flirtatious grin.

The way she bent over the table with her chin resting in her palm made her breasts strain the fabric of her... shirt. If you could even call it a shirt. It was more like a scarf-thin, silk fabric wrapped around her midsection, then bunching and flaring from her hips. Like you would expect one of those Greek goddess statues women to be wearing. It looked as if her giant tits were about to burst free.

Despite myself, my face flamed, and I had to quickly look away when I realized I was gawking. Even Conri was looking, but his thoughts were more centered on what type of material the fabric must be to not break. He was more impressed with her shirt than what the shirt was holding.

"*Watch it,*" Phoebe mind linked me.

"I didn't do anything." I turned my face away, holding my hand over my mouth and chin so she couldn't see the pink hue of my cheeks.

"What is this mate business the two of you are speaking of? Rian said the growling girl was his mate? That really is the equivalent of a spouse, correct? I heard my aunt has a mate partner who is a werewolf Alpha. You both have mates as well?"

"Well," I murmured, exchanging a glance with Phoebe. "We will."

"Oh? When?" Parisa tilted her head curiously.

I bit my lip. This would sound weird to anyone, but maybe if she knows I'm waiting for someone, she will stop with the boob straining and flirty smiles. "In ten years."

"Oh, my," she giggled. "That is quite a long time."

"Yeah, it is," Phoebe groaned. "Shit. I'm nearly twenty years older than her."

I knew exactly how Phoebe was feeling. It took me a while to accept the age difference. I'm just twelve years older than my mate.

"You're a vampire. You don't age like humans do," I reminded Phoebe. "Your moms have a huge age difference too."

"Yeah, but Addi never saw Steph when she was still in diapers."

"Our mates are not still in diapers," I countered.

"Close to," Phoebe smirked. "You know, you go down to Florida an awful lot. You always have, even when they were babies."

"So?"

"So..." Her grin turned wicked, "Are you going to be able to say that you changed your mate's diapers?"

"Fuck you!" I snapped. "I have never changed Harley's diaper."

"No? What about the other one?"

"Harper? No. I was twelve when they were born. Most twelve-year-olds aren't asked to change the diapers of babies they aren't related to."

"Harper," Phoebe said the name and smiled. Then her face turned into a sudden scowl. "You better not have changed my mate's diaper."

"Why are you being so damn weird?" I groaned. "No one changed any diapers."

"That seems unlikely," Parisa grinned. "We would all be lugging around soiled nappies till we were old enough to take them off ourselves, if that were the case."

I smiled at the princess's attempt at a crude joke. It was almost funny. Then I hurried and looked away when I noticed her tits again. She needs to put those damn things away.

Phoebe just rolled her eyes, not amused. I don't think she likes Parisa very much. She has been standoffish towards her since they got here.

"Do the twins' parents know?" Phoebe asked me.

"Know what?"

"Know how to juggle bowling pins," she said sarcastically. "What the hell do you think I mean?! Do they know that you are Harley's mate?"

I frowned, and Conri huffed angrily. "Uh, yeah. They know now."

"Why do you say it like that?" Phoebe lifted her brow at me.

"Because it wasn't a pleasant experience, them finding out. I got told to leave the resort and never come back."

"Why? What did you do?"

I folded my hands on the table and stared at my fists. "Nothing. Not really."

"Not really means you did something," Phoebe bumped me with her hip. "What is it? What did you do?"

"I really didn't do anything, though. I mean, not intentionally."

She stared down at me with that look like she was waiting for me to continue. I sighed.

"I was carrying Harley to the rec area with her sister and Mitch when she kissed my cheek. She does that a lot, and it's never a big fucking deal, but she's a seer. It seems she has finally gained her abilities and her connection to this realm, though. This time when she did it, magic crackled between us and it absorbed into me."

"Isn't that normal?" Phoebe rubbed my head, sensing my distress. "You are a witch. I'm sure those Meyers brothers could understand that."

"Mitch didn't like it. He told her to not kiss me anymore on the cheek, and even took her from my arms and told her to run ahead with her sister so he could talk to me. He asked me not to hold her or touch her any more to keep her safe, since they also know I'm a witch. Conri got offended and I made the small fucking mistake of saying that I would always keep her safe. That was my fucking job. He asked what I meant and when I froze up he figured it out." I groaned, remembering the look on his face when it all clicked in place for him. "He was pissed."

"Why, though?" Phoebe asked. "Like you said, you're everyone's type. Most were-wolves would kill to have your blonde-headed ass as their son-in-law."

"They're fucking protective," I sighed. "With Harley being who she is, they are extra cautious with her."

"Thank fuck I kept my mouth closed when I saw them," Phoebe scoffed. "I guess I'll be waiting ten years watching them from a distance with you."

"Hadley said her mates would come around," I murmured. "Staying away isn't going to be an option for me."

"Yeah," Phoebe sighed. "Me too. I'm going crazy now just wondering if my mate is safe. I ran into the most detestable of uber drivers while I was traveling alone from the packhouse to the resort. Had to deal with him and leave him for the gators. Now I'm wondering how many more creeps like him are freely roaming the city."

"Geez. You okay?"

"Oh, I'm fine. One less creep in Miami," she shrugged.

Now my gut was twisting with worry, even though I knew the Meyers brothers would never let either of their daughters out of their sight unless they were protected.

The quiet stretched between the three of us, and I felt a bit embarrassed to reveal all this shit in front of Rian's cousin. She was so attentive but quiet. I forgot she was listening. I refused to look her way again because of her shirt.

Now the silence and waiting around was getting a bit uncomfortable and awkward again. I chanced a glance at the fairy princess from the corner of my eye and regretted it instantly when I saw the playful smirk on her face. Like a cat watching a mouse struggle.

"So." Parisa reached across the table and ran a finger across the back of my hand. "Do you have to be, what is the word?.... Celibate? Do you have to be celibate for the next ten years," she fluttered her eyelashes, "Alpha Taegan?"

Her magic sparked on the back of my hand, making Conri moan with need for more. He didn't mean to, but I really depleted him when I poked around in Rosie's head. Even with Phoebe's help, he was still not fully recovered.

I had to fight the urge to draw more magic from her, pulling my hand away because I knew what she was trying to do. Women come on to me pretty often. This fairy princess was very forward, which I needed to be wary of. If it appeared I was returning her interest and her father, who is a fucking king, finds out, that could come down hard on my head.

I'm waiting for my mate. I don't want there ever to be any doubt about that.

After getting over my awkward stupor, I opened my mouth to tell her "I was waiting for my mate", but I didn't get the chance to answer her when the front door opened loudly, making me jump.

"Pussy," Conri whispered.

"Shut up. You're wound tight and your nerves are shot too."

Rian came walking in with Rosie at his side. Both of them with exhausted and wary expressions. Rosie gave Parisa a side-eyed glance which made Parisa recede back to her side of the table. Parisa smiled brightly, but Rosie wasn't smiling back.

"You okay?" I asked Rosie.

She pressed her lips together tightly, shrugging her shoulders. Her eyes were red and puffy. I had five sisters. I knew she had been crying. Rosie never cries. She isn't dramatic and she just doesn't cry. She must have really been hurting.

Rian looked at her from the corner of his eye. He seemed so defeated. I felt so bad for both of them.

Phoebe said that I wasn't supposed to be here. Conri had been saying that from the beginning. I couldn't help but wonder, after seeing both of them now, how true that statement really was.

40

CREEPY STALKER

Rosie

The walk back was tense and awkward, but sitting at the table across from cousin "boobs-for-brains" while she smiled like all was right with the world was even more awkward. No matter how hard I tried, I couldn't stop from glaring whenever she looked my way. Or looked in Rian's direction. Or Taegan's.

Okay, I really just don't like her looking anywhere at all. Phoebe was even sending her nasty looks whenever she glanced towards her or Taegan. Phoebe doesn't like many people, but that level of malice is usually reserved for arrogant or obtuse men. She came here with Princess Big-Boobs and those types of women are usually her type. At least, that is what Taegan has told me. Parisa must have gotten on Phoebe's bad side somehow. That isn't a place I would ever want to be.

I wonder what the fairy woman was saying to Taegan when we walked in. By the way she had her body scrawled over the table, I could only assume she was hitting on my friend. Maybe that's why Phoebe was giving her the stink eye. Phoebe was protective of her alpha. Fiercely so.

Rian reached over and rested his hand on my knee, squeezing it tightly to help me focus and break me out of my negative thoughts about his slutty cousin. He'd been trying to touch me more, I noticed. He kept watching me, like he was nervous that I might start with the waterworks again, I guess.

I'm still confused about where we stand, but we have things to discuss, and a mission to get back to. We never even ate that damned soup. There are so many things to worry about, it feels like the worries between us are overshadowing everything else.

"Do you want to know what happened earlier?" he asked me in a low voice.

"Yes," I replied. He wouldn't tell me anything on the walk back here, telling me he would explain it when we got to the house with everyone else. It's annoying being left in the dark.

Rian pressed his lips together, smiling apologetically. "I want to start by saying I'm sorry, Rosie, before anything else. I'm sorry I didn't notice sooner that this was happening."

"Notice what?" I grimaced. "You're freaking me out."

"He was pretty freaked out too," Taegan muttered, earning him a cold look from his uncle. "What? You were."

"You were too," he snapped.

"Not as much as you," Taegan argued, folding his arms over his chest. "You looked like you saw a fucking ghost."

"You passed out because of whatever you saw!"

I looked towards the ceiling, growing more irritated listening to them bicker. This is all they do now.

"I suggest you both stop your childish shit and get to explaining before she knocks both your heads together," Phoebe muttered.

Rian looked at me with a worried expression. I smiled tightly, not denying what Phoebe had just said.

"Sorry," he squeezed my leg again. "Like I was saying, I'm sorry."

"You have said that already, but you haven't told me what for."

"Well... You said the necklace had been reacting since we got here, but it took me so long to notice. The necklace was... was reacting to a darker magic that was intruding on your privacy."

"What does that mean?"

"It means," Taegan said, "someone was spying on you. Something dark has been watching you since we got here."

My face contorted in disgust. "Eww. Like watching me, watching me? Like a weird fairy stalker?"

"That's one way to think of it," Taegan chortled.

I think back to everything I did after getting to this realm. I didn't go to the bathroom or anything while the necklace was spazzing out, did I?

"It won't happen again," Rian reassured me. "That's what I was doing. I pushed the creature back, blocking him from watching you with his magic again. I put even stronger magic into the stone that will hold up against anything."

"Save, my father," Parisa spoke, crinkling her nose like this was a joke.

"Well, yeah. Except for my uncle and the other rulers of the fae kingdoms. I doubt they would be spying on you."

"You never know," Parisa grinned teasingly.

I'm glad she is finding the humor in my situation. I felt like bugs were crawling all over my skin, knowing I had been watched, but she seemed to be enjoying my discomfort. I really don't like her.

"It was dark," Taegan said, staring at an empty spot on the table. "Whoever it was, they were dark. Their aura was black. And...." He looked nervously at me and then Rian. "He latched onto her. I don't think it was....what you were worried about, but there was a connection there."

"Her meaning me?" I looked from Taegan to Rian. "What latched onto me? What is he talking about?"

Rian hesitantly answered, "Remember when I asked if you had another mate?"

"Yeah?"

"That's why I was asking. I heard the creature's voice, and it kept saying that you were his."

The creepy crawling feeling was suddenly so much worse. It was to where I wanted to scour my skin under boiling bleach water repeatedly with steel wool, then take a bath in acid. Who the hell in this realm is watching me and claiming that I'm theirs?

"So you got mad at me for that?" I raised my brows at Rian.

"No! I didn't get mad at you at all. I was mad at myself that I didn't keep you safe."

"I can protect myself, Rian. I'm not defenseless. I thought you were pissed at me, so you left. I would rather have you tell me this kind of shit instead of just walking away."

He looked down dejectedly. "I realize that now. I'm sorry."

Seeing the disheartened look on his face, a wave of guilt washed over me. I probably sounded harsher than I should have. I placed my hand over his and gave it a light squeeze; the sparks going off through the contact.

He looked up, his smile strained, but he laced his fingers with mine tightly, like he didn't want to risk me letting him go.

"I'm not mad at you, Rian. I just don't like being out of the loop. I understand now why you reacted like that."

He ran his thumb over mine rhythmically. "I was scared. Scared something was trying to take you from me."

My heart swelled. His revelation lifted a lot of the tension inside of me. I was struggling to think he was only going along with me because of the bond, but hearing him say that he wanted me, and he was reacting the way he did because he feared losing me, reassured that part of my heart that it wasn't just the bond. He wants me.

"I've been scared, too," I whispered.

"Of what?"

"The same thing," I admitted. I then looked at Parisa from the corner of my eye. She smiled back brightly, waving her fingers at me in that way prissy girls always do.

I want to bite those fingers right off her prissy little hand.

Taegan sighed loudly. "I'm scared too."

Rian and I both gave him a viscous look. "Fuck you," I growled.

"What? I'm feeling left out." Taegan looked up at Phoebe with puppy dog eyes. "Will you hold my hand and tell me everything will be okay?"

Phoebe held her hand out with a smirk. When Taegan placed his hand in hers, she locked their fingers and bent his hand back, making him yell.

"Fuck! Uncle! Uncle! I give!"

"You give your uncle what?" Phoebe chuckled darkly. "I don't understand what you're saying."

"You know very fucking well what I'm- AHH! I'm Sorry!"

Phoebe and Taegan bickered until Phoebe finally let go of his hand. Taegan always knows how to lighten the mood. It felt heavy there for a second, and I'm glad he butted in when he did.

There is something about Parisa that makes you forget she's there. I was more open than I ever would normally be around a stranger, or even not around a stranger. I don't share my feelings well with anyone but Sophia. Even though I wanted to gouge out Parisa's eyes and staple her hands to a goat's ass, then kick it in the shin, it felt like I could open up about anything under her attentive gaze.

She's annoying.

I sighed, feeling exhausted while trying to make sense of what Rian told me. It's hard to wrap my mind around it. "Why would something attach itself to me? What did I do?"

"That's what I want to find out." Rian looked at his annoying cousin. "Parisa?"

41

PILLOW TWINS

My glare as Parisa stood and walked over to me did nothing to deflect her annoyingly cheerful mood. Her tits bounced with every step that she took. They looked like giant water balloons. I want to pop them. No one's boobs should be that bouncy.

Taegan was making a point of looking away, looking uncomfortable. Phoebe looked unimpressed. Parisa just kept going with her bouncy booby walk around the table, happily not noticing the awkwardness it was causing.

"So," she stood behind me, her giant knockers pressed into the back of my head. I jerked away, but she quickly grabbed my head and pulled it back. When she touched me, a wave of calmness shot through my body, making me relax against the pillow twins. "Rosie. That is such a beautiful name. Roses are the most magnificent of flowers. They can be so resilient, versatile, and are always exceedingly gorgeous. Their beauty often comes at a cost, but if you can get around the thorns and handle them with care, they can gift you with more than just their beauty. I personally love rose oil and rosehip tea."

Parisa rambled on about my name while messaging her fingers on my scalp. It felt so good. She and her giant boobs can do this to me whenever she wants.

"What the hell is she doing?" Phoebe muttered in a low, cynical voice.

"Hush," I slurred, not wanting my scalp rubbing boob-pillow time to be interrupted.

"She's connecting with her, in a sense," Rian answered.

Parisa laughed in her high musical way. "I have to ease myself into her mind. If I don't, I could hurt her or there could be side effects."

"What kind of side effects?" Phoebe asked.

"Oh, you know, headaches, migraines, night terrors, bad dreams, memory loss. Nothing horrible."

"Memory loss isn't horrible?" Taegan scoffed.

"Or night terrors?" Phoebe added in an intimidating voice.

Parisa just giggled. "I won't hurt your friend. I'm taking special care of my cousin's special person," she smiled sweetly down at me. I returned her smile for once. Her fingers were now skimming the back of my neck. "Does that feel good?"

"Yes," I murmured, "so good."

It really felt amazing. There was a euphoric feeling traveling all over my body, making my toes curl and my belly button tighten.

"Hmm," she leaned down and rested her head on mine, squishing my head even more between her boobs. "I could make you feel so much better. Would you-"

"Parisa," Rian groaned.

She giggled. "I'm just teasing you. It would make a fun story to tell later that I pleasured your partner before you. All it would take is a single little...." Her hands traveled down the back of my neck, over my shoulder, then glided over my collar bones before Rian stopped her. That sent her into another fit of giggles. "Oh, you are the jealous one now, dear cousin." Her hands moved back to massage my scalp. I felt a bit disappointed, but I couldn't figure out why. "Are you not fond of sharing your things any longer, cousin?"

"Not her," Rian said coldly. "If you want compensation for your help, ask for it, but not from her."

"Oh, relax," she said. "I really am just teasing you. I wouldn't do that to your mate. I'm getting plenty of compensation just by devouring all the raging emotions exuding from your werewolf friends." She looked over at Phoebe. "Your vampire friend as well, though her mind is more similar to a werewolf's than a vampire. I would know." Her smile stretched, showcasing her perfect teeth. "I'm well acquainted with Lady Delilah." Her eyes glazed a bit as she sighed. "Very well acquainted."

"You're fucking a vampire ruler?" Phoebe asked. Leave it to her to be the most direct.

Parisa giggled but didn't answer.

"How did you meet Lady Delilah?" Taegan asked with genuine curiosity.

"My father," Parisa gleamed. "He gave me the task of alerting the ancient vampire of her old friend's descendant returning to her rightful place beside the Alpha of the original pack."

Alpha of the original pack? Wasn't that Blue Cliff Pack?

"When was that?" Rian asked.

"Soon after you came to us, right after your mother's banishment to the human realm."

I could feel Rian's shock. His hand on my knee tightens. His presence beside me is tense. I wanted to look over and offer him a smile or some level of comfort. Even just to put my hand over his again. Whatever Parisa is doing to me is making me too sluggish to do anything but just sit there, wedged between her boobs.

"Are you talking about my grandpa's first mate?" Taegan asked, leaning forward, invested in her answer.

"Of course," she grinned. "But by the time I had told Reika's old friend, the original sacrifice had already died from her own stubbornness and the curses effects. Time works differently between our worlds, so we only had to wait a few years for your mother to find your father. Your world had to wait decades. Lady Delilah, the progressive leader that she is, has always been deeply invested in the happenings of the werewolf world, especially when it came to your pack. It was her original lover's pack at the beginning of your kind."

"Her original lover?"

The fog was growing thick in my head, the euphoric feeling turning into drowsiness, but I clung on to hear the rest of what Parisa had to say.

"Oh, my. Do they not teach you your own history in your pack?"

Why would a vampire's werewolf lover be something we passed down in werewolf history? That's too personal. My grandma Elena is best friends with Lady Delilah. I wonder if she even knows those sorts of things about her friend?

"Time works differently in their world, as you have said. The time between the start of their kind and now is far too great. Honestly, though, I didn't even know this history." Rian sounded offended. Or maybe exasperated.

"Well, Lady Delilah's original lover, the first imprinting from a vampire, was to a werewolf from the original pack."

"What happened to him?" Taegan asked.

Parisa went quiet for a while, and then said, "He was killed by her. She has been trying to atone for killing her most cherished person ever since."

"Vampire venom can kill a werewolf," I slurred. "It poisons." My eyes were now struggling to stay open.

"That it can." Parisa's features looked crestfallen at that moment. That was the first time I had seen her with anything other than that gleeful smile.

Her fingers glided through my hair. She was whispering something under her breath, and within seconds, my eyes won the battle against my will as they slid shut. There was a warm feeling building in my center. It felt amazing, but not near as good as the sparks that were shooting off on my knee, letting me know that my mate was still there beside me.

42

Invaded Memories

Parisa

Rifling through this young girl's mind filled me with so much power. She had so many raw emotions to feed on still lingering in her memories.

All it would take is one change, one morphed perception into any of her thoughts, and I could change this girl's life forever. I could make it where she soiled herself when she heard a dog bark, make her believe spiders were living in her ears, change the way she speaks. Anything. The possibilities are endless. That sort of power always gives me a thrill. I know better than to use it on my cousin's lover, but just knowing I could gave me a drunken taste of superiority.

The more I searched her memories, the more I realized it was a lost cause. I needed to get to the connection the impressive alpha male had mentioned. I needed to search her soul.

The darkness was definitely there. I recognized the dark string he mentioned. The magic was dark, but powerful. I usually love a challenge, but this one may be too much. Even for me.

As I followed the connection, I could detect the type of magic this being possessed. He possessed. Only a man could be this arrogantly resistant to my dominance. When I thought I was finally about to break through the veil of protection he cast over himself, I was forced back with a vicious growl.

***

Rosie

"Rosie." I felt a tingling on the side of my face. "Rosie? Can you hear me?"

"What?" I tried to say, though my voice came out muffled.

My head felt dizzy, my body was heavy. It felt like the time I was waking up after surgery when I broke the bone in my leg as a child, before I got my wolf.

"Maybe she has that memory loss shit we were talking about," I heard Taegan's undeniable voice.

"Fuck you," I muttered, remembering what had happened.

Parisa's sensual head rubbing bull shit. It felt so incredibly good at the time, but now I was pissed. She didn't even ask me. She just squished my head between her massive tits and started rubbing away, saying all kinds of cringy shit about pleasuring me. She said that crap to her fucking cousin. My mate!

I tried to force my eyes open to find her and strangle her, but when I was met with the harsh light, I quickly closed them again and groaned.

"Easy, Rosie. I know that was a lot for your mind to go through." Rian was cradling my head in his lap. It was like déjà vu, only I was in a much more desirable lap this time. The sparks were helping me to feel better.

"What happened?"

"I went hunting," the girlish giggle of Parisa made me growl.

"Hunting for what?" I snapped, still struggling to open my eyes.

"Why, a man, of course," her flirtatious laughter bubbled out, and I wished I was unconscious again.

"I'm going to bite her," I warned Rian.

His fingers rubbed soothingly on my face, circling my eyes and relieving a lot of the strain. His magic was seeping into me, relieving my other symptoms from the brain fuck I just endured.

"Biting is always fun," she giggled at my threat.

When a deep growl rumbled in my chest, her giggling stopped. She must not pick up on social cues, or she just enjoys pissing me off.

"She was looking for the connection Taegan saw," he whispered, his voice like velvet. "She was tracing it to the source to see what was watching you. Who was watching you."

"And?" I finally was able to open one eye. His handsome face was right above mine, and I was lost in the beauty of his eyes. I'm staring at his lips.

"And it was a demon-bred fae creature. One that was exiled to the forbidden seas with all the other undesirable remnants of our dark history," Parisa told me, sounding more serious this time. "He wouldn't reveal himself to me, but I could explore his connection with your soul. The connection was built before any other connections were made. Not even the connections with your parents."

"Eww, has it been watching her for that long?" Taegan asked.

"Most likely," Parisa shrugged.

I felt like I was going to be sick. Did it watch me when I peed and shit like that, too? When I showered? When I... when I was alone at night? Doing things you can only do when you are alone?

I'm fucking mortified.

"Why?" Rian said gruffly. "Why would the connection be there before one with her own parents?"

"Your guess is as good as mine. She had no memories of the time she was in the womb for me to look through. I tried, but there were only muffled noises."

"You looked through my fucking memories too?!" I yelled, having the strength to sit up. Rian held me back, probably sensing my murderous rage.

"I had to," Parisa shrugged, seeming unafraid. "I didn't study the one unrelated to this. I did notice many of your memories were tainted with the dark energy of the demon. He must have been watching you at those moments, but there was never anything to tell me why he was watching you or why he started this infatuation with an unborn babe." She then turned a radiant smile towards Taegan. "I saw a few of those tainted memories with you. Sweat and grime fit you well, especially when you're in the nude."

"What the hell?!" I snapped.

Rian gripped me tighter, glaring at Taegan. Taegan looked confused, staring between Parisa and me.

"Were you watching me change or something? That's creeper as fuck you stalker."

"I didn't fucking stalk you! I'm not the fucking peeping Tom! She is!" I thrust a finger at Parisa, who was smiling angelically.

"Could this have been a memory of training?" Phoebe piped up, looking at all of us like we were idiots.

"Perhaps," Parisa giggled.

"What the fuck, man? You're just trying to stir shit up," Taegan complained.

"I do enjoy seeing the jealous side of my cousin," she winked at Phoebe. Phoebe just rolled her eyes and shook her head.

"I can't with her," I muttered to Rian. "I need air, or I'm going to pop her head like a pimple."

"Yeah," he looked warily at the way Parisa was smiling at Taegan. "I think I do too."

43

BUTTERFLIES

"Where are we going?" I asked Rian as we walked through the busy village streets.

"Somewhere less busy," he said, his voice sounding nervous. "Somewhere I think you will like."

His grip on my hand was firm, like he was scared that I might let go. Ever since we left that pond, he has been touching me in some way relentlessly. Either by holding my hand or resting his hand on my knee. There was always some kind of contact between us. I liked it. I liked the small show of possessiveness.

We passed a stall run by a creature that looked like a tree. He reminded me of Groot from the Avengers. His booth had delicious smelling skewers of some kind of sugary treat. They looked like little doughnut holes, but had nuts on the outside. The warmed sugar and cinnamon smell made my stomach growl loudly.

Rian laughed, stopping to stare down at me. "We never got a chance to eat, did we?"

"No." I shook my head, my cheeks growing warm from his gaze. "I don't think I've eaten more than a granola bar today."

"We can't have that," he murmured, turning us around to head back towards Mr. Groot.

Rian bought six of the skewers, then got us drinks from a stall next to the tree person. The drinks came in woven leaves, folded at the top like a pouch. You had to pinch the corners to get it to open up. The contents inside were a glimmering pink, and it tasted of berries, but not like any berries I had tasted before. It was like a raspberry, but a bit more acidic. Almost like a lime. The shimmers were a ground nut I had never heard of, and Rian told me it was used in place of a sweetener.

"These are delicious," I told Rian when we reached the outskirts of the village, venturing back out into the forest we had come from when we first arrived on the backs of the Pegasus horses.

The balls were doughy, with a tart red paste in the center. The outside was coated in cinnamon and the nuts were the same sort of sweet nuts that were in our drinks. They were just whole and roasted instead of ground up.

"I'm glad you like it." Rian offered me his last skewer as I finished mine. I gladly took it.

"Can we get more on the way back?" I asked. "I could eat ten more of these."

"If you want," he grinned, resting an arm around my shoulders. "We should take some of the nuts back to Miami with us. My mom taught me how to make these. I can make them for you whenever you like."

I bit my lip excitedly. I liked hearing him talk about our future together in Miami.

"So, you are coming back with me?" I softly asked.

He gave me a perturbed expression. "Why wouldn't I? Did... did you not want me to go back with you?"

"Of course I did. I just thought.... I mean...." My face was probably redder than the red paste at the center of the bread ball. "I know you were pretty set on coming back here."

"What do you mean, coming back here? Coming back to Alfheimr?"

I looked at the skewer in my hand, examining it instead of meaning his eyes. His hand pressed into my shoulder, making the tingles erupt. It made it so much harder to voice this concern. I really don't want to lose these sparks.

I need to know, though.

"Calum told me you were leaving our world and rejoining the fairy court after you guys were done with your visit to Miami. I.... I wasn't the nicest to you in the past." I cringed at my own words. "So I thought you might still have thoughts of leaving."

"Rosie," he stopped us and turned my body towards his. His hand rested on the side of my neck, right over where a mark would go if I were mated to another werewolf. Strangely, I was not getting the tingles there that I heard of between unmarked mates. The desire to mark and be marked is usually so strong that even looking at each other's necks can make a person submit to the bond.

I had an urge to bite him. It's the same urge I have had since I felt the bond click into place. It never goes away. When I flash my eyes at his neck now, I notice goosebumps popping up on his skin and a shiver traveling over him.

What made me get that uncontrollable urge to be dominated was when I felt his magic on me. Like when we were in the sky and he was helping me to calm down. When I first put on the necklace, I felt it too.

I wanted this man. I wanted him as my mate so badly. I prayed to the goddess that he felt the same way.

"I have no plans to leave you. Ever." Rian's voice was laced with sincerity. I could feel the resolve in his words. "You're mine," he stressed. "Mine. I can also say that I didn't really go out of my way to get on your good side back then. But I'm going to now." He pulled me close, making it really hard to not drop the skewer or my drink. "I will do anything I have to do to make sure you feel for me the way I feel for you."

His eyes were like galaxies again, and I was already lost in them. His lips were just a breath away from mine. I could feel the air of magic surrounding him morphing to surround me.

"How...how do you feel about me?" I asked in barely a whisper.

His shimmering eyes looked down at my lips, then back up. He licked his bottom lip slowly, biting its corner. The most airy moan left me as I watched the sensual movement. He groaned, resting his head against mine.

"I feel like every breath you take is a gift just for me. I feel like the very ground you walk on must be a holy place, because I endlessly desire to just worship at your feet. I feel... I feel like my world shifted when I saw you at your party. You are the axis on which my world spins. You are my center. You," he gripped my face between his hands. "You are all I need, in any world we may reside. All I need is you, and I feel like my soul will be complete."

"Rian," I whispered. I lost the fight to keep my food in my hands. The only thing I hunger for is him. I hurriedly gripped the front of his shirt and pulled him towards me, crashing my lips to his and welcoming the dominance he once again displayed in his returning kiss.

His lips were tender but demanding. His tongue urged my lips to part before it dove right in. My entire body felt like it was on fire. I was burning for him.

As he lifted me in his arms, my legs wrapped around his waist. I was moving my body impossibly closer to his. I wanted nothing between us. I have never felt so desperate before. The sparks and the bond are maddening enough, but the way he was reading my body, anticipating my every movement, reacting to make cords of pleasure shoot through my center made everything about this more intense.

"Rosie," he moaned, pushing my back against a tree and grinding his firmness between my legs. I gasped. The sensation was like nothing I had ever felt before. I gasped again, the sound coming out whiny and wanting. "My Rosie," he husked, bucking his hips again.

I was going insane. The urge to bite him was overwhelming. He lowered us to the ground, and now I was grinding myself on his lap, my lips moving hungrily with his, devouring the sounds both of us are letting escape.

He leaned back, shaking a bush behind him, and then suddenly the sky was filled with glowing blue butterflies, stunning me for a moment.

Both of us stopped our attacks on one another to watch as hundreds of glittering blue butterflies, glowing more brilliantly than the moon, came out from the bush where they were resting. As they flew higher in the sky, more butterflies joined them from the trees and other plants around. It was the most beautiful and magical thing I had ever seen. I was stunned and grinning with amazement at the sight.

"Beautiful," I gasped.

"Yes," Rian husked, gliding his hand to the back of my neck. "You are."

That brought my focus back to him. He was one to talk. His face was painfully beautiful in the glow of the butterflies around us.

44

KING OF HER WORLD

Rian

Watching her face transform with the most lovely smile, her beautiful eyes lighting with delight, made my spirit soar. She loved the butterflies. I knew she would.

I couldn't take my eyes off of her. Every little action of hers brought me such joy. Every expression on her face made my heart sing.

She's mine. I'm growing more and more confident that no one will be able to take her from me. She wants me and I want her. Everything else will soon fall into place as long as we both remember that.

"Mine," I groaned against her lips. "You're mine."

"Yours," she breathed. "I'm yours."

A sound of deep satisfaction left me, and she moaned with the sweetest voice in response. I meant for us to just talk, to clear the air, but this desire for her, this need to make her mine in every way that truly matters, surged through me. I want to claim her. I want to leave my mark on her so that no one can ever change or take away. I want to leave no question as to who she belongs to, because there was no question that I belong to her. Entirely.

The moisture building inside her shorts was making slick noises as she ground against me. My dick stirred, imagining how warm and inviting that place would be. My fingers flexed into her waist as thoughts of diving into her wetness filled my mind.

I hesitated to go further, not sure if she was ready. I was ready. I want nothing more. That wasn't why I brought her out here. I needed to tell her everything that Parisa found without her making my mate any more aggravated than she already was. Then that moment shifted into the scene we are in now. I didn't know what to do. Keep going and finally fulfill all of my desires, or pause and talk?

The internal battle doesn't last for long. She made the choice quite clear as she lifted my shirt with a low, possessive growl. Her fingers glided over my abdomen and chest. Her excitement showed in her breathing and the fevered way she was moving on top of me. Her voice caught as she fully pulled my shirt over my head, her eyes roaming over my bare chest hungrily.

When she stared at the sensitive spot on my neck, I could feel her eyes caressing my skin like the softest of tingling touches. I could feel her thoughts.

She wanted me as much as I wanted her. For once, I'm not going to overthink this. I'm going to do what we both clearly want.

"I want you, Rosie," I moaned next to her ear. I undid the loosely tied cape around her throat, pushing it off her shoulders.

"Yes," she gasped. "Yes. Please." She ground her pussy right over my hard dick, and it flexed against her in response, wanting more.

She's never done this before. With anyone. This will be her first time. I want it to be more magical than anything she has ever imagined. I wanted to drive any thoughts she had ever had about anyone else right out of her mind, surpassing them with the pleasure I could give her. I wanted to override every single desire and dream she has ever had and make every one of her future dreams about me. I was about to carve myself into her heart, her body. All of her.

I want her.

"Rosie," I moaned, pulling her shirt over her head. "Rosie." My lips attacked hers, devouring her whimpers as I unhooked her bra and slid it down her arms. Her breasts fit perfectly in my hands, her soft skin like velvet. I pinched her tight nipples between my fingers, making her cry out, grinding wildly in my lap. She pushed her chest more into my hands, so I squeezed tighter, watching as her face transformed with the sweet pain.

"Fuck," she groaned when I bit down on her soft chest. I sucked on her sweet-tasting skin, loving every reaction it brought out of her.

"Lay down," I told her, pushing her down to lie upon the cape she had just been wearing. Her back arched as I moved my kisses down from her chest, nipping at her toned belly. Then I met her gaze as I slowly pulled down her shorts, taking her underwear off with them.

She was stunning. Every inch of her body looked carved by angels. She was shivering under my admiring gaze. I would have to do everything I could to warm her body back up. I was looking forward to the task.

Still holding her gaze, I placed open mouth kisses right above her beautiful blushing center. Her back arched as I moved further south and my lips met hers for the first time.

She tasted as sweet as the rest of her. The smell alone was intoxicating, but combined with her flavor, I felt like a starved man devouring my first meal. Her hole was so tight. It squeezed around my tongue. I continued to lap up her juices, massaging her walls. I was humming against her delicious pussy, holding her body in place as she trashed about.

She was fighting me, but also gripping my hair, holding me in place. Soon, her body was rocking, riding my face, making me impossibly more turned on. I could do this all night. I'm sure in the future, I will. She is sweeter than any exotic face nuts and desserts. I'll feed her any of those as long as I always get to eat her like this. She is my new favorite meal.

"Fuck, Rian," she cried. "Yes. Fuck, yes. Wha-what's...."

Her legs began to shake, her walls getting tighter, her pussy pulsing against my tongue. My thumb was furiously rubbing against her slit, and in seconds, she exploded in my mouth. I moaned, consuming every part of her. Everything that she gave me. All of it is for me.

"Rian," she whimpered. Staring down at me with a glazed expression.

My dick was throbbing, pressing painfully against my zipper at seeing her wonton state. I made her like that. Me. No one else has ever seen this side of my Rosie. My Alpha mate. My entire life I have lived in the shadows of Alpha's, but this one before me makes me feel like I'm the king of her world.

45

BELONG TO ME

Rosie

R ian's eyes were glowing. They were hooded with passion, but glowing as he stared down at me. He was licking his bottom lip, his glowing eyes moving to catch every little movement in my body. Every little shiver and tremor. My body was still exploding with them after what he just did to me.

His lips were shining with my cum. He ate me out in the most carnal way, with no reservations whatsoever. The way he was licking his lips, it was as if he was savoring every drop of my essence and wishing for more.

My back arched, the lingering effects of my first given orgasm making rolls of pleasure still vibrate through me. My pussy felt tense and swollen, but I was still desperate for more. More of what this man could do to it.

He moaned when I ground my pussy against his front, his hardened member jumping behind his zipper. His thumb circled my oversensitive clit a few more times, making me jerk back and whimper. He then moved one finger inside me, and then slowly inserted a second. I thrashed and moaned from the invasion, crying out when he pumped them in and out, then spread them apart, stretching me. He did it several more times, then curled those fingers inside of me, the sensation making my hips circle against his hand.

My body was so overwhelmed. I had never done any of this before. I had only heard and imagined what it would be like. Nothing my mom or friends told me could have prepared me for this. Everything was so much better than I thought it would be. Even the painful invasion of his fingers felt good. Too good. My mind couldn't even process how good everything felt.

"I can stop if you need me to," Rian husked. His glowing eyes where my moving galaxies rested were burning with his desire. "If you want to wait, tell me now," he bit his lip, "but I don't want to." He pushed his erection into my thigh, making me gasp. It felt so much harder. So much bigger than I imagined.

I wanted it, I didn't want to stop either. We probably should. In the back of my mind, I knew this was selfish of me, and that I should be thinking about the mission we were on, the creepy stalker that had been invading my head, praying that Julia was alive and that we would find her soon.

All I could think about was Rian, and how I never wanted this moment to end. How I couldn't stop, no matter the reasons I should. I needed this. We needed this. We both needed this assurance that our feelings were the same. That our hearts and our bodies belong to one another. That our souls would forever intertwine.

I needed this, and Rian did, too.

I shook my head adamantly. "Don't stop," I begged. "Please, Rian. Don't stop."

He groaned huskily. He stared at me with total devotion, unfastening his pants and letting them fall to his knees. When I saw it, his thing, a pathetic whimper escaped my lips. He looked like a god, like one of those carved statues in the history books of Greek deities. There was no way a fig leaf could hide what he was gliding his hand over right now. He was pumping his thick dick in his hand, coating it with the wetness from his fingers that he took from my pussy. I ran my hands over my body, watching him.

He leaned over me, sucking one of my nipples into his mouth while rubbing his thickness against my warmth. His mouth traveled up my chest, nibbling on my sensitive neck. He groaned, centering himself at my center while kissing my wanting lips. My folds parted, and the head of his dick stretched me to the point I finally felt the pain I heard would happen during my first time. It ached, and I whimpered pathetically.

"Shh, Rosie," Rian whispered roughly. "I got you, baby. I'll make it not hurt. I got you, Rosie."

His large hands gripped my sides, tingling magic moving over my skin and sinking into my core. He was using his magic to take all the pain and discomfort away, leaving only the pleasure and this insanely satisfied relief. As he moved his thick dick deeper into me, I felt the tearing of my virginity, but I got none of the pain. I cried out solely from the blissful acceptance my body had of my mate.

We were one. Our bodies were fused together in the most intimate way. Tears filled my eyes, the bond inside me singing in triumph.

"Does it hurt?" Rian asked, nuzzling and then kissing away the tears from the corners of my eyes. "Does it hurt, baby?"

"No," I said, my voice catching in my throat. "No, it doesn't hurt. I'm just....so happy," I choked. "This feels so right."

He smiled softly. "I'm happy too. You're mine," he said once again. I could hear the bliss and fulfillment in his voice. "All mine. This is how we were meant to be."

I choked on a sob, smiling as I wrapped my arms around his neck and pulled him in for a kiss.

His hips began to move. His thrusting started out slowly, and then picked up the more intense our kiss became. We were soon just moaning into one another's mouths. I was meeting his every thrust now, rolling my body into his movements, that mind-numbing friction building in my nerves.

He pulled me into his arms, sitting back so I was sitting on top of him, my body bouncing with his upward thrusts, coming down hard so the pleasure exploded deeper and deeper inside of me.

I cried out incoherent pleas, never wanting this pleasure to stop. I felt so full. So stretched. My body felt so attuned to his. Both of us were moving in this most exotic and intimate of dances. His hands roamed my skin, and I was clinging to his neck. His magic was still flowing into me, but it felt different now. It wasn't soft and soothing. It was dominating and possessive. It was moving to every corner of me, filling my soul. It was transforming all of me and making me his.

The more the pleasure built inside me, the more possessive his magic becomes. It was taking all of me, and I was freely giving myself to it.

My pussy was tightening with those same rolling currents of pleasure from before. My center was ready to explode. Rian seemed to know it too, because he was relentlessly grinding his dick inside me, hitting this same spot over and over again. It made my legs shake and my belly tighten uncontrollably.

"I want to mark you," he husked. "I want to imprint myself on to you forever."

"Yes," I moaned, my voice coming out in a garbled cry. "Yes, Rian. Mark me."

My teeth were tingling, desperate to do the same. My tongue started to mindlessly trace that delicious smelling spot on his neck, the place where his scent was the strongest. He shivered, gripping my shoulders, holding me in place. I cried out against his skin when his magic seeped into me stronger than before. The buzzing on my shoulder burned sweetly and traveled down my back. My teeth sank into his neck as my orgasm rocked me entirely.

Fireworks were shooting off inside my head. He groaned in the deepest, sexiest voice, letting all of himself out inside me. I felt it seeping out around him as my pussy twitched with its own ongoing orgasm.

I marked him, and I was sure that he marked me. I felt it in our souls. I felt that connection snap into place. Our souls were mending together, the bond being fulfilled.

"Rosie," he husked, holding my head in place. "My Rosie."

I could feel him. I could feel the peace inside of him now that he knew I was his. Forever.

After our orgasms died down, I retracted my fangs, licking the wound clean. My mark was glowing on his skin, catching the moonlight as it scarred over with the permanent mark.

"Rosie," he roughly whispered my name again.

I laughed breathlessly. "I like the way you say my name," I told him. We collapsed to the ground together, Rian holding me on top of his chest.

"I want even your name to belong to just me," he admitted. "I want to claim every part of you."

"I think you just did," I giggled, my voice hoarse from my cries and moans.

46

Baby Girl

Carli

Bailey, Parker and I were now sitting in my pissed off husband's office. Alpha Max and Thyra stepped over to her world to find our kids while the rest of us went back to the packhouse. Bailey was staring at her phone, looking depressed as shit. Phoebe wasn't picking up the phone. Bailey was getting that same out of service message she got every time she attempted to call her son, or I got when I tried to call Rosie.

Simone and Vincent went to see Lady Delilah to find out what happened to the Beta. I had my suspicions already, and by the look on Bailey's face, I knew she was thinking the same. If Phoebe was still in this world, Bailey's phone calls would go through to voicemail at least.

Parker was fuming. He drove Bailey and me back, and didn't say a word the entire drive. I could tell he was just waiting until we were alone, then he was going to explode. He wanted to check on our daughter multiple times in the last few days. He actually threw a tantrum like a brat when I told him Rosie would be gone for a week to finalize things with her new mate. Overprotective father that he is, I had to threaten him to get him to leave her alone. I could see every time that he looked my way that he blamed me a bit for the disappearance of our daughter.

Bailey pressed her phone to her ear again and sighed. "Damn it. I can't just sit here and wait. I'm going to go talk to Court to see if she has heard anything from Phoebe. I'll be back."

I smiled tightly, understanding how she felt. I was fucking pissed the other night about not being able to do anything when Rosie's friend went missing. The feeling was so much worse when it was your own child.

As the door closed, it was like a switch was flipped inside of Parker. He growled deeply, leaning over his desk and glaring at me. He'd been waiting for this chance to unload. He was waiting to turn off being a diplomatic alpha so he could be a pissed off father instead.

"That punk kidnapped my fucking daughter." His hooded eyes were so cold and vicious. "That fairy brat stole my daughter, and you pushed her right into his arms."

"Uh, I would check your tone with me right now. You aren't going to lash out at me because our daughter chose to go to the fairy realm to save her friend. You and I both know that is what she is doing. Back your ass up, and try again."

"You stopped me from checking on her," he snapped.

"They were supposed to be making me my grandbaby," I huffed. "I didn't know he would whisk her away on a magical honeymoon."

Parker's nostrils flared. "Listen here, woman," he shook his finger at me. "I-"

"I know you are not shaking your fucking finger at me." I raised my eyebrows.

He remained pissed, but slowly curled his finger in.

"She just turned eighteen. She doesn't need to be mated yet. She sure as hell doesn't need to be making a baby when she still is one herself."

I scoffed. "Yeah. Because you sure waited to mark me when my eighteenth birthday came."

The muscles in Parker's neck ticked, his jaw tense. He was going to give himself a hernia or hemorrhoids if he didn't calm his ass down.

"That was different."

"You're right. It was. You knew we were fated mates for four years and left me in the dark, abandoning me during the worst time in my life. I think you like to demonize any other men that might be interested in your daughter because you still remember the shitty stuff you did. Your attitude is not helping and your anger is irrational. Don't act like Rian is a bad guy. He's not. He did nothing wrong and you are being a hypocrite."

"HE KIDNAPPED OUR DAUGHTER!"

"HE DID NO SUCH THING!" I slammed my hands on his desk. Parker jumped back in surprise.

He looked hurt, probably because of me calling him out on the shit from the past. I dealt with those demons years ago, but Parker never fully did. I know he's so overprotective because of me. Because of those four years of hell and the effects they had on me later.

He was being a hypocrite. I was going to call him out on it. Not to start shit, or because I haven't forgiven him, but because I love my daughter, and by extension, I love Rian now, too. Reese is allowed to do all kinds of shit Rosie isn't allowed to do, like stay out all night, have Karina sleep over, not tell us where he was going and who he was going to be with all the time. He can't be overprotective of one kid and not the other just because of their genders. Parker named Rosie his heir. It's time he started to treat her as one. He still sees her as his little girl.

He treats boys who are Rian's and Taegan's age that even look Rosie's way like they're guilty of all the shit Parker did when he left for college after finding out we were mates. He, for four years, lived like a shitty mate and just assumes that other men will do the same to our daughter. Maybe because he hasn't forgiven himself or something. I don't know. I just know that I'm not going to allow Parker to demonize Rian.

"You know as well as I do she wanted to go save Julia. She wanted to do something instead of accepting that there was nothing to be done. That boy, all he is guilty of, is doing all that is in his power to help her set forth to do what she believed was right. He is being a good fucking mate already. While you like to put Rosie and me in this protective cage, guarding us out of fear, it looks to me like he elevated her and let her spread her wings. Yes, she is our fucking daughter, but she is an Alpha first."

"She is still a child," he growled.

"No. She's not. The sooner you realize that, the sooner she will start talking to you about shit like this, too. You were going to fucking punish her for getting a simple tattoo. On her own adult body. If she can't even talk to you about shit that you don't agree with, she will never be comfortable talking to you about shit that really matters, like going to a fairy realm with her mate to save her friend. The more you continue to treat her like a child, the more of a rift you are going to cause between you. Shit, I feel like I'm constantly telling her "I'll talk with your dad," or "I'll deal with your dad". When she's Alpha, her mom isn't going to be able to be a buffer between the both of you anymore. She will just leave you out of the loop all the fucking time. And," I leaned in closer, my voice turning cold, "if you keep this shit up about her mate, she might cut you off completely. There is no choice between a person's mate and their parent. You should know that better than anyone. She will choose him."

Parker's brows pulled down. He looked like he wanted to argue, but he knew I was right. I know I'm right. These were hard truths that needed to be said.

Yes, she is his daughter, but she is my daughter too. I know her strength and I know her resilience. I know she will be fine and will make it back home after accomplishing what she set out to do.

"She's still my little girl," Parker said in a much weaker voice. He looked ready to break. Or break something. I didn't know, but I went around his desk, pulled his chair back, and plopped myself down in his lap, to calm him and put him back together like he always does for me.

"I know she is. She is my baby girl too. But she is more than that now. You can't treat her like your little girl forever. Not when she needs to be an Alpha first."

"You act like you're an expert in Alphas," Parker muttered, wrapping his arms around me, his hand sliding on my neck to rest over my mark.

"I have been dealing with one for most of my life," I laughed dryly. "One that is a particularly huge pain in the ass."

"You're one to talk," he snorted.

I smiled, resting my head on his. I closed my eyes and let his scent and the bond overwhelm me. "I love you, Parker. I love you so much. I forgave you so long ago for the stupid mistakes you made when we were still kids. I know you forgive me for my stupid shit daily. Rian is a good kid. He will be a great mate for our little girl. Hurry up and forgive yourself now so you can see that too."

Parker was quiet for a few moments, running his hand up and down my arm. I felt his emotions shifting. I felt his inner struggle and the anger morphing into pure guilt. It breaks my heart to know he is still carrying this guilt from so long ago.

"I'll try," he said meekly. "No promises."

I smirked, knowing my husband. If he said he was going to try, that meant he was going to do it.

"I'll try if you quit pushing your obsession with babies onto our daughter. Deal?"

My smile fell from my face. A fierce growl tore out of me. "That is not the fucking issue right now."

"Oh, it's one of many," he chuckled, holding me in his lap when I tried to push myself away. "I'll quit painting him as the bad guy if you quit micromanaging their...." he cringed, "their relationship."

"Sex life." I pushed against his chest. "Is it that hard to imagine your daughter having a sex life? Sex makes babies. I'm just preparing."

"No, you're meddling. Let her graduate college at least before demanding grandbabies."

"Fuck you!" I snapped, pushing against his chest.

"Okay," he growled, lifting me in the air and roughly laying me across his desk. "You want a baby so fucking bad, I'll give you one."

"YOU CAN'T!" I yelled. "You can't reverse the snip snip. Remember, asshole?"

"I can," he smirked, bending over me to kiss my mark. My body shivered, and the fight left me. "Make me another baby girl so I can let our first one go."

Fuck. He's convincing me already.

He pushed his dick between my legs, and I groaned loudly, biting his ear as my last act of defiance.

Just then, a mind link came in from the border patrol. *"Alpha, Luna,"* Cole, one of Matt and Lilly's boys, said.

Parker and I both groaned in annoyance at the disruption. *"What?"* Parker tried to keep the annoyance out of his voice.

"Uh, a very pissed off Alpha just passed through demanding to know where Luna Bailey was."

Parker sighed, resting his head between my tits. *"Okay. We'll deal with it."*

"Looks like Axel is here," I smirked.

"It looks like it. We'll come back to this later."

47

MATE SWAP

Parker and I made it out to the lobby right as Axel was pulling up. He didn't even bother to find a parking spot. He parked right outside the packhouse doors, slamming the door before he walked in, radiating the aura of a fucking pissed off grizzly bear.

He looked like he came right from the job site. His blonde hair was thick with dust and dirt. He had smears of grime all over his arms and neck, though his face and hands looked like they had been washed a few times. His buffalo plaid, Cabela's work shirt and Carhart jeans were stained with grease and whatever else can be found in the Alaskan wilderness. His Richie Bros hat was so dirty that the logo that I'm sure was supposed to be orange was dusty gray. He looked like a hot mess. Emphasis on the hot, but a mess. Maybe I should get Parker a plaid shirt and have him roll around in some dirt. Bailey likes herself a dirty man. I don't blame her.

Shit, Canada must me wild. Even Casey, who just wore workout attire and Nikes when he lived here, dresses like some kind of sexy lumberjack most days. I'm going to suggest to Bailey having our men swap clothes for Halloween. I wonder what Axel will look like in Tommy Bahama or Armani? He probably won't look half as good as Parker, but I'm dead certain that Parker will look fucking yummy as heck in Axel's dirty attire. I hate being dirty, but wouldn't mind getting a little dirt on my knees if Parker was willing.

Fuck, I needed to calm down. Parker got me all excited with his talk about putting a baby in me. I was letting my mind wander. I'm still asking Bailey later, though.

"Alpha." I pressed my lips together for a few seconds to hide my amusement. "To what do we owe this surprise visit?"

"Where is she?" Axel snarled, looking around like a madman. "Where the fuck is Bailey?"

I wanted to mess with him so badly and tell him something like she had just left to fly back to Canada, but Parker squeezed my shoulder in warning and told me in a mind link to behave.

"She's with Courtney. I can take you up there if you'd like," Parker said.

Axel looked ready to storm up the stairs without waiting to be led by anyone when Aly came into the room with her cousin. "Daddy!" She squealed, running towards him. "I thought you were in Alaska?" She hugged him around his waist.

I noticed Axel looked noticeably calmer upon seeing his eldest daughter. I thought with Alpha Max coming, along with most of this part of my Canadian family, that Alpha Axel was on board with their sudden visit. Looks like that wasn't exactly the case. No wonder why Parker didn't get a call from him, as is customary for Alphas to do. They're family, so I figured that with the situation going on with the kids and everything that they just forgot.

"I hurried back," he hugged her shoulders.

"Oh. Since you're here now, can we go swimming with the dolphins? Mom is freaking out about Tae and Gramps and Grandma just left. I really want to do it again. Please?"

"Just left?" Axel looked back at me and Parker. "Where the hell did my fucking dad go?"

I was so eager to tell him. I could see his top about to explode. The vein in his head was pulsing. Bailey was wound so tight right now, a little explosion from her mate might be just the thing she needed to settle the fuck down.

"Behave," Parker growled at me.

"Behave my ass. You behave, you bossy jerk." I elbowed him. "Bailey could use some angry sex right now."

"Not everything is solved with sex," he retorted.

"I'll remember that," I snubbed, not even hiding my amusement anymore.

"Alpha, I think we should talk with your mate," Parker said, ignoring me. "I don't know what she told you yet."

"Not a damn fucking thing," he growled.

Aly's little teenage nostrils were flaring, and she had on this disgusted face while staring at her dad. "Daddy, you smell like gas and buttcheeks." Aly sniffed his shirt, then pulled away.

"How do you know what buttcheeks smell like?" Conner asked, covering his smile.

Aly shrugged. "You smell like buttcheeks and I'm always with you."

"I do not," Conner whined.

"Do too. Go sniff someone's butt, then sniff yourself and you'll see I'm right."

"So you're saying that you sniffed someone's butt," Conner growled.

"I told you, I just know what you smell like, and you smell like dad's shirt. Minus the gas. Your butt probably smells like gas, though. Gas and buttcheeks."

"Aly," Axel grumbled, pinching his temples. "Just take me to your fucking mother. I'm not in the mood for any more shit right now."

"I imagine not smelling like gas and buttcheeks," I mumbled.

Aly giggled, but Parker gave me a look like I was about to get some angry sex myself. Too bad he already told me that sex doesn't solve everything. I'm going to torture him with that for a few days now.

Two tense alphas and two bickering teenagers make for a fun walk up the stairs. I was enjoying myself more than ever now.

Aly was the one who led everyone up the stairs, talking her dad's ear off about beating Conner at some game on the flight over. She then told Axel about how Conner was to scared to ask any girls for their numbers. He was apparently really awkward around them at ddinner,and she wanted her dad to know every detail. Conner tried to defend himself, but Aly, sassy as can be, shushed him every time he tried to talk and then continued on with her story.

When we got to the second floor, I noticed Reese arguing with one of his friends outside of the apartment lived in by Sophia and her family. I quickly recognized the friend as the boy that took Sophia to prom. My mind went frantic, desperate for the juicy details of what's going on there.

Then, two floors up, we ran into Calum, who looked freshly showered, heading downstairs.

"Alpha," Calum looked surprised to see Axel. "What are you doing here? Luna said you weren't coming."

"I'm sure she fucking did," Axel groaned. "Is she up there?" He pointed, indicating the Alpha floor.

"Yeah. She and mom are on the phone with Aunt Simone. Pheebs went missing now."

"No fucking surprise. Not one of you mother fuckers can be where you're supposed to be at any given fucking time or tell me shit about it. I had to drag my buttcheek-smelling ass all the way here to figure out this shit. Where the hell are you going now? Your ass disappearing, too?"

I couldn't blame Axel for being so frustrated and angry. Bailey obviously came without his permission and he was left out of the loop. As an Alpha, it's got to nerve-wrackinging for your Luna to leave and take all your offspring with her without approval. I would never do something like that.....

"No sir," Calum looked nervous under Axel's hostility. "I, uh, found my mate. I'm just going to check on her."

"Oh." Axel's face softened just a bit. "Congrats," he said curtly.

"Thanks," Calum ducked his head, then hurried the rest of the way down past us and down the stairs after weaving through our crowded group.

"Uh," Aly's eyes lit up, "I think you know the rest of the way. I'm going to follow him," Aly grinned excitedly.

"Me too!" Conner sounded just as excited. I could hear them murmuring to each other down the stairs. "That boy from the dining hall that was flirting with Sophia was outside her door. That was him, right?"

"Yeah," Aly agreed with her cousin. "Calum's going to punch someone."

"He's going to kill him." Conner sounded way too excited, suggesting his brother was about to turn homicidal.

Parker sighed, then looked at me. "Can you deal with that?"

I pressed my lips together while thinking. Which would be the better fight? Axel and Bailey or Calum versus the other boy?

Calum was the winner. I won't be allowed to do anything but watch if I go with Parker and Axel anyway, and with the angry sex in their near future, it wasn't worth it.

Putting on my most hospitable smile, I said, "Of course, hun," then skipped down the stairs. I could feel and hear Parker's sigh of exasperation behind me.

48

TEAM CALUM

Sophia

"Uh oh," Karina mumbled to herself, lying across my bed. Her red hybrid eyes were glowing like she was getting a mind link. It was probably from Reese. That's who she has been waiting for while hanging out with me, talking up her cousin every chance she could.

"What?" I asked.

Dad took mom out for dinner, since they knew I was with Karina. It's just us in the apartment.

I was sitting on the floor, painting my toes to distract myself from the fact Calum hadn't come to find me since I left him with his family earlier. Karina and I even went down to the dining hall for dinner, and he wasn't there. Isawe his brother and cousin there, but they were arguing at a table full of middle school girls, not paying any attention to me.

"Oh, uh, nothing. Reese is just….trying to take out some trash."

"Trash? They have a trash chute."

"Not that kind of trash," she muttered.

I put the nail polish brush back in the bottle and turned to look at her. "What kind of trash?"

Her smile was apologetic. "The kind that tried to get you to go out for froyo with him after dinner."

"Jason?" I gaped. "Reese and Jason are friends." Jason was a bit pushy, but that's why we left and came back here. Where is Reese that he can be arguing with Jason? I thought Reese was with Calum.

"Yeah," Karina shrugged. "But Reese likes his family more than his friends. He's team Calum," she giggled. "We're getting t-shirts made."

"Team Calum?" I huffed. "I feel like Calum isn't very team Sophia right now. He hasn't come to see me at all." Or explained who it was that he was making sisters with, even though he said he was going to wait to make babies with me. I was a little freaked out by his huge family, but I'm more upset now that I haven't heard from him since they got here.

"Girl, he was busy. Seems your bestie went and ran away with her princely mate."

"Nuh uh," I gasped. "Where? Did they go to the Keys?" There's an entire fairy village on an island down there, hidden from the human eye. We've always talked about going.

"Nope. Not Key West. I think they went a little further than that."

"Where?"

"One might say where they went is a world's away," Karina laughed. "She's using the fact that her mate is a fairy prince to the fullest as our future Alpha. I'm a bit impressed. It's not like her to go this far against her daddy."

"Is it worse than her getting her rebellious tattoo?"

"So much worse." Karina grinned, seeming thrilled by whatever or wherever it is that Rosie and Rian went. "Alpha Parker had a melt down."

"Tell me," I urged, bumping my shoulder on the bed.

"Well," she turned over, looking ready to spill some juicy gossip. "It seems she-"

"WHAT THE FUCK DO YOU WANT WITH MY MATE!?"

Karina froze, and I turned to stare out my open bedroom door towards the front door. That sounded like Calum.

"Uh oh." Karina jumped off my bed then raced for the door. I followed, and cringed when the sudden movement messed up my wet toenails.

Jason was standing on the other side of the door, but so were Reese and a very angry Calum. Calum's face was rigged, his brows pulled down, shadowing his eyes. His muscles were flexed like he was ready to attack someone.

Was it wrong for me to think he looked so hot right now? I'm biting my lips, trying not to show how attractive I find him right this minute, since I'm still a little upset at him and I have no clue what's going on.

"Calum, man, he was just leaving." Reese was barely holding Calum back. "He didn't know."

"I knew," Jason spat. "She's unmarked, dude. She's not taken yet."

Calum growled, and now Reese looked pissed.

"You know what? Fine." Reese raised his hands in the air and stepped aside. "You wanna fuck with the bull, you get the horns. He's a Gamma and a Childes, man. Your funeral."

Jason suddenly had the smarts to look scared, probably realizing he had messed up. Gamma Childes still led many of the training sessions and was known for being crazy strong. He's Calum's great-uncle. Calum's dad is known for how crazy strong he is too, and I hear that Calum's grandfather has even more of a reputation.

I could care less if Jason gets his face bashed in, but I don't want my parents to think badly of Calum for it being done at our front door. As Calum stalked towards Jason, trapping him in the corner by the door, I rushed out to wrap my arms around Calum's waist.

"He's not worth it," I squeezed him tight, staring up at him. "He's not worth the fight."

Calum's nostrils flared, his body tense and sprung tight, ready to react. I could see the effort he was putting into trying to calm himself, but that killer aura was still pouring out of him.

"I say, let him get at least one good punch in." Rosie's mom startled everyone, appearing at the end of the hall. "I heard what you said you brat," she glared at Jason. "You knew Sophia found her mate but still decided to chase her?"

Jason looked ashamed at last. "But she's not claimed, Luna."

"She's still seventeen you dipshit. Of course she's not. She has to wait until she can feel the bond too."

"She was alone. I thought maybe she didn't want him," Jason said as an excuse.

I scoffed and rolled my eyes. I told him I had found my mate and said no to his offer. Karina and I left when he chose to sit at our table and tried to keep talking to me.

This asshole took me to our Junior Prom, and it was a horrible mistake. I thought we were going as just friends, since Rosie had a just friends date too. Jason decided on his own to get a hotel room for after the dance, and spent the whole night trying to convince me to go there with him after. Rosie punched him in the gut at the end of the night and told him to take a hike. When he's between girlfriends like I'm sure he is now, he will try asking me out again, but I always say no.

We don't date pack members. Luna Carli has always stressed that it isn't a good idea. I never would have gone to get froyo with Jason, even if Calum wasn't my mate.

"Did she say she didn't want him?" Luna Carli asked.

I felt Calum twitch, then his entire body was still waiting for the answer.

"Not really," Jason looked sheepish. "She didn't say she didn't want him. I just assumed."

"You know what they say about people who assume?" Luna Carli raised a brow. I bit back a laugh, knowing the saying. Rosie uses it sometimes.

"No." Jason looked guilty and scared. Luna Carli wasn't a woman to mess with.

"You would know if you went to training in the morning," Reese said, looking disappointed in his friend.

"That's an idea." Luna Carli smiled. "Training in the morning. You two will settle this then." She patted Calum on the back.

Calum still looked tense, and I realized he never got his answer.

Jason began to walk away, looking shaken up. Before he got too far, I called out, "Jason!" He stopped to look back at me. His lip quirked up, looking a bit smug when Calum groaned. He was probably expecting me to apologize, then come with him or something. I'm not doing either of those things. "For the record, I want my mate. I want him more than anything."

His face fell. He finally looked defeated. Calum's arms wrapped around my shoulders, and his deep laughter caused me to stare back up at him.

"Good," he murmured. "I'm glad you want me, because I'm not letting you get away."

Crap, he's super handsome. I don't even remember why I was so upset.

"Team Calum," Karina chanted, throwing a fist up in the air, making Reese laugh.

I smiled. I guess I'm team Calum too.

49

PISSED ALPHA

Axel

"I'm sorry, Alpha. Had I known you were unaware your mate was here, I would have reached out."

"It's not your fucking fault," I growled.

It's the crazy woman I'm mated to's fault. I swear, when I get my gas and butt cheek smelling hands on her plump ass, I'm going to leave handprints on it. Not only did she not listen when I told her to wait, she even stole all our fucking girls and smuggled them over the border without letting me know. She knew I would tell her no. That's why she didn't tell me shit.

"Do you have an idea of what's going on right now? Where the kids are? All of our kids?" Parker asked.

"I know that they're all grown ass adults and don't need their mamas hunting them down just because of a bad fucking feeling," I grumbled.

"Hmm," Parker grunted, not sounding like he agreed with me.

We walked into the Alpha suite, and I growled, seeing my wayward mate clutching her phone in her hands, standing next to my breastfeeding cousin. Courtney saw me first and nudged her. Bailey looked away from another phone sitting on the table to look at me.

Her eyes went wide in surprise upon seeing my angry mug. "Axel? What are you doing here?"

Without saying a word, I marched over to her, dipped down, and tossed her over my shoulder with a possessive snarl.

"Hey! What the hell?! Axel!" She pounded on my back. Her phone slipped out of her hands, falling to the floor.

I smacked her ass on reflex, which made her moan. I smirked, looking over my shoulder so I could see her face in the reflection of a mirror on the wall. She pressed her lips together, embarrassed by the sensual sound. Her cheeks turned bright red, and her adorably sexy dimples showed.

Court had her free hand over her mouth, suppressing a laugh. "Guest room is right there," she pointed to the first room down the hall.

I nodded, taking my mate and heading that way. My strides were long and purposeful. I was on a fucking mission. A mission to put my mate in her fucking place.

"Really, Courtney?" I heard Parker say.

"What? Did you want him to screw her right here?"

Screwing isn't exactly what I planned on doing. I'm going to beat some sense into Bailey's stubborn ass. Literally.

I slammed the door shut with my foot and then aggressively threw my hostile wife on the bed. She huffed furiously, clearing the hair out of her face.

"What the hell, Axel?!"

"You," I grabbed her chin, leaning over her curvy body, "had me fucking worried sick. I told you to fucking wait for me."

"No!" She jerked her chin out of my hand and pushed her finger against my chest. "You said I couldn't leave the kids with my mom or go by myself. I didn't do either of those. The girls are here and your dad and Casey came too."

I growled deeply, pushing my body against hers, pushing the most dominating aura from me, but she didn't look the least bit intimidated. She never does. That's what makes it so much more satisfying when I get her to submit to my will.

"You know damn well that you weren't supposed to leave our pack until I got home. You manipulated everybody to get them to do what you wanted to do because you can't get your fucking tit out of our son's mouth."

"Thyra was determined to come, too! It wasn't just me! You don't even know what's going on!" she yelled right back at my face. "He's missing and you don't even care!"

"He's an adult," I said, my face barely an inch from hers. My hot breath fanned over her face, making her dazed. "I don't give a shit where the brat is. He's a grown ass man. He can do what he wants. He doesn't need his mama chasing after him every time he leaves the house."

"You don't even know where he's at! He's in the fairy realm. This isn't like he just flew up to Miami. He's in an entirely different world. A different world, Axel! He could get in so much trouble and you don't even care!"

"No, I don't, because I know that boy. If he's in the fairy realm, there's probably a good reason, and he doesn't need us to save him. If he gets in trouble, it's on him. We will help him then if he asks, but only if he asks. If he didn't ask for your help, you don't need to show up here and force it on him. Are you going to keep doing this shit after he becomes Alpha? You going to show up to every business meeting, every mission, every fucking little thing to hold his hand through it? Do you know how fucking worried I was when I got home and you weren't there?"

"I'm fine," she huffed. "I'm a big girl. I don't need you to babysit me."

"Oh, honey," I purred. "You need to be babysat more than anyone. You are so wrong and you fucking know it. You knew you weren't supposed to leave the pack lands without me. I told you."

"I was with your dad!"

"And now you're not. Casey isn't even here right now. And I had no fucking idea that you wouldn't be there when I got back home."

"I told you! It's not my fault that you do not listen to me!"

I listened to her. I listened to her for a fucking hour about why she thought our son was in trouble. That kid can do and see shit the rest of us can't even fathom. I know for a fact that he is fine and doesn't need our help. If he did, he would ask for help. Bailey is doing nothing but making herself worry.

"Your stubborn ass is asking for it." My face was tense, my jaw set. So many sadistic thoughts were running wild in my head.

"Asking for what?" Her eyes were telling me she already knew the answer to her own question. We've done this dance before.

Still, I took her by surprise, grabbing her by the waist and rolling her body over. I smacked her ass hard; the slap echoing around the room. She yelped, but backed her ass up, arching her back like she liked it. I know she liked it. She knew this was coming. She knew, and I could see that she actually wanted it. She always does. She likes it when I get pissed like this, because rough sex is usually what we both need.

I spanked her again, this time lower, so I could feel the swell of her pussy lips against my palm. Her yelling groan made my dick hard as a rock, pushing against the zipper of my pants.

Slowly, I pulled her leggings down, revealing her plump, round ass. Her wet lips made the most satisfyingly sexy sound from the moisture clinging to her panties. I licked my lips, knowing how she would taste.

I wanted her ass and pussy red and ripe before I partake in them. This was going to be torturous for her. It was going to be torturous for me, but the anticipation and seeing her frustration will make it so much more satisfying for me.

My hand winded back. I anchored her curvy body over one of my grimy knees, loving the way her soft flesh molded around me. When my hand came down, her answering scream made me shiver. She looked so hot, staring back at me with that fire in her beautiful eyes. The challenge in them was always something I loved to step up to. She was daring me to push her to her limits.

She must have been feeling as frustrated as I was. As desperate for the right kind of release as I was. Her mouth was open, her tongue pushing against the back of her teeth. After I beat her ass until it was juicy and red, as ripe as a fucking apple, I was going to fuck that sweet mouth of hers and shoot my first load down her tight throat. All the while, I would devour her dripping pussy, cleaning the mess my hand was making, slapping against it repeatedly. I wanted to feel her legs shaking around my head, her thighs suffocating me in her pleasure.

This was about to get so damn hot. Soon, this whole fucking packhouse would know how much she likes this rough game we were playing.

50

Rage Fuck

Bailey

"Axel," I groaned, clenching my thighs together when his hand came down again on my ass. "This isn't the time or the place."

I didn't know why I was still fighting this. I knew there was no turning back for him now. I knew the moment he walked in that this was the only thing that would calm his anger. Honestly, there was no turning back for me, either. The buzzing between my legs was uncomfortably throbbing and so, so wet. It was getting more wet with every hit.

"You're right. The time and place would have been at home the second I got back, but you chose to leave," he said venomously. I started to roll my eyes, but then his hand came down again and they just rolled upward at the pleasure.

I love rough and angry Axel. It makes it worth it to get him riled up like this. The circumstances still suck. This would be a lot more pleasurable if I wasn't so worried about our son. Not just our son, but now Phoebe was missing, too.

"I would focus on me right now, Bailey." Axel's deep voice made my belly clench and my heart race. He lifted his knee under me, making my ass go further in the air just as his hand came down again. As I was still screaming from the sharp stinging pain between my thighs and ringing against my lower lips, he shoved two fingers deep inside me, turning my scream into a guttural moan. "Fuck, you're so wet," he hummed, pumping those two large fingers in and out of me.

I was breathless, backing into his touch. I could no longer think about anything else but him. He was overwhelming me like he always did. His scent was all I can smell. His touch was all I could focus on. His voice was making every inch of my skin prickle with goose bumps.

"Damn it, Axel," I moaned, rotating my hips, riding his fingers. I growled when he pulled them away. His deep chuckle pissed me off, and when I turned to glare, I could tell that was his intention.

He slowly unbuttoned the top few buttons of his shirt, then pulled it over his head. His body was grimy and dirty. Muck creased into all his delicious muscles. He must have come here straight from the job site without a shower or anything. He looked so sexy like that. I love my mate looking all good and dirty. He knows it too. That gleam in his eyes and his knowing smirk were so fucking annoying, but I couldn't help but to lick my lips, wanting more of the incredible view.

His hands trailed over his perfectly sculpted abs, teasing me, slowly unfastening his belt. I groaned weakly when he pulled the belt free from his waist, then coiled it around his hands.

"What are you going to do with that?" I eyed the belt wearily. I liked being spanked, but being hit with the belt seems excessive.

"What do you want me to do with it?" He challenged, looking domineering, standing over me.

"Put it back on," I lied.

"Hmm," he crawled over my body, running a hand up my curves, squeezing my chest, then wrapping his hand around my neck, making me gasp. "I think it would look so much better on you."

"You took my pants already," I glared at him, though my heart wasn't in it. My heart was too busy pounding in my chest with the anticipation of what he was going to do to be angry anymore.

"I did. I'm going to take more than that from you here pretty soon." He gripped my neck tightly, running his tongue over my lips. My mouth parted, inviting him in. "Mmh, you taste fucking amazing." He licked his lips. "I bet you taste even better down here." He moved his hand from my neck down my body, teasing me, making sparks explode in the most sensitive places. Then he cupped my sex. I moaned loudly when his fingers pushed between my folds, diving into my wet center.

"Why don't you see for yourself?" I moved my pelvis against his fingers. They were curling inside of me. I wanted his tongue in there, too.

"I will," he smiled darkly, "but not yet."

He jumped up, straddling my body, pinning me to the bed. I swung my hands at him to throw him off, but he just captured my hands, holding them in his. First one, and then the other. I struggled, but he tied my hands together with his belt, a satisfied and cocky smirk playing on his lips. He held my tied hands above my head while one-handedly unfastening his pants. He shimmied them down his legs. His large, hard dick sprung free. My eyes focused on that throbbing muscle as it came closer and closer to my face.

"This guy is pretty pissed at you, too. Why don't you kiss him and make up first?"

"I'm gonna bite it," I growled.

"No, you're not. You love him too much."

Damn it, I do. I can already imagine how he would taste and the feeling of his head pressed against the roof of my mouth.

"Say ah." Axel pushed his dick in my face.

That little comment just pissed me off again, and the hunger I had is dwindling into rage. I snapped at it with my teeth. He barely pulled himself away in time.

"Fine," he growled, letting out a claw to rip down my shirt. It tore through the front of my bra, making my breasts spill free. He licked his lips, his eyes darkening. "Rough it is."

He flipped me onto my stomach roughly, making my hair go into my face as I yelled for him to stop. My hands were still tied, and before I could right myself, Axel lifted my butt into the air, spread my cheeks apart, then slammed his cock into me. He thrusted into me so hard that I fell onto my face, screaming, then sucked in a mouth full of my hair. Getting myself right was impossible. There was nothing sweet about the way he was hammering into me. He was being harsh and savage.

His nuts were slapping painfully against my clit, his dick pounding against my cervix. I couldn't breathe or figure out which way was up. I was drowning in the rough pleasure, disoriented by my flailing hair and the twisting way he was controlling my body. I couldn't even move my hands to help myself. Every time I tried to pull them out from under me, the thick belt would scrape against my heavy breasts, making it painful. I was defenseless to his rage fuck. I was simply his tool.

And in some fucked up way, I loved it.

Axel's grunts made the rough pleasure I was feeling so much more intense. I wanted to see his face. I bet it was beyond sexy right now. I might just cum from his expression.

He twisted my body, throwing one of my legs over his shoulder. He slapped my bare breast, making me mewl and hiss. He did it again and again, my perky nipples screaming at the sweet pain. He was taking all his anger and anxiety out of my body. This was a punishment from him, but I was loving it too much to actually learn the lesson he was trying to teach. That my body was his. His to command and look after. He could look after me like this whenever the fuck he wanted. I was still going to do what I wanted.

"Fucking hell, I love this pussy," he moaned. "It's the only part of you that can never lie to me. It always listens. Look how fucking wet you are for me."

"I...I can-can't see....anything....you sh-shit!" I said while being jostled roughly back and forth.

He leaned over my body, bringing my leg with him, pushing his dick all the way to the hilt inside me. I felt so full, so stretched. He moved his hands gingerly over my face, moving my hair back. His hands were so tender, his thumbs poking and rubbing against my dimples and my jaw, but his lower half was still relentless. He liked fucking me hard enough to see my thighs jiggle, and that's what he was doing right now. He loved my soft, giving body, but my face was like a treasure to be handled with care.

His breath mixed with mine, the mood and our desires tense. When he passionately met my lips with his, it was as carnal as the way he was fucking me. He was dominating, driving moans and guttural cries from my mouth. His tongue explored and controlled me. My breath hitched as he took what he wanted from me, giving me mind-blowing currents of torturous pleasure in return.

"You're still sucking on this dick before I let you go," he threatened, then bit my lip. "I'm going to fuck this sweet, defiant mouth of yours."

"Not a fucking cha-AHHH!" I screamed as he picked up his pace. The sound of flesh slapping roughly together was almost as loud as my cries. This was violent and torturous. My entire body was buzzing with raw pleasure.

He snarled, nibbling on my neck. Then I felt his canines elongate, sinking into my mark and forcing me to cum. I screamed so loudly, but he didn't stop with the violent pounding until my orgasm bled into another. I had tears streaming down my face, my body shaking uncontrollably. The tremors were as powerful as the orgasms.

"Fuck," Axel groaned, licking my neck while slowly pulling out of me. His seed was seeping out of my pussy. There was so much. I just knew I was going to end up pregnant again. There was nothing careful about us this time, and angry sex always leads to me getting pregnant. "Mmh," he looks down at the mess he made inside of me flowing out onto my thighs. "You made a mess."

"What!?" I shrieked, pushing against his chest. With him still, I finally could pull myself out of the restraining belt. "You're the one that did it."

"Only because you wouldn't suck it," he smirked. He tried to kiss me, but I snapped and bit his lips together.

"Clean up your mess," I growled, pushing his head down. His deep chuckle tickled my skin and made butterflies flutter in my chest.

"Okay. Up you go," he grunted. He surprised me by picking me up, wrapping my legs around his waist, and holding my ass to keep me in place.

"Where?!"

"Bathroom," he smiled, running his lips along my jaw. "Your daughter told me I smell like buttcheeks and gas. Let's shower and I'll get you clean from the inside out."

"This isn't our room, Axel," I hissed.

"Too late to worry about that. It smells like Calum's been sleeping here. I'll warn him to change the sheets."

Great. Calum was going to love that.

I stopped fighting Axel, going along with his shower idea, since I probably need one too. I breathed a sigh of relief. I was freaking out all day, but I finally felt calm. Axel got my mind off Taegan really fast and now that I was more rational, I could see that Axel was right. Taegan could take care of himself. I'm sure he's fine right now.

51

HUNGRY MAN

Carli

"Alright you two." I looked around the stairway at where Aly and Conner were hiding, hoping for a fight. Both of them looked very disappointed. I placed my hand on my hip and clicked my tongue at their shameless spying. Such little instigators. "Up. Let's go. Maybe we can still catch the fight between your parents." I nodded at Aly.

"Ew, no," she wrinkled her nose in disgust. "We'd rather go downstairs."

"Yeah. You should too." Conner gagged.

"Why?" I looked between them.

Just then, Parker mind linked me. *"Trade me. Holy cow, trade me."* I could feel his discomfort.

"Everything is fine here." I looked over at Calum whispering into Sophia's ear, then the two of them walked back into her apartment with Reese and Karina. *"It was pretty uneventful. The guys will fight it out at training in the morning. Are Axel and Bailey fighting that bad?"*

"I don't think they're fighting," he groaned. *"Office. Meet me in my office. Don't come home."*

Fuck that. I wanna know what's going on now. Even if Aly and Conner are running the other way and with Parker's warning, my curiosity won't let me just let it go.

I took the stairs two at a time, but when I got to our floor, I almost tripped on the last step when a loud throaty scream startled me. Parker opened our door, leading a giggling Courtney out. Bailey was screaming and moaning so embarrassingly loudly. I was blushing just hearing her. Axel growled loudly. I was suddenly scared for his mate. What the hell was he doing to her? Parker looked mortified.

"Are they always like that?" Parker asked Courtney.

"When Bailey pisses off Axel, they are. So....yes," she giggled. "If she grocery shops without telling him, he can get like that."

"Sheesh, that's intense."

"We raise our men rougher up north," Courtney joked.

"They're definitely a lot dirtier." I bit my lip. "In all the good ways."

Parker growled, grabbing my hips and pulling my body back against him. "You want me to be dirty and rough?"

I smirked, giving Courtney a side eye, and then said, "No thanks. Sex isn't the answer to everything. Remember?"

"It's the answer to a whole lot of things," Courtney said. "Why do you think I have so many kids?"

"According to Parker it's not." I sighed, like the thought depressed me. Parker's fingers were digging into my flesh, and I could feel his regret at saying those words. Not only was I right and Axel laid it down on Bailey the moment he saw her instead of them having a discussion, or even a regular fight like I'm sure Parker thought they would, but now Parker knows I really am going to use those words against him until I feel he is properly tortured and practically begging for some nookie.

"What a foolish thing to say." Courtney shook her head, looking amused. "If that's the case, you must be free tonight to have drinks with me and Simone? Bailey's going to be preoccupied for a while since, you know, her mate does believe sex is the answer to everything."

"I would love to go for a drink!" I grinned, feeling Parker getting angrier and angrier behind me. "I think there's a Magic Mike show in town."

"Carli," Parker said in a warning tone.

"Hush, sweetie." I patted his hands, then pinched them when he wouldn't let me go. "I already invited you and you said no."

"Casey will love that." Courtney sounded truly excited. I don't know if it was for the men's strip show or about what Casey would do to her when she told him she was going.

"We'll take Elena too and make it a girl's night! The men can babysit."

"I love the way you think." Courtney passed the baby to a pissed-off-looking Parker and then linked her arm with mine. "Let's go."

"You will not like what happens when you get back," Parker warned me.

"Oh, I think I'll enjoy whatever you've got planned."

***

Parker

I watched my irritatingly defiant mate, with her swinging hips and a flip of her auburn hair, walk out the door of the packhouse with Courtney. The two were probably heading to Simone's to get ready for their sinful night on the town.

If she really thinks I'm just going to let her go to a male strip show, she was in for a surprise later.

I moved the baby to my hip and then pulled out my phone, calling Casey first. I already knew what he would say, and I knew he would be down for what I was planning on doing. I just needed to make sure Vincent would get on board and not ruin my idea by telling his mate.

That man would hire male strippers to come to their condo if Sim wanted it. He always gives her everything that she wants. The only thing Simone ever wants is him, so he has no worries, unlike me. Carli will have no qualms with getting dances from naked men just to irritate me. I said something she didn't like, so she's going to try and punish me.

Jokes on her. When she gets to that club and the show starts, her excitement will die right away when her own father is the one on that pole.

***

Sophia

"I can do it," I told Calum. He had my feet in his lap, and he was gingerly taking the messy nail polish off my toes with a cotton ball and acetone.

"I got it." He held my feet firmly under his arm, not letting me wiggle free. "I like your toes."

"She does have cute feet," Karina said, sitting on the other couch with Reese's head in her lap. She was combing her fingers through his hair while he nuzzled his face between her thighs. "They're so small that no one can borrow her shoes."

"That's not true," I murmured. "Rosie has small feet too."

"Rosie doesn't wear anything but slides and trainers. She wouldn't borrow your shoes."

That's true. Rosie doesn't wear sandals or heels. She dresses for comfort.

I sat still, watching as Calum re-painted all my toes. Reese and Karina left after Reese got a call from his dad telling him to help babysit with Aly and Conner. Calum got a phone call from his dad too, but he said he was busy with me, so his dad let him go. Calum gagged at something else his dad said, but when I asked what, he told me that he just had to find somewhere else to sleep tonight. His room was taken over by his Alpha and Luna.

I got a call from mom saying she and dad were going to stay on our boat tonight. Dad thought Calum was busy with the search for Rosie after hearing some rumor from the other warriors. I didn't correct him. I decided to use the rumor to my advantage. I'll thank Rosie later.

"Hey, Calum?" I said, wiggling my toes as he massaged my feet.

"Hmm?" He looked over with his big brown eyes, his handsome face making my heart race.

"Um, you can stay here tonight if you want."

His eyes looked surprised, his mouth opening slightly. He was thinking, and I was suddenly nervous that he would say no.

"Your parents don't care?"

I pressed my lips together, not wanting to lie. He gave me a disapproving look.

"I'm not going to get on your parents' bad side, Sophia. I don't want to start off on the wrong foot with them."

I pouted my lips. "So you can make sisters with another girl but can't even spend the night with me, your mate?"

"Hey," he leaned over and pulled me into his lap. "I didn't ever make sisters with anyone. My brother didn't know what he was talking about. I kissed a girl and he saw it, but it wasn't enjoyable and I never saw the chick again. I sure as hell didn't touch her like that or ever spend the night with her. I never...I never did that with anyone," he admitted sheepishly. "You saw my family. They're intimidating as hell. And Alpha Axel is really big on us future leaders not touching the girls in our pack. Taegan extended that to not touching the girls in our fucking town. I didn't have the interest anyway. I always knew I wanted to wait for you."

My face heated at his confession. My chest felt light and my heart beat wildly in my chest.

"I still want you to stay over," I pouted, though you could hear the smile in my own voice. "We could make a pan of brownies and watch a movie. Don't you want to fall asleep beside me and wake up with me in your arms?" I wrapped my arms around his neck. "I want that, and you just told me you had to find somewhere else to sleep tonight." I let my fingers trail over the sensitive hairs on the back of his neck.

"Fuck, I do want that," he mumbled. He kissed my nose, and then my chin as he thought. "Brownies?"

"Brownies," I smiled. "With ice cream and hot fudge on top."

"Mmh, now you're talking," he kissed the soft spot on the side of my neck. "Fine. But I'm just staying because you added ice cream to the menu."

"Is the way to your heart through your stomach?" I giggled.

"I'm a hungry man," he growled, surprising me by suddenly pinning me underneath him on the couch. His hands roamed down my body. "A very hungry man. When the time comes, I home you're able to keep up."

52

Boy's a Natural

***R**osie*

"They're pretty," I whispered. My voice was hoarse and rough. There was no helping it after all we had done for the past few hours. We were supposed to go on a walk and talk, but we did very little talking. We did a whole lot of something else.

I was waving my hand through the air, trying to catch one or two of the glowing butterflies fluttering around us. Even the way they flew was magical. They weren't exactly fast, but every time my hand came close to touching one of them, it would disappear from one spot and reappear in another. Rian was chuckling under breath watching me, holding my body lazily as I laid my head on his chest.

"You're so pretty," he whispered, running his fingertips up and down my spine.

I laughed softly. "You say pretty words when you have me naked."

"I want to say pretty words to you all the time. Things have just been… tense since we felt the bond."

"Yeah," I mumbled. I absentmindedly started playing with the smooth skin of his chest, running my nail down between his pecs. He wasn't bulky like most werewolves, but I liked his leaner muscles so much better. They weren't exactly lean like a human's. They're still more than impressive. If he was human he would be considered really buff. He's lean compared to Taegan or Calum, or even my brother, who were all just disgustingly huge. Rian was perfect.

My finger trailed down his chest, through the center of his abs, around his belly button, then moved the extra cloak he laid over us so I could gaze at everything impressive about his body. Who knew that a man's dick could be something I would think of as pretty, but his was. It was pretty fucking amazing what he could do with it, and how much pleasure a single muscle in his body could give me.

"Would you like more of that?" Rian asked when I let my hand wander to its base. It jumped against my hand as I traced it to its tip.

I bit my lip while smiling. I really wanted more. The satisfaction of making love was like nothing I had ever felt before. My entire body was still buzzing with the afterglow.

"I like it," I admitted, pressing my face against his chest to hide my shy grin.

"I'm glad you do," he chuckled. He grabbed my waist and rolled my body on top of his. "It would be a shame if you didn't."

"And why is that?" I asked playfully.

"Because you're mine." He kissed my nose.

He traced his fingers over the glowing imprint he left on my shoulder, his name sprawled right over my butterfly tattoo. The rolling script looked to belong to the artwork. It made my shoulder glitter and glow just like the butterflies flying around us. Every time he touched it, my pussy would throb and the tug on our bond would tighten in a delicious way.

Mom was wrong. It didn't matter where he put his mark on my body. Being over my vagina would not have mattered. The effects were the same. I felt the sparks in my core just like I could when he touched me directly down there.

Rian pressed himself firmly against my pelvis, making me groan loudly. "All of me, including this, is all yours."

"Mmh, I like that." I moved up his chest to kiss his lips. "That means I can do this whenever I want then."

His eyes glowed with delight as I pushed myself against his body. I lifted my hips, moving my waist to rub his dick between my folds. He licked his lips, watching me with hooded eyes. The swirling galaxies in those eyes trailed down to my leaking center, watching as I grazed my pussy over his length over and over again, then rode it to the very tip, rotating my hips until it squeezed inside of me. Then his eyes rolled back from the bliss of being inside me.

Fuck, I felt so fucking full and so, so good. I sat back, squeezing my breasts as I started moving up and down his mass. He groaned so loudly, his mouth slightly open, his tongue between his teeth. He looked so sexy and seductive. It flared my desire. I wanted all of him. Forever. I never wanted this moment between us to end.

Rian sat up with me, gripping my hips and guiding me up and down him. His mouth on mine was pure passion. His tongue teased mine, but his lips were more forceful and demanding. We were breathing the same air, but only when I remembered to breathe at all.

"Rosie," he moaned. Just his voice was enough to make my body grow in furious need. "My Rosie."

My movements were now frantic. I was crying with pleasure feeling his chest pressed against mine. My nipples were so hard, the friction pulsing in them tightening that band inside me. I felt ready to snap. When his lips wrapped around one of my nipples, sucking hard and nibbling on the tip, I screamed out as the pleasure snapped and exploded inside of me.

His dick was pulsing against my walls, the slick sounds of our cum mixing and leaking out of me had my orgasm colliding with another. He was rolling his fingers in rough circles over my clit, not stopping until my entire body spasmed and I fell backwards, every one of my muscles feeling like jelly. Currents of pleasure were still vibrating inside of me, but he ceased his spark-inducing torture. His breath was heavy watching me come down from my high.

"Beautiful," he whispered, his breath still coming out in pants. He ran his hands down my front, making me shiver. He slowly pulled out of me, massaging my thighs while spreading me wide open. I was still too high in my pleasure to be surprised when his face dipped between my legs. He stared into my eyes as he sucked my swollen clit, twitching and flicking his tongue against the tip.

"No," I whimpered, pushing against his head. I didn't think my body could take any more.

"Yes," he groaned, sucking and kissing my clit more. "More, Rosie." He flicked his tongue against me. "Give me more."

I didn't know if I had any more to give. My body wouldn't listen to me any longer. He's in complete control. He's not just eating me out. His mouth was making love to my lower lips. He's hitting every nerve ending, licking every part of me from the inside out. It's the dirtiest thing I have ever seen and it's turning me on more than I ever thought possible. He had no reservations. Just insatiable hunger.

Right when I felt myself about to give in again, he pulled his face away, licking his lips, then sliding his dick back inside of me. I was a crying, shaking mess, right on the cusp of another raging orgasm, but he held back just enough to prevent me from tipping over.

His hips slowly rotated, circling so his dick pushed all around me. I was trying to meet his every rotation of his hips, but my body still felt like jelly. I was completely at his mercy.

"This is mine," he moved his thumb over my clit. "Tell me your pussy is mine."

"M-my pussy i-is yours," I cried, "Rian, please," I begged.

"Please what, baby?" He kissed my lips, our salty taste still thick on his tongue.

"Please, Rian," I mewled. "Please. I-I want to cum."

"Mmh," he groaned, picking up speed.

That sweet, tingling spot inside me was getting a steady torrent of friction and pressure. I was close. So close. He gripped my shoulder, his fingers brushing against his imprint, and that was when I finally fell. He pounded into me the entire time, only stilling as his seed started shooting deep into me once again.

"Mine," he mumbled against my skin.

"Yours," I agreed in a croaky voice. I didn't want to leave any doubt that we belonged to each other. I never want to give him up. I coughed, trying to clear my airway. It didn't help much. My voice still sounded rough. "I'm going to lose my voice if we keep this up."

"That would be a shame," he chuckled, rolling to tuck my body alongside his. "I like hearing your voice."

I liked his voice too. I liked everything about him. Butterflies seemed to be the theme of our relationship, because everything about him gave them to me. I could feel them fluttering around inside my chest just as they are fluttering around in the air around us.

I wonder if he knows I got my tattoo because of Taegan? I wonder if that would upset him, seeing as he put his imprint on it. I know butterflies will just make me think about Rian from now on, but he seems to get jealous of Taegan a lot. I don't want there to be a misunderstanding again because of the reasons for my tattoo.

"What are you thinking about?" Rian asked.

I smiled shyly, propping my chin on his chest. "Butterflies."

He grinned, rubbing his fingers over my shoulder a few times, then trailing them to my necklace resting between us from around my neck.

"Roses and butterflies. They fit well together."

I don't know why, but I blushed under his gaze. His eyes were so intense. So adoring.

"I love your eyes." I ran a finger under his right one. "They make me think of the universe. They look like dancing galaxies."

"Are you telling me you can see your entire world in my eyes?" He smirked.

I giggled, "Maybe. Would that be okay?"

"Mhmm. I see my entire world in your eyes too." He combed his fingers into my hair, pulling my face up towards his.

Right when my lips were about to meet his, a deep voice startled me, making me jump back and hurry to pull the cape over my body.

"See, honey. I told you the brat didn't need his mama's help to get between her legs. Boy's a natural."

"Max," Thyra hissed, slapping the large Alpha's chest.

Rian's parents were on the trial just several meters away, his mother looking embarrassed and stunned, but Alpha Max looked way too amused.

"Mom?" Rian sat up, moving the corner of the cape we were laying on to cover his junk. He held an arm out in front of me as if to block their view of me, but I think there wasn't much of me they didn't already see. I've never been more embarrassed in my life. "What... How are you here?"

"Hello to you too," Alpha Max smiled mockingly.

"Max." Thyra pulled his arm. "Come on," she started to lead him away. "We'll see you at the house, Rian." She gave him a stern look, then turned a smile towards me. "It's good to see you again, Rosie."

"You too," I called out, my voice cracking. Shit, shit, shit this is horrifying. "Fuck," I groaned. "Could that have been more embarrassing?"

"Yes," Rian scoffed. "It could have been your parents finding us instead of mine."

53

TAEGAN'S MISTAKE

*T*aegan

"They're sure taking their sweet time," I groaned, lying on the couch and weakly throwing some weird-looking fruit up in the air often to keep my muscles from locking up. I was bored and feeling unsettled. My magic still wasn't where it should be and I had no way to fix it until Rian got back. I didn't care if I had to tackle him to the fucking ground and kiss him. He was helping me get my magic back up.

"They had a lot to talk about," Phoebe said, cleaning under her nails with a paring knife.

"I don't think they're doing much talking," Parisa giggled, biting her full bottom lip.

"What do you mean?" I stupidly asked. When she raised her thin brows, tilting her head, it suddenly came to me. "Fucking hell," I groaned. "We have important shit to do. It's not the time for that," I groaned, running my hand down my face.

"They are mates," Phoebe told me. "She's an Alpha. Leaving him unmarked must have been torture."

"How long does it take to bite someone?" I grumbled.

"There's more to mating than just biting. You should know that," she smirked.

"Yeah, but where would they even do that? Are there rent by the hour hotels here or something?"

"Why would one rent a hotel by the hour?" Parisa tilted her face, her eyes dancing with magic and mischief.

"Umm." I pressed my lips together, trying to find a delicate way of answering her.

"Sometimes you only need a bed for an hour." Phoebe shrugged. "In our world, they're used for hookers and prostitutes, sometimes to have an after work affair. You'd be familiar with them if you lived in our world, I'm sure."

Damn, Phoebe was openly taking shots now. I knew she didn't like Parisa, but she's not even trying to hide it anymore.

"An hour seems too short of an amount of time," Parisa tilted her head in the other direction, missing the insult completely.

"Your cousin must feel the same," Phoebe checked the odd-looking clock on the wall, then checked the window, seeing that it was now completely dark outside. "If I go look for them, are you going to be okay here by yourself?" Phoebe raised her eyebrows, staring straight at me.

"We'll be fine," Parisa giggled, making Phoebe roll her eyes.

"I didn't ask you. I asked him." She then asked in a mind link, *"Are you going to be fine with Princess Prostitute Barbie or do you want to come with me?"*

I smiled weakly. *"I don't think my body is up for walking around. I need Rian to help me get my magic back up. I feel unstable without it. Conri is weaker too."*

Conri was quietly observing in my mind, conserving the rest of his energy.

"I'll hurry then. That whore has her sights on your dick. Don't let her use that head fuckery on you."

"Okay, mom," I grinned lazily. "I'll be fine," I answered out loud.

Phoebe looked at me for a long time, probably studying my aura. She then looked at Parisa with a cold stare. "You keep your hands off him. He's not yours."

Parisa bit her lips, containing her smile. She made a show of holding her hands behind her back, looking as innocent as can be. At least as innocent as she could manage with her tits spilling out of her top and her legs spread just enough to show anyone willing to look that she had nothing on under her outfit.

Phoebe sighed heavily, but left. I hoped she could find them fast. Conri was weakening more and more without his direct connection to the goddess, awith noany way to pull magic in. He needed a boost, and only Rian could help him right now.

It was quiet for some time as I continued to throw the fruit. I suddenly missed catching it and it rolled on the floor towards the fireplace. I wish Rian would hurry his ass up. I need his fae energy so badly. I can't even bring myself to lift my head now.

"My cousin isn't the only fae being here, you know," Parisa said, lying back seductively in her chair, giving me a flirtatious smile. "I have plenty of magic. Maybe more than him, seeing as both of my parents are royal."

"I'm good," I muttered, looking away when the pink flesh of one of her nipples made an appearance. How did she know what I was thinking?

"She's a damned succubus. That's how. One touch is all that it takes to fuck with your head," Conri warned me. I started to think about when she could have touched me, but then I remembered sitting at the table earlier, how she leaned towards me and placed her hand over mine.

Fuck.

I saw how loopy and turned on Rosie got when Parisa was fucking with her head. Is she going to try that shit on me now? Should I tell Phoebe to come back?

"Relax," Parisa grinned. "I was simply offering you my help. I can tell you're struggling. I just wanted to see if you needed a little pick me up to get you back on your feet until my cousin returned. You can say no." She let her magic flare into the air, sending little sparks off around her face. Conri flinched inside me, wanting to latch on to that magic and siphon from it.

"How would you help?" I raised my eyebrows, averting my gaze when I noticed her nipple again.

"Same way my cousin would," she shrugged. "I'd just let you siphon what you needed from me. Simple and easy. My magic would restore almost instantly. Actually," she paused her small fireworks display to send me a radiant smile. "I'm feeling a little overfilled at the moment. The emotional energy coming from you and your friends is astounding. I'm overflowing with power right now. You could take what you needed and I wouldn't even notice."

It was tempting. Too tempting. Conri wanted to say no, but he hated being so weak. We were going to take power from Rian, anyway. Would it really be that different to take it from Parisa, his cousin, instead? I take power from Thyra and Rian without any issues. This shouldn't be any different.

Parisa went back to shooting off those enticing fireworks above her. The magic was close enough for me to feel but just far enough for it not to touch me so I could siphon from it.

"Fine," I growled, the need was too great right now. Conri was zoned out on the magic sparkling in her hands, and it was all we could concentrate on. "No funny business. I don't want to be a lusty freak like Rosie was."

She grinned widely, pushing her tongue between her lips. "That was different. I was searching her head and body, intruding on her consciousness. I needed her to relax. I'm just giving you some magic." She shrugged like it wasn't a big deal. "No need to be so cautious."

"Hmm," I stared at her with untrusting eyes, watching as she got up from her chair and made her way over to where I was lying. "How are you going to do it?" I lifted a hand, because that's how Thyra and Rian would give me power. They would simply hold my hand and let it seep into me.

She shook her head softly. "Unfortunately, your Beta forbade me from touching you with my hands. She explicitly told me to keep them to myself."

"Then what the hell are you going to do?" I looked away, her nipple now fully out.

"This."

Since I was looking away, I didn't know what "this" meant until her lips were already pressed to mine. The surprise and resistance only lasted a second, because the rush of power was too great to deny. Conri latched onto her, siphoning what he needed. I held her face to mine, deepening the kiss to get more from her. The raw energy was so satisfying, quelling every inch of my body as magic filled my muscles and flowed through my bloodstream once again.

I don't know how long we were like that, her lips to mine, her tongue twisting around my tongue and her breath breathing magic deep inside me, but I was filled to the brim with magic once again when I heard a sudden gasp.

"TAEGAN!" Thyra shrieked.

I startled, falling to the ground, away from Parisa's glowing features and completely exposed chest I hadn't realized was pressed against mine. What the hell just happened? How did I lose myself so completely?

"Jeez, you idiot." Phoebe was shaking her head with disappointment, holding her face in her hand. "I fucking told you, and look what happened."

"I..." I looked between Phoebe, Thyra, and my stoic grandpa. How did they get here? Why are they here? Grandpa didn't look pissed exactly, but I could tell he was annoyed. I was having a hard time wrapping my head around everything at the same time. I felt dazed despite the shit Parisa said. "I don't know what happened."

"Parisa." Thyra stared at her wide-eyed. Her eyes then moved down to her large chest. "Cover yourself!"

Parisa had the nerve to fucking giggle. I was stuck on the ground, mortified, but she looked as pleased as she could be with what just happened.

"I told you to be careful," Phoebe told me.

"I really don't know what happened. She was supposed to just be giving me power. I didn't realize she would kiss me until it was... it was happening."

Phoebe shook her head. "What about your mate, Taegan?"

Conri growled deep in my chest, fully energized and feeling the full brunt of regret. Parisa just had her chest completely out while grinding over my body and I was oblivious to the whole thing, overwhelmed by the magic. She could have crossed that line and I wouldn't have been thinking clearly enough to stop her. I can't believe I was so stupid.

"Did both these brats just come here to fuck around?" Grandpa growled, rubbing his temples. "I didn't spend an hour riding the gluestick to walk in on my son and my grandson in the span of twenty fucking minutes."

"Hello, Aunt Thyra," Parisa skipped up to her after she fixed her shirt. "I didn't expect to see you here as well."

"I didn't expect to see you either. So much of you." Her eyes drifted down to Parisa's outfit.

"What's going on?" Rian chose that moment to walk through the door with Rosie holding his hand, hiding behind him.

"Your nephew can't keep his shit in his pants either," Grandpa growled. "Is there something in the air here? Are we supposed to fuck in the open too?" He looked at Thyra.

I tried not to gag, but Rian had a harder time hiding his disgust. He then looked at me curiously, his eyes gliding over my aura, then he looked at Parisa. When his eyes went wide, I knew he had figured out what was going on.

"You and Parisa?! What about your mate?!"

"Mate?" Grandpa growled, his expression getting angrier. "You have a fucking mate?"

54

TAEGAN'S REGRET

Rosie

My embarrassment at facing Rian's parents faded as the chaos broke out inside of the fairy's house. Parisa, that slutty fairy bitch, looked far too pleased with herself for putting Taegan in this situation. I've been under her magic. I know how little control you have while in her hands. I wanted to punch the whore right in her smug face.

Alpha Max was berating Taegan, screaming in his face with spit flying everywhere about how stupid and irresponsible he was for doing that after he found his mate. I get it. If his mate was of age, or close to it, she would have felt that and it would have torn her apart.

I've seen it plenty. Every time my Grandma Mary gets intimate with Lady Delilah it hurts my grandpa. He hides it from us, but there have been a few times where I have seen him excuse himself from a room quickly while clutching his chest, then breaking down in agony the moment he was alone. Dad or mom go to comfort him when they can, dulling the pain with their auras. Even though Grandma Mary is consumed with her role as the vampire leader's sire, grandpa won't reject her so he can be without pain. He just lives with it.

I would never condone putting your mate through that kind of pain, but I feel for Taegan. I know, without even truly knowing, that this wasn't his fault. I was about to step up and say that, but Rian took a step forward before I could.

"Dad, it isn't like that." He stepped between Taegan and Alpha Max. "Taegan wouldn't intentionally hurt his mate. You know him better than that."

"I KNOW WHAT I SAW!" Alpha Max was still seething. "You don't do that shit if you have a mate. I don't care about the fucking circumstances."

"She's a succubus, honey." Thyra placed a calming hand on his shoulder. "I'm sure that she overwhelmed him with her abilities."

Thyra didn't look too pleased with her niece. When Parisa tried to hug her earlier, Thyra remained stiff.

"That's no fucking excuse!"

Taegan was zoned out, looking lost in his own thoughts, just wincing every once in a while from either his grandfather's words or, more than likely, the inner dialogue he was holding with his beast.

"Alpha Max," I stepped up beside my mate. "Um, I was under her spell too not too long ago. I don't think Taegan had much choice in the matter. I didn't." I glared at the fairy tramp standing across the room, her eyes dancing with amusement. "I hate the bitch and still couldn't stop myself from being swept up."

Yeah, I just admitted to hating one of Rian's family members, but his own mother didn't look too happy with her presence here. Why should I hold back when my lifelong friend is getting attacked for something that wasn't even his fault?

"The woman has been on his nuts since we got here," Phoebe said. "I never should have left them alone together."

"Why did you?" I asked, confused about how this happened.

"He needed magic, a heavy dose of it." She narrowed her eyes at Parisa. "I told her to keep her hands to herself, but didn't think I needed to clarify that meant her tits and lips as well." She curled her lip in disgust. "I thought something was up with this chick. She kept asking me questions about Taegan, not Rian, after she brought me here. I thought it was because Taegan had his reputation of being the goddess's descendant, or maybe because of the shit that happened when we were kids, but then when we got here she came onto him every chance she got."

Alpha Max looked at Phoebe for a long time, then looked down at his mate, who already seemed tired of all of this. After some communication passed between them, he turned his head to stare down at Taegan. Taegan looked so broken while sitting on the couch.

"I'm pissed too," Taegan murmured. "I'm so mad at myself. I shouldn't have even come here. I should have just let them come alone." He nodded towards us.

"Taegan." I rested my hand on his shoulder. I could see how torn up he was about this. Honestly, I don't think it's that big of a deal, since it wasn't his fault, and I would be more than willing to stick up for him to his mate if there were a problem later.

"Parisa, what were you even doing?" Rian stared at his cousin.

"You knew he had a mate," Phoebe added. "We talked about it for a long time in front of you."

"Oh, I knew before you said anything," Parisa giggled. "I knew before we left your world."

Phoebe gave her a confused look, as did Thyra. Alpha Max seemed to be turning his anger on the bitch, steam practically coming from his nostrils as he glared.

"I think it's best if you leave now, Parisa," Thyra said, gripping Alpha Max's arm to hold him in place. "I will come see you in the courts to discuss this at a later time."

"There will be no need," Parisa pushed off against where she was perched on the stair railing. "I shall come to you later, Aunt Thyra. Until then," she giggled, waving goodbye to the tense room. Phoebe stared her down with a hostile expression when Parisa slid past her to exit through the door. Parisa seemed as unaffected as always, which I found beyond annoying.

"Taegan, it's okay," I urged him, sitting beside him on the couch and rubbing his arm. "If you're worried about your mate, I can tell her it wasn't your fault. Rian will too." I looked up at him, telling him with my eyes to agree with me.

"I'll take the blame for bringing her here," he said. "I knew she could be a bit manipulative."

Taegan still looked torn up. Who was his mate that he was this worried about this? Is she someone so unforgiving?

"She wouldn't have felt it," Phoebe told him. "You know she couldn't yet. I know you're pissed at yourself, but a child can't feel the mate bond or the effects of a betrayal. It's not possible."

"A child?" Alpha Max looked back at his grandson. "What the fuck? Who the hell is your mate?"

Taegan looked worriedly up at Rian, who smiled tightly. Phoebe just looked exasperated.

"You can tell them, idiot. It's not like it's a secret from the goddess anymore. You're an adult."

"The goddess? Fucking gluesticks. How long have you known?" Alpha Max looked more concerned now than he was angry.

"A long time," Taegan sighed. He rubbed his eyes with the palms of his hands. "Since before she was born. Since we were in the goddess realm."

Thyra was clutching her chest with one hand, looking worried, and holding onto Alpha Max with the other.

"How old is she?" Alpha Max asked.

"Young," Taegan said. "Too young to have felt anything."

"How young," Alpha Max pushed.

Taegan looked lost for a moment, his eyes glowing as they often did. "She's twelve years younger than me. We still have ten years before we can claim them," he looked at Phoebe. Ten years? With how old he is now, and that bit of information, I'm already wracking my brain to figure out who he's talking about. The way he and Phoebe are staring at one another, I have a suspicion already.

"We?" Alpha Max turned to his grandson's Beta.

"I'm mated to his mate's twin."

"The Meyer's twins," I whispered. "Is that who?" It would explain so much. It would explain why he always had to come down to Miami. Why he was always with the Meyers brothers.

"Yeah," Taegan sighed. "Harley."

The little purple-eyed twin. She is the one who is more sheltered. Harper comes to the classes for kids at the warrior center, but Harley never does. I knew she was different, and wouldn't have a wolf, but my dad hasn't told me why yet and I never cared enough to ask.

"And Harper is mine," Phoebe added. "I just found out before coming here. I haven't known as long as he has."

"That's why you stopped going after all the mates," Alpha Max said. "You spoon carrying little shit." He didn't look mad anymore. He seemed almost impressed, maybe even proud.

Taegan snorted. "I forgot about that."

"Having a mate does that to you. Even at her age now, I'm sure her safety and wellbeing is all you can think about. Even the possibility that this may hurt her is probably eating at your ass right now."

"It's eating away right here." Taegan hammered his fist against his chest. "If she had felt that, I never would have forgiven myself."

"She's eight." I rested my hand on his. "She couldn't have felt it."

"But what if she did," he hissed, running his other hand down his face.

Alpha Max shook his head, then looked back at his mate. "That trampy girl was your niece?"

"She is my brother's daughter, yes." Thyra didn't look phased that her mate just called her niece a tramp.

"I don't want her anywhere around my kids again. Not my son, grandson, or daughter-in-law."

My heart fluttered a bit to hear him call me that.

"What about me?" Phoebe smirked at her alpha.

"I think it would do that girl some good to try and fuck with you," Alpha Max snorted. "What did she mean about knowing before she brought you here? Knowing about Taegan's mate?"

Phoebe thought deeply for a few seconds. "I don't know. Mitchel Meyers did come along with us to see Lady Delilah. Maybe he said something? They talked for a while, but I did't hear anything off in their conversation." She tilted her head to the side as if something had just happened to her. "There was one thing, though. Now that I'm thinking about it..."

55

EAVESDROPPING

Phoebe

"*P*hoebe?" *Vincent leaned down to peer into the car.*

I barely rolled the windows down, but the smell of blood was getting strong in the hot climate. Even with the air conditioning on, the blood spilled from the human I killed in the back seat was beginning to sour.

Vincent looked shocked, then I saw the wheels turning in his head. Before he could land on the idea that I might have murdered someone in cold blood for thirst, I said, "Seems my Uber driver has a habit of sexually assaulting and then killing his female clients. I put a stop to that. I hope you don't mind." I smiled sweetly, like I truly did him the kindness of ridding the town of the vile man.

"Oh, dear." Vincent rubbed the back of his neck, straightening up to look back at the men standing at the front of the resort with their twins. "Men, it seems we have a minor hiccup in our agenda."

"What's that?" The brother with the short buzzed haircut, I think Mark, came to lean into the car window as Vincent had.

The brothers have identical faces, but their other features have always made them appear very different. From their hairstyles, to the way they dress and their facial hair. I believe Taegan said that Mitch has longer hair and a more rugged appearance, and that fits the other guy with a man bun waiting at the resort door with his hands on the shoulders of the twin girls. Mark was in a suit with a clean-shaven face, and Mitch was just in dress pants and a linen shirt, unbuttoned at the top, with a short beard and piercings in his ears and eyebrow.

"Oh, dear indeed," Mark smirked. "Stop for a bite along the way?"

"She stopped a predator along the way," Vincent corrected him.

"In that case," Mark grinned widely, a smile I'm sure would charm the panties off of any other woman. "Thank you for helping to clean the streets of Miami. As a father, I can rest better at night."

I looked over at the twin girls. The gray eyes of the slightly taller twin were on me, tension between her little brows, like she was brooding over something. My breath caught in my throat from the storm brewing behind those eyes. I could almost feel the goddess's influence inside of her in her dormant wolf.

I knew one day she will be a fierce warrior. Her sister and her are as different as their fathers. They may be twins, but their eye-color isn't the only difference between them. I could envision the beast hidden away inside the gray-eyed little girl, and knew one day she would be strong. Very strong. She had the aura of a protector.

"Phoebe?" Vincent's voice brought me back to the present.

I snapped my head to the side. "Sorry. What?"

"Mark is going to take this car for us and get rid of it. You and I will ride along with Mitch." Vincent had a slight smile playing at the corners of his lips. I could tell from his knowing eyes that he had caught on, but he was silently vowing not to say a word.

"Ralph is coming to get the girls to take them up to mom," Mitch told Mark. "I'll help him then be right back."

"He still worries more than the norm, doesn't he?" Vincent looked amused, watching as Mitch guided his daughters back into the resort.

"At least he doesn't worry about pipes bursting in the walls and somehow hurting the girls anymore."

"That was a silly worry," Vincent chuckled. "What ever will he do when your girls find their mates?"

"What will we do, you mean?"

"Ah, yes. What will both of you do?" Vincent looked over towards me and winked subtly.

Mark's face turned a bit sour. "We'll manage. If the goddess gifted them with mates, we have to trust her judgment, right?" He then muttered under his breath, "Even if her timing sucked."

"Of course. Your goddess has the best of judgment," Vincent held his hands out to his side. "Just look at me. Could Simone have been blessed with a better mate?"

"*I think that is the other way around,*" *Mark snickered, trading places with me as I got out of the bloody car.*

"*Ah, you are right,*" *Vincent twirled his wedding ring on his finger.* "*There is no greater joy than finding you were blessed by the goddess with one of her children. I'm sure when your daughters find their mates, you will recognize the gift they are being given.*"

"*Hmph, maybe,*" *Mark scoffed.* "*Doesn't mean I won't give him hell.*"

With that, Mark rode off in the car, leaving Vincent and myself on the curb.

"*Give her hell,*" *Vincent grinned.* "*I don't think they have considered the possibility their daughter's mates could be a man or a woman.*"

"*You're toying with me,*" *I narrowed my eyes at the vampire beside me.*

"*I would never. I just wanted you to see what you were going to be dealing with soon. I expect that even when your mate comes of age, her fathers will still be overprotective. That is the way of most fathers.*"

"*Is that the way you are?*" *I lifted my brow. I know Reese and I know that Reese believes he is mated to Vincent's daughter.*

His smile faltered "*That's different.*"

I laughed to myself. "*It always is when it's your own daughter.*"

"*Certainly,*" *he snickered.*

Vincent then asked me to go over all the details of my encounter with the Uber driver. He typed away at his phone quickly as I spoke, and I had a feeling he was already informing the Alpha of what had happened. They're dealing with it quickly. I wondered how this would be handled in a city this size, but it seems even the police were influenced by the supernaturals in Miami.

Mitch came back and drove Vincent and I to the building where Lady Delilah resides in the city. I sat quietly in the backseat as Vincent and Mitch talked among themselves. My head was somewhere else anyway. That pair of stormy gray eyes were still consuming my thoughts, as well as murderous thoughts about Taegan. He knew. He had to have. He knows everything.

Mitch pulled up to a curb outside of an elegant building. Nothing like the dark and gothic building of Lord Antonio's coven. To my surprise, Mitch stayed, going in with us.

"*I'm old friends with the management,*" *he told me with a glint in his gray eyes. I was momentarily disarmed by those eyes, reminding me of his daughters. I just nodded and smiled tightly.*

She's so much younger than me. Taegan is a lot younger than me, but those little girls were still babies. Why would the goddess let there be so much of an age gap? Taegan reminds me often that I don't age like werewolves. I'm twenty-nine but still look like I'm in my early twenties. Still....

I'm old. Shit, I have never felt so old.

"I'm going to go ahead and talk to Lady D," Mitch said with a playful look on his face, but something in his eyes almost looked sinister. He jogged ahead, leaving me and Vincent to wait.

"Look at him," Vincent snickered. I turned in time to see a raven-haired woman with delicate, but still somehow fierce features embrace Mitch in a strong hug. I could tell by her eyes that she was powerful. I could feel it in the air that her first generation blood was the purist it could be. She was timeless and beautiful, and her aura was something I had never encountered in a vampire before. Mitch didn't even flinch. He was unfazed as he hugged her back.

"They seem close," I muttered.

"Lady Delilah has always had a soft spot for Mitchel. He is a sensitive soul and highly affected by the outside world. She protects him and dotes on him."

"His mate doesn't mind?"

"Have you met Hadley? She welcomes the help of keeping her mates in line. Lady Delilah's affection is motherly. Nothing a mate should worry about."

I watched Mitch's face turn serious as he whispered low in her ear. I could barely hear anything he was saying. Barely. I could still hear some words.

".....worried... protect the girls....... seer...... he will expose her......"

"What are they talking about?" I asked, interrupting Vincent, who was staring down at his phone.

"Uh," Vincent looked over at Mitch and the vampire leader, then shrugged. "I'm sorry. I wasn't paying attention, but it doesn't appear to be about the reason you are here. I think they are just catching up. She's asking about his girls." Vincent scowled at his phone again. "Alpha Parker is on his way here. We are heading to investigate the man you snacked on. It seems the man that the car was registered to fit the description of a serial rapist running rampant in the city. Good job."

I smiled tightly, not sure how to handle that praise. It wasn't my intention to be praised for killing a man.

Vincent left soon after, leaving me to eavesdrop with ease. I slowly eased closer, not sure, trying to seem nonchalant.

"I'll see what I can do. I'm sure we can discuss this before she leaves," Lady Delilah was telling Mitch, patting his arm reassuringly.

"Who leaves?" I asked, now just a few feet away.

"Uh...me," Mitch smiled warmly, but his eyes were still tense. "I need to get back home to my girls. I hope you have a pleasant journey," he patted my shoulder. As he made his way towards the door, a look passed between him and Lady Delilah.

***

"I waited around for about an hour after that. Lady Delilah disappeared for some time, then came back with Parisa to escort me. I didn't think much more of it. It was odd, him coming in and leaving like that, but I don't know them well enough to tell if that was just weird to me but normal to them."

"Mitch was the one that figured out that I was his daughter's mate," Taegan whispered. His blue eyes looked so worried and disheartened. "Do you think it was me that he was talking to the vampire leader about?"

"Only one way to find out," Alpha Max grunted. "We will ask the woman when we get back. As far as Parisa is concerned, you stay the fuck away from the glittering, tree-covered tramp."

"Max," Luna Thyra patted his arm.

"She's a hussy, Thyra. I want the woman away from my kids."

"You don't have to worry about that, grandpa. I don't want shit to do with the girl again."

Because of the guilt-filled, broken look on his face, I hope I never see the girl again either. I might just knock her fucking glittering lights out for taking advantage of my Alpha.

56

SHIT DROPPING

Rian

"She's a bitch, Taegan. It wasn't your fault," Rosie told Taegan again.

She was holding his hand, tracing his thumb with hers. I was trying not to let it bother me. She's mine. My mark is on her and hers is on my neck, but it didn't make the possessiveness go away. I don't care if he's family. It still irks me to see her sitting so close to him, treating him gently while nursing his guilty feelings.

I felt bad for Taegan. I really did. I even felt a bit guilty for bringing Parisa here, but my mate coddling him was irritating me.

"Hey." My dad placed a hand on my shoulder, squeezing it gently. "Why don't you and I go somewhere and talk?"

I couldn't tell if the hardness in his eyes meant he was mad or concerned. No matter how old I get, I will always be wary of my dad's anger. I haven't faced it often, but I've seen it plenty. Discipline and my dad go hand in hand. Taegan is usually the one getting in trouble, not me.

"It's just a talk," dad said, giving my shoulder another squeeze.

"Okay," I said quietly. "We can go to the kitchen."

He nodded, then followed me to the other room. Mom gave me a soft smile as we passed, then went to sit on the other side of Taegan. Not only my mate, but my mom is going to baby him now. It was one kiss. It doesn't sound like it was anything more. Everyone is acting like he impregnated her or something.

"Keep walking, boy," Dad murmured, pushing me through the kitchen door.

"I was walking."

"You were glaring. I could see every fucking thought in your head on your face."

I scowled, wondering what he meant. He motioned for me to sit at the table, then sat across from me.

We sat awkwardly, and I still had the sinking feeling that I wouldn't like this talk.

"So," Dad started, strumming his beefy fingers on the delicately carved wooden table. "Got yourself a mate now, huh?"

My goodness, is this going to be one of those talks?

"Yes...."

Dad nodded, continuing to nonchalantly strum his fingers. The tension was mounting....

"Did you figure out where to stick it?"

"Are you kidding me?" I huffed, cringing and throwing my hands back. "What the hell kind of question is that?"

"I just wanted to make sure," he chuckled. "You looked a little lost earlier."

"I wasn't lost," I grimaced. "We were..... uh..... finished."

"Oh, we heard her finish. I'm sure the whole fucking forest heard her finish."

"Dad..."

"Good job, by the way."

"Could you not?" I groaned, covering my face with my hands.

"What? This is what dads do, right? I had the same talk with Axel when he started, you know, putting his pecker in-"

"DAD!" I yelled, cutting him off. As much as I don't want to hear a sex talk about my own life. I sure as hell didn't want to hear one about Axel.

"Come on, kid. I'm just trying to help."

"I don't need help."

"You sure about that?" Dad smirked. "You looked like you were in need of a bit of help just a minute ago."

"Help with what?" I didn't even do anything but stand to the side and watch as my mate got all protective over Taegan.

"There." Dad pointed at me. "That fucking face."

"What fucking face?"

"That face like you just got shit on by a fucking eagle or something. Better yet, a pegasus shitted on top of your pretty head. You look pissed at the whole damn world."

"Did you think that I was maybe making this pegasus shit face because of the uncomfortable conversation we are having right now?"

"No, because I know you, kid. And you were making the same shit dropping face earlier when your mate started to get all caring towards your nephew."

I grimaced. "Probably because my mate has been in love with my nephew her whole life and I hate seeing it."

Dad crossed his arms over his chest. "You know that's not the case for her now, right?"

I pressed my lips together, not wanting to answer. Deep inside, I know it's not the case for her anymore, but I still hate seeing it. I don't want to get jealous like this, but she's mine. Only mine. Not only is some demonic fae being trying to claim her, I have a family member that is always too cozy with her, too. It makes me feel...

Frustrated. So damn frustrated.

I thought this would calm down now that we mated, but I want even more to imprint myself all over her. I want to override every touch she makes with Taegan, and any other male. She's mine, and I just don't know how to control this possessiveness inside me.

"I see you, Rian," Dad muttered, a smirk playing on his lips. "I see the jealousy inside you. Hard to control, right?"

I narrowed my eyes at him. "Is this normal?"

"Sooooo fucking normal," he chuckled. "Your mom still gets her panties in a bunch when the she-wolves start flocking to me."

I scoffed, unable to keep the smile off my face. No she-wolves flirt with dad. He's devoted to mom and the whole pack knows better than to try to disrespect mom like that.

"Alright. It might be the other way around." His fist tightens on the table, and his jaw goes tense. "I get so damn homicidal when a guy even looks at your mom. I'm made a fool of myself plenty of fucking times, acting like you are now. Worse. You know me. You know this cheery demeanor I have all the time fades the moment someone looks at my woman."

"Cheery demeanor?"

Dad's face turned stone cold. "Are you saying I don't have a cheery demeanor?"

"No, no," I laughed softly, shaking my head. "I'm in total agreement."

"Damn fucking right." He smirked. He then exhaled. "It's normal to get possessive of your mate. Hell. I still get the shit dropping look daily. I know you're struggling right now. It's not in your nature to have the overbearing possessiveness of a werewolf. You're not just mated to one. You are mated to an alpha female. Your drive to possess her is just going to get stronger now that you are marked. Her DNA is going to keep changing you, changing the way your body reacts."

"So.... this is normal?"

"So fucking normal. It's going to be hard, but I know you're going to make an amazing mate for that girl. You are an amazing son to me and your mom, and even if you are annoyed with the punk right now, you're an exceptional friend to Taegan too. You've had most of your life to get used to supporting an Alpha. You elevate Taegan instead of holding him back, as you do with all your nieces and even the other ranked wolves. I know it was hard growing up in our pack being different from everyone else, but I truly believe that your upbringing is what is going to make you perfect for being her mate."

My chest felt a little lighter at my dad's encouragement. I didn't know if I deserved the praise he was giving me. I've felt pretty shitty most of today, and felt like a failure more than I ever have before. Still.... A smile was playing on my lips now, and I felt like I could breathe again.

"You are going to do just fine. She's crazy about you too, so don't let shit like her comforting a friend get to you."

"How do you know she's crazy about me? You haven't gotten a chance to see us together."

"Boy," a devious grin took over my dad's face. "You had that girl screaming for all to hear how crazy she is about you. No woman screams the way she did without being enraptured by their mate."

"Oh my goddess," I groaned, covering my face with my hands.

"I'm just saying, she seemed pretty fucking happy to me."

"Just stop," I begged.

He chuckled, then got up and patted me on the back before giving my shoulder a good squeeze. "You got this. The jealousy will get easier over time."

"Really?" I clung to that hope.

"No," he snorted. "But if you ever need help, you've got me, Axel, shit-head Casey, Nate, and so many other guys in your family that love you enough to help you through it."

57

— • —

FAIRY ITCH

I felt a little better after talking to my dad. Hearing that all the irrational jealousy I was feeling was normal was a relief.

Stepping back out into the living room, dad gripped my shoulder one last time, then walked to the couch to trade places with mom. Mom had that knowing smile, and I knew Taegan was about to get an inspirational cringe-filled talk with him, too.

"You okay?" Rosie came walking over to me with a worried expression, smoothing out frown lines I didn't know were still showing on my face. Just the sparks from her touch chased away so many of the negative feelings inside me.

"Yeah." I placed my hand over hers, giving her a soft smile. "I'm okay now."

I used to think of Rosie as a hard woman, and absolutely ruthless, but the sweet smile gracing her lips just for me sent my heart into a racing speed beating against my rib cage. I would dare to say that this smile was only for me, because I have never even seen her give this tender look to my nephew or anyone else. I prayed it was reserved for me. "We should give my dad space to talk to Taegan. Let's head upstairs."

"Space? Why would they need space?" Rosie looked back at my dad, who was whispering something in Taegan's ear that made Taegan turn bright red and covered his face. Phoebe started snickering in the corner. Her hearing was better than anyone else here, and I'm sure by the look on her face that I didn't want to overhear the conversation between Taegan and my dad. He doesn't sugar coat words, and he is excessively crude when making a point.

Plus, I would just like some alone time with Rosie after feeling insecure again.

"Trust me," I groaned. "They need space." I leaned down, then whispered in Rosie's ear, "And I wouldn't mind getting you to myself for a little while again."

Now Rosie's cheeks were turning bright red. She looked adorable; a word I'm sure no one would have dared to describe her before. She's adorable just for me and because of me. It fills me with pride to know this.

"Okay," she said meekly. If I was like her, I would have growled deeply at the feeling that one little "okay" stirred inside of me.

We slowly walked upstairs, my hands resting on her hips. I couldn't stand taking my hands off her for even a moment to walk more comfortably, but we made it up. I had only been in the room my mother had prepared for me at this house a handful of times for very short amounts of time. Never longer than an hour because of the time difference between worlds.

I still felt shy when Rosie walked into the room and took note of everything around her. My mother had prepared the room to my liking as a small child. The walls were a soft green and wooden carvings of fairy knights and elvish warriors were lining different floating shelves shaped like tree branches. There was a curtain hanging over the window that looked like the tongues of flames raining down. In the daylight, it cast flame -shaped shadows on the wall in the sun's rays. Even the bedspread was knit to mimic the armor of the fairy knights, like wooden shingles knit closely together. I watched as Rosie touched the blanket in wonder, feeling how soft it was compared to how it looked.

"It's a child's room still. I've never spent a night here, so I've never had a chance to update it."

She bit her lip, suppressing a smile as she ran her fingers over the carved figurines. "Are these like fairy power rangers?"

"I have no idea what power rangers are."

"You don't know power rangers?" She gaped at me. "Everyone knows power rangers. Didn't you grow up with a million kids all around you?"

"Taegan's sisters," I shrugged.

"I guess they would be into TV shows about monster fighting masked ninjas and crap like that."

"No," I chuckled. "I've seen plenty of princess and barbie movies, but never power rangers."

"What about my cousins?"

"Callum's brothers?" I laughed softly, scratching the back of my head. "They don't have the attention span for TV shows. Unless dad is hovering over them with that look like he is about to skin them alive, they don't sit still." Now that I think about it, both sets of twins are the same way. They would only be calm and restrained with me and mom when we helped them. There is something in that family's blood that just makes them overly excited all the time.

"I can see that," Rosie smiled, knowing Callum's family as well as I do. "I guess I'll have to show you myself one day what power rangers are." She pressed against me with a coy grin, resting her hands against my chest. "Maybe with our own kids?"

"Mmh," I pulled her close, wrapping my arms around her waist. "I like the sound of that."

Power ranger, barbies, anything else that Rosie wanted to show me and the kids, I would love to see just because I was watching it with her.

***

Taegan

"You look like shit," grandpa told me as he sat down beside me.

"I feel like shit," I groaned, wiping my hands down my face, wishing I could go back and just tell Parisa no instead of giving in to the temptation of her magic.

"Good. You should. If you didn't feel bad for letting something like that happen after finding your mate, then we would have issues."

"We already have issues," Conri growled. He feels sick, and having Parisa's magic flowing inside of us is making everything so much worse. Her magic is darker than we expected, even though it is so strong. She must have gotten it from feeding on the negativity around all of us for the past few hours. It feels and tastes almost sour; spoiled and decrepit. The way she administered it to us makes everything so much worse.

Grandpa leaned in close and whispered in my ear, "Is there some sort of fairy STD test you need to take now?"

"Grandpa," I groaned, covering my face with my hands.

"What? If there was a fairy that had diseases, I think it would be that woman. Fucking trash was what she was."

"Max," Thyra gave him a warning look.

"Don't fucking look at me like that." Grandpa narrowed his eyes at his mate. "You saw as well as I did what your fucking niece did."

Thyra gave him a cold, leveled look. I could feel grandpa's body tense with regret at his words.

"I mean, I'm sure she could be, uh, nice, if, uh, you like women like that. I still don't want the wh-... I mean, girl around my kids."

"I agree she shouldn't be around Taegan or the rest of our people again, but if you start with your mouth at me, you're not going to like the outcome."

Grandpa looked sheepishly at his mate, the only person in the world who could talk to him like that. Well, mom usually can too, but he doesn't submit to anyone, even mom, the way he does to Thyra.

"Sorry," he mumbled. "I'm just saying."

"I know what you are saying, and I agree, but some things should be worded better. Especially in this world. Her mother isn't very fond of me. Because I didn't follow through with the marriage I was being forced into, she was taken as one of my brother's concubines."

"Wouldn't women in this world desire to be married off to the king?"

"One of the many wives of a king is not something to strive for. It's loveless, and a succubus. She could not get her magic the way she desired, since wives are required to stay monogamous and the husbands can take as many wives as needed. The Queen of the South, Queen Aisling, is the only woman who has accomplished turning the tables on the system here, and she had to become ruthless to do it."

"What does any of that have to do with your niece being a hussy?" Grandpa muttered.

Thyra shook her head. "Just be careful with your words. I know Parisa and her mother well enough to know that if they want to harm our family, they'll find a way."

"Do you think the vampire ruler of Miami said something to your niece to make her act like that?" Phoebe asked.

Thyra was silent for a moment and then smiled sadly. "I'm unsure. That would be a question for Lady Delilah and the owners of the resort when we get back."

My gut twisted in my stomach. "Do you think Mitch Meyers was trying to prove something by making Parisa do that to me?"

"I think that if he did, he's going to answer to me," grandpa growled.

"He will have to answer to a whole number of people. His own mate included. You don't tamper with the mate bond," Thyra said. "He could be the most powerful hybrid witch in existence, he wouldn't be safe from the consequences."

"No, he wouldn't," Phoebe looked deadly. "It isn't just your mate. You bet your ass I will make sure the goddess punishes him for fucking with us."

"We don't know for sure that he did anything yet." Thyra tried to calm us down. "It may just be a misunderstanding. Parisa is... promiscuous. She may have just really wanted to see what it was like with someone as powerful as Taegan. I'm thankful we walked in when we did."

"Me too," I murmured. A shiver traveled down my spine. "I can't even imagine how bad things would have gotten if you hadn't."

"We left Miami just in time." Thyra patted my shoulder.

"How did you guys even make it to Miami? How did you know I was here?"

Thyra smirked. "A mother always knows. Your mother knew too. She's back in Miami waiting for us to bring you home."

"So is dipshit Casey and the rest of your cousins and all of your sisters."

Oh, goddess. I bet they're all wrecking Miami right now.

"So," grandpa clapped his hands. "How do we test for these fairy STDs? Is there a clinic nearby, or..."

"Max," Thyra pinched the bridge of her nose, closing her eyes in exasperation.

"I'm fucking serious? I felt the itch just looking at the tramp."

"The itch?" Phoebe lifted her eyebrow with a smirk. "What kind of itch, Alpha Max?"

"Don't encourage him." Thyra gave Phoebe a warning look. "And there is no fairy itch you need to worry about."

"*I have the itch to fuck up a certain fairy,*" Conri growled. "*And not in the way she would enjoy.*"

"I would rather stay way the fuck away from her and not deal with this shit again. I'm more worried about what mom and everyone else is doing in Miami."

58

CARLI'S SURPRISE

Carli

"Do you know where you're going?" Simone laughed as I missed my turn again, circling around the block of clubs and missing the parking garage.

"Yes!" I snapped. "I've been here before."

"Parker doesn't mind you going to male strip shows?" Courtney giggled in the backseat.

"She went with me for my birthday the first year these shows were in town," Elena said, pressing her curled fingers to her lips, leaning against the door frame beside Courtney. "Your dad got us the tickets to mess with our mates."

"That's something dad would do," Courtney laughed. "He was the one that tried to organize a stripper for my bachelorette party. Joke was on him when Axel set him up to have Casey strip for me instead."

"I remember," I chuckled.

"Me too." Simone looked disgusted, even though she laughed more than anyone when she realized the stripper was going to be her brother. It was a fun night. That was about the time Axel started really trusting Casey as his gamma and the two formed the relationship they have now.

"How would your dad react if someone tried to get Fiona a male stripper?" Simone asked.

"He'd lose it," Courtney giggled.

"Sounds like Aunt Fiona is overdue for a vacation to Miami," I smirked, meeting Elena's eyes in the rearview mirror. She's got that grin on her face. I knew she was thinking the same thing as me.

Eventually, I pulled into the right parking lot. Lilly was already there with Hadley, Hillary and even Vivian Meyers, the triplet's mother. She has always been one of my favorite people and I'm excited to see her.

The club was packed; the line stretching around the block. Vivian called ahead, and we were ushered inside to the VIP seating at the front of the stage. The bachelorette party in the row behind us was snickering, complaining about their change of seating, so I guess Vivian jilted these seats from someone else. I almost felt guilty, but the more they ran their mouths, the less guilty I felt.

"Sheesh," Simone leaned in and whispered in my ear. "By how eager that bride is to be close to strippers, I don't think she needs to be getting married."

"We were eager to be close to the strippers," I reminded her dryly, a smile playing on my lips.

"No, no, sweetie. That was just you and Courtney."

"Oh yeah," I laughed.

"Hell yeah, it was," Courtney grinned. "I've been watching these videos online. I want to see it live."

"My brother would be more than happy to give you a live show."

"Eh." Courtney waved her hand dismissively. "Been there, done that. I get pregnant every time he even looks at me a certain way."

"So it's Casey's excessive stripping keeping you knocked up?" I asked. "Maybe Parker should take up stripping."

"I thought he had a vasectomy?" Courtney asked.

"He did," Simone smirked at me. "He had to because this one gets baby fever way too often."

"He didn't have to," I grunted. "He could have just said no." That doesn't matter anymore. Seems my mate was now set on getting it reversed. I'm not the only one with baby fever anymore. His daughter, being mated now, must have him missing baby Rosie. Baby Rosie was freaking adorable. I can't wait for mini-Rosies and mini-Rian running around the packhouse.

"Tell you no," Simone scoffed. "I should record your reaction the next time someone tells you no to anything."

"What's that supposed to mean?" I glared.

"It means you don't take the word no very well. It's like a cuss word to you."

"It's true," Lilly leaned over to poke my knee. "I see it daily."

"Excuse me for going after what I want."

"Please," Simone rolled her eyes. "I've seen you freak out on Parker for telling you no to buying your drunk ass pickles on some weekends at two in the morning."

"That's a legitimate complaint. I like pickles," I grumbled. I only really like them when I'm drunk or pregnant. I'm okay without them any other time. Parker knows this. "He should have known I would want pickles when he dragged my ass back home."

"You should have known your ass would want pickles before you went out and got them for yourself," Simone said in defense of my mate. "You are the only drunk person to ever stomach pickles with alcohol in your stomach."

"They're yummy," I declared, waving for the server to bring us drinks. "I hope Parker has some at home for tonight."

"Jeez," Simone shakes her head.

We were sipping martinis as the rest of the crowd started trickling in and taking their seats. As we continued talking, the party behind us got louder and louder with their complaints.

"Whose dick do you think they had to suck to get the upgrade we were supposed to get?"

"They all look like whores. They probably took turns sucking off the owner of the club."

"We're being punished for not being sluts like them."

I was gripping the seat of my chair, and so was Courtney. Simone had her amused grin on her face, just waiting for me to blow my fucking lip on these bitches.

"No class at all. Look at what they're wearing. That redhead is just in a sports bra and shorts. Women like them, I bet, couldn't get guys without paying. You're getting married at the Meyers resort ballroom and they probably couldn't even afford to spend a night there. We should have just splurged on the VIP tickets instead of assuming you could get the upgrade."

"You should also pay extra to get those report owner brothers to personally attend the wedding. I hear they're married, but I'm sure one of us could bag one of them. Then we would be set for life with a hot guy at our side."

"Hell, I'd be satisfied with just having one last fling with one or both of them," the bride snickered.

Hadley and Vivian exchanged a glance, then turned to the women. "Excuse me. May I ask what day you are getting married?" Vivian asked the bride.

The woman in the tacky veiled headband turned her nose up in disgust. "I don't see how that is any of your business, but if you must know, being a nosy old hag, my wedding is next Saturday."

"Did we have a booking for next Saturday?" Vivian asked Hadley.

"I think we did. I guess I'll have to clear that up when we get back."

"Clear what up?" A woman with a silk cami top that said MOH on the front glared.

"Oh, I'm sorry." Vivian grinned widely, looking the epitome of class and decorum. She turned to hold her hand out as if to shake the bride's hand. To no surprise of anyone, she didn't return the gesture, so Vivian curled her fingers in, widening her smile. "I'm Vivian Meyers, the original owner of the resort. The one you just mentioned getting married this Saturday. This is my daughter-in-law, Hadley Meyers, the current owner and wife of the men you were just discussing. This is Lilly Meyers, the wife of my other son," Vivian waved at Lilly, who giggled and waved back. "We'll let you know in the morning about the status of your reservation. I think Mitch mentioned something about the pipes in the wall?" She played pensively while staring at Hadley.

"He did go on about exploding pipes in the walls," Hadley agreed.

"So unfortunate. I hear the justice of the peace downtown or the courthouse can take short notice weddings. Maybe give them a call? Do you need the number?" Vivian pulled out her phone as if to really give it to them.

"Are you fucking serious?" The maid of honor asked with a horrified expression.

"You can't do that," the bride whispered, looking as white as a sheet. "I paid a deposit."

"Oh, I can get that back to you now. You can use it to buy the VIP seating at this club tomorrow. I own this club too, by the way," Vivian grinned. "I actually own all the buildings on this block. And Simone, down there." Vivian pointed to Simone, who giggled at the attention. "She and her husband own most of the clubs on the other side of the street. You ladies were just bad-mouthing the most prominent women of this city. Next time you decide to turn your jealousy into hateful words, remember this moment, because you might be speaking within earshot."

All the women behind us were ghostly white, except for the bride, who seemed to turn bright red from embarrassment.

"And those men you just want to bag as a last fling," I leaned forward, wiping my finger on my tongue and swiping it down the bride's bare arms. A fake orange glow smeared all down my finger. "They hate fake tanners. Even if they weren't happily married and completely obsessed with their wife, not one of you would be their type." I turned completely in my seat, displaying my bralette that looked a lot like a sports bra. "And I look so fucking hot in this sports bra. Do I not?" I challenged. The glint in my eyes made it impossible to disagree with me.

Before they could answer, the lights dimmed, and I smugly turned in my seat for the beginning of the show.

"I think you look hot in your sports bra." Courtney wiggled her eyebrows at me.

"I know I do," I shrugged. "That's why they said shit in the first place."

The music hammered into the stale club air; the lights flickering with the tempo. As the smoke machines went off, everyone cheered as nine men ran out on stage dressed in not the usual stripper outfits, but leg warmers and cufflinks covered in different colored fur that matched fur covered shorts each of them were wearing. They all had on wolf masks, too.

"What the fuck?!" I yelled above the music, getting hit with several familiar smells. The tattoos all over the masked men standing before us looked all too familiar. Especially the tallest man standing at the head of the group.

Then the dancer in the front removed his mask, throwing it right at me, and the crowd went wild seeing his face. I just sat silently, gaping, completely in disbelief.

"Parker?!"

"You did say you wanted Parker to take up stripping," Simone reminded me, laughing and cheering with the rest of the crowd. I recognized Vincent on the stage after following Simone's gaze. I can't believe our men did this.

"This was not what I had in mind!"

59

MAGIC PARKER

"What the fuck are you doing, Parker?!" I yelled above the noise of the crowd. His cocky smile said that he heard me, but he gave no other answer. He simply blew me a kiss, then looked back at Vincent, who now had his mask off too.

Vincent nodded at the DJ, then went back to sending Simone sultry gag-worthy glances. Simone was a whimpering mess beside me. She had no issues with her mate showing up on a girl's night, unlike me. Out of all of us, I was the only one who was pissed. All the other women were swooning with the rest of the crowd.

"You've got to be shitting me," I muttered when *She Wolf* started blaring through the speakers.

"Oh my, this is better than I expected," Courtney giggled. Casey was on the other side of Parker, thrusting his hips in tempo with the beat. He still had his mask on, and his tattoos were still colored in with markers by the kids. He always lets the kids use him as a living coloring book. Courtney loves it. She has fucking hearts in her eyes right now.

"I thought you said you didn't want him stripping for you because you didn't want to get pregnant again."

"Getting pregnant sounds pretty fun right now," she grinned, biting the tip of her nail. Casey took off the mask and threw it at her, giving her a panty-dropping wink. Smooth mother mucker. She could get pregnant from the look alone.

"Ladies and all the fabulous men present for tonight's show." The host's voice echoed in the speakers. "We have a special treat for you tonight. Allow me to present our special guest just for this one honorary night, the Alpha, and his wolf pack!"

I cringed inwardly at the lack of creativity, along with the truth in the name, but high-pitched screams pierced my ears from the human women's excitement. All these men look like wolves, and leave it to Parker to not mince words when coming up with a stripper name. At least he didn't try to call himself 'Magic Parker' or anything stupid like that.

Then my dad came into view. "Goddess, this is too fucking much." I covered my eyes, trying to unsee my dad shaking his hips and biting his bottom lip while staring at my stepmom.

"Look at Uncle Tommy go!" Courtney laughed.

"Fucking kill me now," I groaned.

"Ah, let the old man have his fun. Elena loves it!" Courtney yelled, then went back to eye-fucking Casey.

Mitchel and Mark had already dragged Hadley on stage, sandwiching her between them, while running her hands through the bulges in their fur. They wasted no time getting her between them, even though their mom was in the audience.

Vivian was too distracted with her own mate to notice or care. The triplet's father jumped down from the stage, and was obstructing Vivian's view of anything but his fur-covered junk grinding in front of her face in time with the music. He was a beautiful man for his age, and fit the stripper stereotype a little too well.

"Eyes on me," Parker's voice rang through my head.

"What the fuck are you even doing here?"

"Giving you what you want," he said darkly. A shiver traveled through me from the dark look in his eyes. When the tempo picked up, and Sia started bellowing about a she-wolf with yellow eyes and falling to pieces, all the men simultaneously pulled all their fur shorts, revealing fur thongs underneath.

A possessive growl ripped out of me when the women all around us went crazy. I was on my feet, about ready to rip Parker off the stage and drag him out of there, but he jumped down and got in my face before I could.

"You fucking ass hole," I snarled, glaring up at his smug, handsome face. "Cover your shit."

"What shit?" He took my hands, moving them down his bare chest. He then tugged me forward, making our bodies press against one another, and moved my hands to grip his ass. "This shit?"

"All of it," I huffed in his face. "It's all mine."

"It is," he agreed with a crooked grin. "And this," he grabbed my ass, lifting me swiftly in his bulging arms, making it where I had to wrap my legs around his waist, "is all mine. Did you really think I was going to let other guys take their clothes off in front of you?"

"Yes," I answered honestly. "You jerk."

"Hmm, you are so wrong," he ran his tongue up my neck, lingering over my mark. My legs tightened around him in reflex, my underwear getting damp from the effects of him using the mate bond to subdue my anger. "I can smell you getting wet for me, baby."

"Shut up," I growled, trying to resist temptation.

"Make me," he said in defiance.

His coy smile stayed in place as he carried me up to the stage. His eyes were locked on my face, the fevered lust behind them clear for all to see. I felt nervous, but I was trying not to let it show.

All the men were working over and dancing on their mates now. Hadley was pinned to the ground, Mitch dancing with his junk over her face and Mark kissing his way up between her legs. The show was way too much for the audience, but they didn't care. Mitch and Mark never cared. Hadley is the one who keeps them in check, but she was being overwhelmed by both of them, and she was probably trying to prove something to the bitchy bride that the men were hers.

Casey was giving Courtney a lap dance, Courtney laughing her ass off and cheering him on. Daryl was making out with Hillary, Hillary's hand over his furry crotch. Matt had Lilly giggling, hoisting her over his shoulder to drag her to the stage like his brothers did with Hadley. Their mother and father were in their own little world. Vivian was lost in her mate's sensual dancing, not noticing anything else around her.

Oh, fuck me. I gagged seeing dad bent over the side of the stage, letting Elena smack him on the ass. No daughter should have to see their dad doing that shit.

"Where the fuck did Simone go?" I looked around, distracting myself from Parker's gaze so I would quit getting caught up in his game.

"Vincent wasn't going to let any other woman ogle him, he had said. He probably took Simone to the back room."

"What a fucking gentleman," I growled, glaring at Parker.

"I'm just giving you what you want," he reminded me again. "You wanted a show."

"This isn't what I wanted."

"Isn't it?" he grinned, dropping me onto a chair that magically appeared at the center of the stage.

"What the hell do you have planned?" I raised an eyebrow, giving my dad and Elena a wary look. I had an idea of what he was about to do, and I didn't think it was safe for parental supervision.

"You came here for a certain type of strip show. I plan on giving it to you." He smiled, standing up straight as the DJ changed the music to the all too familiar Ginuwine song.

"No you are not! My dad is right there!"

"Is he?" Parker looked over his shoulder, and that's when I noticed my dad and Elena were nowhere to be seen. I looked around the room, squinting through the glare of lights, and saw them leaving through the back door, Elena draped over his shoulder, giving me a little wave with a sated smile on her lips. "He was just here to get his mate."

"Fuck," I gaped in disbelief.

"Mmh, I love your dirty mouth." Parker leaned down, pressing his lips to mine, making the crowd cheer wildly. "Makes me want to make the rest of you just as dirty."

Parker then took my face in his hands and thrusted his pelvis towards it in time with the music. When he let go, I growled and watched as he sank to the ground in front of me, arching his bbackand jerking his hips in my direction. If I wasn't so pissed, it would have been hot as hell. With the crowd going crazy for his almost naked ass, I couldn't enjoy this at all. I wanted to strangle him.

As if he could read my thoughts, he leaned forward, grabbing my hands, staring up at me with a heated gaze. He wrapped my hands around his throat, squeezing his hands over mine, then gliding my hands to the back of his head. He moved my legs wide open, diving between them. His hot breath could be felt through the fabric of my shorts. My pussy was getting wet, despite my pissy mood.

He glided his hands over my thighs, gripping my waist, then listed me in the air. I was straddling him in a daze. His hips were rotating and gyrating towards me. I could feel how hard his dick was. You could see those lickable lines leading down to it. I couldn't stop myself from touching them.

He lifted me, turning us around, so I was back in the chair. He lifted his leg, thrusting his hard dick right in my face. His scent and his touch were too much, and my possessiveness, combined with the cheers from the crowd, were about to break me.

"You have five seconds to get me out of here, or I'm fighting you on this stage," I snarled.

He laughed breathlessly. "As my Luna commands." He lifted me in his arms. "But first...."

He laid me on the ground, and I gave him a puzzling look. He had a smile that I didn't trust in place. He lifted my knees, then turned around so his back was to me. As he hooked his legs through mine, I realized what he was about to do, but it was too late. He twirled me around on the ground and had his dick planted between my ass cheeks. He was tugging on my pponytail jerking my head back to kiss me deeply. The buzzing in my head drowned out the screams of the excited crowd.

I was breathless, delirious, and completely out of sorts. Parker came here to throw me off guard and overpower me, and he accomplished that. He can do with me whatever he wants, as long as this show continues in private.

He was smiling at himself, carrying me in his arms as we descended from the stage.

"OVER HERE! OVER HERE!" the bitchy maid of honor yelled out as we passed by. "She's getting married soon! Can she get a dance too?" She batted her fake eyelashes. "Or even me?"

"Sorry," Parker snorted. "I don't dance with cheaters and sluts. Only for my wife." Parker kissed my forehead. "Condolences to your future husband."

The bride turned bright red, and the maid of honor's mouth dropped. The entire group looked embarrassed, since many were now mocking them, pointing and laughing out loud. I didn't care anymore. I just wanted Parker alone as fast as possible.

With that, we left the club, Parker carrying me while he was still half naked all the way to the employee lot where his truck was parked. He used the door code to get in, then I helped him get rid of the rest of his ridiculous outfit before returning the favor and grinding my crotch in his face until he made me scream.

60

— • —

Bathing Suit Areas and Tattoos

Rosie

"I've got a strange feeling," Thyra said as we all sat around the kitchen table after Alpha Max finished whatever pep talk he was having with Taegan.

"Not another one of your damn feelings again, woman. I'm not riding the glue stick again until our asses are heading home."

"Not that kind of feeling," Thyra scoffed, waving her hand dismissively at her mate.

"Glue stick?" I leaned over and whispered the word as a question to Rian.

"Don't ask," he grinned crookedly and made a dramatic roll of his eyes.

"I don't want to hear shit about any more of your damn feelings. I'm still trying to wrap my head around this one."

"It wasn't a bad feeling, you grump," Thyra slapped his arm. "I just got the sudden feeling that I was missing something great happening back home."

"Something great?" Alpha Max raised his eyebrows. "What something great? The greatest thing you've got happening is right here," he said, waving his hands up and down his large frame.

I couldn't help but to laugh at Alpha Max's playfulness with his mate. Alpha Axel is the serious type, and I thought Alpha Max was the same, but the more I see him with Thyra, the more I see a lot of Taegan's character in him. Taegan was playful like that, too. Especially with his sisters.

Thyra offered me a warm smile, catching my amusement. "Forgive him, Rosie. I know you have pressing matters to attend to, like finding your friend."

"You're the one that brought up your fucking feelings!" Alpha Max huffed, sounding completely offended.

Thyra glared at him, but he just blew her a kiss. They were cute together. I never thought I would see anything about Alpha Max as cute.

"Did you tell her everything?" Taegan asked Rian, refocusing the conversation on the reason for this little table meeting we were having once again in the kitchen of Thyra's house. These meetings haven't ended well the last few times we have tried. Hopefully, this one goes better.

"He did," I answered for Rian.

"Found time to talk as well, huh?" Taegan smirked, his eyes zeroing in on the mark on Rian's neck.

I growled defensively. "He told me while we were upstairs while you were getting your safe fairy sex talk from your grandpa, you ass."

"So you didn't have any time to talk when you were out for your little walk?" Taegan's eyes glistened with amusement.

"I heard a lot of screaming, not not much talking," Alpha Max muttered.

My face went bright red, and I tried to hide my embarrassment behind my hands.

"Max!" Thyra backhanded his chest.

"Dad!" Rian pulled my chair closer to his, tucking my face to his chest to help me hide my embarrassment. "Why?"

"What? Why what?" Alpha Max looked around at all of us sitting at the table. Even Phoebe was snickering, covering her mouth on the opposite end of the table. "Can't a dad brag about his son?"

"No!" Rian and Thyra said together. "Not about that, dad," Rian went on to say.

"Ah, it's nothing to be shy about. I make your mom scream constantly."

"MAX!" Thyra stood up, grabbing him by the ear roughly. Alpha Max cried out in protest. Taegan and Rian were both hanging their heads with disgust at hearing about their parents', or grandparents', sex life. Phoebe was bent over, trying to suppress her giggles. "We need a talk about what's appropriate to say and what's not. You're embarrassing poor Rosie."

"I'm fine," I lied, smiling tightly.

"Still," Thyra gave me an apologetic smile, then turned a cross expression to her mate. "Get your ass up and follow me."

"Why!? I was just stating the truth!"

"You need an attitude adjustment. That's why," Thyra fumed, dragging the hulking man out of the room, still tugging on his ear.

"I It's too damn old to be trying her patience like that," Taegan groaned, shaking his head. "She should use a spoon on his ass."

"I agree," Rian muttered. He still looked disturbed. I would be too if I heard my dad say that shit about my mom. I have the opposite problem. Usually it is my mom who over shares shit like that.

"Come on. They're fucking hilarious," Phoebe chuckled. "Alpha Max has never had a filter."

"No, he hasn't. I'm sorry he embarrassed you like that," Rian whispered in my ear.

I smiled shyly at him. "It's okay. I think they're funny too. I didn't know your dad could be like that. I thought he was no-nonsense and serious all the time."

"Not around family," Phoebe said. "You're family now, girl. Be prepared to see more of that same blunt, no-filter Alpha Max in the future. He's now your father-in-law, after all."

I bit my lip, liking what I was hearing. I gained an amazing mate and two powerful in-laws, too. I've seen Alpha Max dote on Taegan's sisters and even Luna Bailey and Thyra. I feel like I'm about to be privy to some Alpha Max persona that only the most special of women to him get to see.

"Are you weirded out?" Rian asked me.

An uncontrollable grin stretched on my lips as I stared up into his mesmerizing, galaxy-twirling eyes. "Not at all. I'm happy. I get to have you and your parents are adorable."

"Adorable?" Taegan scoffed. "I can't wait until Grandpa hears you call him that."

"Luna Bailey calls him adorable sometimes," Phoebe reminded Taegan.

"Mom calls me adorable, too. She's a poor judge of what adorable truly is."

"You used to be adorable," I teased him. "Then you grew into a fucking giant with a giant ego and not a humble bone in your oversized body."

"My body is too full of awesome-sauce to be filled with anything else," he smirked.

"See," I laughed, shaking my head.

"So, I see your mark on Rian," Phoebe said, changing the subject. "Where did Rian end up putting his imprint on you?"

"Ooh, yeah. Did you get a tramp stamp like my grandpa has?" Taegan sounded too enthusiastic to find out. "Let me see."

"Did you just ask to see my ass?" I growled. I felt Rian's arms tighten around me.

"No," Taegan scoffed. "I just want to see the skin above it."

"I didn't mark her there, and if I did, you wouldn't be seeing it," Rian said in a leveled tone.

"Where did you mark her then?" Taegan smirked, crossing his arms over his chest, making his muscles bulge. He really is too big, with far too much muscle. I can't believe I ever found that attractive. I much prefer Rian's body. I grimaced and felt sorry for Taegan's poor shirt. It looked ready to bust at the seams. His chest was bigger than mine.

"None of your business," Rian snapped.

Taegan's smirk became more mocking. "You left your mark on her ass, didn't you?"

"Maybe it was her chest?" Phoebe offered.

"Or the other bathing suit area," Taegan snickered. "Sounds like he spent a lot of time focused on-"

"It's on my shoulder!" I yelled, cutting him off before he could finish that sentence. "Fuck, you're annoying."

"Lies. You would show us if it was really just your shoulder. It probably really is on your vaginal area."

"Vaginal area?" Phoebe raised her eyebrows.

"Rian would be upset if I called it her pussy," Taegan shrugged.

"Oh, I'm getting plenty upset already. Keep talking about my mate's bathing suit parts and I might start leaving my magical marks all over your ass, too."

"See," Taegan chortled. "I knew it. It's on her ass."

"Fucking hell," I snarled, turning around and pulling the back of my shirt up so they could see Rian's name over my butterfly tattoo in its glowing, intricate script. "It's on my fucking sshoulder,you dipshit. Quit talking about my ass and pussy."

"And your tits," Phoebe added. "Those were mentioned too."

"By you," Taegan scoffed.

Both Taegan and Phoebe leaned over the table to inspect my mark. I was facing Rian now, and he had a look of pride on his face as I showed off his name embedded in my skin. I could see how much he liked having a claim on me, and proof of it. I'm glad he put it on my shoulder and not on my vag like mom suggested. I can show this off all the time easily, so everyone can see who owns the other half of my soul. Seeing the pride on his face makes me want to show his mark off to everyone.

"I like your tattoo," Phoebe said, running her fingers over it. "Looks familiar."

"It looks like mine," Taegan said, pulling up his own sleeve and showing off the butterflies mixed in with his tattoos.

"It does," Phoebe said, looking from Taegan's arm to my shoulder. "The butterflies are identical."

"You didn't have that last time I came to visit," Taegan said. "When did you get it?"

"The day of my birthday party. I got it that morning."

"Did you mean to make it look like Taegan's?" Phoebe asked. "I mean, they really are identical."

"Uh," I looked nervously at Rian. The proud expression was fading away. His eyes were spinning their orbital beauty, but there was tension in the corners of them. "I guess so," I couldn't help but to answer honestly. I didn't want to make Rian feel my lie in the bond. I could feel his troubled feelings and didn't want to add to them. "I just liked the butterflies, so I thought I'd get one too."

"Hmm," Phoebe hummed.

I pulled my shirt back down, then turned around, too embarrassed that my little crush on Taegan caused me to permanently mark my body to be like his.

Phoebe and Taegan were staring at one another, their eyes glowing. They were mind linking about something, and when their eyes kept flashing at us, I had a feeling that I knew what they were talking about. My crush on Taegan wasn't a secret.

Rian was getting more and more tense as they continued to mind link. His hand was no longer holding on to me. It was draped loosely on the back of my chair, and losing contact between us was eating at me. It was the first time he willingly stopped touching me since we mated.

"Uh, so," Phoebe smiled nervously, clearing her throat. "About your friend. We should probably map out all the details that we know so you can get to work on finding her tomorrow."

"Yeah," Taegan smiled tightly, then ran his hand over his jaw. "You had some creepy demonic fae creature lingering in your soul. We should figure that shit out, too."

The conversation felt forced, and when Thyra and Alpha Max joined us again a moment later, they were looking around at all of us like they could tell something was off.

The soul feeling in my gut prevented me from even finding amusement in the state Thyra's appearance was in. She looked like she did anything but talk to her mate. Her lips were swollen and her hair was mused. Even her mate mark was bruised with a large hickey on top of it.

"Are you okay?" I eventually mustered the courage to ask Rian.

"Fine," he answered flatly.

Shit. He was pissed about the tattoo, just like I knew he would be.

61

— · —

SAME FIGHT

The room was stuffy. I felt so uncomfortable sitting there, trying to discuss the shit going on with me and how we were going to find Julia while the tension was so thick.

Rian had barely said a word to me. He barely said a word at all to anybody. He answers questions, but that's it.

And he still hasn't touched me. Not once. His arm wasn't even draped over the back of my chair any longer.

Alpha Max and Thyra walked in at the start of the tension, but no one revealed the cause of it. I'm not even sure the cause is something worth telling. I'm too embarrassed to admit that my mate placed his mark on a tattoo I got to mimic his nephew's during the time I thought I would still be Taegan's mate. My previous crush on Taegan was never a secret, even to them.

The older, burly Alpha was staring at each one of us while the rest of us talked, his thick brows furrowing deeper and deeper with every passing minute. I knew it was coming, but I still jumped in shock when he finally exploded.

"What the fuck is going on?!"

The entire table went silent. Phoebe scratched her forehead, looking everywhere but at Alpha Max and Thyra, and Taegan had his arms crossed tightly over his chest, playing dumb.

"What do you mean, Grandpa?" Taegan looked like an overgrown child, bouncing his leg on the floor nervously.

"I mean with all of you," he pointed his beefy finger in a circle at the four of us. "Did one of you let out a fart before we walked in?"

"No one farted," Taegan smirked.

"You sure? Because something fucking stinks. What the hell is going on?"

"They're all probably just tired, honey," Thyra patted his arm. "It's getting really late and they've had an extremely long day."

"Hmph," Alpha Max grunted, then stared pointedly at Rian and me. "Is that it? You're tired?"

I smiled tightly, then nodded, too scared to use words. If I said out loud that everything was fine, it could piss Rian off more. I'd be lying to his parents, too.

"Maybe we should pick this back up in the morning," Thyra suggested, giving me a sympathetic smile.

Alpha Max continued to stare at Rian, no longer looking at all at me for answers. There was some deep communication happening there, but I knew they could not mind link. It was a hidden message being passed from a father to his son.

"The rest of you get to bed then. I think Rian and I need to talk about one more thing."

I hesitated to get up, staring back at Rian as I did. He didn't spare me a glance. He just stared back at his dad, a stony expression set on his face.

"Come, Rosie," Thyra held her hand out in my direction. After a second of hesitation, internally begging Rian to look up at me, I gave up and took her hand, letting her pull me out of the room with her while she ushered Taegan and Phoebe out of the door in front of us.

"Hold my hand too," Taegan whined, swooping his large form down to grab her other hand. "You're making me jealous, grandma Thyra."

"Silly boy," she beamed up at him.

"I want a hand too," Phoebe teased.

"Here you go," Taegan held his free hand out to her. He had this cocky smirk while wiggling his fingers at her.

The hallways in this house were far too narrow for the four of us to be holding hands at the same time. Phoebe must have realized that obvious fact, too. She took my free hand instead, pulling me ahead, so Thyra let me go and I was just with Phoebe.

"Go ahead and soak up Grandma Thyra's affection, you overgrown baby. I'll take Rosie instead."

She pulled me ahead of them with her, up the stairs and into Rian's room. I didn't protest, having no reason to, and because I was silently grateful that she took me away from what could be an awkward conversation with my mate's mother when he was clearly upset with me again.

"Phew," Phoebe plopped down on the bed. "I feel like I can breathe now. It was stuffy as shit down there."

I smiled awkwardly. "Yeah," I agreed.

"Hey," she patted the spot on the bed beside her. "I'm sorry about earlier," Phoebe said as I slowly sat down. "I didn't think before I asked about your tattoo. Rian usually isn't the jealous type, so I didn't think he would be upset about it when I noticed. I was trying to tease you both and took it too far."

I couldn't really say it was okay, because it felt like the complete opposite of being okay right now, but I smiled softly at her apology. "I've seen mostly that side of Rian since we found out we were mates," I admitted. "I thought now that we were mated he would feel more at ease with the past I had stupidly obsessing over Taegan, but I guess not."

"Yeah, I didn't think it would be such an issue either. It's not like you two slept together or anything. I guess it's different when you find your mate," Phoebe said in a dry tone. She then sighed deeply. "I'll have to be careful in the future now too, so I don't make my future mate jealous."

I cringed, feeling ashamed. "I should have listened to Taegan the thousands of times he told me we weren't mates. Maybe Rian wouldn't feel so threatened by shit like this now."

"Maybe," Phoebe shrugged. "Personally, I like seeing Rian be possessive and jealous. He never really fought for anything he wanted in the past. He was always too kind and too giving. Some of the wolves in the pack that didn't really know him thought that he didn't have a backbone because of it, but we all knew that wasn't the case. He just always put others before himself. Him acting all defensive about you shows that he's not going to roll over and let someone else threaten his bond with you. If he wasn't upset at all, I'd be more concerned."

I pressed my lips together, staring at the ground as I thought about what Phoebe had just said.

"I feel bad about the tattoo. If I had told him before, he might have put his mark somewhere else."

"I think that tattoo is the perfect spot to put his mark on," Phoebe smirked. "It's overwriting the last attachment of your childhood crush with a part of him that will last forever. His brand is the dominant feature on your skin. I'm sure he will see it that way too once he cools down. He can't blame you for having a crush," she shrugged. "Just like you can't blame him for having a past before you."

I narrowed my eyes, a soft growl emitting from my chest. "What past before me?"

She burst out laughing. "Ah, you two are hilarious," she patted my back. "Don't worry. He didn't have any long-term crushes lingering around him. Alpha Max didn't let his boys mess around with women in our pack."

"Then outside of the pack?"

"That," she tapped the end of my nose playfully, making me growl, "is none of my business."

"But it's mine."

"See," she chuckled. "This jealousy you are feeling right now is what he feels when you are around Taegan. It's natural and healthy with mates. Now," she stood up and stretched her arms above her head, "I'm going to go to bed. It really has been too long of a fucking day."

I was still raging about the idea of Rian with a past, but managed to tell her goodnight before she left the room. Maybe I couldn't blame Rian for his feelings towards Taegan and me, since I was getting this pissed off by some imaginary girl I'm conjuring up in my mind. Even the idea of Rian having a history with another girl is souring my mood.

I was rifling through drawers, trying to find something to change into now, fuming still on the inside. I found a shirt that looked way too small for Rian, but would fit snugly on me. After washing my face and getting as cleaned up as I could without my toothbrush that Rian still had stored away with my things in his magical hidden locker he can conjure up with his magic, I went back to his room and started stripping out of my dirty shirt.

I had it off, along with my bra, by the time Rian came in.

62

DOING THIS ALONE

O ur eyes met, and the surprise on his face almost made me smile. But then his eyes scanned the tattoo on my back, and they turned cold again.

I rolled my eyes, pulling his childhood shirt over my head and down my body to hide the tattoo. Hope had flared for a moment that he might prefer that I keep my shirt off, but with the issue of my tattoo still weighing heavy on us, that was clearly not the case.

"Rian," I said, pulling on his arm when he tried to walk toward the bathroom. "We need to talk."

"About what?" He wasn't pulling away from me, but his entire body had become tense because of my touch. The sparks were flaring stronger than ever before, but he seemed unaffected by them. That hurt.

"Rian, please," I tugged lightly on him. "I don't want to fight over something stupid."

"I'm not fighting," he said through gritted teeth. "I'm just wondering how much more my nephew will hang over us."

"He's not hanging over us."

"Really?" Rian's eyes snapped at mine. "So my mark isn't branded over a symbol of your feelings for him, that you willingly put on your own body the morning that we found out we were mates?"

"I didn't know we were mates then!"

"No, you thought you would still be mated with Taegan. You still had hope that it would be him and not me."

"I didn't think if my mate wasn't Taegan, it would be his uncle!" I snapped back. "That's not fair and not my fault."

"No," he huffed, shaking his head. An irritable smile softly graced his lips. "You never even considered me before that moment."

"Did you consider me?!" I yelled. "You were making out and hooking up with my friends every time you came to town. Apparently, you even have a past in your own damn town too before me. I never even touched another fucking man before you. Not even your nephew, so this whole fucking fit you're throwing at me is stupid."

"My feelings are stupid? Did you really just say that?"

"No. This fight is stupid. I don't want fucking Taegan. The tattoo is meaningless now."

His eyes were blazing, the galaxies in them flamed with his anger. "Maybe my mark on it is meaningless too?"

"What?!" I scoffed, letting him go and backing away. "Are you fucking serious right now?"

"No!" His eyes went wide for a minute, like he had just realized what he said. He covered his face and started rubbing circles on his forehead. "I didn't mean it like that. I'm just tired. Let's talk about this tomorrow."

I couldn't speak. I turned my back to him as he walked towards the bathroom so he wouldn't see the angry tears in my eyes. "Fuck it," I snarled, wiping them away with the back of my hand. I wiped the hot moisture away from my hands on the fabric of my shorts, and that's when I felt the stone still resting in my pocket that Kret had given me at the pond.

With all the shit that kept happening with Rian, I almost forgot why I really came here. Guilt and dread weighed down on me, my selfishness and the warring emotions that keep stemming from the mate bond caused me to just be angry with myself.

I'm a fucking Alpha. Not some pubescent little girl who can't get a hold on the dramatics.

Talking with Rian and Taegan wasn't getting us anywhere. It just caused us to fight every damn time we tried to do anything as a team. Maybe it's time I did this alone. I got a solid lead, the only one we've gotten the entire time we have been here. I did that by myself after the last major fight we had.

All this other shit can wait. The dramatics, the arguing, and the constant battle Rian is having alone with his own fucking nephew. I get it. I get why he is mad, but Julia could be dying while we sort this other shit out. The issues between Rian and me could wait. I'll deal with this all later. For now, I need to do my job and do what I can to bring Julia back.

Rian came out of the bathroom as I was gathering up my bra and shirt, about to sneak out of the room.

"Where are you going?" he asked, staring at my clothes in my hand, the other hand on the doorknob with a deep scowl.

I walled up my emotions, trying to keep my face passive. I didn't want to start another fight. "Downstairs."

"You're not sleeping in here?" His expression seemed hurt, but that hurt was quickly replaced with anger. "Are you sneaking over to Taegan's room?"

"What?!" I couldn't believe he just accused me of that. "No! Are you...." My heart hurt so fucking bad hearing him ask me that. "Fuck you!" With that, I stormed out, slamming the door behind me.

I thought mating and marking each other would help overcome this kind of shit. I guess not. I'm not going to keep having the same argument over and over again. Not when I have work to do.

Thankfully, no one was downstairs when I quietly descended the stairs. I quickly got my clothes back on, throwing the small borrowed shirt on the couch before slipping on my cloak and my shoes, and silently leaving the house. I pulled the stone out of my pocket as I traveled through the sleeping streets of the fairy village, rubbing it between my fingers. I could feel its magic and the power inside it humming in my hand. It was so different to Rian's magic, but it wasn't unpleasant. Right now, I actually liked it. It helped me to center myself again.

The necklace around my neck started pulsing softly against my throat. Kret said the magic wouldn't mix, and I had to take the necklace off before I could call for him. I dragged it over my head before pulling my hood back up to hide my face. The butterfly's stones were glowing gently. Staring at the pendent reminded me of the tattoo and the stupidness of the latest argument with Rian. I pocketed the necklace before I could get myself even more mad.

I turned off those petty emotions and urges as I neared the pond. It was the dead of night, and I know Kret said to wait until tomorrow to call him, but it was likely tomorrow already. I could only hope he wouldn't be too upset with me for calling him at this hour. I needed to get going before someone realized I was gone and everyone tried helping in their overbearing ways again.

With a steadying deep breath, I tossed the stone into the pond, hoping that Kret would come. This was my only lead to Julia. I had to find her. Soon. The sooner I found her and finished my duty as Alpha, the sooner I could deal with the issues with my mate.

"Why, hello my treasure," the deep, comforting voice of Kret startled me, not coming from the center of the pond like I expected, but from the forest behind it. "You are seeking me out much sooner than I expected."

His bulking frame looked more imposing with the dark magical forest behind him. His expression was as friendly as it was when we met before. He didn't look upset at all.

"I.... I was feeling desperate to do something. I'm sorry. I know it's late but..."

"No worries," he smiled easily, helping my heart to settle down. "I'm happy you sought me out in your time of trouble. It reassures me you feel comfortable enough with me to call your newest friend for hto with your matters of the heart."

"Matters of the heart?" I was confused for a moment, but then I remembered the excuse I had given him for seeking out the demonic merman. For a moment, I thought he was seeing right through me and maybe sensed the shit that had just happened with Rian. Kret caught me last time in this same spot when I was stressing over a fight with Rian. "Yes! My heart. So, uh, were you maybe able to find out anything?"

"I think I might have," his smile beamed, relaxing me again. "Follow me, my lovely, and I can take you to the likely place you will find this merman who stole your heart."

I stared at the dark water in front of me, nervous again because of Taegan's warning. Does Kret want me to swim across to him?

Then, Kret raised his hand, a dark cloud of magic smoking from his fingers. The smoke traveled across the pond in a steady stream until it reached me, and then it solidified, making a bridge for me to cross.

"I noticed you were without a proper swimsuit again, my treasure. We can travel on foot. For now. Hurry across, Rosie, and I will help you to find what you seek."

63

— ◆ —

Max's Shit

Max

Earlier...

"I don't need another talk," Rian said stubbornly.

He was scowling at the door where his mate had just disappeared with his mom and the others. When Taegan demanded someone to hold his hand too, right before the door swung shut, Rian looked ready to jump out of his chair and follow after them. I knew then that this was the same jealousy I saw earlier when Rosie sat beside Taegan on the couch.

This boy. He's so affected by that girl and doesn't have a damn clue how to deal with his emotions just yet.

"Did I ever tell you about my previous mate? Axel's mom?' I strummed my fingers on the table, trying not to appear too serious. The boy was ready to close himself off, and I didn't want that. That would cause him and his mate to just fight more. No woman will react rationally to their mate closing them off. I know that all too well.

"No. You never talk about her," Rian muttered.

"For good reason. We had a shitty relationship, and even now, the guilt can weigh on my chest like a stack of bricks when I talk or think about her."

"Why?" Rian was still scowling, but he seemed curious now. "Axel told me once that it was his mother who made all the mistakes. He said she made you miserable."

"Harriet made many of those," I said, hating the foreign taste of her name after not saying it for so long. "But I was the one who fucked up first."

Rian raised his brows, waiting for me to continue.

"I... I wasn't in a great place when we mated. She was my chosen mate, and I picked her out of duty after losing my first mate to the curse placed on the goddess. I went through the motions and did my duty as her mate from the outsider's perspective, but kept her at a distance with my emotions. For years and years, she tried to get my attention and to secure her place. Instead of reassuring her, I took the backseat in our relationship and let her do whatever she wanted. I never, not once, opened up to her. By guarding myself, I hurt her pride repeatedly. She felt she was rejected repeatedly. When I noticed the damage I had done, it was too late. We were never able to repair our relationship, and in her desperation to prove herself and find a place to belong, she made rash and shitty choices."

"Why are you telling me this?" Rian looked confused.

"Because watching you close yourself off with your mate sitting right beside you, seeing her so obviously desperate for your attention, you reminded me a lot of myself just now. The me back then who couldn't get control of my feelings unless I closed myself off to them completely. I don't know what the hell happened this time, but I can see you pushing her away."

"You don't even know what happened," Rian scoffed.

"No. I don't. So why don't you talk so we can figure this shit out?"

"Because there is nothing to figure out, dad!" Rian sounded exasperated. "Talking isn't going to make this okay."

"Make what okay?" Anxiety was gripping my chest. Or maybe it was just heartburn. I ate three huge burgers with extra jalapenos and greasy bacon before we left our world to come to this one. I had to. Thyra eats too much green shit for my taste and I figured green shit and bird food were all I would find here. I made Callum and Rosie's brother get me something normal before I took a ride from hell on the glue stick to come chasing these brats.

That reminded me I should probably find the bathroom down here before going up to bed with my woman. That would be a fast way to ruin my chances of playing chess tonight.

I tried to ignore the rumbling in my belly and focused on Rian and his issue again. "What did she do to make you this pissy, Rian? I don't get it. She's your mate."

"Yeah," he scoffed, crossing his arms and leaning back in his chair. "She may be my mate, but I know I wasn't the one she wanted."

"Is this about Taegan again?" I groaned. "Come on, boy. I thought we had talked about this. I thought you were okay now."

"I was, until I found out that I placed my imprint over... over," he pressed his lips together, steam almost coming out of his ears and nose. He looked more mad than I had ever seen him before. Rian never gets this mad. Whatever happened, it's hurting him. Bad. "She got a tattoo just for Taegan. Did you know that? It's fucking identical to the one he has."

"No. I didn't know that, but she's with you now. Unless his name is written all over her ass, I don't think that's anything to hold over her." I'd be pissed too if my woman had a tattoo because of another guy, but I wouldn't stone wall her for it. I'd whine my ass off until she did everything in her ability to make me feel better. I'd cum all over that tattoo until I felt better.

Fuck. Dark thoughts were coming into my head. I wonder what Thyra would think about getting a tattoo....

"I marked her over the tattoo," Rian mumbled. That pulled me right back out of my dirty thoughts about cumming all over my mate. "She didn't tell me. I thought she just liked butterflies. I didn't know she only liked them because Taegan had them tattooed on his arm. I... Fuck," he hung his head, covering his face. "I thought it was our thing. I thought it was in some way for me. I put my imprint right over the mark she put on herself for another guy, my damn nephew of all people, and I somehow thought that it was fitting because butterflies were our thing. It was never our thing though," he groaned. "It was theirs."

Well, shit. Yeah. If I was my son, I'd be pissed as hell, too. I would have fucked the other guy up, family or not.

"No matter what, it feels like Taegan is always going to be this wall between us. I could never measure up to him before. How can I get over this barrier when it is always fucking him?"

"Well," I wracked my brain, trying to come up with some kind of advice. I was a little stuck on how to help. No impressive words of wisdom came to me. Maybe Taegan will take one for the team and let Rian get a few good hits in to help get over his anger. Maybe Rian can move his imprint somewhere else? I don't know if it's possible, but his mom would know.

That won't fix this underlying issue Rian and Rosie keep having concerning Taegan. I was suddenly glad that Rosie would be taking over as Alpha of her pack, because that meant Rian wouldn't have Taegan close by to make him feel insecure like this all the damn time.

Taegan should never have gone on this trip with them. If he hadn't, I feel like shit would have been easier for this newly mated couple to sort out. They might be communicating by now.

"What will help you get over this, Rian? What do you think needs to be done between you and Rosie to work past the issue of Taegan? Something has to give, or the two of you will just keep drifting further and further apart."

Rian stared at the ground silently for a long time, then his eyes lifted to look at me. He looked so hurt and vulnerable at that moment.

"I don't know, dad. I'm scared of demanding anything from her. She... she didn't want me as a mate. She wanted him. If I keep pushing her, what if she.... what if she...."

There was fear in his voice. As pissed as he was, I could see he was still scared of losing her. He's not stonewalling her just out of anger, but out of fear that he still might get rejected.

"Before that girl left his room, she was staring at you like she was pleading with you to forgive her. I don't think you need to worry about that girl ever not wanting you. She does. Don't fight tonight. Don't say anything if you can't get your thoughts in order, but don't close her out any more. Just....just be there with her, and let the mate bond mend some of the hurt between you two tonight. In the morning, when your emotions aren't so heightened, that's when I would have a real conversation with her about the mark and the tattoo."

He nodded his head, looking defeated.

I wanted to stay and talk with him more, but my stomach was gurgling loudly now. I needed to find the fucking bathroom quickly.

"I'll see you in the morning, kid," I patted his back as I stood up from the table. I was clamping my butt cheeks together, and I couldn't wait around to coddle him more. Rian was a man now. At twenty years old, he can sort the rest out himself. Hopefully. These young men were testing the limits with their stupidity, but I had to deal with my own shit. Literally.

I found the fucking bathroom downstairs. It was as tiny as a fucking broom closet. I thought my ass was going to crush the tiny toilet. The entire time I was sitting on it, I was trying to support my weight as much as I could.

No fucking plunger. Great.

I cracked open the door, about to call for Thyra, or maybe even Rian, but before I could make a sound, I heard a movement in the living room. I looked around the hall, then peeked around the corner to see Rosie pulling on her shoes and getting on one of the cloaks used to hide our werewolf identities. Her eyes were red and I could tell she had been crying. She slipped out of the house silently before I grasped what she was doing.

Shit. That kid. One kiss, one touch, was all it would have taken to settle the bond between them again. What the hell happened between them now? What happened to make her leave on her own in tears in the middle of the night?

64

Tug Of War

Rosie

I stared across the bridge at the smiling Kret, apprehension weighing on me. I expected to find information, or directions to the ocean, where I could find the dark merman at best. I didn't think Kret would ask me to go with him. I was set on doing this alone. Being told to cross a strange bridge that appeared out of a magical black cloud over a large body of water, all to enter a forest that appeared to be anything but welcoming was leaving me apprehensive.

"You can find this dark merman?" I clarified one last time while heavily weighing what I was going to do.

"Oh, I can. I can do a great many things, my treasure. I am a powerful man. I will graciously use my power to help you in any way I can. That's what a friend does. Am I correct?"

His eyes darkened, and I felt a pull inside of me that told me I could trust him, but I was still apprehensive. The longer I stood there staring at him, deciding what to do, the less trusting I actually felt. The pull inside me was still there. It was strangely getting more and more nagging, and there was something about his smile. The longer he held it, it got tighter and tighter. It didn't appear friendly any longer. It seemed strained.

"I don't know if I can leave without at least telling my friends first..."

Maybe I should go back and get Phoebe, or maybe Thyra to come along, too. Rian was still upset with me and was hostile about Kret. Asking Taegan would make things worse with Rian. If I could go back and get someone to back me up, maybe going with Kret wouldn't be such a dangerous option.

"Rosie." There was a hardness to Kret's voice now. "If you want to find the one you seek, we need to hurry."

I bit my lip, still torn about what to do. Would he really not wait for me to go get Phoebe and come back? I wasn't even supposed to call on him until way later. Why is he in such a rush now? Despite the nagging feeling in my chest telling me I could trust him, this is starting to not feel right. That tugging sensation in my chest started to irritate me, like a rock in a shoe. It was just grating on my nerves now, and my back, where Rian's imprint was burning. There was a war going on with something inside me. My head was trying to make sense of too much at one time, all with the nagging feeling tugging on my chest.

"Rosie." Kret took a step forward, out of the dimness and into the light of the moon. His ashen face was sharper than I remembered, and I took a hesitant step back. "Come," he demanded. He wasn't asking now. He lifted his other hand, and suddenly that tugging inside my chest became a force that was moving me against my will.

I took an involuntary step onto the bridge. A black string extended from the palm of his hand, shining in the moonlight and stretching out across the pond to me. It connected to my chest, right where I was feeling the tugging. It was now a pulling force. Too strong to resist.

"What the hell?" I growled, trying to grab hold of the string to pull against it, but my hands couldn't touch it. They swept through it like air. It made me panic. "FUCKING STOP!" I demanded, but the pulling pain caused me to take another step onto the bridge. I was almost over the railing of the pond now on the incline of the bridge. Another step and I would be over the water. That water looked so much more enticing in the daylight. It looked like a lifeless black hole now. Staring down at it made my hair stand on end.

"What are we doing here?" a deep voice broke from the shadows behind me.

My forced steps onto the beginning of the bridge halted. Kret dropped the hand with the black string extending out of it. Kret's face was no longer friendly. It was no longer comforting to gaze upon as it was before. I felt hostility, not friendship, towards the man.

I looked behind me to see Alpha Max, and I breathed a sigh of relief, almost crumpling to the ground, trying to back off of the bridge. I thankfully caught myself on the fence surrounding the pond, or I might have accidentally fallen into the menacing water.

Alpha Max was in a cloak like mine, but his huge build and presence were telling of his powerful aura hidden underneath. His eyes were glowing a strange green I didn't expect. It looked like Thyra's magic. His glowing eyes were on Kret, hostility radiating out of them. He looked every inch the Alpha he was. As Alpha Max walked towards me, Kret let out a low, menacing hiss.

"Rosie," Kret called out, his voice laced with a rough desperation. It made that tugging feeling inside of me hurt and I cried out when he said my name. "Come. Now. We have no time to wait."

"I don't think I'll be letting her go with you anywhere. Who the fuck are you supposed to be? You got a black van with 'FREE CANDY' spray painted on the side over there somewhere? What kind of Fabio-demon looking fucker tries to lure young women into a dark forest in the dead of fucking night? You want someone to come over there and join you? I'll volunteer. I'll tie your cunt flaps to a tree and we can have a long chat about boundaries, you shit stain." Alpha Max placed a protective hand on my shoulder as I rubbed my chest.

"ROSIE!" Kret sneered. "COME! NOW!"

Kret raised his hand, and the black string appeared from my chest again. It was thicker than before and I still couldn't grasp it to pull against the force. It was still untouchable for me. I screamed out when it tugged tightly forward; the jerking causing me to flail over the railing of the fence at the banks of the pond. I got a face full of mud and I almost fell in, the string painfully forcing me forward more and more. Alpha Max caught me though, and held me tight, snarling at Kret.

"What the hell is this?!" He tried in vain to grab the string too.

I was screaming from the pain, feeling like my body was the rope in a game of tug of war. The bridge was evaporating. Kret wasn't pulling me towards it, anyway. He was trying to get me in the water.

"Hold on, Rosie," Alpha Max groaned, linking his arms under mine to keep me on the bank.

I couldn't hold on. I couldn't do anything but scream. I didn't want to go with Kret, but the pain was tearing me apart. I felt I was about to be torn in two.

"Just hold on. She's almost here," Alpha Max strained.

I couldn't ask who. I couldn't do anything. My insides were being ripped apart by the force of the black string.

"You got this, Rosie, just hold on. You-"

Suddenly, a blast of heat flew past my face. It hit Alpha Max on the shoulder, causing him to stumble back and loosen his grip on my arms. The force in my chest caused me to topple into the pond, blackness surrounding me so I couldn't tell which way was up.

The sensation of descending as my lungs struggled to keep the air from my last shortened breath inside made me nauseous. I wanted to scream. I wanted to yell out at Kret, begging him to stop. I wanted to let my wolf tear out of me, clawing the blackened string to bits.

I couldn't do any of those things. Not without drowning.

"Rian," I cried out to him, since it seemed the only thing I could do now. It felt like I was facing my end. I don't want the last memory he has of me to be my irrational anxiety-driven anger. *"I'm so sorry. I'm so sorry, Rian,"* I cried. *"I....I love you, and I am so sorry."*

65

— • —

TAKEN

Rian

"No," I gasped, feeling the mark on my neck throbbing painfully. "Please, no." Rosie was in trouble. Not just Rosie, but something was hurting our bond.

"Max," mom gasped, her eyes glowing with her magic. She was pushing herself to run alongside me, and I could see the fear written all over her face. She didn't tell me what was going on, but somehow I knew. I felt something was wrong with my mate, and I could see something was also wrong with hers. Wherever Rosie is, that's where dad is too.

When I first felt the irritating feeling deep in my chest, I thought it was stemming from my anxiety after Rosie left the bedroom. I was pacing, trying to sort myself out enough to face her without us fighting once again. Talking to her angrily just made it worse for both of us. I didn't want to crawl in that bed without her, but I was scared she would get fed up for good if I approached her without cooling down first.

Then, mom burst into my room and said that we needed to go. Immediately. I knew just from seeing the panicked look on my mother's face that something bad was happening, and then Rosie's mark on my neck burned. Not just throb. It was burning.

Mom was desperately racing beside me, and somehow I just knew where we were heading. Rosie left again because we once again fought over Taegan. I knew she was hurting, and all I wanted to do was get to her. I didn't care about the stupid tattoo or anything else anymore. I couldn't lose her.

"Rian. I'm so sorry," her fearful voice invaded my mind. My head was flooding with her feelings of guilt and fear..... and her regret. *"I'm so sorry, Rian. I-I love you, and I am so sorry."*

It wasn't just an apology. It was a last plea. It was a desperate attempt for forgiveness. It was a goodbye.

It was the first time she said that she loved me, and I choked, praying it wouldn't be the last.

"Rosie, I'm coming," I tried desperately to call out to her. "I'm almost there." I could see the abandoned mill and the pond just ahead. "Please, don't leave me."

The connection was gone. All my attempts to reach her were answered with silence. My neck was burning now, the connection to her sizzling to something so fragile I was scared to tug on it for fear it would snap.

The pond and the forest beyond were cloaked in dark magic. It was rancid in the air, the thick black smoke left over from it lying in a thick fog over the water.

"Where are they?" Mom looked around desperately. "MAX! ROSIE!" She sounded scared. "MAX!"

Something massive broke the surface of the water, a hulking frame emerging from the black fog.

"Max," mom went over the fence to help dad get to the shore.

"He took her," dad growled. He was staring at the forest across the way, then searched all around the pond. "HE FUCKING TOOK HER!"

He was pissed, but then so was I when I realized what he meant.

"WHO!" I demanded.

"That fabio fucker. He pulled her into the water." Dad shook off my mom, telling her to get help, and then dove back down to search for Rosie again.

My body was moving before he was under, jumping over the fence and diving into the water too. Mom threw a blast of her magic into the pond, illuminating the water from within, making it easier to see. She got rid of the black dark magic lingering on the surface as my dad and I tried desperately to find my mate.

My body's shape changed. My clothes drifted away when my tail and fins appeared. I swam desperately to the deepest depths, combing the floor for some sign of her. There were concentrations of black magic everywhere, but particularly in one spot. Whatever took her, it must have made a portal, like it did when it took Julia.

As my fingers were searching through the muddy bank, I felt a familiar jolt of power travel up my arm when my hand conneted with a hard metal object. Lifting it from the mud, my heart wretched seeing the necklace I gave to Rosie, the stone that held my magic broken in half.

***

Rosie

"Take a lick," mom said in my memory, turning on the new lamp she bought for my room. "It's a salt lamp. It purifies the air. It tastes like the ocean. Take a lick."

"That's weird, mommy. You're not supposed to lick lamps," I told her in my six-year-old voice.

"Just try," mom urged, holding the glowing pink rock out towards me.

I did as she said, hesitantly sticking out my small tongue and flicking it over one of the salt lamp's hard edges. My mouth exploded with the salty flavor.

"Yuck!" I giggled, trying to wipe the powerfully salty taste off my tongue. Mom laughed with me, even when I panicked.

The taste wouldn't go away. The more I wiped it with my hands, the more I tasted the salt all over my mouth. It was spreading to the back of my tongue, my throat, the roof of my mouth. When my nose burned, as well as my chest, fear set in on my little body. My eyes watered and I clung to my chest. My mom and my six-year-old me's bedroom faded away. The world around me was grainy and dark. Salt had overtaken all my senses, but now I feel the grainy, rough ground beneath my body.

My eyes flew open, a scratching burn in my chest making me cough and heave as I sat up straight on a sandy shore. I spat and coughed up so much water into the dark sand. It was pooling beneath my face. My eyes were burning as hot tears streamed down my cheeks. My throat burned and felt like sandpaper.

Where the fuck was I? I thought I had drowned. Fuck. Alpha Max. What happened to Alpha Max? He was with me.

I'm gasping for breath, ignoring the burning pain in my throat while face down in the wet sand, sucking in lungful after lungful of the rancid-smelling air. My limbs are too heavy to move right now. My body wasn't recovering like it should. It's like my wolf's side was suppressed.

When I could finally lift my head, I looked up to the desolate ocean ahead, fear running through me. I had no idea where I was, but I knew it wasn't Florida. I was staring at the ocean, but it seemed devoid of life. The waves were dark and menacing, full of malice.

The air tasted foul. It wasn't the sweet ocean air I loved. The scent that smelled so much like my mate.

I managed to push myself onto all fours, crawling away from the water to drier land. It was dark, and my werewolf senses weren't with me, but I could make out rocks and trees further inland. I couldn't see any trace of Alpha Max, and I didn't know if that was a good or bad thing. I pray that when Kret took me, he left Alpha Max alone. Alpha Max said to wait and hold on for something. I bet he called for help. Kret knew that. He had to have. That's why he was desperate to take me then, before more powerful people came. Hopefully, Kret fled once he got me into the water like he wanted and he left Alpha Max alone, but I saw no signs of Kret here on this foreign and spooky island either. I seemed to be alone.

I came upon what I thought was a long rock, but when my hand bumped against it when I crawled past, it groaned like it was in pain.

"What the-" I jerked away. I stared at it until my wolf's senses faintly came back to me and I could see better in the darkness.

It was a person. Their back was to me, but it was definitely a person. I could tell it was a woman because of her smaller build and long, matted hair. All I could smell before was salt, but as my wolf genes strengthened a bit more, I picked up the girl's scent. It was a familiar scent that sent me into a panic.

"Julia? Julie!" I crawled back to her, turning her on her side so I could see her face. It was her, but she looked dead. Her face was bruised and her jaw looked like it was out of joint. She was naked, her bikini in shreds. Worse than her face were her legs. They had bite marks all over them and one looked infected. It was clearly broken and puss was oozing out of an open wound.

If she hadn't groaned when I rolled her over, I would have assumed she was dead already. She looked like she was at death's doorstep. Her skin was ashen. She had lost a lot of blood from whatever she had been through.

I know there are races of sirens that feed on blood like vampires do. They were the result of the fall of the fae when the fairy kingdoms first tore the veil between the realms. The fairy knights my parents work with have to deal with those types of sirens at times. Lady Delilah has a special prison for them.

Was Kret the thing that took Julia? Was I tricked from the beginning?

When I first met him, I felt such a connection to the man. It was strange how comforting he felt. It doesn't make sense to me now, but I had thought I could trust him then.

He....he felt familiar. I don't know how to explain it. It seems so absurd now. It's fucking insane. How could a man in this realm be familiar to me?

Unless......

Shit. I was too scared to finish that thought, but I suddenly knew the answer to my own damn question.

"What did that asshole do to you?" I whispered, timing Julie's pulse. She was in such terrible shape, I didn't know what I could do to help her. We're stranded on a fucking island.

"She's going to die," a deep, raspy voice choked from somewhere close by. I looked around frantically, and then I saw him. That demonic fish from the cove. I could only see his face. The rest of him was covered in a thick black slime, like tar, and he was stuck to the side of a tropical tree similar to a palm tree in the human world, but its trunk was spiraling and the leaves were rounded. "Now that you are here, he will kill her," he rasped out. It sounded like he was struggling to breathe, let alone talk. "He will kill me, too. He has what he wants."

"Who?" I asked, pulling Julia into my lap and cradling her limp body to my chest. She was ice cold from blood loss. I needed to get her body heated up.

"Slarkrethel," the demonic being spat the name like it hurt him to say it, then went into a coughing fit. His black eyes were bulging from his face. I thought he had some kind of tattoo on the side of his face, but it was blood. It was so dark that it looked like ink.

"Who is Slarkrethel?" I demanded to know. "What the fuck does he want with me?"

The man attempted to cackle, but it caused another coughing fit. He wheezed and huffed until he got enough air to say, "You. Are. His."

"The fuck I am," I snarled. "Where's Kret? Where the hell did that coward go?!"

Suddenly a deep cry, like a blaring siren's call, shook the ground and made me cover my ears to keep my eardrums from bursting. I tried to cradle Julia's ears to my body with my chest and arm, but her whimpering told me she was hurting from the sound. The demon fish stuck to the tree was screaming in pain.

The water closest to the shore began to gurgle and foam. A whirlpool was forming, sucking all the debris floating on the water in the inverted funnel. The wailing cry stopped, but the ground still shook. The decaying smell of swampy waters made me want to gag, but I swallowed down the bile in my throat. This wasn't a swamp, but it sure as hell smelled as horrible as one.

Something was about to emerge from the water, and whatever it was, it was huge and vile. When a soft, bulbous head that was the size of a house started to appear, along with huge, spike-covered tentacles, I let out a blood-curdling scream.

66

THE KRAKEN

I shifted. I don't know how I found the strength. Maybe it was fear. Maybe it was instinct. I just shifted after I screamed, and I stood over Julia's body, shielding her from the horrifying monster climbing its way onto the shore.

It was monstrous. Grotesque. The sky rattled and then lightning broke behind the dark clouds, followed by rumbling thunder. The weather became more menacing in his presence. He terrified everything around him.

It shrieked. The same ear-splitting, ground-shaking cry I heard earlier, only ten times worse now that it was on land. My canine ears felt like they were bursting. My ears flattened back against my skull and I stood my ground, ready to defend Julia and myself.

"MASTER!" the dark merman screamed, still stuck to the tree. "MASTER! AH-HHH! STOP!" He was flailing about, blood dripping from his ear, running from his nose.

The giant squid-shaped monster, with its bulbous head and eight hideous tentacles with spike-filled suckers covering its repulsive slimy skin, also had spikes along the top of its head, staggered to where the tallest spike was in its center, stopped the ear-splitting roar spilling from his beak, staring down at us with beady eyes. Its grotesque shape fluidly moved along the bank, even though it was gigantic in size.

My hackles raised as steaming drool dripped from my exposed teeth. My snout burned as hot air mixed with the stench of the massive creature. It smelled like death. I could taste death in the air. Death for me, Julia, or even the bastard stuck to the tree, I wasn't sure.

Then, its massive form shrank in size. Black smoke overtook its large body, clouding over its slimy, hideous form. The blackness of its body faded into the stark white skin of a human. The flowing black hair and coal-like eyes made me snarl furiously with recognition.

Kret. Slarkrethel was Kret. He's the one that thought I was his. I would bet anything he was the one Taegan and Rian discovered spying on me, too. So many things clicked into place, but it was too late. I was facing the monster responsible for everything, but I was powerless. Why did I think I could ever do this shit alone?

It all makes sense. All of it. Julia was taken that night, but if Rian hadn't dived into the water first, I would have tried to save her. That demonic merman called Kret master. He was sent to get me. He had to be. He was sent to get me, and Kret was this dark being tied to me in some way, invading my privacy and the cause of so much mayhem and discord.

"Hello, my treasure," Kret smiled in that easy, calming way, but it wasn't calming to me anymore. I remembered thinking it did before, but now it infuriated me. I snarled, keeping my stance over my friend. His smile only seemed slimy to me. Deceitful. Why did he feel so trustworthy and authentic when I met him at the pond the first time? He felt like a lifelong friend then.

Now.....

"I will not harm you, my Rosie. I would never harm you. I just wanted to bring you home. Where you belong. With me."

He tried to take a step towards me, but I growled out a warning. My wolf and alpha aura still weren't at their strongest, but I could feel another power rising inside of me, filling the gaps in my strength.

Kret raised up his hands in a calming manner. "I really won't hurt you. Not a hair on your head. Why don't you change back so we can talk?"

Like hell I will, I thought, barking and snapping my teeth when he took another step.

"Here," he raised his hand in the air, letting his black magic pour out of it.

It created a small opening, a portal to a store that looked like one from my world. It was lined with racks of clothing. It was dark, so it was probably nighttime wherever it was. He bent down and picked up a long jagged stick, then used it to reach in and take out a robe. When I didn't move to take it from his extended hand, after he took it off his retrieval instrument, he tossed it to me, then used his magic to close the portal back up. Why didn't he reach in and take it with his hand? Why the stick?

"Please, my treasure. Change back and we can speak about this in a calm manner. We do not need to start off this life together now that we have finally been united in such a hostile way."

Still standing over Julia, I shifted back quickly, tugging the bathrobe around my body the moment my arms were formed so he wouldn't get the chance to see my body naked. His weird claim that I was home, and the way he called me his, was vile enough.

"That's better," he smiled, his eyes crinkling in the corners like he was truly pleased. "Welcome, Rosie. I told you I could help you find the man that," he smirked, waving his hand at the siren stuck to the tree, "stole your heart." He said mockingly.

He knew that was a lie. He knew what I was after all along. The merman I was thinking about as I told that lie was never the demonic one behind me, but the prince who took my breath away as his powerful siren body moved in the ocean back at the cove while trying to save my friend. Rian stole my heart. These men just kidnapped Julia, and now me.

"What did you do to Alpha Max?" I hissed between clenched teeth. "Where is he?"

"That large brute of a man that was clinging onto you tightly? I simply gave him the nudge he needed to throw him off your precious body, my treasure. I was fearful you would get hurt. He is perfectly fine."

"I don't believe you," I snarled. Look what he did to Julia.

"See." He held an orb of magic smoke in his hand, the blackness turning translucent as a picture appeared. In it, I saw Alpha Max on the bank of the pond, Thyra beside him as both of them stared down into the water.

I don't know if I was relieved not to see Rian there too, or disappointed that I wouldn't get to see his face one more time.

I thought I was going to die. I still might. I don't know what this asshole wants with me. If I was about to die, I didn't want my last words to Rian to be from anger. I wish I could go back and carve this fucking tattoo off my damn back instead of saying "fuck you". Or... maybe I should have let him go. I didn't deserve him. After the way I treated him before, I had no right to try. I was just hurting him.

But I don't regret it. I may never be good enough, and I may never be able to earn his forgiveness and trust, but I will never regret being with him. I only regret hurting him the way I did.

His parents looked broken up because of my disappearance, which was making me regret everything so much more.

"I lost her. I can't believe I let that fucker throw me off of her like that. You've used more fucking power on me during foreplay. I should have held on." Alpha Max had his hands over his face. *"Damn it. I should have held on."*

"*We will find her,*" Thyra said. She had tears skimming down her cheeks. My heart ached seeing them like that.

With a wave of his hand, the picture disappeared. I wiped the burning moisture gathering in my own eyes to glare.

"Take me back to them. Now."

"I can't do that, Rosie," Kret angled his head to the side, his expression tender, but laced with something dark. "This is where you belong."

"I belong with my family. They won't give up the search for me."

"That may be so, but this place isn't accessible to the normal fairy folk. It certainly wouldn't be to werewolves from another world." His telling smile sent shivers down my spine.

"It was you," I whispered. "You were the one watching me."

When his smile stretched, I felt physically ill. I felt violated. My skin was crawling. I hugged myself, and if it wasn't for Julia, I would have probably run.

"You're fucking sick. Disgusting." He was there watching me. I asked my fucking stalker for help. That thought made me sick.

67

JULIA'S ESCAPE

His smile faltered. "You are mine, Rosie. You were promised to me. You have always been mine. I was watching you to protect you."

"For how long?" I snapped. "How fucking long have you been watching me like a creep, you fucking demonic squid? You....you fucking stalker!"

A deep, menacing warning sound left him, like a mix of a snarl and a hiss. It was a lower, softer sound, similar to the shriek I heard from him before, but his message was clear.

"You were always mine. That has not changed now. Not even with that meddlesome brat who thinks he has a claim on you as well."

The insult towards Rian was met with a growl, and then his words sank in. "My whole life?" My eyes went wide. "Have you been spying on me my entire life? Since I....since I was....a baby? Wh-what the.....that's so.....you're disgusting."

"Think what you will," Kret paced around me, not getting any closer, but he looked like a predator on the prowl. I moved my body to protect Julia, blocking her body with mine. "You will have an easier time if you accept this as your fate."

"I don't understand why you think that this is my fate, but I will never accept it. Look at what you did to my friend. Why the hell would I trust you?"

His eyes flickered at Julia, then back to me. He shrugged as if my friend on the brink of death wasn't a big deal. "A misfortune for her, but a necessary sacrifice to get you to where you belong."

"This isn't where I belong. What do you even want with me? Is there a shortage of fucking girl squids at the bottom of the ocean? Why not go after a whale or octopus instead? A fish?! Why me?"

He chuckled darkly. "Ah, but you are the one who was promised to me. Our destiny has been intertwined since before your birth."

"How?" It didn't make any sense? Who the fuck would promise me to a devil-squid from another world? I know my parents would never. If mom were here, she would be threatening to turn Kret into enough calamari to feed the Miami Dolphins, or half our warriors on a Friday night. Dad would just straight up filet anyone who threatened to promise me to anyone, let alone this disgusting monster.

His expression almost looked sympathetic. "The creatures of your former world are cruel and selfish. Vindictive. The one who tied our fates was likely trying to save you from the misery you would face there."

"No misery would be worse than staying here with you. Send me back. Send us back."

Kret was still prowling around me, but I noticed he was now getting a fraction of an inch closer with every step. While resting his large hand on his chin, he keeps looking between Julia and me. "I can't send you back, but what if I send her? Will you be more agreeable, then?"

"What? You... Really?" I gaped, still moving my feet and turning my body every few seconds, circling around Julia to guard her broken form from Kret. "You would send her back?"

"Of course. I never wished to take her, anyway. My... friend was the one that took it upon himself to steal her from your world. He even hurt her while I was busy trying to help my lonely friend, who felt abandoned in a new world." He gestured towards me. He was talking about when he came to first see me at the pond. That was just hours ago. Maybe eight in total. Many of her injuries looked much older than that.

I scoffed, seeing that moment by the pond so different now. He'd been playing with me. I couldn't trust anything he said. Why did I not feel this sense of wariness when I was with him before? It's obvious how creepy he is to me now.

"Then do it. Send her back," I said, challenging his intentions.

"I will," Kret smiled, chancing a full step closer to me. "But only if you agree to give me a chance. I do not wish to fight with you. Or hurt you, Rosie. You are my treasure. Allow me to treat you as such."

"That's it?" I scoffed in disbelief. "If I agree to be more reasonable you will send her home?"

"Well," his smile stretched. "I do want one thing."

"What?" I glared.

He tapped on the space on his neck below his ear. "I know how your kind attach yourselves to one another. If you agree to become mates with me, I will let her go back home."

My mouth dropped in disbelief. He wants my mark? He was watching me, wasn't he? Does he not know that I already have a mate? Did he... did he not see Rian and me mate?

No. He didn't. The necklace. I was thankful he couldn't spy on the most intimate moment in my life. Damn it, I never should have taken it off. Rian said it would keep the dark entity spying on me from being able to attach itself to me again. Fuck, I'm so stupid. I took the necklace off and ended up in the fucking water.

I glanced down at my torn clothes scattered on the ground from my sudden shift. I didn't see the necklace in any of the mess. It was gone. It probably fell out of my pocket in the pond. I lost my cloak in the pond as well.

Damn it. My necklace... Tears were swelling in my eyes, thinking I may have lost it forever.

"You can take your time to get used to the idea," Kret said in a hurry, taking another step towards me. "I will still send her over now, as a testament of my goodwill and consideration I feel towards you." He probably thought my tears were from his request, and not my heartbreak from losing something so precious to me.

I stared up at him through my burning tears. He looked apologetic, and almost kind, but he still gave me the creeps.

With a wave of his hands, and more of that black smoke, Kret made another portal door, this one leading right along the busiest streets of Miami. My body tensed with the urge to put Julia over my shoulder and make a run for it, but he was blocking my path. I wouldn't make it.

He snapped his fingers and the black substance around the dark merman holding him in place against the tree melted away. He fell to the ground with a groan.

"Take her home." Kret's eyes glowed eerily.

The man, now with legs and not a tail or fins, stumbled forward. I growled when he got closer to us.

"YOU SAID HE WAS THE ONE THAT HURT HER!"

"Yes," Kret said slowly and carefully, like he was talking to a child. "And he was punished. If you want her to go home, he will be the one to do it. I can not leave this place and I will not risk you taking her yourself."

The man hesitated, but kept creeping closer and closer. I snarled deeply at him when he was only a few feet away.

"If you hurt her, or she dies, I will skin you alive, then carve you into a million pieces, leaving your vital organs for last. I know a sketchy sushi place in Model City that will serve you raw with soy sauce and wasabi for $4.99."

"He will not harm your friend. You can watch alongside me to make sure," Kret said, nodding at the merman as he stooped to lift Julia in his arms. I didn't move as I stared at him, daring him with my eyes to hurt her in any way. I didn't trust him, but I also didn't trust Kret. I just knew that if Julia was going to live, she needed to get home immediately.

Julia groaned, sweat beading and dropping from her ashen face. I resisted the urge to cringe seeing the dark merman's hands on her bare body. Her mangled legs hung limply, one of them twisted in at disturbing angle. The man took her and walked through the portal, and I prayed to the goddess that someone from my pack would find them soon.

"You will be happy here," Kret said with confidence, coming to stand beside me. He closed the portal, and I closed my eyes tightly, feeling repulsed by his nearness, but not wanting to piss him off just yet until I knew Julia was safe. "Follow me," he bent down to whisper in my ear. He moved his hands horizontally, sending a burst of magic to illuminate the entire island, and then walked over to a pool of water at the island's center.

Feeling like I had no choice, I followed him. He was twirling his hands over the pool, and then a picture appeared of the merman carrying Julia down a dark alleyway, and then onto the busy street that I saw. He was stopped immediately by patrolling police officers. I sighed with relief to see they were some of our men working under my dad.

"See," Kret practically purred. "She is now safe, and the one who hurt her shall be punished by your former people. I am benevolent and just." He lifted his large hand and placed it on my back as I continued to stare down at the pool of water. Julia was being placed in the back of a patrol car, then it rushed off. The other officer had the merman pressed against the side of a building, handcuffing him with iron cuffs before a pack's SUV pulled up alongside him. "Now, we can focus on us," Kret said, his hand moving to my shoulder, right over my tattoo and Rian's mark.

Suddenly, he screamed, jumped back and cradled his hand against his chest. It was burned, a green glow radiating from it. My shoulder was pulsing with Rian's magic, and Kret's black eyes were swirling with fury.

"He didn't," Kret looked at his hand, then back at me. The green magic was still burning him, and his teeth were clenched as it tried to shake it away. "Tell me he didn't."

"What?" I took a step back, not liking the look he was giving me. I clutched the robe tighter around my body.

"DID THAT BOY PLACE HIS SEAL ON YOUR BODY?!"

Rian's mark..... Is that what he meant? Did the mark do that to him? I...I shouldn't say anything, but he already knew the answer to his own question. I was doomed. I knew I was. His promise to not hurt me was already about to be void.

My silence was broken as I fell back into the pool of water. I yelped and the robe became heavy with the weight of the water.

The ground shook with his anger, and then his body exploded, his massive true form breaking out. He shrieked his ear-piercing roar. The sky cracked with lightning, the thunder beating in the sky behind his wail. Covering my ears, I was taken by surprise as one of his thinner tentacles wrapped around my body. My scream was drowned out as I was flung into the air.

The heavy robe was hanging off me, and he used a barbed sucker on the tip of a tentacle to rip the sopping wet robe completely off me. My body was being flung around the air, making my stomach spin and my head fog as I grit my teeth, trying to keep it together.

I was knocked back to the ground, naked and unprepared, when another tentacle wrapped around my throat and slammed my front against a tree. A cloud of smoke choked me, squeezing my body tight. It felt like a rope was wrapping around and constricting me. He was binding me to the tree.

The giant squid monster let out another wail, but soon it was my own scream piercing the dark air as fiery pain exploded on my back. Something wet and searing hot blasted against my shoulder. It felt like my skin was melting away.

68

NAUGHTY TAEGAN

Rian

There was nothing I could do. I had been swimming in this filthy pond all night, but there was nothing I could do. When the sun came up, Mom and Dad were waiting for me on the bank of the water. Dad was sitting on the ground, his hands pressed to his head as he rubbed his temples. His mutters told me he was pissed at himself.

Mom had Taegan and Phoebe on the other side of the fence. Taegan looked terrified. He was worse than I had seen him before. Even after Parisa forced herself on him.

"We need my brother's help, Taegan. If you and Phoebe are here when the knights arrive, it will be no small matter. They could punish you severely."

"No." Taegan shook his head fervently at my mom. "No. I can't leave. Not until we find her."

"Taegan." Phoebe pulled his arm. "I was sent to get you to bring you back home. You aren't supposed to be here, anyway. You could fuck things up again."

"You don't know what he's going to do to her," Taegan said with a ghastly look in his eyes. "You didn't see it."

"See what?" I demanded, stepping onto shore. I jumped over the fence, then stormed up to Taegan, grabbing him by the collar. "What did you see, huh? What the hell are you not telling me?! AGAIN!" He was always keeping the important shit to himself.

There was no question in his eyes or in his statement that he knew who had taken Rosie, even though he was in bed and unaware of the shit happening here until Mom woke them up with a mind link for help. He knew shit, and he wasn't talking.

He knew shit all along. I could see it on his frightened face. This was why he insisted on coming. Taegan had to try and save the fucking day like he always did, but this time he fucked up. He couldn't keep this secret, whatever it was.

"Talk or I'll make you. I swear to your fucking goddess, Taegan, I will make you."

"I can't," he said in a broken whisper. "I... I'm not... I-"

Suddenly, his eyes glowed, and his Lycan pushed to the surface. Conri's deep voice took over.

"He wasn't supposed to see," Conri said. "We can't reveal what has been disclosed, or snooped on, in the books, or Reika could place us in purgatory. You could be put there as well."

"As well?" Mom looked confused. "But, if he knows what took her or how to find it, wouldn't the goddess want us to know?"

Conri gave mom a sad expression with Taegan's face. "She wants nothing more than to help, but fates can be altered when there is intervention. We can not say anything or there could be a great loss for all."

"If I lose her..." I closed my eyes, loosening my grip on his collar as the pain of that thought crippled me on the inside. "If I lose her, there will be no greater loss. I would rather be damned for eternity than be without her."

Conri's glowing eyes were so full of sadness, but he understood. He had a mate, too.

"I can not tell you. Neither of us can. But..." Conri's glowing eyes dimmed and narrowed. "We couldn't stop you if you took that memory from us. Our magic is weaker here. We would be powerless to stop you."

Mom's sharp intake of breath didn't stop me. I knew what Conri was telling me to do, and even though it was invasive and could be dangerous to the person it was acted upon, I wouldn't hesitate when my mate's life was on the line. I was not naturally blessed with this power like Parisa. Conri knew that. This ability was not my own, but one held by my uncle. The moment I withdrew from his power, he would know. It was power I accessed only because I remained a prince in his court. But I was willing to doom us all for Rosie's sake. I would give up my rights as a prince, and everything else for Rosie. Nothing was too high of a price.

My hands stretched to grip Taegan's face, and his glowing eyes clouded over before rolling into the back of his head. Phoebe caught him as his body went limp, and then slowly lowered him to the ground. My hands never left his temples, and mom didn't urge me to stop. She heard Conri, just like I did. She knew this was vital to getting Rosie back. Conri wouldn't have suggested it if it wasn't.

"What's he doing? What the hell is the boy doing?" Dad demanded.

"He's invading his memories, Max. He's doing what he has to do to find his mate."

***

"So, I can see anyone in these books?" A mischievous looking Taegan asked a beautiful woman with an ethereal glow surrounding her. She was dressed in bright, shining robes, her eyes brilliant and radiating her authority. She looked familiar. She could have been Bailey's sister. Maybe even her twin. She wasn't Bailey, but the goddess Bailey descended from.

"Yes, my child," she smiled tenderly, running her hand over Taegan's little head. This was the appearance of the Taegan I first met. He was a young child of six or seven, but already he had that look in his blue eyes showing he was wise beyond his years. Taegan was never truly a child. His fate and destiny didn't allow for it, and seeing him in the goddess's presence made that all the more clear to me.

"So I can see Rosie in this?" Taegan tapped on a giant aged book opened on an intricate wooden stand.

"Taegan," the goddess looked at him disapprovingly. "I already told you that you wouldn't be fated for your little friend. She is destined for another. You will be with-"

"I know, I know," Taegan huffed. "I still want to see. Can't I just see my friend? I just want to see who she will be with. They have to be someone, like, really awesome. She has the weird power in her, remember? She can't be with a normal, boring person. They have to be strong."

"They will be," the goddess reassured him tenderly. "The one she is destined for is perfect for her in every way, and he will have the strength that she lacks. He will be stronger than all who threaten her. He will be her perfect pair, just like your mate will be for you. Do you not trust me, Taegan?" Reika looked at him with mild offense, though she was still smiling with her eyes. She looked so much like Bailey at that moment.

Taegan shrunk down in a chair with a shameful expression. "No. I just like to know things. She's my friend."

Even though he was so young, I was still irritated at how attached he seemed to Rosie. The goddess had clearly told him he wasn't her mate, but his interest in her didn't wane.

"*Your thirst for knowledge isn't always a good thing, Taegan. Sometimes knowing too much can be your doom.*"

"*Really?*" He cocked his head to the side in disbelief.

"*Really.*" Reika closed the giant book and set it back on the shelf in a massive library.

The entire scene seemed surreal with how heavily the memory was laced with a supreme magic that I could never fathom obtaining. Even the library seemed sovereign in its power. You could tell it was the home of a truly powerful being. She was a goddess, so I guess it was. Seeing the memory in Taegan's mind myself gave me a better understanding as to why Taegan was the way that he was. He casually sat with his goddess in her realm, discussing matters over my head. I still didn't understand the business with the books, but the way they sat on the shelves wasn't normal. They held the same aura as the goddess, and the fact Taegan was just touching them left me in awe.

A knock came from a massive, beautifully carved wooden door. Then, a creature with the head of a dog and a human body entered the office.

"*My goddess, there was an issue with-*"

"*I felt it, Dante. Thank you. I will be right there,*" the goddess smiled sadly, then turned to look at Taegan. "*Will you be alright here on your own for a moment, Taegan, or do you want to take a stroll in the gardens?*"

"*Can I not go with you?*"

"*No,*" Reika sadly shook her head. "*This is another time when too much knowledge can doom you.*"

Taegan puckered his lips in disappointment. "*I'll stay here then. I can read the other books, right? I want to read the one on dragons again.*"

"*Of course.*" Reika ran a hand over his head. "*I shall be back.*"

A few moments after the goddess left the library, Taegan, with a crooked grin, was pushing a chair to the shelf containing the giant ethereal books. "*I'll just have a peek. Just one look can't hurt.*"

He was just a little too short to reach, and I thought he was about to give up, but then he stooped down and retrieved a long wooden spoon he had hidden in his sock. He used it to wedge the third, newest looking book off the shelf just enough for it to fall into his arms. It was too heavy for his small build, but he just grunted and managed to plop down on the cushion on the chair instead of falling to the floor. Even at this young age, he was skilled at maneuvering his body in the way of a fighter.

He carried the book to the floor, grinning proudly at himself as he rifled through its pages. He moved his hand over one of them. "I can't see Rosie now because she has no wolf, but she will have one later. I have to see her later with her wolf." Taegan was talking to himself, trying to figure out how to get the pages to show him what he wanted to see. "Living words. You showed me cousin Courtney and brother Casey. Why won't you show me Rosie?"

He grew frustrated, but then his eyes glowed blue with his magic and the words on the pages started to swirl together and create a picture. His smile returned, excited and triumphant.

Then, his face changed to a look of horror.

"Wha-what is.... that?"

The picture that formed was not just Rosie, but Rosie being squeezed by the barbed tentacles of a giant monster. I knew instantly what it was and felt horror, too. It was a kraken. The kraken was screaming at her, flailing her body through the air and down to the ground.

Rosie's body was broken and bleeding, but her face was a ferocious mask of defiance.

"BITE ME!" The giant monster's words shook the pages. "MARK ME!"

"No!" Rosie screamed, another barbed tentacle wrapping around her neck. "Rian," she cried, her eyes going wide.

Then, the monster choked her so tightly that her face turned a blazing red. She was mouthing my name over and over until her eyes rolled to the back of her head and she fell unconscious, and then the monster let out a shrieking cry before throwing her naked and broken body to the ground.

She looked dead, but with her blood-matted hair covering her face, it was impossible to tell if she was.

Taegan closed the book after that, and I could feel his fright and horror at what he had just seen.

***

It all made sense why Taegan was so determined to come along. That scared him to his core, and now I felt the same horror. She looked dead. If she dies, I don't know what I will do. He wanted her to stay behind.

"No," I gasped, falling backward after letting go of Taegan's face. "No."

"What?" Mom was over me as Dad and Phoebe helped Taegan, who was just gaining consciousness again. "What did you see?"

My horrified eyes moved to hers. "A kraken. Mom... she..."

"A kraken?" Mom looked stunned. "That's what took her?"

I didn't get the chance to answer, because right then the ground shook with the steady beat of hundreds of feet marching our way. When I looked up to fairy knights surrounded us. There, in front of them, was my uncle.

69

COUSIN'S COUSIN'S DAUGHTER

Bailey

"Will you stop it?" I grumbled, rolling to the other side of the bed. I was dead asleep after being assaulted by my grumpy but sinfully sexy husband for the last few hours. Now the stiff-dicked, insatiable and inconsiderate man was groping my breast and kissing my mark while trying to push his dick between my thighs.

"No," he said stiffly.

"Axel, I need sleep," I griped, swatting away his hand after he grabbed my breasts and used them to pull me back against him.

"Sleep then," he grumbled. "Don't mind me."

"With you sticking that thing between my ass cheeks, how can I not mind?"

"Sounds like a personal problem," he mumbled against my skin, trying to nuzzle his way back to my marking spot. He knows once his teeth start to graze against it, I'll be lost to him again.

Not going to happen. My vagina needs rest. "If you don't quit squeezing my thighs, I'm going to-"

"Going to what?" Axel growled in my ear playfully. "Wanna wrestle?"

"I've had enough wrestling with you. Go to sleep."

"Yep. Closing my eyes now."

"No, you're not," I hissed, his fingers kneading my soft flesh.

"They're sealed tight. I know your body so well that I don't need my eyes. Just my hands... or tongue. Want me to switch to my tongue?"

"Nope," I growled.

"Hands it is."

"I hope you don't need those hands for anything else because I'm about to chop them off."

"You wouldn't," he said in a challenging tone.

"Shh. Go to sleep." I grabbed a pillow and swung it back at his face. That was the wrong move. War broke out as he tickled my sides, and I continued to hit him with the pillow.

"Fine! I give!" I cried out when I couldn't take the tickling any longer.

"Good," Axel's deep throaty laughter filled the room. "Open them legs, woman."

"That's not what I'm giving in to," I giggled when he tried to shimmy between my legs. Sleep had evaded me, but I was still too tired to go another round. My vagina couldn't.

"Just let me cuddle you," he whined. He pried my legs apart and settle his large body between them, using my pudge as a pillow. One of his hands wandered to my boob, but I let it go since he was just gently squeezing it and not messing with my nipples. "Mmh, this is my favorite way to sleep."

"Oh, now you're going to sleep. Now that you have got me wide awake."

"Shh. Sleep," he mumbled.

I took the pillow and hit him upside the head again one last time. He just laughed and snuggled more into my flesh.

"We're going to have to get a house here now. You know that, right?" he mumbled sleepily. "My cousin's cousin's daughter is now my sister-in-law. We're going to be coming down here a lot more often. Dad isn't going to manage well without the girls."

"I didn't think about that," I whispered, running my fingers through his hair.

"Thyra is going to want to visit Rian, and when Rian and Rosie start having babies it's going to be hard for them to divide their time. We should make it easier for them and just get a house built here on pack lands. I'll ask Parker about it in the morning."

"You mean in four hours?" I scoffed. "It's almost morning."

"Later in the morning. Like, before lunch and after the girls find us and force us out of this room."

"I wonder who has them," I mused. Ali can babysit just fine, but she's going to be upset in the morning about it and hunt us down herself.

"Casey mind linked me and said they were with Reese and his girlfriend for the night. The old Alpha here is helping to watch all of them, too. Ali and Conner are there, so they're fine."

"I should have brought my mom," I sighed. "I didn't think your dad and Thyra would have to leave for Alfheimr as soon as we got here."

"My jet can only hold so many people, babe. If you brought your mom, Lord Dipshit would have come too and brought all his vampire cronies. The girls are fine. I'll get up first in the morning and go find them so you can sleep in."

"You're such a good mate," I giggled. "I'm holding you to that."

"Please do," he mumbled, kissing my tummy.

"So, what did you call your cousin's cousin's daughter before she became your sister-in-law?" I giggled, breaking the silence right before I felt him going to sleep.

"Rosie," he mumbled, now acting like the tired one.

"No, like, she's some kind of cousin to you, right? Your cousin's cousin's daughter? Aren't you supposed to, like, twice remove her or something?"

"I think it should be once removed," he mumbled. "I don't fucking know. I'll just call her my sister-in-law and save the confusing shit for you to think about."

"Hmm." I kept moving my fingers through his hair, making it stick up wildly. "Our sister-in-law is younger than our oldest child. At one time, we thought our sister-in-law was going to be our daughter-in-law. That's fun to think about. Makes me feel young having a sister-in-law that's only eighteen."

"You are young." Axel turned his head to stare at me. "That's why I just put baby number seven in you."

"Jeez," I giggled at his proud expression. "Maybe we can finally get the girls that little brother they all want."

"Poor kid," Axel smiled. "He's going to be a nightmare with so many big sisters treating him like a doll."

"He might be worse than Taegan," I agreed.

"Taegan's only bad because you baby the shit out of the boy. Being away from his mom and making mistakes is good for him."

"Take that back," I growled, tugging at a chunk of his hair.

"That's how he will grow up. That's how he will be a better alpha."

"He's my baby."

"He's a grown ass boy. His mama doesn't need to follow him to clean up his mess everywhere he goes."

I rolled my eyes, not wanting to argue with him. He might be right, but I'm not ready to admit it. Taegan will always be my baby. It would take something drastic for me not to baby him anymore.

Both of us were almost asleep when there was suddenly a knock at the door, pounding away and making Axel leap out of bed butt naked to answer it in a huff.

"WHAT?!" he roared to Calum, who was standing on the other side.

"Um, Alpha? I think we have a problem you might want to be present to see for yourself."

"What? What the hell is it? Are the girls okay?" Axel left the door open and started hunting for his boots. Thinking something had happened to our girls, he was putting on his boots before underwear or pants.

"It's not the kids, Alpha. It's the missing girl. The one that was kidnapped that Rian and Taegan went after with Rosie. They found her almost dead in the streets in Miami and she wasn't alone."

"What do you mean? What happened?" I asked, wrapping the sheet around my body and getting out of bed to get ready.

"The thing that took her brought her back, and he's spilling his fucking guts trying to get his life spared. He told us what was behind the kidnapping and it seems the girl wasn't the original target. It was someone else."

"Who?!" Axel yelled, getting right in Calum's face. "Spit it the fuck out!"

"Rosie! It was after Rosie. It seems it got her and is going to force her to mate him. Alpha Parker is raising hell. Luna Carli is on a warpath. I think you should come down. Dad sent me to get you since your block was up."

"Fuck," Axel hissed.

"What was it? What took her?" I asked, moving around the room to pick up clothes I could wear. I took one of Calum's shirts to put on and a pair of his sweats. Axel was kicking off his boots to put his dirty jeans back on without the underwear.

"A kraken," Calum said solemnly. "I think we're going to need all the help we can get."

70

FIGHT FOR ME

Rosie

"It burns," I cried, feeling like my skin was being peeled away from my shoulder.

"It doesn't," Kret said through gritted teeth. He's peeling away black tar-covered leaves from my back again.

It's been the same routine for two days now. At least I think it has been two days. With the constant darkness, it was impossible to tell. It felt like it'd been two long, excruciating days of hell.

I screamed when he peeled the last leaf off. My throat was dry, my lips cracked from lack of water, but the pain from what he was doing to my back was worse than any other pain I had.

Hunger, thirst, my aching body from being tied to this tree in the same spot for two days, and my dizzying headache didn't compare to the pain he's been inflicting endlessly on my back. My wolf still had not recovered and I didn't know why.

"You did this to yourself," Kret hissed, dumping salt water on my open wound. Then he roared loudly, infuriated again that Rian's mark was still there. It wouldn't go away no matter how long he soaked it in his acidic, black, tarry ink. My tears and screams just aggravated him more. When I told him it wouldn't work, no matter what he tried, it fell on deaf ears.

"Please," I begged. "No more." My throat was burning and my voice was barely a rasp. I know he heard me. He was just choosing not to answer. "Just kill me," I tried to beg instead.

"You were promised to me," he snarled.

"By who?!" I demanded. "Who promised me? Because I know it wasn't me."

"Those witches always sacrificed to me, but it was the first time they offered the living. You are mine. Mine. I will take what is mine!" He hissed, taking a blade and trying to cut away the imprinted flesh.

I screamed so hard that I blacked out. I didn't know how long I was out that time, but the night was even darker when I opened my eyes. Night or day, the sky was dark, but this was the darkest I had ever seen it. The lifelessness of my surroundings was haunting. No birds. No insects. Nothing. There was nothing living here except for me and the one torturing me.

"You're finally awake," Kret grumbled. I couldn't see him. He had to be behind me, probably in the water. I was too weak to turn my head. "I will only ask you this once, Rosie. Do you know how to rid yourself of the mark on your shoulder?"

My silence stretched, and he snarled in frustration.

"DO YOU?!"

"Yes," I croaked.

"THEN HOW?!" he demanded. "HOW DO I GET RID OF THAT OTHER MAN'S MARK ON YOUR BODY SO I CAN MAKE YOU MINE?!"

If I had the strength, I would laugh. I could tell him a rejection, but I know rejection for a fairy doesn't work the way it does for a wolf. Once your imprint is on a partner in the fae world, it is there for life. It can not be undone. Even if it could, that would never be an option for me.

"Death," I said, my hoarse voice capturing my finality in the answer. I would rather die as Rian's than live on as someone else's.

Kret surprised me by asking, "Your death or his?"

I didn't need to answer. There was no answer to that. The answer was the same either way. If he killed Rian, I would never be able to live with myself. Instead, I let my pain fade into unconsciousness once again.

***

"...*Rosie*," a voice invaded the peaceful blackness of my mind.

My battered body and exhausted mind didn't want to emerge from the darkness just yet.

"*Rosie..... Please, honey. Answer me.*"

I knew that voice. I loved that voice. That's the voice that has carried me through all my moments of defeat that I have ever felt in my life. He was the one that has sheltered me and loved me since before I was born. I wanted to cling to the voice, but the pain when I emerged from the wall that was numbing my mind was making it hard to cling to anything that would drag us away from it.

"Rosie. I'm begging you. Just let me know you are okay, baby girl." Dad was hysterical.

I was not okay. Nothing about me was okay. I tried to find the ability to tell him that, but I couldn't. I couldn't speak. I couldn't move. I couldn't do anything but rest in the dark numbness or the pain will come back and break me. I could not face that pain again.

"Rosie, baby. It's your mom. Can you hear me, Rose? Rosie?!" My mother was pushing into the numbness that I was trying to maintain. *"Damn it, child. ANSWER ME! You answer me, Rosie, or else."* She had real fear in her voice. My mother, who never cries, is crying in my head. *"My baby. Please just answer me. Just one word. Rosie..."*

I couldn't. I couldn't say anything. My wolf side was still numb. I felt like I was swimming in the numbness now, trying to break free, but there was no strength left in me to break anything.

I was swimming and swimming, but it still just felt like I was sinking further into the nothingness that was expanding inside me. There wasn't anything left to swim for. There was no surface to break. I wasted away in this torturous place, and all that was left was to just give into the darkness that was trying to consume me.

"Rosie..."

I felt a jolt inside me at the sound of that voice. That sweet, deep, velvety voice.

"Rosie..."

The voice came a bit louder this time. A light appeared in the center of the darkness. A brilliant green swirl of something stirs, like the beautiful galaxies of his eyes.

"My Rosie. You are mine. Nothing can take you from me. Nothing. I'm going to find you, and I will never let anyone harm you ever again."

"Rian," I cried, the darkness around me being overcome by the warmth of his energy filling me from somewhere deep within.

"Rosie!" His voice was more urgent. *"Rosie! Oh, my Rosie. Are you okay?"*

"No," I breathed. I had never been less okay. With the blackness fading away, the pain was coming back to me. Rian groaned, our connection resurface. I was sure he felt it too. That thought filled me with dread. This pain was too much for me. I didn't want it to touch him in any way.

"Oh, goddess. Rosie. We're coming. We're coming to save you, baby. I'm coming to save you. Just hold on."

"I can't," I whimpered, searing fire-like pain spreading to every pore, every cell, every tiny atom in my body. The tarry ink was back on my shoulder. I could feel it. It was going to kill me this time. I knew it will.

"You can, Rosie. You are the strongest person I know. You can do this. We're coming. We're coming to save you."

"Please hurry," I sobbed. *"I just want to die."*

"No, Rosie. You can't. You're mine, remember. I'm telling you to fight. You gotta keep fighting. My Alpha wouldn't give up. She would never let anything defeat her."

I'm already defeated. *"It hurts. It's going to kill me this time."*

The long silence between us was full of fear and heartache. I tried to stifle my cries of pain.

"I love you, Rosie. I love you too, so you gotta keep fighting. For me."

71

COMING TOGETHER

Rian

"Y ou heard her? You really heard her voice?" Carli asked me, sitting beside me in my uncle's court.

I nodded solemnly.

"Thank fuck," she murmured. She wrapped her arms around her friend Simone's shoulder and cried heavily again. "Thank you, goddess."

Simone rubbed her back, smoothing her snot and tear soaked hair out of her face. Simone was crying too, but not like Carli. I'd seen the Luna plenty of times and never thought she could cry like she has since she came to this world. Guilt was crushing me on the inside.

Alpha Parker was irate, yelling at my dad again. He snarled at me, but dad and Axel put themselves between us. Luna Carli told him to stop, and she hasn't left my side since. I didn't feel like I deserved her protection from her angry mate. If I could have kept myself from showing my intense jealousy, Rosie would never have left.

"THIS IS ON YOU! YOU AND HIM!" Alpha Parker was in my dad's face, his eyes red and his hair standing on end.

My dad didn't look much better, blaming himself as much as Rosie's dad was. Alpha Parker's been a whole range of extreme emotions. He was usually so calm and relaxed. When he felt the Alpha link to his daughter fading away, ready to snap like her death was near, panic coursed through him. I don't blame his anger, and I know dad doesn't either.

"Parker, man. That's enough." Gamma Casey pushed against Alpha Parker's chest to move him away from Dad and Axel to calm him down. "Rian got through to her. She's still there. We will save her."

"She almost... She almost... FUCK!" Alpha Parker marched off, running his hands through his hair angrily and choking on a sob.

It scared all of us, feeling her connection about to snap. Any attempt I made to reach her was met with silence. Then I felt her dying. If not for my uncle's help, we wouldn't have been able to break that veil to reach her. Even now, I couldn't mind link her. The pain she was feeling cut off from me when he had to close the veil again. But her death wasn't looming like before. Whatever she was facing, she was enduring it again. She wasn't giving up.

"Shit." I buried my face in my hands, choking while remembering her pain. It was crushing. Please, goddess, just keep her safe. Please.

"We're almost ready, Rian," mom whispered in my ear. "Your uncle had to make arrangements to permanently break the veil keeping the Kraken in his abyss. He wasn't the one who put him there."

"I know," I whispered roughly.

I didn't know what we would have done if not for my uncle. When this Kraken was made an outcast, a spell was cast to keep him out of all the kingdoms. But in turn, the place of his banishment was protected from any wandering being from venturing into it. It was powerful magic that only a king or the queen that placed him there could break.

My uncle acted quickly. Once we told him everything, he declared that the only thing that mattered for the time being was the abduction of a princess from his kingdom. As my mate, that was what Rosie was. He used that as a reason to open a portal from his court to Crystal Moon Pack, allowing the werewolves through. It had never been done before, but he declared that through the mating of a prince and the pack's future Alpha, that gave them the right to travel through. The mark Rosie placed on my neck was proof of Rosie's right to be here, and in turn, it was her pack's right to save her.

After the stunt Parisa pulled, I didn't expect that from my uncle. I was beyond grateful for the lengths he was going to help. Whatever happens afterward, if there is any fallout or discord for this, I will shoulder all of it gladly as long as Rosie is saved.

"I've never seen anything like this," mom murmured to herself, looking around at the werewolves preparing for battle alongside the fairy knights.

I blinked through the guilt and rage pooling in my eyes to see. This had never been done before. No one from the human realm has ever been granted entry into Alfheimr.

"Gather round!" Oberon, my uncle's lead knight, the commander of his first order, stood tall on a platform, his knights gathering behind him. "Werewolves of the human realm. Our people are familiar with the evils and dangers of facing a mutant birthed from the demons mingling with our kind, but I am sure you are not. The Kraken, Slarkrethel, is from the highest powers of both the demon and the fae realms. He was banished out of our populated lands, using strong magic cast by a neighboring kingdom. His dark energy was such that he plagued our people. It seems, in his confinement, his loneliness grew to an unmanageable state.

"The curse confined him to the dark waters in which he reigns, which was how he managed to break into our kingdom without our notice. The water reservoir in which the princess discovered him is tainted with the energy his kind creates. Another part of the curse is that he can only be in his true form in the prison that he is in, so if he manages to enter any of our kingdoms, he can be easily subdued.

"Last, the curse of his purgatory was that time moved at the rate it moves in your human realm. It has been but hours for us, but it has already been days where he is keeping Princess Rosie. Time is the madness he has had to endure, and because of this, having Princess Rosie to watch and keep him sane has likely been the reason for his desperation to bring her to him.

"He is already a powerful being, but his desperation to keep her with him will make rescuing her even more dangerous, especially for your kind, who does not possess magic. Your ability to heal and manage your wolves will not be as strong. The veil separating him from us acts as a blocker. Even after that veil is taken away, his dark energy affected all of his domain. Our King asks that to protect each other, we pair up; a werewolf to every knight."

Oberon's severe face turned grave. "I have heard many murmurings about this just being a giant squid, so I must warn you now. Do not underestimate the kraken. He is horrific. Both in demeanor and strength. We are coming at him in his own territory, which will make him stronger than any of us. His power resides in the waters he rules. His body will be massive; so big that it would not even fit in the place we stand.

"His limbs will be outfitted with thousands of barbs, able to stab through and kill a person instantly. He has a scream that is at a decibel to kill, though he will likely not use it in the presence of Princess Rosie. He could use it to burst eardrums and to incapacitate. The interrogation of his accomplice already suggested he will use this power. Be prepared, because this battle, if you run into it without the understanding of what you are about to face, will get you killed."

"Dibs." Luna Carli wiped her nose on the back of her hand and grabbed hold of me.

Alpha Parker snarled, staring at us, but then Oberon approached him and he turned his focus on my uncle's lead knight. I watched as all the werewolves found someone to pair up with.

Taegan and Phoebe were the only ones without a fairy knight, but that was because they were huddled together in a heated discussion, staring at the brothers who own the resort. Simone's mate, the vampire, was beside the brother, looking ferocious while hissing something at the two. The fairy knights paired with the brothers were staring at the vampire with stunned horror. I couldn't even imagine what was being said over there, but whatever it is, Taegan and Phoebe didn't seem to like it.

"Reese and Beta Trevor are prepared for the worst," Carli was telling Simone. "Make sure if something happens, you and Vincent help Reece maintain our pack."

"Just bring our Rose back home. Don't worry about anything else. Vincent and I will be right here, waiting for your return."

Simone, her mate, and Bailey came through the portal, but were staying at my uncle's court, not joining the fight. Bailey was currently in an intimate bubble with Axel, tears flowing softly from her eyes.

When my uncle entered the court, all went silent. He was in full armor, his presence and aura showing his immense power. He walked through the center of the court, approaching an ivy-covered wall at the end.

He didn't even have to lift his hands. His eyes shone, and a portal formed where the wall once was. It's a portal to the field where our pegasus horses graze, all of which were already saddled for battle with attendants handling them.

"Not the fucking glue stick," dad muttered to my mom.

"I'm taking Philos," I said with determination.

72

LAST BREATH

Rosie

"Please," I tried to cry, but my voice was just a rough gasp of air. "Stop."

"I'm doing what needs to be done." His voice was thick with frustration.

Kret was peeling away the tar-like acidic filth from my back again, and this time, I was beyond the pain. I felt numb, a calm stillness traveling through my body. I could feel a throbbing numbness, like pins and needles, where he was scouring my body for at least the tenth time, but it was not like before.

Maybe because my body was so close to death, there was not enough strength for true pain any longer. I was fighting not to pass out again, fearful of actually dying, but my body already felt like it was giving out. If he did anything else to me, I knew it would be my end.

"Why won't it work?" he hissed. His claws were scraping at the wound open and gaping on my shoulder. I let out the weakest of cries, but nothing more. There was no point. "What do I have to do to make it go away?"

He lifted the knife in his hands, and I thought he was going to cut away at my back again, slicing through my flesh in his attempts to slice off Rian's name. That's his usual ritual after peeling off the drying black ink. I braced for the slicing of my flesh as well as I could in my weakened state, but that ended up being in vain and a total waste of the little energy I had left in me. Instead, Kret used the knife to cut me free from the tree I had been tied to for so long.

My legs gave out instantly. Everything was numb and useless. My groan as I crumpled to the soggy ground was as broken as my body. It was so out of it I didn't notice I was lying in my blood. Filth mixed with the last stagnant water that was dumped on me until the scent hit me moments later.

Just as I was about to get my bearings enough to push myself up, a powerful stream of water was dumped on me from overhead. I fell back face first to the ground, too pathetic to even verbally protest any more. Kret kept dumping water on me until I could barely smell anything but the salty brine. Then he leaned over me.

"There's only one way to do this now," Kret said venomously, grabbing my limp body by the arm and tugging me up against him. I would have thrown up from the sickness stirring in my stomach from being so close to him, his face directly in mine. I didn't know what he wants, but if it would make this all stop, I might actually do it. I have nothing left to give, anyway. "Bite me."

Except that.

"W-w-what?...."

"Bite me, Rosie. We can deal with the offensive mark on your back after. If we continue going like this, you could get hurt."

Jeez, really? If I had the fucking strength to punch him, I would. Does he not realize I am on the brink of death now?

"Mark me and make me your second mate. I know it can be done. I have seen others around you with multiple mates. If you do the same to me, then we can still be together. I will just deal with the one who left that mark on your back at a later time."

"I-I c-can't." I forced the words to leave my parched lips.

"You have to," he urged, his dark eyes getting impossibly darker. "It's the only way we can be together." The urgency in his tone scared me. "Your mortal body can not last in my domain much longer if you don't."

My mortal body couldn't last longer, but arguing with him would be meaningless. I would not mark him. Even if I could, I wouldn't. I would rather die having one mate, knowing that he loved me before I go, then live in this hell with this monster being a permanent part of me for the rest of an agonizingly long life.

Kret's presence became stifling the longer I went without responding to him or moving to do as he commanded. He couldn't force me. He can cut me, burn me, torture and abuse me, but he can't make me mark him. I won't do it.

His grip on my body becomes painful, his nails sinking into my raw skin. I whimpered, but wouldn't open my mouth more than that, for fear of him trying to force my canine to come out and mark him without my consent. He has done so many other things to me without my consent. Why wouldn't he stoop that low?

"MARK ME!"

I closed my eyes, trying to remain numb and pull on that darkness that had tried to overtake me before. Death would be better than succumbing to this freak.

"ROSIE!"

"No," I accidentally whispered. I meant to say 'no' in my head, but in my dizzy state, it left my lips instead.

He dropped my body. I went limp in the rotting sand; the grains cutting into my skinless back. Moving made it worse, so I was forced to stay still as the horrible sounds from Kret grew louder and louder. His dark energy was stifling, and I could feel the ground quaking beneath me. He was changing into his true form, hopefully to finish me off so we could be done with this. I saved my friend. I know Rian said they were coming to save me, but that felt like forever ago. I can not hang on any longer. Just knowing he was trying is a comfort to me now, and I hope that he one day forgives me for not being able to do what he asked.

I couldn't fight. I had no fight left in me.

The monstrous squid let out another of his terrifying screams. I couldn't cover my ears or do anything to shield myself from the noise. My brain was rattling in my head. The scream faded into an endless whining hum in my ears. I couldn't hear anything else.

When his tentacles wrapped around my body, lifting me into the air, I didn't even move. I had nothing in me anymore.

That's what I thought.

One of his suckers sank into the festering wound on my back and a fire raged under my skin. My eyes flew open and I let out a scream I didn't know I had in me. I knew the monster was yelling something at me. I felt the vibration of his words, but all I could hear was my scream echoing in my head and the ringing in my ears.

This was it. He was really killing me this time. My heart was racing, about to explode in my chest. "No," I tried to say. I was demanding my body to scream out the words, begging him to stop, but this only seemed to anger the bastard more.

Another tentacle wrapped around my neck, squeezing and closing off my airway. I couldn't believe that this was it. This was my end.

"I'm sorry," I whimpered inwardly at Rian, knowing it was in vain. I haven't been able to mind link him again. *"I am so sorry I couldn't fight."*

"Rosie!" I thought I heard his reply, but my mind was a delusional mess. Even now, my eyes wide and bulging, desperately trying to suck in even the smallest amount of air, I could see hundreds of shapes behind Kret's bulbous head. The one in the front looked like Rian, fierce and desperate, riding on a flying horse. My head was imagining things that couldn't be there now.

My Rian. My mate.

"Rian," I tried to move my mouth to say his name one last time. Over and over again, I was mouthing his name, desperate for his face to truly be the last thing I saw before I died.

Then, my eyes rolled in my head. The darkness was taking over again. My body felt like it was flying, no longer in the immense pain it was just in.

Not flying. Falling. I felt like I was falling into nothingness. When my body crashed to the bottom of the blackness I was falling into, I couldn't feel anything again.

I was dying, but I was grateful that the last image that my mind produced before the blackness took over was of Rian coming to save me. Whatever purgatory I end up in for coming to a world I didn't belong to in the first place, I will be thankful to the goddess for at least granting me the sight of his beautifully fierce face one last time.

73

No One But Me

Rian

"Rosie!" I screamed her name into the stale, brinyy air, looking on in horror as the Kraken strangled her. Her eyes went wide, and I knew she was saying my name. This was the same scene Taegan saw in that moon goddess's book. I knew what was coming next, and I was powerless to stop it. "Damn it. Rosie!"

Her mother, clinging to my back as we soared through the air, was vibrating with fury. She was about to shift. I could feel it with every one of her snarls. All the werewolves behind me, riding with their fairy knight partners, were snarling at the scene of their future Alpha being tortured before them.

Philos was pushing through the wind, ready to descend on the monster. When he flung Rosie to the ground, my direction changed.

She looked dead. I knew she wasn't dead yet. I could feel her again. I also knew that she was close to death. If I didn't get to her first, it would be too late.

The kraken, having heard us, or maybe feeling our approach, reared back and let out the most awful scream. The snarls turned into pain-filled cries.

"SILENTIUM!" Oberon shouted, and a golden light exuded from his body. The light stretched out to cover all within several hundred feet of him and Alpha Parker, who was riding along behind him.

Others repeated the spell, protecting our ears and the ears of our werewolf partners from exploding. I didn't care if my ears exploded. I don't think Carli did either, as she gritted her teeth. All I wanted was to get to Rosie, but I still managed to murmur the spell for Carli's sake.

Barred tentacles came flying towards us, the Kraken shrieking his deadly cry. Philos easily dodged them, skillfully diving and soaring through the mess of water and flesh. The monster's black, inky eyes were the size of my face as I got closer to them. I could see that he knew who I was the moment his giant eye locked on me.

"Look out!" Carli shouted, and I turned just in time to see a spiky, snake-like tentacle heading straight for me.

I braced myself to use my magic to stop it from hurting Carli, but then my mother and dad soared down from high in the sky. Dad leaped off the back of Nelly as mom continued to drop in the air. He shifted into his massive wolf in a split second, tearing the tentacle off with his teeth, then falling back onto the back of mom's pegasus after shifting back into human form. I had never seen mom look so fierce.

"Thank fuck," Carli murmured, her claws sinking into my sides. She was ready to shift too, but my dad beat her to it.

Alpha Parker and Oberon mimicked dad and mom when a tentacle went flying for Gamma Casey and another knight. The battle was underway, but everyone was holding their own.

"GO! GET ROSIE TO SAFETY!" Dad yelled out to me.

I nodded once, then I wasted no time in turning Philos back to my original goal.

All the fairy knights and warriors were attacking the Kraken at once, so with him distracted, we could fly down safely to the shore. Two warriors from Rosie's pack were using powerful purple magic on the Kraken in their wolf forms, literally leaping and walking on the water as they attacked with purple fire, singing the barbs off the tentacles as they fought.

Taegan had an older knight with powerful magic with him. The fairy was lending him all the magic he needed and Taegan too joined the two purple glowing wolves running and fighting on the surface of the ocean. When he shifted into Conri, many of the knights looked on in amazement, especially when one of the purple glowing wolves didn't notice a black spear of dark magic flying toward him, and Conri easily absorbed the magical spear into his own body, saving the wolf.

Those two wolves must be the Meyers brothers. That's why Taegan fought with them so well, but they were still no match for Taegan's powerful goddess-derived magic.

The pack and the knights were handling the beast. I needed to save my mate.

"Rosie!" I screamed, seeing the blood pooling under her still body. She was sickly pale. Her skin always had a sun-kissed glow, but the only color to her now was the red of the blood spilling from her wounds.

Carli and I ran to her, dropping on the ground beside her. I pulled her to my lap, moving the hair from her face and body so I could see the extent of her injuries, and then I fell sick.

Her back, her entire shoulder with my imprint was exposed down to the muscle. Even her muscles looked like they had been dissolved and sliced through. Her tendons were showing, and blood was still streaking down her back. There were festering sores all over her middle. Puss was oozing out of them with streams of blood. A rope or something had been tied around her naked body for a long time.

One side of her face was worse than the other. Her eyes were both crusted with pus, but one was black and bruised. That side of her face had scrapes and little festering sores. She was way worse off than I ever imagined.

And her neck.....

I thought her neck was broken. The angry lines from the squid's tentacles made it hard to tell if she was even breathing.

"My baby," Carli cried, checking her pulse. "Why can't her wolf side heal her?"

"Because this place is infected with dark magic," I reminded her, moving my hands over the welts forming on her neck. "It's toxic, and the veil my uncle tore kept any other power or energy from getting in."

"How do we heal her then?!" Carli panicked. "She's going to die. She can't die, Rian. I can't lose my daughter."

"She's not going to die," I said with determination. "Only one thing is going to die today, and it's not going to be her."

My magic flared to life, seeping into Rosie from my hands. Her neck was the first thing I healed, her crushed airway keeping her from breathing properly. There were so many other injuries, it was hard to find the worst of them. Except for her back. Angry tears burned in my eyes as Carli helped me to roll her daughter over so I could heal her back as much as possible. It would never be the same.

All my bitching about that damn tattoo, and now my mate didn't even have skin there any more. The only skin that remained was the thin weaving of my name, but its intended structure told mme itwas the monster's goal to remove this all along.

A fae's imprint can never be removed. He sliced and carved away the tattoo and the surrounding skin, but my name remained through it all. The pain in my chest because of my own past pettiness made me choke.

"Her leg is shattered," Carli said, fighting back angry tears. "She fell at least thirty feet. Her head, Rian."

As Carli worked to straighten her leg and brace it with strips from her shirt and a fallen tree branch, I used my magic on her head, praying that there wouldn't be any lasting damage there.

The ground shook, and a treacherous scream rang through the dark, rancid sky. I cringed, and Carli covered her ears. I looked up to see the Kraken coming towards the shore, his devilish black eyes trained on us. The knights and warriors were trying to attack, but he was too big for any blows to do lasting damage to him, his magic healing him as fast as any wounds were inflicted.

Carli shifted, snarling and standing over her daughter protectively. I stood to fend off the impending attack, but then a golden Pegasus dropped on the beach before us, my uncle descending from his mount.

The ground around him crackled with the power he possessed, fighting off the darkness plaguing this place. The air stilled, and the cloudy sky cleared above his head as he lifted his arms above him. His hands to his shoulders were cackling with electric, golden magic, building until he let it go, aiming it for the creature's head.

The Kraken screamed, blood piercing shrieks. Black acidic ink plumed in the water around it and black magic seeped from his pores and he pushed back against my uncle's power.

He was no match for my uncle, the King of the Septentrional Kingdom. It soon retreated into the safety of the dark ocean in which it reigned, knowing no one, not even my uncle, could follow him there.

No one but me.

74

It Can Only Be Me

I looked down at Rosie, breathing steadily now and the color returning to her face. I knew what I needed to do, but leaving her seemed impossible. What if there was another grave injury I missed? Fear for her was the only thing keeping me from chasing after that heinous creature that sank into the blackened sea.

"Nephew." My uncle's hand came to grip my shoulder. "Your princess is in my hands now. Do what you need to do, for you and I both know if this doesn't end now, she will forever be his prey."

She was no one's prey. She was my mate. Mine to protect. Mine to keep safe.

"I can't lose her," I whispered.

"You won't. I will finish what you started. You finish the battle that has already begun. It can only be you."

It could only be me. A part of me, deep inside, throbbed steadily, hammering in my chest at that realization. It could only be me. Staring at my broken mate, something broke inside of me. For her, it could only ever be me.

Carli stepped back, shifting into her human form as I bent over her daughter, gently stroking the sand off her face.

"Keep fighting, Rosie. My heart can't survive without you." I kissed her lips, shutting my eyes tightly as I relished the sparks. They were stronger than ever, giving me hope she was going to be okay.

She would be okay, as long as I ensured her future was safe.

It could only be me.

"Come back to us, Rian," her mother grabbed my arm as I got up to walk away towards the sinister ocean. "Be careful."

I was going to do what needed to, whatever the cost, but I nodded just so she would drop her hand and let me go. Her gaze was unyielding, holding the same fear for me she held for her daughter. It strengthened my resolve even more.

"I'll ensure her life. You ensure her future," my uncle whispered, then bent to lift Rosie into his arms, encasing her in a rainbow display of light.

Warriors and knights were landing all around us on the beach, but no one could approach my uncle as he worked to completely heal Rosie. Her injuries were grave, but his power was immense. I knew she would be safe with him and with so many watching out for her now.

"Rian," I heard Taegan yell out to me, half shifted into his normal self as he ran along the shore. "Here!" The black magic he had absorbed came out of his palm in a thick cloud, elongating and then forming a spear once again. He produced two more, then panted breathlessly. He tossed them to me, one by one. "The water is toxic now. Be careful."

I could see the hair around his ankles melting away. The brothers, still engulfed in purple light as they shifted back to their human forms, were hissing as they crawled out of the water as well. They were using up much of their remaining magic to heal themselves from the acidic waste. It was only Conri keeping Taegan from suffering from the toxic ink coating his skin. A goddess's power could not be tarnished by a demon's power.

Neither could the power of a siren prince.

"I will," I said, taking the first spear, illuminating it with my magic and stabbing it in the blackening angry waves.

A clear path broke on the water's surface, my power exuding from its tip after traveling through the dark weapon. I used the clearing to dive into the water, determination pushing me through the acidic ink. It began eating at my skin, but some seething magic under the surface of my fairy magic was breaking free. It's spreading inside of me, healing me and making the sting of the ink not affect me any longer.

My tail and fins took shape, ripping the clothes right off my body. My usually soft flesh of scales felt heavier and stronger than before. My siren body felt as firm as my resolve. I opened my mouth, arms pushed forward as the dark spears extended before me, and expelled a raging burst of magic that cleared the ocean of the toxic ink, making it to where I could finally see to the ocean floor.

There he was, fleeing to the caverns hidden deep beneath the sea. His massive body was escaping through a narrow tunnel. I sent a burst of power to stop him, but it just shattered the walls around the outside of the cave as his tentacles slithered the rest of the way in.

He was trying to escape, most likely to hide until another day. Another day to spy on and plan the abduction of my mate.

I would not let him get another day.

One more blast, and I crushed the tunnel further along the cavernous bottom. His unyielding scream vibrated in the souring briny water. My siren body didn't need shielding from his cries. Not in the water. His power did not match my own.

He pushed his monstrous squid body out of the cave before it completely collapsed, his toxic ink clouding around him. He turned in circles, his rubbery head moving with the currents, until he spotted me.

"You," he seethed. "It was you!" His echoing voice traveled through the water, bouncing against my inner ear. "You stole what was mine."

"She was never yours," I said, the rage inside me reaching new heights. "She never will be. You will die for trying to destroy what belongs to me."

"Ha! You may have a tail and a bit of magic, boy, but I have been ruling these seas longer than you have been alive."

His beak had razored, fang-like protrusions along its edge. His rubber skin quivered and sharp spikes sprang out, armouring his body. His tentacles, some still heavily damaged from the battle, were swelling with black energy, and even the trails of his black blood ribboning from the wounds were boiling the water around them with his darkness.

"Death is the only thing that can separate you from her? Too easy," he cackled, then pushed his heavy body towards me, flying through the water.

I had a dark spear in each hand, and I slammed them together, making my magic explode into a golden and green swirl of massive energy. It struck out like a thick beam of pure lightning, and the kraken could barely dodge the attack.

His surprise was obvious. He reared back, spinning to stare at the golden outline exuding from my aura. I would have been surprised as well at the change in my magic, but I was beyond the ability to be surprised at the increase in my power now. The omnipotent surge of vitality that was swelling up in me was new, but welcome. It couldn't have come at a better time.

"You... you were a lowly prince. How?...." His tentacles shifted frantically around him, his plaguing eyes drowning in his own disbelief. Then, a vibrating scream shook the ocean around me, the waters rushing past my fins.

"I'm her prince." I ground my teeth, letting the energy flowing in my body build up in my limbs. "And you are nothing."

Like a flash, I pushed my body to spring through the water faster than ever before. He roared, moving in a rush, evading my first couple of attacks. With a flick of his tentacles and a blast of his magic, he tried to lose me in a whirlpool, but I stilled his every attempt. He couldn't outmatch me in the water. It may be his purgatory, but the water was my domain. It was the source of my true power; a power that could not be suppressed by any attempts by him. His inky discharge simply brushed against my steel scales, no longer affecting me at all.

He had no choice but to break the surface to get free. My repeated blasts had taken off five of his tentacles completely already, and there was no sign of their regrowth. He was finished, and he knew it.

As he neared the surface, just about to break free, I sucked in a massive stream of water, implanting my will into each molecule and making it spread to the next as I pushed the water back out. It was like a live wire in the sea. All that was dark, all that was evil and toxic, was eradicated by my magic.

When the green and golden streams reached his last remaining tentacles, just as he was bursting free from the surface with a deafening scream, his limbs dissolved into nothing. The power moved up his body, encasing his bulbous black head with spidering gold and green veins.

I brought the two spears of his own changed magic above me and launched them toward the center of his body, aiming for his heart.

He exploded into the dark sky, this body raining down in vapors over the waters that were his prison for so long. There was no recovery for him. There was nothing left to repair. He was gone. The dark sky cleared, the imposing clouds parting and folding in on themselves. The blast from the explosion cleared the air of the rank stench that was plaguing it.

I had no time to be amazed at the sudden clarity of the world around me. I started swimming towards the shore. I wasn't going to feel any relief until my mate's eyes opened and I heard her voice again.

75

DREAM VISITS

Rosie

When I fell into the darkness and the numbness again, I thought I was truly dead. I felt nothing. No pain. No anguish. Nothing but numb nothingness, void of all restraints or the world.

And then, a silvery light took shape in the darkness. It started out small, then grew larger and larger, flowing towards me. I thought it was just a brilliant light, maybe some entrance to the afterlife. When it got close enough that I could see past the brilliant glow, I saw it was a woman. A beautiful woman with a very familiar face. Her long, flowing robes blended into the silver light. She looked angelic with her heavenly aura. Everything about her made me feel at ease.

"My child." She grinned.

Even her voice sounded the same as the one she reminded me of. My chest swelled with happiness when she called me her child. I felt like her child, as much as I felt like my mother or father's child. In some way, I was hers, and she was here to bring me comfort as I faced my death.

"Are you ready to give up already?"

"Ready?" I repeated, my voice floating into the nothingness around me. Giving up was never in my plans, but I'm already dead. Aren't I?

"The Rosie I know would never throw in the towel so easily."

"Easily?" I had to fight the urge to scoff. *"Really?"*

"Your fight may not have been easy, but you seem to be so ready to be guided into the light? Are you giving up? Is there nothing you wish to return to?"

I didn't want to hurt anymore, but I never wanted to die. I never wanted to give up. I wanted to keep fighting, and for one reason. *"Rian,"* I whispered.

"Ah, yes. The miraculous fairy prince. He was an anomaly to his world already, not bearing the arrogance of his peers and having the kindest of hearts. It is not a common trait in the fairy realm. He is a treasure indeed."

I cringed at the word 'treasure'. *"I don't like that word."*

"I suppose you wouldn't. It takes a demon to make a fine word like treasure into a form of a curse. Maybe Prince Rian is more like a prize? Or maybe a precious gem? Like the one you once wore around your neck."

"Yes," I replied sadly. *"That was my most precious possession of all. I lost it. Just like I lost my life. That squid, he...he took everything from me."*

"Did he?" The woman tilted her lovely face, her dimpled cheeks protruding out with her gentle smile. *"He took your flesh. He took your peace. He took your sanity for some time. That is for sure. But.... Rosie, I think you have gained so much more from the endurance you have shown in this chapter of your life."* She came impossibly closer. So close, her brilliance brought with it this urge inside of me to cry. Not from sadness, but from the warmth she had. *"You, my child, will do great things with all you have gained from this. In you, I am already extremely proud."*

Her face, lovely and perfect, came closer to mine, until her lips pressed against my face that before I could not feel. My eyes closed tightly, and when I opened them again, she was gone. She was gone, but I could see.

The colors. I was in darkness, but now I feel as if I'm being hugged by all the colors, even ones I had never seen before. Ones that were on a different spectrum that I could feel more than see.

My everything, right done to my soul, felt like it was coated in the colors of this dream. The range of emotions that erupted inside of me with every new ray made me want to cry. Shamelessly cry. It felt like I was being embarrassed in some form of unwavering, all-encompassing love.

My body was changing. I knew that, but I don't know how I knew. I couldn't see anything. I could only see and feel the colors and the brilliance of each of them.

"Take this new life, my princess, and use it well. It will be extensive, but inspiring. You will be the change to our worlds, dear Rosie. Wake, for your prince awaits."

That voice. I have never heard it before, but the love in it was unmistakable.

My body slowly gained feeling, but the first place I felt anything was my shoulder. That same warmth I felt while bathed in the colors was pressing against my shoulder, then moved to my arms, my head, down my spine, and then pressed into my heart. The tingles made me gasp, longing for one person weighing down on me.

I was in someone's arms, but that wasn't where the tingles were coming from. They were coming from my shoulder and nowhere else.

"Rosie! My baby. Is she okay? Is she going to be okay?" I heard my mother's frantic voice and felt her familiar touch. "Rosie, baby. Open your eyes."

"Move!" My father's voice was commanding in the distance. I somehow knew he was trying to make his way towards me, even though my eyes had yet to gain the ability to open. "Get the fuck out of my way! Rosie! Rosie!"

"She's alive," that loving voice that was just in my head told my father, his voice more firm than before.

"Why won't her eyes open?" Mom asked.

"Rose. Rosie, sweetie. Open your eyes for daddy. Please. Please open your eyes."

I couldn't. I couldn't even move yet. I could feel. I could hear. I could not open my eyes to see, or open my mouth to speak. My body, my entire soul, was waiting for something. Someone. It was no longer my mother or my father that held the greatest place in my heart. It was another.

"Is she okay?" I heard Thyra's mellow voice, full of concern. I felt fingers brushing against my face.

"She's fine, sister. She is waiting for him." That voice sounded loving again as it spoke to my mate's mother. He called her sister. My brain was still slow, but I was coming to realize who he was.

"Thank a mother duck," Alpha Max sighed somewhere close by. My heart panged hearing him near, knowing he was really okay. He seemed so upset in the image Kret showed me, but sounded better now. Exhausted, but no longer devastated.

"A mother duck?" Thyra asked in a monotone voice.

"What? You told me I couldn't cuss in front of him," Alpha Max murmured in a low voice that I'm sure everyone could hear.

"He's here!" I heard Taegan's voice ring out. "Rian! This way!"

"Wow," Mom's voice was barely a whisper, and then a growl escaped my dad.

"You and the damned mermen. Look away, Carli. Shit."

If I could, I would laugh. Dad sounded like he was wound up tight.

Then I felt him. Everything shifted under me, and tingles broke out all over my body. My fingers twitched first, wanting to cling to the one taking me away.

"Rosie," the most beautiful, deep and agonizingly perfect voice spoke my name, and just like that, my eyes broke their seal, opening to the most perfect and beautiful face. "My Rosie."

76

---•---

DEBTS

"Rian," Rosie's weathered voice sounded so sweet, speaking my name. "Rian." Tears began to spill down her lovely cheeks.

She was healed. The gnashes, and wounds that were taking over her body had closed. She was still a mess, but cleaning would have to wait because I was never letting her go again.

"Thank the goddess," her mother gasped, covering her mouth with her hands. Alpha Parker had tears glistening in his eyes, wrapping his arms around Carli's shoulders as she gripped his arms.

Mom was patting dad's back as silent tears reluctantly spilled from his eyes. He was staring up at the sky, trying not to let them show.

All of our family, friends, and pack mates were all around us, along with my uncle and his army of Fairy knights. Even in this crown, it felt like it was just Rosie and me.

She was clinging to me, her hands tightly wound around my neck. I was pressing her body as close to mine as possible. She was safe now, and would forever be. She was mine. Only mine. She always would be.

"I love you," I whispered, bringing her face close to mine. "I love you so damn much. I would have died if I had lost you."

"I love you too," she smiled. A genuine smile that made her entire face light up. "I'm sorry, Rian. I'm so sorry for everything. I thought..." Her face suddenly fell as new tears brimmed in her eyes. "I thought if I could get Julia home, we could all go home and then we could work on us without... without distractions."

Distractions, meaning Taegan. Taegan was no longer an issue for me, though. I don't think he will be, ever again.

"I shouldn't have gotten mad," I whispered roughly, closing my eyes tightly at the reminder of our last conversation in person. "I never should have been that way."

"It's in the past, now," she said. "We have an entire future to look forward to. I don't want to spend it stuck in the mistakes of my past."

"No," I breathed, feeling so much relief. "I don't want that either. I just want my future with you."

Her hand rested on my face, her thumb strumming my bottom lip. Her eyes were traveling, memorizing every feature. There was something different about her eyes. Some magic that wasn't there before. The green glow was of fae royalty, not the same magic you would find in a person from the human realm.

When she pulled me in for a kiss, I eagerly met her lips, ignoring her dad's huffing protests, even as I deepened the kiss. Her kiss, and having her safely in my arms was everything to me. She's safe, and now she always will be.

***

Rosie

Rian held me on the beach, both of us lost in each other. Being with him felt like a miracle after everything I went through. I didn't want him to ever let me go.

Eventually, he had to. A tall knight, like a real-life version of one of the figures I found in Rian's room, came to let Rian know his uncle had opened a portal back to the fairy court and we were being asked to go through it before it was closed. Neither of us had noticed that we were the last on the beach.

The moment we stepped through, my father appeared and stole me from Rian's arms. I tried to cling on to my mate, not ready to be away from him, but then my dad pointed out I was too naked for his liking and Rian was called away by his mother and uncle. I relented and let Rian go and went with my dad.

"Dad, I'm fine." I tried to push my father away as he smothered me in another over-bearing hug. "I missed you too, but this is too much."

"Don't fucking start with me, Rosie. Do you have any idea how fucking worried I was? You're grounded when we get home. For a year."

"I'm an adult now, dad. You can't just ground me."

"Oh, yes, I damn well can. You may be an adult, but I am still your father and your Alpha. You're grounded."

"Mom," I groaned, looking at my mom, who was standing off to the side with Aunt Sim and Vincent.

"Oh, I wholeheartedly agree with your father on this one," she said, though there was a glint in her eyes that made me think she was up to something. Simone's little giggle didn't help my suspicion.

I wasn't going to win right now. Not while my dad was so worked up. He's always been a bit overprotective of me, but now, with this happening, he was worse than ever. He wrapped a robe around my body after taking me from Rian, but I noticed the look in his eyes as he stared at my shoulder.

He looked horrified, and I could only imagine what the damage was like to my body. I felt fine. Better than new. No matter how I felt, or how much I was healed, I knew the torture my body endured wouldn't be completely repairable. My shoulder was literally sliced away over and over again. I was scared to even ask what that scar looks like.

As my dad continued to be an overbearing butthead, smothering me with his over-protective love, I looked across the courtyard to Rian, who was standing with a very commanding fairy, with long hair swept back from his face, and pants that looked like they were woven from pure gold. His pointed ears had golden tips, and his eyes were identical to Thyra's and Rian's.

He must be Rian's uncle, the fairy king.

Seeing the three of them together, there was something different about Rian and his uncle compared to Thyra. There was a golden hue around both men. I never noticed it with Rian before. I didn't notice any hues around anyone before, but I was catching them now all over the place, with all these different fairies.

Then there were Mitch and Mark Meyers. They had a purple and green swirling hue surrounding them, but their green was different from Thyra's and some of the other fairies present. It was a darker, almost dirtier color, and not as luminescent. Taegan had a brilliant blue hue surrounding him, shining almost as brightly as Rian and his Uncle. There was a silver lining to it that reminded me of the woman I saw in my dream.

That was a beautiful dream. That woman, the carbon copy of Bailey, stopped so much of the turmoil inside me. Even now, thinking back to that dream, I feel a peace I didn't think I would feel after all that had happened. She called me her child. I wonder if that was just a beautiful dream, or if it was deeper than that. I want to ask Bailey about it, but she seems stressed talking to Taegan and Alpha Axel right now. I'll maybe call her when we get back to the human world.

"I'm not drinking any more of this damned nut tea and rabbit food!" Alpha Max roared from another area in the court, Gamma Casey and a few of the Blue Cliff warriors with him as a slim fairy woman offered them a tray of drinks and food. "Get me a fucking coffee. Not nut tea. Coffee. If you can't do that, send us home! I'm ready to go home!"

"Max." Thyra rushed over to him, apologizing to the fairy woman and giving him a stern look. "Watch your mouth."

"My mouth wants coffee! How the hell does an entire species survive without it. I've been here for two days now without a single fucking cup. If you want me to watch my mouth, coffee needs to go in it first. And meat."

"We... we don't," the fairy woman stumbled to find a response.

"Don't mind him," Thyra smiled, dismissing the woman. "You!" She stabbed her finger in the center of Alpha Max's chest. "Behave. We're wrapping things up with Rian, and then we can head back. All of us. Patience and behave or you will regret it."

"Zap my ass and call me a dog. I don't give a shit. If I don't get coffee in the next ten minutes, I'm taking the next best thing, and you can't say no."

The look that passed between them was all too familiar. My parents got that look when they were frustrated with each other all the time.

"He's going to fuck her right here," mom whispered to Simone. "Right in front of everyone. Lucky duck."

Dad groaned, rolling his eyes. "I'm ready to get home, too."

"I think we all are," Vincent said, though he looked worried, staring back at Taegan, who was still arguing with his parents. Alpha Axel was looking around the courtyard, his face a mask of fury. When his eyes landed on the Meyer's brothers, I knew something was up. I just didn't know what.

"We can discuss things later, sister. We have plenty of time." Rian's uncle made me gasp when he spoke loud enough for Alpha Max and everyone else to hear. His voice was the one I heard over and over again in my dream. "I can prepare the portals now for everyone to be on their way."

"Not everyone," a sickly sweet voice invaded the energy buzzing between the warriors and knights. "There is one here who can not yet leave our world, father. Not with the debt that he owes me."

Parisa, the skanky bitch, came striding in the yard dressed in impossibly less than she was wearing last time I saw her. Thin vines were wrapped around her chest, their leaves barely covering her nipples, and a slightly larger leaf was covering her vagina, while the rest of her was exposed with a see-through veil.

There was another woman, maybe a bit older, otherwise she could be her twin, standing beside her. This new woman had cat eyes, with yellow irises.

"One of these wolves owes our daughter a payment for her services, my husband," the new woman said. Her cat eyes searched the crowd until they landed on Thyra, then a twistedly sweet smile spread on her face. "I expect you to see to it that it is paid before he departs."

77

DOGMATIC RIGHTS

"Padina," Rian's uncle gave the woman a warning look. "Now is not the time for your unwarranted aggression."

"Oh, my king husband. Whether you think this is unwarranted or not, I just want what is due to our daughter. She was quite used by one in your company. She was treated with nothing but hostility while granting a favor for your beloved nephew." The way the woman's nose turned up when she said nephew, I knew she held no affection for my mate. "After she was used, abused and tossed away like filth, I think the least you could do was to hear her out."

"There is no need for this. Rian is an heir, more so than she," he gave a sideways glance to Parisa. "You know as well as she that you can not play these tricks on an heir to my throne. You have been warned repeatedly in the past."

Padina's sickly sweet expression turned sour for a moment, her cat eyes flickering to Thyra again, and then my mate. A deep growl rolled through my chest, and that flickering of warmth I had originally felt spreading from my shoulder was not moving in my body once again. Dad even loosened his hold on me, staring at me like I had grown a second head. I could see a green glow reflecting from my body in his eyes when I spared him a quick glance, but my eyes didn't waver from my mate and the bitch glowering at him long enough to figure out what the green glow was about.

"You have expressed your favoritism toward the bastard child, yes, but it is not he or his mother who have wronged our precious daughter, dear husband. It was someone else."

That sharp, pointed gaze of hers turned towards Taegan, and a smile spread on her face. As she raised her pointed finger, her razored nails like a sword threatening Taegan across the courtyard, everyone gasped.

"That one there. The one touched by the goddess. He willingly took from our daughter magic of this world. Since he is not of this world, there is a price to be paid. A price that must be completed before you may permit him to be sent on his way."

Bailey snarled, and it was the first time in my life I heard such a menacing sound from the Blue Cliff Luna. Alpha Axel blocked the bitch's view of his son and his body shook, like he was ready to shift and tear off the bitch's head. Many others were ready to follow him in that fight, even our warriors.

My eyes landed on the Meyers brothers. Mark was equally as pissed as most everyone else, but Mitch had a guilty expression on his face. Vincent and Phoebe were glaring at Mitch with hostility that matched his guilt.

There were suspicions, but I had thought there was no way Mitch or anyone would tamper with a mate bond, no matter how protective they were over their child. Now, I wasn't so sure. Something was going on with Mitch or he wouldn't look so guilty right now.

"Dad," I said, just low enough that my voice wouldn't travel. "Mitch Meyers. He did something. This isn't all on Taegan."

"What isn't all on Taegan? What the hell is going on?"

I knew. I think Taegan suspected too, because the look on his face said it all. I knew then that Parisa's ploy to kiss him wasn't as innocent as she had claimed. She wasn't just trying to help him. He was a victim. She targeted him for this purpose. This was some kind of twisted scheme, and I wanted to know Mitch's part in it.

"He didn't take shit, you cat-eyed tramp!" Alpha Max yelled. Thyra was pushing against his chest to hold him back as Padina smiled at his insult. "Your hussy of a daughter forced her bowling ball tits on him and shoved her disease ridden tongue down his throat."

"Max," Thyra tugged on his beard to get his attention. She sounded sad more than scolding, but she was still trying to deescalate the situation.

"What?! Who the fuck would want that!? Look at them! They're disgusting, loose cunt hussies with weird fucking eyes and weirder fucking tits! This is fucking extortion! Miss herpes fairy is trying to trap my grandson!"

"I agree about the extortion, but that is still my brother's daughter and one of his wives."

"That's not my fault! It sure as hell isn't Taegan's. Why are they coming after my grandson?!"

Parisa's sweet smile faltered more and more at Alpha's Max's insults, but her mother just narrowed her creepy eyes at Alpha Max and Thyra. Parisa seemed unsure now, looking back and forth between her mother and father. It was the least confidence I had seen in her as of yet.

"Maybe your grandson has forgotten the events that unfolded between him and Parisa." She then looked towards her daughter. "Show them." Paris hesitated for a moment, but her mother's eyes flashed for a moment which spurred Parisa on. She stepped forward and held her hands above her head, projecting an image for all to see.

It was of her and Taegan at Thyra's cottage. They were all alone and he looked drained. In his weakened state, he agreed to taking magic from Parisa, and when his lips locked with hers, the magic that flowed between them became dark. I could see his aura changing, becoming tainted by her.

I looked over at him and his aura wasn't that polluted. It was blue and silver, with a lining of red. The lining seemed to be from his emotions and not his power or energy.

He was pissed. Rightfully so. Parisa was showing everyone here something he was so ashamed of that he looked traumatized by the event.

The longer the image showed the scene, the more into kissing Parisa Taegan became. If I couldn't see the energy moving between them, I would think he was enjoying himself, but I knew that wasn't the case. I knew that it was the dark magic making him drunk in its power, causing him to do things he wouldn't otherwise do.

Her tits were completely exposed, and now I know why Alpha Max was going on the way he was about them. She was smothering him with them, and they looked as heavy and imposing as fucking bowling balls.

"Fucking bitch," I muttered under my breath.

"I hate to say it, honey, but it looks like he was in fact asking for it."

I shook my head at my dad. "He wasn't. It's her magic. I was under its spell once too. It makes you deliriously lustful. He doesn't want her at all. It's the magic making him do it."

"He's unmated," mom said, her hand over her mouth, looking appalled by the scene. "It does look like she is the one in control, but he's single anyway. Why does this shit matter so much?"

Because he found his mate. I wanted to tell her, but now was not the time. Not with so many around us who might be listening. I didn't want to sully Taegan's reputation by making anyone think less of him. I knew this wasn't his fault, no matter what Parisa and her mother were scheming.

I chanced a glance at the Meyers brothers. Mark was inflamed, just like Taegan, with a red lining to his murky aura. He was looking at Mitch now and now the image, and Mitch looked like he was about to be sick.

The image was suddenly cut off, without showing Phoebe or Alpha Max interrupting them and the way Taegan acted afterward. She left it where it seriously looked like they were getting carried away with a dirty make-out session, and Taegan was as guilty as she was in the act.

"YOU FUCKING BITCH! SHOW THE REST!" Alpha Max yelled, spit flying from his mouth. "YOU MANIPULATIVE FUCKING CUNT!"

Thyra wasn't holding him back any longer. She was glaring at her niece. "You are purposefully not showing the rest because you want to make it look like he is not the victim that he is, but I will not stand for that."

She moved to stand on Taegan's other side, holding his hand. His eyes glowed as she lifted her hand in a similar way that Parisa did. Only, the image was all from Taegan's point of view, not from a bystander's view. It even had some of Taegan's thoughts.

Like I saw from their auras, Taegan didn't even realize what was happening with Parisa. He had no magic and was drunk on hers, trying to get more. He was clearly manipulated from the images in his mind, and then when it showed the aftermath, Phoebe's outburst when she walked in with Alpha Max and Thyra, you could see how disgusted and horrified he was by the reality of what had happened.

There was no lust, only disgust.

Parisa's body language seemed flustered, She was looking at her father like she was worried.

"In our world, we call that sexual assault," Alpha Axel's voice was firm, his eyes blazing with fury. "Seems to me like you are trying to manipulate all of us like you manipulated my son. If we were back home, what you did would be punished severely." He rolled his neck, cracking it. "Very severely."

"Ah, but we are not in your world, Alpha wolf," Padina moved stealthily towards her daughter, placing her hands around her shoulders. "We are in Alfheimr, where women are the victims of the unequivocal rights of the men we are assigned to. Dogmatic may be a term your kind is more understanding of," she scoffed. "Your son came into this world without the proper authority or even the courtesy of letting my husband know. Then he took magic from my daughter, clearly stating he wanted it. How he got it is not the issue. He took it." Her voice was firm and cold. "That is the issue. Since he was not able to fulfill the task she wished for as payment because of their interruption, another payment is needed."

"What is it that you want?" Thyra said, standing to block Taegan, like Alpha Axel and Bailey.

Padina's sweet smile returned, and she craned her head, now looking at her husband. "He will stay in this land. It is the law after taking magic from your daughter. He has to stay here until some payment she finds acceptable is made. That is what I am after. As the ruler of this Kingdom, you can not deny Parisa, your daughter, that right."

78

CONSEQUENCES

"You spoke of no payment," Rian stepped forward, the lining of his aura thick with gold. "You showed it yourself. You didn't ask for anything in return."

Parisa and her mother stared at Rian, Padina looking displeased and Parisa seemed surprised.

"No payment was voiced because she was taking it from a willing man," Padina jutted out her chin, looking arrogant in her stance. "If they were not interrupted, she could have taken payment the succubus way, but she was denied that right."

"I trusted you." Rian turned his focus on Parisa, his eyes burning with fury. "Were you trying to trap Taegan the moment you showed up? Why? Why stoop this low? We're family. Cousins."

Parisa's bubbly face was long gone, replaced with an expression that was a mix of indifference and coldness. Her aura was yellow, and I felt that there was guilt in her too. She was just doing a good job of hiding it.

"I never considered you family."

Rian's raging aura burned brighter, causing Parisa to drop the cold persona and take a hesitant step back. Her mother stopped her from retreating further with a forceful hand on her back.

"Judging by your nephew's transformed magic, I can see you finally decided on the future generations, leaving our daughter out of your consideration." She took a forceful step forward. "You owe her at least this. You say you are just, and the laws bind you as well as the rest of us. He took magic freely from our world. The price must be paid. My daughter, YOUR daughter's magic was taken from her. He is bound to her now."

"Fucking tosspot, pusswit, cat fucking, cuntwa-"

"Dad," Alpha Axel raised his voice, using a command of all things to calm his father. He pushed his father back to stand with their women and Taegan as he stepped forward to face Parisa and her mother.

Poor Taegan was a fucking mess of emotions. I could tell he was hurt, but that extended to the witch hybrid brothers behind him more than Parisa.

"You obviously want to hurt Thyra and Rian by hurting their family. Fine. If you think you will feel even an ounce of satisfaction by doing so, then punish me instead."

"Are you offering your body to my daughter, Alpha wolf?" Padina's cat eyes roamed Alpha Axel's shirtless form, causing Bailey to snarl softly.

"No. My son would never agree to offering his body either. We hold ourselves in higher regard and have more self-respect than the both of you do. That is clear." Parisa and Padina scoffed at Alpha Axel's insult. Padina just looked offended, but there was true hurt outlining Parisa's face. "I also have a mate I am fully devoted to. I know things work differently here, but we do not betray our mates. We do not betray our family. If you want to punish someone, punish me, but know you will never get that physical payment you desire from anyone in my pack."

"None of us want your damn fairy STDs," Alpha Max muttered under his breath. "No telling what about of coffee-less torture we would have to endure to get rid of them."

"Your devotion to your son is praiseworthy," Padina lifted a thin brow, eying Bailey and waving her fingers in a slow, taunting motion. Bailey's eyes glowed as her lips curled maliciously. "As disappointing as that is to hear you would refuse something as simple as your body for a single night, your body isn't the one that took my daughter's magic. It was your son's. He and he alone can repay my daughter, and until that payment is met, he can not leave."

"Then none of us leave," Alpha Axel snarled. I could see his restraint was about to snap.

The tension was mounting, and as the warriors from both of our packs prepared for whatever the next battle was to come, the fairy knights were visibly distraught about what to do. Padina was one of the King's wives. That had to make her a queen, or at least a concubine. We had an heir on our side too, because of my mate. They were looking at their king for guidance, but he was stoically watching Padina and Alpha Axel face off.

Then.....

"This wasn't what I wanted," Mitch Meyers stepped forward. Dad growled low in his chest, now knowing I was right. "I don't know why you are taking this so far when it's not what I wanted. This isn't what Lady Delilah told me you would do."

"Ah." Padina slipped back into a sickly smile. "You must be my daughter's vampire lover's pet wolf. The one that asked for the future mate of your child to be banned from entering your city until she came of age. What was that city called, dear daughter?"

Parisa hesitantly answered, "Miami."

"Miami," Padina giggled, her whole body jiggling with the action. "A silly little human name for a silly little human town."

"Fucking hell. Miami is a huge city," my mom muttered. "Ignorant bitch."

Padina went on like she didn't hear a thing. "Miami," she repeated. "You wanted Parisa to use her magic to prevent the goddess-touched alpha wolf from coming to Miami. This was exactly what you wanted."

"I'm going to kill him," Gamma Casey mumbled. Most of Blue Cliff was glaring at Mitch Meyers like they were ready to kill him, Alpha Max and Alpha Axel especially. Our pack was gaping in disbelief. You don't prevent a wolf from seeing their mate. That's a huge violation of wolf law, going against the goddess's wishes itself.

Taegan looked so hurt, and I swear there were tears glistening in his glowing, icy blue eyes. My eyes met Rian's as I looked away, and the communication in our stare sent my heart racing. This would not end well for Taegan. I could see it on Rian's face.

"You went around pack code to try to ban another Alpha from entering our city?" My dad asked with a voice so steady and deep that it was frightening.

"My daughter needs to be protected. I thought I was doing what was best. As her father."

"THAT'S NOT YOUR CALL TO MAKE!" Spit flew from my dad's mouth as he let his fury break free.

"SHE'S MY DAUGHTER!"

"And he's my son!" Alpha Axel turned to stare at Mitch with a look that made my heart contract. "You doomed your own daughter's future mate out of fear. How are you going to face her after this?" He shook his head, his eyes brimming with disappointment. "How can you face yourself?"

Mitch looked sick with guilt, as he should. No amount of his guilt can change what he did. If I were his daughter, I could never forgive him. Especially if Taegan didn't get home safely from this.

"Let us stay here instead," Mark stepped up next to his brother. "One or both of us. If it is magic you seek, we have it ourselves. Let my son-in-law go and one of us will stay behind instead."

"Leaves and vines," Padina said in exasperation, pinching the brim of her nose. "Not one of you is hearing me. Talking to dogs," she shook her head. "I might as well be talking to a tree or a rock. They would better comprehend words. Only the goddess-touched boy and pay for what he has taken. No substitutions will suffice. He is to stay." Padina looked at Thyra and smirked. Her cat-eyes batted gently. "The laws of Alfheimr can be harsh, but can not be evaded. Is that not right, Thyra dear?"

"You twit-brained bitch," Thyra hissed. "All this because of the adverse effects of a mistake I made so long ago?"

Padina simply shrugged. "Adverse effects are tricky, because you never know how many could be your victim."

"You are no victim. You're a snake," Thyra hissed.

"Be that as it may. It changes nothing." Padina looked to the king, who had stayed stoically observant through all of this. "As king, it is your job to ensure our laws are held."

King Aengus remained quiet, staring coldly at Padina. Her smug face faltered the longer she stood in his gaze, his ethereal aura pouring out of him. She tried to maintain her arrogance, but it wasn't working.

Paris bowed her head, finally having the fucking decency to look ashamed as her mother was being glared at by every person here. Even the knights seemed to hold disdain for one of the wives of their king.

"Is this truly the road you wish to travel, Padina?" Rian's uncle finally said.

Padina jutted out her chin, looking defiant in her stance. "Yes. It is."

The fairy king didn't seem surprised. He just turned his gaze to Parisa. "And you? Are you sure your mother's schemes would be worth the fallout from what you are both forcing my hand for?"

Parisa squirmed in place, seeming scared of her father's words. Then, her mother hissed something in another language under her breath that made Parisa startle and take a tiny step back.

"I'm sure, father."

"No," King Aengus seemed deeply disappointed and shook his head. "Father is not a term you will be permitted to call me from this moment on. If this is what you both are sure of, then so be it." He raised his hands in the air, a golden light erupting from his fingers. His eyes were beaming so brightly that they looked like beacons in the sky. His mouth opened, and it was like a siphon, sucking the aura right from both Parisa and Padina in front of everyone.

Padina wailed, falling to her knees and then screaming in protest. Parisa looked scared and whimpered softly, the green energy from both being sucked right out of their bodies.

He was stripping them of their royal pedigree. They were being left as commoners after he was done. Not a trace of magic was left in either of them.

"I hereby banish the two of you from the courts of Septentrional. Entrapment of a child of a goddess is a law of nature that I can not overlook either." He then turned his stare to Parisa. "For your sake, because you were once known as my daughter, I hope you find redemption for this crime, because the purgatory of the gods is not a favorable position to hold. From this day forward." He then turned his gaze to Rian. "You, Rian, will be my crowned heir."

79

SENTENCE FROM A PRINCE

Rian

"You, Rian, will be the crowned heir."

I was left stunned when he spoke those words out loud. I have always been grateful to my uncle for taking me in and making me a prince during the short time that I was without my mom. Those few years I spent as his prince were far easier because of the title he gave me, but I never expected more than what I had already received. How could I?

"No!" Padina hissed from the ground where she lay in a crumpled heap. "NO! I AM YOUR WIFE!"

"That makes your corruption even more sinister. The power you held as my wife will be no more, Padina. Oberon," he looked towards the seasoned knight, "remove these two from the courts. Arrange a dwelling in the lower region."

"In the slums?!" Padina seethed.

"With the common fae. The terms of your banishment from my court will be discussed with you later."

He nodded at Oberon and the knight, along with four of his men, came to take Padina and Parisa from the courtyard. Padina fought and demanded to be released, telling my uncle this was against the law of marriage. My uncle stood his ground, not saying a word. He watched in silence as his former wife was dragged out of the courtyard, kicking and screaming.

Parisa was quiet, staring at the ground with glimmering tears in her now muddled eyes. The vibrant magic of a royal was no longer there.

"What about my son?" Axel asked once my cousin and aunt were gone.

All the werewolves were watching with anticipation, dad and mom still guarding Taegan alongside Bailey.

All the wolves but my mate were anxious about Taegan. Rosie was staring at me, biting her bottom lip. I could feel her worry, and it wasn't at all for Taegan. It was for me. I could guess why, but didn't have the answers yet to reassure her. I was as shocked and worried just as she was, but as the next Alpha to her pack, the announcement my uncle just gave would be harder for her.

One thing was for sure to me, among all other uncertainties; Rosie's first concern was me. Taegan was in the midst of something terrifyingly life-changing, but Rosie was more concerned about me. I felt like such an idiot for ever thinking I was not her first priority, or below Taegan in her heart. Her priority. Her first worry. Her first for everything; everything that truly mattered. That is my place in her heart. The undying love I felt coming from her for me mixed with her anxious worry, had me feeling breathless.

"King Aengus, please," Mark Meyers stepped in front of his brother, tears filling his eyes. "It was a mistake. My brother or I will pay the price. We will do whatever we have to do. Please. Just allow Taegan to go home."

"It was me," Mitch said, staring at the ground as if he feared meeting the eyes of those around him, the weight of guilt heavy on his neck. "I acted out of fear. My... my little girl. She is a seer, and too young to be exposed as one yet. Being together with him made it apparent what she was now that he was of age. I got scared for my daughter and just wanted them to be separated until she turned of age too. I didn't mean for this to happen."

He slowly raised his head and met my uncle's stoic, all-knowing gaze. The purple fuel of seer energy from Hadley was churning with the dull green magic of a mortal witch or the human realm. Looking in his eyes or Mark's, you could tell he was powered by his seer of a mate. He was telling the truth, but he also confessed to intentionally breaking werewolf law by trying to keep Taegan away from his fated mate.

I knew what my uncle would say, even before he said it, because he really didn't have another choice. Not with Parisa and her mother demanding payment for the magic Paris had given Taegan.

Parisa never gives favors without something in return. I should never have trusted her from the beginning.

"I do not hold the authority to carry out the punishment of your sins against your kind, Gemini Wolf. I can only uphold the laws of Alfheimr and my kingdom. Your transgression may have led to the young Alpha's violation of the laws here, but it is still on his shoulders. Not yours." Uncle looked at Axel, too. "Not yours either, Alpha. I will grant him the comforts of family to the crowned heir here in my courts, but unfortunately, I can not permit him to leave. Not until the debt is paid."

"No!" Bailey wailed, burying her face against Taegan's chest and gripping on to him with all her might.

"Mom," Taegan wrapped his arms around his mother, kissing the top of her head. Tears were dropping from his eyes into her hair.

Mark Meyers was staring at them with a gut-wrenching expression, but his brother looked dead on his feet. His eyes were zoned out into space, with deep shadows underneath, his magic flaring with defeat and despair. When his legs gave out and he fell to the ground, not even his brother moved to help him. The way Alpha Parker, Casey, and many of the others were looking at him, I knew they were not going to let him off easy for this. If his guilt didn't destroy him first, they just might.

"There is nothing you can do?" Axel asked, his voice quivering.

His eyes were glossy and red, an expression I had only seen him make when his daughters were born, or that time that Baily started working out and she had noticeably lost weight in her thighs. This is the expression that made Bailey give up her "hot girl summer bod" and workout kick with Courtney, and had dad giving him slack when both sets of twins came into the world. If I could, I'd change the fate of Taegan just to ease his and all the rest of my family's hurt, but just like my uncle, there was nothing I could do.

"I will do all I can during his time here to appease the hurt this may cause you and your family," my uncle said.

***

The Crystal Moon warriors left in a portal my uncle temporarily made back to their pack after many of them wished Taegan a heartfelt goodbye.

The Meyers brothers were forced to leave. Mark approached Taegan and his family to apologize, but none of them were having it. Axel was barely holding himself together, and dad didn't hold himself together at all. Taegan himself had to pull dad off Mitch when dad grabbed him by the throat, trying to kill him right at that moment.

Alpha Parker then commanded the brothers to leave and wait for him in his office at the packhouse until he got home.

The only ones left from the Crystal Moon Pack were my mate and her immediate family. Her mother's friends had gone back through.

My uncle had asked me to wait with him to finish discussing what he had said before Parisa and her mother interrupted us. He was talking to me about Rosie being a princess, and the change her body went through in order to come back from the brink of death. He and mom needed me to understand the changes to better prepare her for the effects she may face when we go back to her world, but now I think he had a bigger plan for her transformation in all this all along.

You never know with my uncle what is truly going on. Much like the moon goddess, our fae rulers have a divinity that allows them to know things they are not permitted to outright say. It made me wonder how much of this whole ordeal my uncle was aware of, but held back from getting involved in. I don't want to offend myself by asking.

"Your cousin and her mother were a tragic pair," my uncle suddenly said, closing the portal after the last of the warrior wolves went through. It was just my family and Rosie's here now. "Padina, though greedy and egotistical, was far more affected than most women in a situation such as hers. It hurt her pride to be a tool in her incubus father's political schemes. Your mother was always willful and noncompliant with our ways, something I found humorous and charming, but the king before me found to be a burden. She refused to become one of the Incubus King's concubines, and I was highly against it as well." My uncle showed a rare, genuine smile, his eyes glowing with affection. "Thyra would have cut the king in his sleep, and left him without a means to increase his vitality."

I chuckled low under my breath, knowing what he meant. Mom would not have done well being one of hundreds of concubines solely used for sex. She would have broken all his bones and slit his throat in his sleep.

"Before the former king could try to barter your mother's innocence for the chance to be rid of her, and to gain an alliance with the Incubus King, I volunteered to take one of the King's daughters as a wife instead. I thought it would be the best solution to everything, since I had no interest in forcing a woman against her will, and your mother could have several more years of freedom.

"I didn't know at the time that Padina, the eldest of the Incubus King's daughters, was hoping for an agreement of marriage from the Siren King instead. She was cheated out of the marriage she desired, one where she would have been a consort with hundreds of other wives and husbands to the Siren King she could have relations with freely. It would have been a succubus woman's dream.

"When I could no longer interfere with your mother's marriage talks, it was that same Siren King who sought her hand and wished to not just make her a concubine, but to make your mother the official queen. That alone angered Padina, but then, when your mother ran away from the marriage with a knight, Padina took it as the ultimate offense."

I was gaping at my uncle, never having heard this story of my mother's past.

"Parisa was always so kind to me."

"I thought when I punished your mother as I did for the crimes she committed, it might have sated some of Padina's anger, allowing for Parisa to show the son of her mother's nemesis' kindness." My uncle smiled sadly at me. "Or maybe Parisa did once hold affection for her younger cousin, who was lonely in this world without his mom. Parents can influence their children greatly, but Padina was not Parisa's only parent."

I know the affection my uncle held for me. I never questioned that, and the events of today affirmed that more than ever.

"King Aengus," Phoebe approached us, looking determined. "I would like to stay with my Alpha. I would like your permission to stay here in Alfheimr for the time being."

My uncle feigned a saddened expression, but I could see the amusement in his eyes. Amusement about what, I wasn't sure.

"I'm sorry, young Beta. There is nothing holding you in this world. You do not have fae relations and there is no broken law to hold you in my kingdom."

Her eyes flashed with revolt, ready to stand her ground to stay here. "If I go back to my world without my Alpha, I'm going to unalive the fucker that caused him to stay here, and considering that fucker is one of the fathers of my mate too, I think it is in everyone's best interest I stay with him for now."

"It's not in my best interest," Uncle said, then looked at me. "What do you say, nephew, crowned prince of the Septentrional Kingdom?"

No broken law keeping her here? I smirked, knowing that was an easy fix.

"Like you could unalive anyone if you tried," I scoffed, giving Phoebe a look like she was beneath me. "Someone incapable of saying kill or murder and uses a juvenile term such as unalive wouldn't be able to kill a grown adult, especially since he is a man."

Phoebe's mouth dropped open. "Boy, have you lost your damn mind? Has the sudden elevation of your title filled your head with smoke?"

I shrugged. "I just think it's hilarious that a girl thinks she can kill a man. You couldn't hurt a -"

"Bitch," Phoebe punished me right in the face, hitting me square in the nose. I fell to the ground with her on top of me, knowing I needed to end this quickly, when I heard my mate's menacing growl drawing near.

I pulled on my magic just enough to flip her off me and subdue her with her hands behind her back, smiling to myself as she threw insult after insult at me.

"Phoebe Baptiste, as the crown prince of the Septentrional Kingdom, I am afraid I am going to have to sentence you to serve time here in my uncle's court for assaulting my very handsome face. It's for your own protection, of course. My Alpha mate won't take kindly to you breaking her mate's nose."

Phoebe stopped struggling, her face half-smashed into the ground, turning up into a slow half grin. "You crazy motherfucker. I was about to kill you."

"Sure you were," I laughed, getting off of her and letting her up. I reached down and helped her to her feet. "Uncle, I think she should serve her term being the caretaker of my nephew."

"A fair sentence indeed," Uncle said, trying to look solemn, but his eyes were as amused as before. "May you serve the Alpha well, young Beta."

80

GODDESS'S PLAN

A fter calming down Rosie, who looked ready to unalive Phoebe for punching me, no matter how many times I told her I had provoked the attack, I stood with my uncle and watched everyone say goodbye to Taegan. Rosie didn't want to leave my side, glaring at Phoebe so venomously that I feared for Phoebe's life. I insisted, knowing she would regret not saying her goodbyes.

She did not care for him in the same way she cared for me. I knew that now. I also knew that they were best friends for her entire life and this was still going to affect her. Time moved differently between our worlds. I hoped this sentence wasn't a long one, because time can be a greater prison than anything else. Several years here could be a lifetime in the human world.

"My mom and dad are going to stay here, too. You know that, don't you?" I asked my uncle.

"Oh, I'm sure. I was just wondering how to import coffee for my burly brother-in-law. Things will be interesting now with their frequent visits. As the mother and father of the next king, I can not deny them access to my courts."

"Phoebe is who you really need to watch out for. After Parisa, I don't think she is going to treat many of the women in your court kindly."

"No," Uncle chuckled. "It will be amusing to see how the other wives and daughters fare against her."

My smile faded as I thought about the fact the cousin that was closest to me and her mother was no longer a part of the court, and then thinking about all the things that led up to it. Everything was a chain reaction of hurt and hardships before the current generation's mistakes, mine and Parisa's included. It was sobering to think about.

"If I never brought Rosie and Taegan here, none of this would have happened."

"Yes, but the young she-wolf your mate saved would have been lost. No one would have found her after she passed away. The Kraken would have fed her to the fish. Not only was she found, but she was saved. Her parents will attest to how rewarding your coming here has been."

"Still," I grimaced, watching Rosie hug Taegan as he squeezed her back tightly. The tunic she was given to wear slipped from her shoulder, revealing her scarred flesh. Surprisingly, the scar was shaped like a butterfly. The strips of her flesh that were carved away look like wings, my name at the wings' center. It was humbling in so many ways that the old butterfly that got me in such a rage was gone, but this one would remain forever, and only my name was left unscarred.

"You will never know, my nephew, how far down the line a person's sins will affect their lineage. A father's crime can place a permanent label on his son. I thought I prevented the sins of your parents from affecting you. It seems this time your nephew will suffer, and no one is to blame but the ones that came before you. Even I am to share in that blame."

I watched with a heavy heart as Taegan said goodbye to his family. Bailey was clinging to his waist, wailing like he was dying instead of just being left in the fairy realm. All this suffering was just because of a vendetta Parisa and her mother had against my mother and the circumstances of my birth. I couldn't help but to share that blame, even if my uncle is telling me not to. If I hadn't asked for Parisa's help, Taegan would be going home with us, too.

That damned kraken. The demented squid was the start of this whole thing. We never would have come to Alfheimr if it wasn't for him.

"I just wish we could have found out what the damned kraken wanted with my mate. Why he thought she was hers and how the connection got there to begin with. Rosie mentioned witches, but he never clarified further."

My uncle's face turned solemn. "That too, my nephew, was a chain reaction from the sins of those that came before her. It is over now and I think it is best not to dig more into it, or the fallout from that could be greater. That mistake has been made right. Leave it at that." I looked at him questionably, but he just shook his head and sighed. "Those sins go further back than just her parents, and honestly, they couldn't handle that guilt. Leave it be. The one that started that chain of events is already being punished for a lifetime. Even death, if death ever comes to the woman, will not free her from the purgatory she is to face. A deity's will is not to be trifled with. Leave it be."

"You seem to know an awful lot about the happenings of the human world," I murmured.

My uncle laughed. "My beloved nephew and dear sister live in that world. I make it my business to know. Plus," his eyes light with ethereal magic, "there are perks to being king. I'm sure that one day you will find out."

My heart hammered thinking about being in my uncle's position one day. It hammered even harder when I saw Rosie walking towards me. "Not anytime soon, though. Right?"

"Not soon for you." My uncle's eyes followed mine and a gentle smile broke on his face, seeing Rosie's tears. "You will have a long reign on earth alongside your princess, aiding her like she will one day aid you. But the kingdom will soon welcome you both home."

Home. Home always seemed like such a broad term for me, but watching my mate, I finally know what it truly means. Home is wherever she is.

"I hate this," Rosie said, walking right into my open arms. "I hate that we have to leave him behind."

"You may visit your friend whenever you choose, princess," my uncle said with an affectionate grin. "You are part of this world now, as much as Rian is a part of yours."

Rosie turned her head against my chest. The feeling of having her depend on me in her sadness was astounding. Everyone now knew her strength, and I knew I was the only one who would know her weaknesses.

"It was you," she whispered. "I heard you. In my dream." She grew quiet and I could feel her swell of emotions. "Thank you."

"It was my honor, my princess," he said, eyes glowing with mirth. He smiled, nodded his head, then left to talk with our families.

"What dream?" I asked, curious about what they were talking about.

Rosie looked up at me, resting her chin on my chest. Her beautiful eyes had that royal green glow deep within them, and now I knew why. My uncle blessed her when he healed her, because she would one day rule beside me.

"I had a dream when I thought I was dead. I saw a woman first, one that looked so much like Bailey that just taunted me until I didn't want to let go anymore. She was... she was warm. Loving, but firm. And then... then I heard your uncle. He was what pulled me back to reality. He brought me back to you."

I couldn't help myself. I placed my lips gently on hers, relishing the sparks between us.

"I love you," I whispered when we broke the kiss. "Thank you for coming back to me."

"Thank you for saving me," she said hoarsely. There were tears glistening in her eyes. "I love you too."

Hearing her say that now that she wasn't in harm's way and we were out of the hellish place she was tortured in healed a part of me; that part that still was on edge after she was taken. I kissed her deeply one more time, then rested my head on hers.

"Let's go home."

***

Reika

"You're grinning." Dante watched me with a tea towel over his arm as I strummed my fingers against the pages of my book.

"Am I?" I pressed my lips together, trying to hide my satisfaction. "It's a beautiful day today. It must be affecting my mood."

"Each day here is the same." Dante's sharp eyes crinkled in their corners. "I think something else is affecting your mood, my goddess."

"Perhaps." I let my triumphant smile break free. "Perhaps an idea that has been long in the making has finally come together."

"Your scheming with your children, you mean?"

"Not just my children. The others and I have been working towards this unified goal for quite some time. Every story needs a happily ever after."

"It doesn't look like the boy will be getting his happy ending anytime soon."

"No, but he needed this. He and Conri needed to learn to work together without me. They both needed to be humbled or his power would have ruled him. I refuse to see the corruption of my line's savior. He will be better for this."

"And his mate?"

I looked up at my shelf, seeing my book for the future. "She needs to learn to fight for herself one day or she can never become a Luna to the original pack. She will need to lose her humble personality to win him for herself."

Dante chuckled deeply. "To think, leaving the boy alone one time could cause this chain reaction."

"Things unfolded nicely, didn't they? I knew my child from the Crystal Moon Pack would have the strength to pull through. The reward she will receive from facing that beast when she becomes queen of another world will be the balm to unify our species. The others will be pleased."

"You seemed distraught when she was enduring that beast."

"Of course I was. I am always distraught for my children when they are being tested in the fires of the mortal world. Without knowing real suffering, an Alpha can not effectively lead their pack, and her being a woman would have made it harder for her to earn that respect." I smiled, running my fingers over the pages. "No one will question her strength now."

81

WELCOME HOME

Rosie

With a last hug with Taegan, Rian and I joined the rest of his family and my parents, traveling back to Crystal Moon Pack. Bailey was wailing uncontrollably, and Alpha Axel ended up having to carry her through the portal. She didn't want to let her son go. None of us did, but she was taking it the hardest.

Taegan looked equally upset, staring at his family with a sad smile, blue eyes brimming with moisture. Phoebe leaned her head against her Alpha's arm like they were supporting each other. They would have each other. Hopefully, this wasn't for forever. I didn't know how we were going to get him back home, but I didn't doubt he would be. If not, I would do something myself. He came because he was trying to keep me safe. I'm guilty for him being here, too. If I wasn't so insistent on coming, Taegan wouldn't have followed me. I'm wondering how everything could get so messed up for the one descended from the moon goddess herself. Surely there was a way out of this for him.

Murderous thoughts of Parisa and her mother filtered through my head. I should have killed her the moment I saw her hanging on Rian. Yeah, it would have been a misunderstanding, but she'd be dead and Taegan and Pheobe would be going home.

When their image was lost as we moved through the portal door, the discomfort I felt from the transition from different realms was nothing compared to the grief I felt for the Blue Cliff Pack.

"I wanna be there when you talk to that motherfucker," Alpha Max growled lowly as we stepped foot on Florida ground. "His ass should be the one ripped away from his family, not the kid's."

"I don't know if that's the best idea," Dad mumbled, seeing the homicidal look on Alpha Max's face. "He fucked up, but he is still the father of Taegan's mate. You killing him isn't going to bode well for their future."

"They might not have a fucking future!" Alpha Max bellowed.

"It's going to be us," Bailey looked fiercely at my dad, her face red and blotchy, especially around her eyes. Her determination was unmistakable, though. She was not taking no for an answer. "Axel and I will be in there, or we will be dealing with this ourselves."

"Is that a threat?" Dad's Alpha genes were making him defensive.

"No. It's not a threat at all. I am simply telling you it is in that man's best interest for you to let Axel and I be in that room with you. Letting is a loose use of the term. We will be handling this one way or another. It's up to you if you want to be present or not."

Dad's eyes were tightening into slits, his hackles raised, but my mom calmly touched Dad's arms and looked ahead at Bailey. "You will be there. That won't be a problem. Anything short of death we will agree to. His fate will be in your hands."

Bailey nodded, then met Rian's eyes. I looked up to see Rian's eyes glowing his vibrant green, and Bailey's were shining a pure gold. I had never seen her eyes do that before.

Rian nodded, pulling me close to his side. "We will be there too."

"Then why the fuck can't I be there?!" Alpha Max yelled.

"Honey," Thyra smiled softly, pulling on his hand. "We need to pack, anyway. Let your sons handle things. We need to find the girls."

"Why?" he stared down at her face, and then understanding painted over his. "Oh. Yeah," he sighed, and smiled sadly. "Fuck," he wiped a hand down his face. "Okay. Yeah. Let's go get my girls."

When we walked into the packhouse, there was still mayhem going on with everyone else who had returned before us. Everyone was gone for a week because of the time difference between here and the fairy realm and families were frantically reuniting and kids were crying to see their missing parent again.

Taegan's sisters were standing near the stairs with my brother and Karina. They saw Alpha Max before anyone else and started squealing and crying, barreling at him. All but the youngest pair of twins who ran for Thyra with snotty noses and unkempt hair.

"What did Bailey say to you?" I asked Rian while everyone else was distracted.

"She just wanted to confirm something," he smiled down at me. "We're going with your parents as witnesses more than anything. Bailey wanted to be sure."

"Sure of what?"

He didn't get to answer that question before my brother tore me out of Rian's arms. He's been bigger than me for some time, but was never brave enough to use that strength on me. I felt every ounce of his strength in his embrace as he squeezed me against his chest.

"Thank the goddess, Rose. When you didn't come back with the rest, I thought something happened to you!"

"Can't. Breathe," I groaned, and he tightened his hold.

"Shit, sorry," he held me a bit looser. I could hear the roughness in his voice. He was crying, or had been crying.

"What? Didn't you want to step up and be the next alpha?" I teased, hugging him back.

"Goddess, no. That's all on you," he sniffed. He tried to play off, wiping away his tears and nose by mumbling he had something in his eyes.

"Welcome back, Rosie." Karina's eyes gleamed with unshed tears as I looked at her over my brother's broad shoulder.

"Thanks." I reached for her, pulling her into the hug with us. She wedged her face between mine and my brother's chests and cried softly.

"Don't do that again," she sniffled. "When Julia told us what took her... I thought... I thought..."

"How is Julia?" I asked.

My brother finally let me go to wipe away Karina's tears. Rian came up behind me and wrapped an arm around my waist. He was back to not wanting to let go of me it seemed. He's been touching me nonstop since he finished his discussion with his uncle.

"She's doing better. Her wolf came forth and healed her a lot, but she still has to stay in the hospital. She had infections everywhere, and it made her and her wolf really weak. But," Reece smiled at me. "She's alive. Thanks to you."

I felt so much of a relief hearing that. She was so close to death that I was scared it was still too late. There was also that doubt that she made it back at all. Kret, that bastard, was so delusional and psychotic that I wasn't sure if I should trust that he did what he said, or that maybe I had just imagined him sending Julia back.

"We need to go," Rian whispered in my ear. "Bailey just called for us."

I looked around and didn't notice my parents or Alpha Axel and Bailey anywhere. They must have gone straight to dad's office.

We walked together through the dozens of warrior families, and I smiled my thanks as many welcomed me home. When we got to the less busy hallway leading to my dad's office, Simone and Vincent were outside the office door with my grandpa Jared.

"Hadley, I'm sorry, but I really need you and the twins to come here now. It was worse than what you suspected... No, they haven't yet, but I still need you guys to come... Yes. Okay... Bye."

I frowned at Vincent's phone call with Mitch and Mark's mate. I don't know if the twins should be present for the beat down their dad is about to get.

"Rosie." Grandpa Jared pushed off the wall and hurried over to me, wrapping me in a hug much like Reece did earlier. "I'm so glad you're safe. You made me so worried."

"I missed you too, grandpa." I patted his back. "Rian saved me. I'm fine."

I felt his chest vibrate with a quiet growl. "Yes, well, he wouldn't have had to save you if he didn't take you off in the first place," Grandpa muttered.

I sighed and pulled away from him, shaking my head. "He's my mate, grandpa. Don't."

"I'm just saying," grandpa glared at Rian.

I was getting more than a little irritated, and was about to let it show, but then I heard a ferocious growl emanating from inside of my dad's office.

I pushed past Grandpa and the rest to rip open the door, just to see a beast similar to Taegan's Lycan holding Mitch Meyers in the air by his throat.

82

WEREWOLF LAW

"What the-" my mouth dropped at the sight before me. I knew it was a Lycan, and it was distinctly female. It had a softer build than Conri and was noticeably smaller, but still far larger than my wolf. She was larger than my parents' wolves.

"It's Bailey," Rian whispered in my ear, his body pressed against my back and tense.

I figured it was Bailey, but I had never seen her transformed before. She is always so kind and carefree. This was a side to her I never expected.

Mitch was struggling to breathe. I could see his struggles weren't just from the physical attack by Bailey, but also because his muddled green aura was weakening. His magic depleted in the fairy realm, like Taegan's did when we first got there, and neither Mitch nor Mark have had a chance to refill it.

Bailey was snarling in his face, drool dripping from her fangs. Her eyes were shining bright, and her hair was standing on end. Mitch looked scared shitless. Every time I thought he was going to pass out, Bailey would loosen her hold just enough for him to suck in more air before she restricted his airway again.

"He's sorry!" Mark was being restrained by Alpha Axel. Alpha Axel had a stoic, stony face, so rigid that it made my senses instantly go on edge. No matter our relations, he was a visiting Alpha, pissed off and exacting vengeance on my pack members with his Luna. The instinct to defend Mark and Mitch was hard to overcome. I knew why dad was so uptight earlier now. "He didn't think it would turn out like this! He just asked for help to ban him from the city for now. That's it! He didn't know this was that fairy's plan when he came to Lady Delilah!"

"Did Lady Delilah know the extent of what the fairy whore was going to do?" Mom asked.

"I don't know! I wasn't there, and she didn't say anything to Mitch. She just said she would talk with that fairy and see what she could do."

"Either way, that vampire still had a hand in this," Alpha Axel looked at my dad.

"I'll have it handled," dad nodded firmly.

Alpha Axel scoffed. "Phoebe and Taegan have a vampire lord who is a grandfather to both of them. It may be from adoption and mating, but he now takes his role as grandfather very seriously. I expect he will be visiting Miami soon with my mother-in-law to handle things with her."

Dad grit his teeth and my mom sighed. "Lady Delilah has always acted with consideration for our pack's best interest. She may not have known that this would happen," Mom said.

"I doubt that, mom," I spoke up. "You know she has always had a soft spot for Mitch. If Mitch asked her to do something, she would do it. She was also Parisa's lover. That's how Phoebe got to the fairy realm."

Mom pinched the bridge of her nose. "Elena won't like this."

Grandma Elena is best friends with Lady Delilah. She won't like it at all, but that can't be helped. Seeing Taegan and how heartbroken and betrayed he was as we left was a haunting image.

Bailey tossed Mitch across the room, slamming his body into a large picture of the packhouse that has been up my entire life. Mom hated it because the frame was gaudy. I guess she doesn't have to worry about it anymore. Mitch's body shattered the glass and broke the frame completely.

All of us stood back and watched as Bailey destroyed Dad's office with Mitch's body. Seriously, the entire room would need to be repaired and remodeled. There were even cracks in the ceiling and chunks of the walls missing. Dad's solid mahogany desk was in shambles. Bailey lifted the whole thing and dropped it on Mitch at one point.

Mitch just took it. Every blow and every attack. He wasn't trying to fight back, even though I knew he was capable. Mark was struggling to get free from Alpha Axel's hold to help his brother, but even he couldn't use the last flickering of his magic to force Alpha Axel off.

Bailey threw Mitch onto the broken top of dad's desk, splitting it down the middle, and then she crumpled to the floor. She shifted back into her human form on the way down, wailing loudly as tears streamed down her face.

Alpha Axel let Mark go at last and went to comfort Bailey on the floor. He wrapped his arms around her crumpled form, and she turned her head to sob against his chest. Mark hesitated, looking anxious and guilty at Bailey before moving to help his brother.

Rian shrugged off his shirt, moving away from me just long enough to kiss the top of Bailey's head and give his shirt to Alpha Axel for Bailey. Axel nodded tightly, tears in his eyes, then shifted Bailey enough to get the shirt over her body.

With Mark's help, Mitch sat up on top of the broken desk. His body was a mess, open wounds and blood everywhere, though his wolf was healing him quickly. He looked at Bailey in Alpha Axel's arms with so much regret.

"I'm so sorry," he said with a strained croak of a voice. "I am so, so sorry."

"He only wanted to protect our daughter," Mark added.

Bailey pushed away from Axel, using his shoulders to get herself to her feet. She wiped her tears and snot on the back of her hands, glaring down at the Meyers brothers with a sovereign authority that reminded me greatly of the woman in my dream.

"Just like there are laws in Alfheimr, there are laws that apply to all the moon goddess's children, and you have broken a sacred one. There is a price for breaking these laws under the goddess's eyes, too."

"He's sorry!" Mark cried out. "We all are. Beating him to the point of death won't bring your son back. It won't fix anything."

"Beating him was a mother's wrath. Not the goddess's," Bailey's voice exuded so much authority that everyone in the room felt it. The gold and silver lining of her aura was evidence of her true power that had always previously been concealed. Mitch and Mark were cringing beneath her. "You tampered with a mate bond, but not just any bond. It was the bond of the first pack's Alpha heir, the descendant of the moon goddess herself. It was not just my son you hurt with your insecurities. Your daughter will suffer as well." Bailey's chin rose with dominance. "Both of your daughters. Both of their mates are now trapped in the fairy realm."

Mark and Mitch's eyes went wide, and mom gasped from across the room.

"Phoebe was one twin's mate, and Taegan was the other," Rian said, affirming Bailey's claim.

"You have entrapped the next Alpha and Beta of our pack, and because of that, you have left your daughters more exposed than ever. They are not just your daughters. They are the next Luna and Beta female of Blue Cliff, and because of your intervening in their fate, Blue Cliff will take back control of their fate in all ways we still can. The law demands it."

My eyes went wide at her meaning. Mitch looked horrified, and Mark growled deeply.

"What the hell do you mean by that?"

"I mean, we will be bringing our future Luna and Beta female back with us. Your irrational behavior and breaking of the goddess's laws demands it. You failed to keep them safe, and I will not sit by and allow you to sabotage Taegan and Phoebe's fates any more. Your daughters will be coming with us."

"You can't do that," Mitch begged. "They're our little girls."

"We can and we will," Alpha Axel stood behind Bailey and glared down at the men. "With my son and Phoebe out of the way, you could do something even more drastic to keep them from their fated mates. Blue Cliff will not allow for it."

I get it. Mitch was trying to block Taegan from coming back to Miami. What if he mated his daughters off to someone in our pack, someone he thought he could control while Taegan was gone? Mitch has proven to be irrational, and as much as it sucks, especially for the girls and the rest of their family, it is the law. They broke the law by tampering with an alpha's fated mate bond. Taegan's pack has the right to take the girls until they come of age and can decide for themselves what it is they want to do. They can choose to accept their positions in the pack in Taegan's and Phoebe's absence once they turn eighteen, or they can choose to reject their fated mates and return home. Until they are of age, they will be Blue Cliff Pack's charge.

"Please," Mark's eyes filled with tears. "Don't. Don't take our girls."

Alpha Axel knelt at their eye level, leaning dangerously close to Mark and Mitch. "Unlike my mate and I, you will be allowed to see the children taken from you whenever you wish. They will be living in Blue Cliff. Not another realm. Thank the goddess for that."

A subtle knock came from the door behind me and Rian, and then Gamma Matt, Mark and Mitch's brother, poked his head in. "Hadley is freaking out in my office with the girls. She wants her mates."

"We'll be right there," Dad told him.

Matt looked pitifully at his brothers, then quietly closed the door.

"Hadley won't forgive me," Mitch mumbled, staring at the ground. His eyes were void, like he was dying inside.

"Until our son is home, we won't be forgiving you either," Alpha Axel said, then stood back up to lead Bailey from the room.

83

— · —

WET BOOBS

Mom and Dad stayed behind to handle the transfer of Harper and Harley to Blue Cliff, and to navigate any other transfers that would happen because of it. I suspect there will be quite a few.

"Wow," I said to Rian as we walked alone to the top floor.

"Yeah. I was surprised, too, but Bailey knows what she is doing. She's as in-tuned to the moon goddess as Taegan and Phoebe. Maybe more, since Taegan is too into his own idea of what's right and wrong to listen all the time." Rian sighed and shook his head. "I wish Taegan had just stayed home."

Yeah. It's too late to think about what ifs now. What happened has already happened, and we can't change it. I wish we could too, but we can't. I will never forget the image of Bailey clinging to Taegan in the Fairy Courts, refusing to let her son go. She has to be in tune with the goddess, because if I were her, I would likely have killed Mitch.

She and Axel could have. They had that right. They clearly proved to be more rational than Mitch, and even Mark. Bailey would have had to be more in tune with the goddess's will than her own, or she wouldn't have held back at all or stopped until he was dead.

Even if she wasn't in tune with the goddess, Mitch had already broken the trust between Blue Cliff and him. Blue Cliff, by law, may protect their heir's future mate. Not just Alpha heir. The Alpha and Beta heirs. I don't think either brother expected both of their daughters to be mated to ranked members of Blue Cliff Pack.

Mitch wouldn't be able to go see his daughters for some time. Not safely. Bailey and Alpha Axel let out their wrath and judgment, and they got to say goodbye to their son. Phoebe's moms didn't get that chance, and both are strong warrior women. One is the daughter and heir to Lord Antonio, the ruler of the vampire coven outside of Blue Cliff Pack. I suspect they will be visiting Mitch soon, too. Mitch ultimately damned both of his daughter's mates to be separated from them in a different realm unaccessible to anyone who is not fairy.

What Mitch did was equivalent to if Thyra or Alpha Max tried to ban me from seeing Rian. Unless the mate comes of age and chooses to reject their fated mate, you can not forcefully separate fated mates. Not without cause and an Alpha's ordered protection. Mitch didn't even try talking to my dad. He went straight to an outsider, and should count himself lucky if dad doesn't make him a rogue on top of all this too.

"Don't worry about the girls," Rian rubbed my arm soothingly, seeing the concern on my face. "Bailey just wants to keep them safe."

"I know." I rested my head on his shoulder for a second as we stood at the Alpha suite door. He wrapped his arms around my waist and we just took a moment to calm each other and bask in the bond, letting it unravel some of the turmoil we were both feeling.

It wasn't the girls I was worried about. It was Mitch. He used to get freaked out and overthink about the silliest and stupidest of things. He thought the fucking pipes in their walls at the resort would burst randomly in the girls' bedroom. He went off about it all the time when they were newborns. Then, he would hire bodyguards from the pack to guard their bedroom doors at night, thinking someone would break in and kidnap them. Mark backed him up on that, and they even took turns standing watch outside their door themselves at night when Hadley made them stop wasting money.

There was another time that their father had to step in once, when Mitch noticed a human guest at the hotel with a firearm strapped to his waist and Mitch started freaking out. The guest was a game warden and had the proper paperwork to carry, but Mitch insisted he was lying. My dad had to step in later to keep the state from getting involved.

I was worried Mitch might go off the deep end with this level of consequences for his actions.

With a sigh, I turned the knob to my door so we could head inside and wait for news from my mom. I expected the apartment to be deserted with everyone downstairs, but the undeniable sounds of two people engaged in lust-filled acts were coming from the living room. The scent of arousal was thick in the air.

Did Reese bring Karina up here while our parents were busy with all the pack drama?

Rian looked at me with his lips turned up in a smirk, wiggling his eyebrows suggestively. I bit my lips to keep from laughing as we quietly walked towards the living room.

"What the hell?!" I scoffed, my mouth dropping open when I saw Sophia straddling my cousin on the couch, both of their tops off and his mouth on one of her tits. "What are you doing in my house?!"

"Rosie?" Sophia pushed Callum's face away, quickly pulling up her bra to cover her nipples again. Then a smile broke out on her face. "ROSIE!"

She leapt off Callum's lap, running towards me, then jumping to latch her arms and legs around my body. "ROSIE! YOU'RE HOME!"

"No shit. And so are you," I laughed, then cringed when the smells clinging to her got disgustingly strong with her proximity. "Your boobs are wet. Get off me!"

"NO!" she cried, holding on to me tighter. "You fucking twat rag! I can't believe you just left like that without saying anything to me! What if I never saw you again!?"

Twat rag? Seems she is learning some fun new words from my cousin's side of the family.

"Then you would have more time to get your boobs sucked by my cousin," I groaned, trying to pry her free.

"Oh, no you fucking don't, you bitch," she hissed, then started tickling my sides.

I screamed out, begging her to stop, but she was relentless, even as I fell to the ground. She was growling, attacking all my most ticklish spots, and I thought she was laughing too, but when I got a clear view of her face, I saw she was crying uncontrollably. She soon let up on her tickle attack to just sit on top of me, bawling her eyes out.

Callum came forward to help, but I shook my head at him, sitting up and pulling my best friend closer, letting her wipe all her snot on my shoulder and in my hair.

"I'm sorry," I whispered, a few tears spilling free from my eyes too. "I didn't think things would get as dangerous as they did. I'm sorry for scaring you."

"I thought you were dead!" She yelled, slapping my right boob and making me hiss.

I tried not to roll my eyes. She sure had a weird way of grieving. Or maybe Callum was comforting her and it turned into more. Reese thought something had happened to me too, so maybe it was just the consensus that I was gravely injured or dead.

"It was a close call, but I made it." I took a tissue Rian offered me from the coffee table and wiped away the worst of Sophia's tears.

"Don't tell me that!" she hissed. "That... that's going to make me cry more!"

Now that I see her face closely, it's clear she has been crying all day. She had swollen, blotchy skin and redness around her eyes. Her lips were dry and peeling, like she had been biting them more than usual.

"I'm sorry," I hugged her close. "It won't happen again."

She scoffed, pushing against my chest to glare at me. "No. It won't. I'm going to get my mate to sit on you if you try to leave Crystal Moon without my permission again!"

I smirked, looking up at Callum, who looked so concerned, staring down at his mate. I could see by the way he was shuffling on his feet and flexing his hands that he wanted to reach down and take her from me.

"I could take him," I remarked, knowing I could. Callum may be huge, but I'm me. I survived the damned Kraken, for fuck's sake. And even if I couldn't take Callum for whatever reason, say I lost both my arms or couldn't shift, I have a powerful mate myself who I know is more than capable of keeping Sophia's mate in check.

I smiled at Rian, feeling his warm gaze on me. We're home now, and I don't know how different things will be now that I have a mate, but I know I can rely on him to help me through everything. He saved me from death. There isn't any length he can't or won't go for me, and I feel the same way about him.

84

— • —

INAPPROPRIATE PUNISHMENT

When Sophia calmed down, after another tickle attack and an even bigger tantrum than the first one, Calum pulled her off me, and finally got a shirt back on her. We all sat and talked about everything that had happened in both worlds.

I thought we were only gone for a few days, but it had been weeks here. Callum said that Beta Rick and his mate, Quinn, have been calling several times a day wanting their Alpha and Gamma back. It's the busiest time of the year, and with all three Alphas gone, they were having a hard time managing.

Rian told Calum about Taegan, and I was shocked to see my big burly cousin shed tears for his Alpha. It was a tragedy and left him in a tough spot. Alpha Axel was losing his heir for who knows how long. The Beta heir would be gone too, and according to Calum, Adam, the current Beta's oldest son, had no interest in managing the pack. He was going to university to become a geologist and then was training to take over the mining camps in Alaska and the Yukon one day. Beth, their daughter, was a dancer and wouldn't want to be Beta either. That meant that Calum might need to go back home without Sophia to help his family for now. There was a chance he would be the next Beta, and one of his brothers would need to start training to become Gamma.

That thought saddened him even more.

"You can finish your last year of school online," I told Sophia. "Why don't you ask my dad if you can transfer?"

"I can't until I'm eighteen," Sophia whimpered, resting her head sadly on Calum's shoulder.

Both of them looked so heartbroken that I wished there was something I could do. Maybe dad could ask Sophia's parents to transfer too. I know her dad will insist on it anyway when she mates Calum and moves to Blue Cliff permanently. Why not just do it a bit sooner?

I'll miss my best friend, but I know I couldn't live without Rian now. I don't want my cousin and best friend to have to face that because of someone else's stupid choices.

All of us perked up when we heard the front door open and the sound of my parents' voices. I was sitting on Rian's lap, and quickly slid down to sit on the cushion beside him instead. He smiled crookedly at me with amusement. I know he would have preferred to keep me in his lap.

Sophia was on Calum's lap, but she didn't make any attempt to move. I don't think Calum would have let her. He was still broken up about everything and was using her touch for comfort.

"There you are," Dad said, looking at Calum and Sophia. "We were looking for you both. Your parents need you."

"Why?" Sophia stared up at my dad with concern.

Dad smiled sadly at her. "Your father is being assigned as Harley and Harper Meyers' guard and acting guardian for the time being until their mom sorts some things out. I know this is sudden, but you and your family will be moving to Blue Cliff Pack. Lilly Meyers is sorting out your senior year with your school now, so you will only have to do one more semester online and can fly back to graduate with your class next spring."

Both Sophia and Calum broke out into brilliant smiles, Sophia turning to wrap her arms around Calum, squeezing him with a loud squeal. I was happy for my friend, but I really would miss her.

"So much for making your mate sit on me. Who's going to guard me now and make sure I stay in this realm?" I meant it teasingly, but my dad let out a ferocious growl.

"Relax, honey," mom patted his shoulder. "I got them. She will be thoroughly punished. I promise. She won't be able to leave our realm again by the time I'm through. You handle the transfers. You have got a lot to do."

"Yeah. I do."

Dad never stopped glaring at Rian, not until mom pushed him out the door with my cousin and friend. Then mom sighed and turned back to glare at both of us herself. I gulped nervously, more afraid of my mother's wrath than dad's. Rian must be too, because he was shifting nervously beside me.

"Okay, you two brats. Follow me."

"Where are we going?" I asked, wondering if it would be the training field, or if she was going to get creative and make me battle her and the angry gator in the swamps behind the outdoor field.

Maybe she was going to just take me to the foyer and have me push Florida until she tired of watching me. Push-ups were easy unless you were doing them as a punishment for my mom. She gets creative with the forms and the weights she puts on your back.

Reece wrecked her bike when he was thirteen and she made him do push-ups with a box full of naked baby pictures, and any other photo of him she deemed embarrassing rested on his back. He had to do them in front of Karina and Vincent, and if he broke form, the box would have fallen over so Karina would see all the pictures.

My brother did 1,683 push ups before falling to the ground. The box ended up only having one naked butt picture of him in it, and the rest of the papers were flyers for one of Vincent's restaurants. Vincent enjoyed that punishment so much that he bought mom a new bike himself.

"Mom?" She just kept walking, not looking back at all.

Rian and I met each other's nervous gaze as she led us down to the third floor. She surprised me by taking the hallway to the warriors' one-bedroom suites, rounding one last corner and stopping at the last door on the left. She took a key out of her pocket and opened the door for us, waving her hand for us to go in.

"What the hell is this?" I asked, looking around.

Mom shrugged, folding her hands over her chest, looking pissed still, but there was something in the way her mouth was set that made me think she really wasn't.

Rian and I looked around in confusion. The apartment was completely furnished, as most of these apartments were, but this one was extra with its design. Someone clearly lived there, but all the stuff looked brand new. The more I looked around, I noticed my own stuff mixed in with the new decor and furnishings.

My favorite bucket chair was in the corner of the living room with one of my blankets folded on top of it. It was one Grandma Elena made for me a couple of years ago for my birthday. My bookshelf from my room was next to a desk in the office nook, all my books and pictures arranged just as I had left them in my room on the shelf. I noticed most of the ones of Taegan I held onto for years were missing, but I didn't voice that observation out loud.

Rian went and looked in the bedroom as I got bold and decided to look in the fridge. It was fully stocked with all my favorite foods, plus energy drinks and protein shakes that I usually just stole from mom's office at the warrior building.

"Uh, Rosie!" Rian yelled at me.

I looked up from where I had ducked down in the fridge and saw my mom full on smirking now. I narrowed my eyes at her and then hurried to the bedroom. I stopped and gasped when I saw the bed.

"MOM!" I yelled, staring in horror at the king-size bed with rose petals in the shape of a heart, chocolates, and a basket full of sex toys. OPENED sex toys. They were new, but they were conveniently opened ahead of time to be waiting there for use. I had my suspicions, but this just sealed it.

"MOM! What the actual fuck?!"

"Quiet down! You have neighbors!" A slow smirk then spread across her face. "Not that they can hear you. I had this room extra padded with soundproofing. Even the windows. Once I'm gone, I expect you to be as loud as you can to your heart's content."

"VIBRATORS?!"

"Oh good. You know what they are. I didn't want to explain." She walked over to the basket like it was a basket of treats and not offensive dildos and cock rings. She rifled around and pulled out a large black dildo with a belt on it. "Rian, I wasn't sure what you were into, so I made sure you two would be prepared for whatever. This is her father-in-law's favorite-"

"MOM!" I seethed, stomping my foot. "STOP! Holy hell! What the fuck are you doing?"

"What?" she looked innocently between us. "Did I not buy enough?"

"You shouldn't have bought anything at all!"

"That's true," she laughed, then wiggled her eyebrows at Rian. "I caught a glimpse. You'll do."

"MOM!"

"Sorry! Sorry! My bad. It was an accident." She then winked at me. Rian was beat red, and I was now fuming.

"Mom! What the hell is all this?" I'd rather do a million push ups in the lobby than suffer this moment with my mom and a basket full of sex toys any longer.

"This," she waved her hands around the bedroom, "is your punishment. Both of you. You are grounded to this room until I decide I'm not pissed anymore about you leaving the way you did and almost dying." She glared at me while saying that. "Or until I'm a grandma. Whichever comes first."

"You can't be serious," I gaped. We just got home. I haven't even fucking showered yet.

"Oh, I am. Rian, I gave your parents the room number. They will stop by in the morning to get you both to say bye, and then it's back up to solitary confinement. House arrest. Whatever you want to call it. You both don't leave this room at all for any reason. Got it? Omegas will deliver more groceries and stuff like toilet paper. You will have everything you need." She smiled, looking at the basket and then back at us. "Everything."

"Mom, I-"

"Nope," mom held her hand up. "No arguments. Get started on your punishment," she pointed between us, then walked to the door.

"Mom, this isn't funny!"

"I didn't say it was," she yelled back. "If you have my grandbaby in that belly, Rian will think twice before taking you away from your pack again. You brought this on yourselves."

With that, she slammed the door, and I heard it lock from the outside. I ran back to make sure we could unlock it from inside too, and we could. She wasn't totally psycho. Just about ninety percent.

"Sex as punishment?" Rian raised his eyebrow at me. "I hope she didn't normally punish you in this way. It seems highly inappropriate."

"It is highly inappropriate, but no. This is a first." I sighed, looking around at the apartment I guess was now ours. "She's so insane," I groaned.

"Well," Rian came to me and suavely wrapped his arms around my waist, pulling me towards him. "I'm not keen to put a baby in you quite yet. I don't think that would bode well for getting your dad to like me, but I'm up for a bit of practice." He rested his forehead on mine, and the sparks shot over my skin. His sweet ocean scent made my knees weak, but he was luckily holding me against him. I could feel his firm body beneath his clothes. "I finally got you to myself. I'm not going to let this go to waste."

85

BUTTERFLY EFFECT

The shower together was so calming and intimate, though all Rian did was hold me close, rocking our bodies in a gentle sway under the steaming current of hot water.

I didn't realize how dirty I was. The water was running off me in filthy streams from the dried blood and dirt still clinging to my skin. If Rian noticed, he didn't say a thing. He just rested his head on mine and continued to hold me close, despite my filth.

When the water finally ran clean from running over my body for so long, not from any effort I put in to clean myself, I finally broke the silence with a curious observation.

"No scales," I murmured, running my hands up and down Rian's arms. "I thought gills or scales might appear when you got wet."

"Why would you think that?" he chuckled softly.

I shrugged. "Every time you get wet in front of me, you grow a tail."

"So you just assumed I would shift into my siren form every time I got in any kind of water? Even the shower?"

"Maybe not fully transform, but I thought at least gills would show up." I ran my hands up to his neck, tracing my mark. He shuddered under my touch.

"You sound disappointed."

I smiled shyly. "I like your siren body. It's beautiful."

"And ruggedly strong and sexy," he added with a playful glint.

"Not ruggedly." My smile stretched. "Royally. You look like a prince from another world in your siren body." I played with the wet hair on the back of his neck. "A very sexy and powerful prince from another world."

"Would my princess like for me to transform right now so you can spend some time with your royally sexy prince?"

I bit my bottom lip and shook my head. "No. I like this side of my sexy and powerful prince too. I am curious where this goes in your other body, though," I said, hooking my leg over his hip and rotating my pelvis against him.

He closed his eyes and let out a small moan. "I would love to show you sometime."

My imagination was growing, as was my lust. I was thinking up so many impossible scenarios of where his dick might disappear to. Some were as crazy as simply tucking it into the scales of his tail like they were just a pair of pants. I never actually saw the underside of him, so it could just be hanging out for all to see. Who knows.....

I don't like that scenario at all . That means other creatures in the water could see him exposed, and that part of him is all mine.

Rian kissed the top of my head several times, holding my face between his hands. "Let me wash your hair for you."

"Is it really bad?" I asked, looking up at his swirling, galaxy-like eyes and seeing concern on his handsome face. He didn't answer me, so I took that as a yes.

He reached up and touched a spot in my hair. "Does that hurt?"

"No," I answered honestly. "Nothing hurts anymore." It's strange how okay I feel now, considering how extensive my injuries were before. I was being sliced and burned repeatedly without rest, tied to a tree in the same position for days. I should be feeling some lasting damage or pain, but I didn't. Julia was still in the hospital, and I was walking around freely, taking a shower with my mate like nothing happened and I hadn't almost died just half a day earlier.

"I wish I could have found you sooner," Rian whispered, sounding a bit broken inside. "I wish I hadn't driven you away at all."

"I left on my own, Rian." I reached up and angled his face to look at me and not whatever he was looking at in my hair. "It was my fault what happened to me. Not yours."

"If I hadn't gotten mad about something so stupid," he closed his eyes, and I could feel his guilt as he pressed his forehead to mine.

"You acted like anyone would. I would have flipped out and kicked yours and the girl's ass if you got a tattoo the way I did. It didn't mean anything to me anymore, but I know if the roles were reversed, I would have gone insane." I gripped his face, forcing his strained eyes to look into mine. "Because you are mine. I'm yours too. You had a right to be pissed. I shouldn't have left like I did."

He searched my eyes, the magic behind his drawing me in like it always does. I love him. I love my mate, and I wasn't going to let him blame himself for what happened to me, especially since I knew it was my fault.

"You are mine," he husked softly. "My princess and my Alpha. No more going into danger without me, because you belong to me."

A shy smile made my face burn. "I won't. I promise."

He kissed my lips, soft and tender. I could taste his lust, but then his eyes flickered back to that spot that was distracting him before in my hair. He made this little sound of displeasure deep in his throat, then grabbed the shampoo after breaking the kiss.

Having his hands on my scalp and lathering my hair felt amazing. I could get used to this. Being grounded in this apartment with my mate wouldn't be bad at all. I may ask mom for an extended sentence. I'm sure she would grant it. Dad might revoke the whole punishment thing, but mom has a much stronger will than dad does.

Rian turned my body around to rinse the suds out of my hair. It felt great having his fingers comb the lingering debris free. But the strain and regret mixed with guilt and sadness I felt coming from him overshadowed that. When I opened my eyes, I saw what was disturbing my moment with my mate. He was staring at my shoulder.

"It doesn't hurt," I reassured him.

His brows creased, and he hesitantly ran his finger over the marred flesh. "It did."

That's obvious, so I couldn't deny it. I feared I'd have nightmares of the pain I barely endured in that rank oceanic prison. Hurt was too inefficient a word to describe what it felt like to have my skin carved away and burned for days on end.

"I endured," I whispered. "And so did your mark. No matter how much of my body he tried to strip away, he could never strip you away from me. We won, Rian." I turned and wrapped my arms around his neck, begging him to feel what I was feeling inside. "We won, and this scar is proof that no one can tear us apart."

A half grin lifted the side of his face, his lady-getter smile making my heart beat rapidly in my chest.

"Turn around," he whispered in the most smooth, persuasive voice that had my core tingling. I listened without hesitation.

I felt the warmth of his magic seeping into me as his hand rested flat on my shoulder blade. The tingling in the bond made my breath quicken. Gold and green sparks were flickering around us, matching the energy I felt moving inside of me. The strongest sparks in our bond seemed to expand on my back, moving from the confined space where his name was scripted to cover most of my shoulder blade.

"Rian," I gasped, buckling over as my body convulsed from the torrent of his magic transforming the connection to him inside the imprint he gave me.

"Almost done," his voice came in a panting breath, not helping the convulsions inside of me.

What was he doing? Was he trying to send me into a fucking climax just by using his mark? Was that what mom was talking about with Thyra and Alpha Max? I could barely hold myself together much longer.

"Done," he husked, bending over to press his lips to my skin. The kiss on his mark sealed the deal and my knees crumbled to the wet shower floor. The water raining down did nothing to wash away the evidence of my climax.

When I was done, Rian helped me up, his mouth slightly open and his own arousal standing long and stiff at full attention. He kissed me deeply, his lips urgently molding to mine as I still struggled to catch my breath.

As he broke away from me, his hooded eyes roamed down my body, and then he bit his bottom lip like he was struggling to hold himself back. He looked behind me, opening the shower door so we could see ourselves in the mirror over the double sink. When I looked over my shoulder, I gasped in surprise.

He had transformed his imprint to encompass my entire scarred shoulder, hiding the evidence of my capture with elegant vines and twisting glowing green cords. The vines and cords took the shape of a large butterfly, Rian's name at its center.

"Butterflies are our thing," he husked in my ear. "Now they forever will be."

86

Naked Breakfast

It was still dark outside when I woke up the next morning, lying on top of Rian's chest. I had passed after riding him into oblivion soon after the shower we took together. I was exhausted, and I surprised myself by lasting as long as I did.

My stomach growled. That's what woke me up. We didn't eat or anything yesterday, and it had been a long time since I had an actual meal. I don't think I'd really eaten anything since that night I had the sugary nut powdered drink and dough balls with Rian in the fairy realm. I had felt no hunger after his uncle healed me, but I guess that effect was long gone. I was starving.

I slowly lifted myself from Rian's naked form, licking my lips with a different hunger as I stared down at his perfection. He had both of his hands tucked behind his head, his face turned to the side and the rose petals mom went overboard with scattered around him. He looked like a sexy cover model, even in his sleep. It should be a crime to be so perfect.

When my stomach growled again, I tore my eyes away from my mate. I tiptoed out of the bedroom, closing the door behind me. I was naked, but hadn't had a moment to look through the closet or any of the dresser drawers to see what clothes were available to me. I wasn't going to disturb Rian by doing that now.

I found a loaf of bread and a case of spam in the pantry. I popped a couple pieces of bread in the toaster and sliced up the spam to fry in a pan. Mom knows me so well. Reece hates Spam, hates the texture and smell, so when we were little I used to ask for spam instead of bacon when we went to visit our great-grandparents just to make sure I got more meat than him. It was like a comfort food to me after my great-grandparents both passed away and I love it still. Reece, that pansy-fied simp, only likes what Karina likes now, so prefers smoked salmon or prosciutto, and cream cheese on bagels like she does for breakfast. I get all the bacon, sausage and spam I want while he is always at her side spoon feeding her bites of whatever he is eating.

I wouldn't mind spoon feeding Rian, though. You having him spoon feed me....

I was daydreaming about eating food directly off Rian's abs, bent over in the open fridge to grab the eggs, when I felt sparks traveling up and down my legs, gentle hands now resting on my hips. I sat up and turned to see Rian with a dreamy look on his face, staring down at my naked body. I thought it was lust on his face at first, but then I felt his anxiety rushing wildly in the bond.

"Rian?" I set the carton of eggs on the counter and angled his face to look at me. "Are you okay?"

He blinked a few times, then a sad smile spread across his face. "I didn't enjoy opening my eyes and you not being there," he admitted.

Guilt filled me. "I'm sorry." I went on my tiptoes to kiss the worry creases away between his brows. "I was hungry. I just didn't want to wake you."

"I see that now," he breathed, wrapping his arms around my shoulder and pulling me in close. "Wake me up next time."

"Okay," I whispered, hugging him back. "I'll wake you next time."

"Thank you." The relief was evident in his sighed response. After a few more seconds of holding each other in the kitchen, I felt his anxiety completely dissipate. "What are you making?" he asked, the sizzling Spam getting louder and louder.

"Spam and eggs. Want some?"

"Spam?" A slow smile spread on his face.

I furrowed my brows. "What's wrong with Spam?"

"Nothing," he chuckled, kissing my cheek. "I've never had it, but I heard nothing but bad things."

"From who?"

"Bailey," he shrugged. "It makes her sick when she's expecting. Dad and Axel ordered it out of the packhouse and no one in the family bought it ever to keep Dad and Axel from killing them. That and Courtney would go on and on about how bad it was for you."

"Well, I like it," I grumbled, turning in his arms to flip the innocent meat product in the pan on the stove. "It's comfort food."

"Then I'm sure I'll love it too," Rian smiled against my skin, nuzzling behind my ear.

I finished frying all the Spam, then made two more pieces of toast and fried four eggs for each of us. I was starving, so I'm sure he was, too. Rian sat in the nude on a bar stool across from me, watching as I cooked. I wasn't domestic, or a good cook at all, but fried eggs and Spam were something I cooked often and was decent enough at. I was still a little self conscious of him watching me.

I finished plating our food, and Rian looked at the plates, then back up at me.

"What?"

"Nothing," he chuckled. "You cook like my dad and Axel. All protein and carbs."

My cheeks flushed furiously. "Well, sorry," I said sarcastically. "Feel free to make yourself a salad."

"I'm not saying it's bad. It's surprisingly cute. It's proof you're a full-fledged Alpha." he wiggled his eyebrows, sliding his plate towards him. "My Alpha."

"Damn right," I grumbled, turning my back to get a couple of protein shakes from the fridge, hiding my smile. I guess I don't eat like a typical girl, but hearing that Rian thought that was cute made me feel weirdly giddy. Mostly because I could feel his approval in the bond.

We sat and ate, talking about our domestic abilities, since it looked like we were going to be "grounded" here for a while. I had no complaints, and neither did he, but I had never lived away from my family, let alone with a man before. Rian hadn't either, but Alpha Max seemed to make him do way more than my parents made me do. He even knew how to do laundry. I just threw my laundry in the hamper and it magically appeared in my drawers clean the next day.

I knew it wasn't magically done. We had omegas that cleaned and took care of the house since we were all so busy, but things were done differently in Blue Cliff. I always thought Rian was a pampered prince before I found out he was my mate, but I'm coming to find that I'm the pampered one in this relationship. My parents spoiled the shit out of me.

"I can try to do laundry," I grimaced, thinking about the offensive washing machine with all the dials in the utility room.

"Or," he smirked playfully, reaching over and rubbing his hand on my naked leg. "We could conserve water and energy and just stay naked when home from now on."

I grinned. "I like that idea."

87

---・---

HARD GOODBYE

Rian

I was curled around my beautiful sleeping mate, memorizing every single feature on her face as I listened to the beating of her heart. It was a melody singing just for me.

After our breakfast and my enthusiastic second breakfast served at the same counter, I could see and feel that Rosie was still exhausted, so I carried her back to bed, sated and full. She fell asleep instantly, but I've been lying awake for hours, enthralled by every little thing about her. Her breathing came in soft purrs the deeper asleep she was. It's adorable and primal, reminding me again that she is a pure alpha wolf and those alpha genes will show when she is her normal comfortable self.

I always want her to be her normal, strong, comfortable, alpha self with me. Like hours ago, when I was watching her devour her meal while giggling and laughing, not concerned with manners or chewing with her mouth closed. When we were together at the fairy village, eating the food from the stalls, I realized she was trying to act reserved back then because she wasn't yet comfortable with me.

She was growing more and more comfortable with me every second, which filled me with great pride.

"You're mine," I whispered into the early morning rays beaming against her tanned skin. "All mine." I couldn't stop myself from kissing her nose, her eyes, and even her lips. I tried to keep the touch feather soft so as not to wake her, but she stirred from the spark, nonetheless. I stayed perfectly still, holding my breath as she moaned softly and nuzzled her face against my chest. Within seconds, she was back asleep.

I chuckled silently to myself, using my fingers to smooth the little indent she gained between her eyes. She was back in dreamland, and whatever she was thinking of made her lips pucker and her brows furrow.

Adorable. She's so magnificently adorable, and I'm the only one who will ever get to see her this way.

The sun was rising higher and higher in the sky outside the window. Neither of us thought of drawing the curtains last night, so the sun was making the room incredibly bright. I was raising my hand, about to use my magic to close them, when I felt a familiar pull inside my mind.

"We're getting ready to leave, Rian," Bailey told me in a solemn voice. *"Your parents are coming to get you to say bye for now. I thought I would warn you, just in case."*

"Thank you," I said back. *"I'll see you in a bit."*

I suddenly felt guilty. I was living my fantasy, cuddled in bed with my adorable mate, and the rest of my family was preparing to leave, still grieving Taegan's imprisonment in Alfheimr.

Guess it was time to say goodbye. To think, before the start of this trip, I thought I would be bidding my family goodbye after it was over to return to my uncle's court. It's ironic how everything ended up working out, since Taegan was the one who urged me to come to Miami one last time.

I thought briefly about leaving Rosie to sleep, feeling how deeply she was in her dream, but then I remembered how I felt waking up with her not beside me. She was just in the next room, and I was on the verge of a panic attack. I don't want to make Rosie experience the same thing, and considering she went through so much more than I did because of all she had to endure, I will not lett her feel any level of panic again if I can help it.

"Rosie," I gently shook her. She didn't even stir, just squeezed her eyes tighter together. I smiled to myself and did what I caused her to stir before. I placed kisses all over her sleeping face. "Rosie," kiss, "Wake up," kiss, "open your eyes, baby," kiss.

I continued this pattern until she reluctantly opened her eyes, stretching and groaning in my arms.

"Good morning, sleepy."

"Mmph." She rolled over, grabbing my free arm that wasn't under her head and pulling it, so I was spooning her from behind. "Not yet."

"Yes, yet," I kissed her head. "I have to go say bye to my family, Rose. I didn't want to leave without you."

She stiffened, then turned back to face me. Her eyes were slits squinting from the sunlight. "I'm sorry, Rian. I forgot," she mumbled.

"I forgot too," I kissed the tip of her nose before nuzzling mine to her, soaking in the last bit of bliss we had shared before I faced the heart-wrenching task of telling my family goodbye.

I know I can see them all again any time I want, even Taegan, but Bailey and Axel will not be allowed that same opportunity. Seeing their pain will tear at me, because I know it is in part my fault.

Rosie and I showered together quickly, then went about the task of finding clothes to wear. Rosie had a harder time than I did. Carli had just set my suitcase she must have retrieved from the resort in the walk-in closet. Everything was left untouched.

Rosie's clothes, on the other hand, were hidden in a mess of lace, latex, and sheer lingerie, all of which Rosie claimed she had never seen before in her life. My mother-in-law was something. I'm as grateful as I am terrified. The strap on sex toy was horrifying, especially accompanied with the knowledge she has one she likes to use on her own mate, but I have very much enjoyed my new home with my mate aside from that awkward first five minutes.

Rosie eventually found a pair of acceptable shorts and I just let her wear one of my smaller shirts. It was still quite large on her, and considering she could only find the raunchy lingerie sets and no regular underwear to wear underneath, I knew I was going to have a hard time keeping my thoughts clean towards her in front of my family. The strappy silk thing she cursed at as she slid it onto her tight body had my pants fitting tight, and then when she put on my baggy shirt over it...

I would definitely be thanking Carli later. I might curse her in my head while I try to get myself under control, not wanting a raging boner to appear in front of my parents, but I would thank her for her punishment later.

"Ready?" Rosie looked up at me, her smile soft and serene, knowing this wasn't going to be a happy goodbye for everyone involved.

"I'm ready," I whispered, then ducked to steal one more kiss before we left our apartment jail.

We walked hand in hand to the foyer, most of my family were already there. Courtney was yelling at Calvin and Casper to quit running as she was standing and feeding Carter at the same time. As usual, she was doing so openly, even though her nipple was half out of Carter's mouth. She didn't care. She never does. Everyone has nipples, she says, and if anyone acts offended about seeing hers, then Casey always sweeps in and starts showing off his too. It's not a fight you will win, so no one comments on her open breastfeeding anymore.

Jade and Jana were on either of Axel's hips, both twins beating on his chest, demanding to go to my mom instead. Axel is a pro at ignoring the fits and tantrums of his daughters. My dad, not so much. Dad was staring at the girls, his hands flexing, wanting to take them and give in to whatever demands they had. It's an ongoing battle that he won't win. They always prefer my mom over him for some reason. It drives him insane.

Casey was talking to an older couple I recognized from the resort. The man was a witch. I recognize his energy, since it was similar to his sons. He must be the Meyers triplets' father. The woman standing with him was often with Hadley, so I knew she was their mother. They looked sad, but nodded and thanked Casey for something before walking out the front door right when we made it down the stairs.

"I wonder what that was about?" Rosie whispered to me.

I had no clue, but I'm guessing they were the ones being transferred to the Blue Cliff Pack. They were the ones who easily could be transferred right away in the Meyers family.

My eyes met my mom's as she stood next to Bailey on the far side of the room. There were already tears there, and I knew we were in for a hard goodbye.

88

— ⋅ —

EASIER WITH YOU

Rosie

R ian's grip on my hand tightened, and I could feel his worry for his family in the bond. I wish there was something I could do or say to make him feel reassured everything would be fine.

"I'm here," I ended up whispering, leaning against him to rest my head on his shoulder.

He offered me a small smile that didn't touch his swirling galaxy eyes. I could still see his love reflected at me, but also the love and pain he had for his family. They were grieving, and no words would fix that.

"Thank you for being here," he kissed my head. "I don't know if I could do this without you."

The moment passed when stupid Casey appeared on the other side of Rian, pulling him away from me and wrapping him in an annoyingly exaggerated hug. "I'm going to miss my favorite Kissinger." He pretended to cry, looking ridiculous as he twirled Rian in an awkward circle.

"You tell all of us that!" Rian stressed, pushing away from the burly Gamma.

"Yeah, but I mean it when I say it to you." Casey rubbed the side of his face with Rian's.

"You told me I was your favorite ten minutes ago," Aly scoffed, rolling her eyes as she stared at her phone.

"Dad tells me I'm his favorite son all the time. His words mean nothing," Conner muttered.

"No! I'm his favorite," Casper yelled.

"No, me!" Calvin pushed his older brother to the ground, kicked him in the butt, then ran off around the corner before Casper could get back up.

"See." Conner shrugged.

"We all know cousin Courtney is his only true favorite. The rest of us are background characters." Aly leaned her head on her cousin's shoulder like she was bored.

"Mom and Brother Taegan, but Taegan's gone now," Conner said the words to extinguish the little bit of humor that began to form in the depressed space.

Aly picked her head up, gave Conner the nastiest look, then kicked him in the shin before storming out of the packhouse. Conner looked surprised and guilty, hopping on one leg while watching her leave.

"Aly, I wasn't trying to be mean," Conner followed after her.

The room was now silent, the awkwardness and tension thick in the air.

Bailey was the one that broke that silence, a single tear falling from her eyes. "He's only going to be gone for a little while," she said confidently. "I know he will be back. I know it. He won't be there forever."

"Honey," Alpha Axel rubbed her shoulder, trying to pull her in for a hug.

"No," she held her hand up stubbornly, turning away from his advance. "No. I don't want comfort or pity. My son will be back home. Stop trying to make it sound like he is dead. He is alive and will be home soon."

With that, she came and gave Rian a hug so firm but loving that my own eyes filled with tears. She was often underestimated because she was once human and had a sweet disposition, but I have seen enough now to conclude that she may be the strongest Luna there ever was. Considering who my mother is, that was saying something.

"You will do great here, Rian. I love you, and I am so proud of the man you have become." She kissed his cheek, then whispered in his ear so only he and I could hear, "Please check in on him when you can. Let him know we love and miss him."

"I will, Bailey," he kissed her forehead, holding her tight before she smiled and pulled away to hug me.

"I'm sorry, Luna Bailey. I should have-"

"Things are as they were meant to be," she told me firmly. "Don't blame yourself for anything. And take care of Rian for us." She then somehow said in my mind, *"His parents may be a little MIA for a while."*

I was so stunned by her ability to mind link me that she was already out the door before the words she said fully sunk in. Why would Thyra and Alpha Max be missing in action?

Courtney gave both Rian and I an awkward hug with her youngest child still hanging off her tit. It was weird, but normal for her. The boys asked Rian a million questions about why he wasn't going home with them, but when Casey said some shit about Rian needing to make a sister with me, they all acted like they understood and followed their mother out the door.

"I hope you get lots of sisters," Calvin whispered loudly to Rian, then gave me a creepy smile as he skipped outside.

"Did she get her boob juice on you?" Casey asked, looking at the front of Rian's shirt.

"Gross. No." Rian fake gagged.

"Well, here," Casey said, raising his shirt and wiping his sweaty chest all over Rian. "My parting gift to you. We call those humid-ee-titties down here. You better get used to them."

"What the hell!" Rian actually gagged, pulling at his moistened shirt.

"I have never heard of humid-ee-titties before," I muttered, taking a step back when Casey tried to hug me.

"Bullshit. The same man that taught me the term was your grandpa, so I call bullshit."

"Call whatever you want, but you are not touching me with your man boobs."

"Aw, come on," Casey tried to pull me in.

"Leave the girl alone, you dipshit," Alpha Axel sighed. "Go wrangle your boys before Alpha Parker throws them into a swamp."

"Gator wrestling is good training," Casey argued.

"The fuck it is," Alpha Max muttered, staring out the window like he was suddenly concerned an alligator would randomly appear on our packhouse lawn. I mean, it has happened in the training fields, but never the packhouse.

"Go," Alpha Axel said more firmly to Casey, and Casey reluctantly rolled his eyes. I gave him a side hug, safe from his boobs.

Alpha Axel had red blotches around his eyes. He obviously cried a lot recently. It made the blue in his eyes more prominent than before. It tugged at something inside of me to see such a strong alpha so vulnerable.

He pulled Rian in close. "I'm happy for you, brother. You come see us when you get settled here." Alpha Axel pulled me into the hug too. "Both of you. You still have a home back in the pack, even if you are the male Luna of another."

"Thanks, Axel," Rian said. "I'll come after I check on Taegan soon."

Alpha Axel made a choking sound, then nodded, letting us go to walk off to join his mate.

That was hard, but I know the next goodbyes are going to be so much worse.

"My son," Thyra opened her arms as Rian made his way towards her.

I followed behind, giving them their space. I could feel Rian's sadness, and the gravity of it left me confused. As they whispered to one another, Alpha Max came beside me and wrapped an arm around my shoulders.

"They're going to take this harder than normal. He was separated from her for most of his early childhood. It took a toll on both of them, but I'm happy he found his reason to stay in our world." Alpha Max squeezed my shoulder firmly. "Thank you for being that reason, Alpha Rosie. I couldn't live without her, and she couldn't be happy without him. You are a blessing to my family in more ways than you know."

"I don't feel like it," I murmured, seeing my mate's eyes spill with tears, wiping his mother's tears with his hands. "I feel like I caused your family nothing but trouble."

"Do you regret any of it?" Alpha Max asked me.

I didn't even hesitate. "No," I said, low but firm. Maybe it was what Bailey told me, or maybe it was the fact I wouldn't give up the path that I'm on now with Rian, but I really didn't feel any regrets. I felt guilt and sadness about the situation saving Julia caused, but regret nothing.

"Good," Alpha Max said, pulling me in for a hug. "Don't regret a thing. We know better than anyone. The goddess works in mysterious ways." The way he was looking at Thyra lifted some of my sadness and let peace settle over me. "I've learned to never have regrets, either."

"Thank you, Alpha Max."

"You can call me Max. Or dad even, if you want. Just make sure my grandkids know to call me g-pa. It's tradition."

"I'll make sure," I laughed softly. "You can teach them that yourself, you know. You guys can visit whenever, and we will go up there a lot, too."

Alpha Max smiled sadly. "I don't think it will be that easy."

"Why not?" I looked up at him in confusion.

He pressed his lips together, his eyes glistening, looking much like Alpha Axel's did. "We're going to be with Taegan, Rosie. I need you to take care of my boy and your future kids until we get back."

***

Thyra came and gave me a tearful goodbye as well, saying many of the same things as her mate, but with far more tears. I cried with her, now understanding the sadness that Rian was feeling. We can go to Alfheimr to visit them, but with the time difference, it would have to be perfectly timed and planned.

It really won't be as easy as just popping over to see them for a week or two. An hour in the fairy realm could be a day here. A day could be a week, or even two. Only Thyra's new title as the mother to the crown prince will allow her to bring Alpha Max. She was stripped of her princess title long ago. Because of her past mistakes, going back and forth freely would be difficult on her part as well.

We said goodbye to everyone one last time outside, this time including Callum and Sophia. Sophia cried while clinging to me, but I promised to come see her soon.

When everyone drove off in four different SUVs, Rian and I stood at the door and waved until the cars were no longer visible. Rian had silent tears streaming down his face, and I could do nothing but hold him close to share his grief.

"You knew your parents were going to be with Taegan," I whispered when we made it back up to our room.

"I suspected it. I thought I was prepared to hear the news, but it's still hard." Rian sucked in a shuddering breath. "Visiting won't be so easy now."

"We can make it work, right?" I hugged him around his waist. "We'll go every summer for a few days at least. That should be fine."

"We can work it out," Rian nodded in agreement. "Thank you."

"For what?"

"For being there for me today," he smiled, kissing my nose then my forehead. "It made it easier being with you."

I smiled sadly. "I wish there was more I could do."

"Just being with me is enough."

89

——— ◆ ———

READY FOR CHANGE

"*My* Lady," *Vincent bowed before his leader; the woman he had devotedly followed his entire life. When she called him in secret after the incident, he answered the call without hesitation, despite the scheme she was a part of. He knew there had to be a reason; some sort of an explanation.*

He was right.

"Vincent," Lady Delilah purred, resting her hand on his shoulder. "Is everything taken care of? Have you made the necessary preparations?"

"I followed your instructions according to your will, my Lady," he smiled sadly. "Reluctantly so."

"Change was coming," she turned to her desk, devoid of all its usual paperwork and personal belongings and knick-knacks. All that was left was a single manila folder with the name of the one who would take her place. "I decided to be a part of the solution this time instead of being greedy. I chose this, so don't have any regrets. I don't."

Her painted red lips stretched into a kind smile, one not often seen by her followers. This smile was reserved for her closest friends. Vincent was special to her. He had proven to be loyal and trustworthy, and had earned her favor. Not many would sacrifice their own parents for the good of the world; for the good of their coven. Vincent did that, and ever since Lady Delilah has had her eyes on him and his family. She knew the time was right, so when the opportunity presented itself, she took it.

"My only regret is your leaving," Vincent said, looking around the office that could belong to anyone. Even a human.

Everything was cleared out, tossed away or stored. Lady Delilah wanted to make a clean break, unburdening the coven from the consequences of her choices. The blood bank will be in Vincent's charge until the next leader is ready to take their place. He made all the preparations to ensure the coven would be in good hands for the next few years. She was meticulous and she knew he would carry out her plans perfectly.

The vampire leader of the north had warned he was coming tomorrow for answers regarding his grandchildren. He would arrive to an empty seat in her coven. Vincent knew how to handle that as well. His devotion would be put to the test one last time, but Lady Delilah had no doubts about his loyalty to her. Her coven would be safe. Until the curses upon her people were lifted, she would be safe too. This was the only way. One last tragedy would lead to freedom for them all.

"If it is because of the werewolves that you think you have to go, I can help to smooth things over with them. You know I can. You don't need to go to such lengths."

"I do," she sighed.

She had seen what would happen if she didn't. Very few in the human realm have the ability to fraternize with the gods, but she had earned that. She, the first immortal of the human world, the one original vampire who started it all, knew what she was doing. She knew what she was doing from the start, starting seventeen years ago when she listened to a Gemini Wolf's pleading to spare a vampire that did not need to be spared. The pendulum had swung, and things were put into motion starting then. Those that needed to be in the know were. Wrongs of this world were being made right. First, the werewolves and their original bloodline. It was now her turn. This was the start.

"Why?" Vincent stressed, not ready to let go of his leader.

Lady Delilah smiled sadly. "There needs to be a villain to unite what couldn't come together before." She sat in her chair one last time, sitting back and relishing the comfort of being in her office, in her home for the final moment before everything changed. "You will find all you need in there," she nodded towards the file envelope.

Vincent stepped forward, picking it up. He turned to the first page, then his eyes went wide. "This is why you confided in me?"

"It is," she grinned, pleased with herself. "I could not think of a more worthy successor."

"But.... She's...."

"I know," Lady Delilah's smile softened, knowing his concerns. "That is why it has to be her."

"She might not want it." Vincent's concern was coming out in waves.

"No, she likely won't, but I wouldn't trust someone that did want it. This isn't an enviable position to have. She will have to fight for her place." Lady Delilah laughed softly to herself. "She has strong allies and a stronger will. I know she will be just fine."

"He *might not want this*," Vincent continued, searching through the documents.

"*He will want what she wants. You know that.*"

Vincent snorted. He did know that better than anyone. It was the only reason he had allowed their relationship to develop as it had over the years. He isn't as oblivious as they assumed he was. He was tolerant, only because of the young Alpha's devotion.

"*You will help her?*" Lady Delilah asked, though she didn't need to. "*You will have four years to train and prepare her for what is to come. Him as well. You will have to continue keeping things from your Alpha and friends. Can you do it?*"

"*I can,*" he frowned. "*I will trust you. To the end.*"

Lady Delilah threw her head back and laughed. "*My end. Not yours, dear one. It will only be my end this time.*" She smiled, the thought filling her with hope and pride. "*I'm ready for this change, more than you could ever know.*"

90

— · —

MOST IMPORTANT MEAL

Rosie

K NOCK KNOCK KNOCK

I groaned, rolling over to hide my face against Rian's chest when someone hammered against our door. I already knew who it was. We've been holed up in our prison of bliss and sex for two weeks now and mom mind linked me last night to let me know she couldn't keep dad from bursting our bubble any longer.

"Fucking hell," I cursed when the knocking started again.

I felt Rian chuckling roughly against my face. "He's just going to break in, Rose. At least let me get up to let him in."

"No thanks," I latched onto his waist, not willing to let him go.

"Hmm," Rian kissed the top of my head. "That's not going to win me any points with him."

"You only need points with me," I whined, not ready to leave our happy bubble yet.

It's been a good two weeks healing, and I know the moment we leave this room that it will be back to the stress of the pack again. I'm not willing to share my mate with anyone either. I want to keep him to myself as long as I can.

"Let me just open the door and let him know you will see him later. Will that be okay? I'll come back and give you all the points you want after."

"You're supposed to be getting points from me, not the other way around," I said stubbornly.

"There will be plenty of giving and taking," he husked in my ear.

A lazy grin spread across my face. "Fine." I rolled back over, searching for a pillow without opening my eyes and then pulling it to my chest in a huff. I could hear Rian's soft chuckling as he dug around in a drawer for pants.

My time with Rian alone in this room has been blissfully perfect. I don't feel guilty at all for not wanting it to end.

**

Rian

I pressed my lips together, trying to rein in my lust-filled thoughts after seeing Rosie's beautiful bare back and the top of her firm, round ass when the sheets pulled away from her body. She found a pillow to cuddle in place of me, but she was never worried about the sheet. It makes getting out of bed harder and harder.

After pulling on a pair of pants, I quietly walked out of the bedroom, closing the door quietly behind me. Just then, the knocking started hammering through the apartment once again.

Nerves ate at me. I was not Alpha Parker's favorite. He made it abundantly clear plenty of times in my uncle's court, and we hadn't seen each other much since then. Luna Carli confined Rosie and me to this room, which won't improve the alpha's opinion of me.

I quickly swung the door open so his thunderous knocking didn't disturb my mate again. She gets grumpy when she is woken up. I found ways to sweeten her disposition in the mornings, but I don't think her father would appreciate me using those methods on her now.

"Good morning, Alpha Parker," I tried to put on my most friendly smile, trying to appear relaxed, though I felt anything but relaxed under his spiteful gaze.

"Where is my daughter?" he asked gruffly, his eyes roaming my naked chest like it disgusted him. He was shirtless too, and smelled like he was fresh off the training grounds. I couldn't help but to look at him too, my eyes pointing out the hypocrisy in his judgment.

"Rosie is still asleep. She wanted me to let you know she will drop by your office later once she gets up and going."

"Why can't she tell me that herself?"

"GO AWAY, DAD!" Rosie yelled from the bedroom with an adorable growl.

Alpha Parker grit his teeth, looking at me like I was to blame for his daughter not wanting to come to the door.

He leaned in close. "Listen here, bucko. I don't care what my wife said to either one of you; if you get my daughter pregnant, I'll kill you and toss you into the sea where you belong."

I couldn't help but to smile. "Well, Alpha, I have no intentions of getting my mate pregnant right now or in the near future." I didn't let my voice waver. "Not because of any threat you can make, but because I love her. I want to selfishly keep her to myself for as long as she is willing." I then leaned in closer. "When she does give me a child, it won't be because of you or her mother, but because she made that choice." I stood back up and held Alpha Parker's intense glare. "I hope we understand each other, Alpha. I will respect you as her father, but my actions will be dictated by her needs and wants, not your vengeful threats."

Alpha Parker eyed me up and down. "You are a real piece of work."

"I have my moments," I said.

He can threaten me until he is blue in the face. I grew up with the king of making threats and had an entire family that had a colorful way of adding to them. There wasn't a thing Alpha Parker could say to phase me. Yes, I wanted my father-in-law to like me, but I was raised with more of a backbone than to let anyone talk down to me for malicious reasons.

"I bet you do," Alpha Parker sighed, taking a step back and finally looking less aggressive. "Look, I miss my little girl. Just have her come see me sometime today. And," he hesitated, "treat her like the princess she is. She may be tough as nails for the rest of the world, but she is still my baby girl."

"HURRY UP!" Rosie yelled at me from the bedroom. "I CAN'T SLEEP WITH YOU TWO TALKING! YOU MADE ME PROMISES, RIAN! HURRY UP!"

I stifled a laugh, amused by her lack of decorum in front of her dad. That's a trait that has Carli's genes all over it.

"My rude and brash baby girl, but still my baby girl, nonetheless."

"I don't think she's anything less than a princess, Alpha Parker," I smiled, staring back at our bedroom door. My adorable Alpha mate was my princess and the entire world to me. Her father would see that in time.

Alpha Parker was staring at me with a less harsh expression. After a few seconds, he held his hand out for me to shake. I couldn't contain my grin as I took his hand and shook it, proudly and firmly, like my dad always taught me to do. Fae don't shake hands in the fairy realm. This is something strictly done in the human realm that I didn't think would apply to me when I left home. I'm more thankful than ever for my dad teaching me what I'll need to know to hold my own in the life of being mated to the Alpha of a strong werewolf pack.

"Welcome to the family, Rian," Alpha Parker said.

"Thanks, Alpha."

"Call me Parker," he muttered before retreating down the hall.

When I walked back into our bedroom, I couldn't keep the grin off my face. Rosie had her eyes open, waiting for me, a sly smile on herself.

"I don't think you have ever sounded sexier than you just did talking back to my dad."

I scoffed, kicking off my pants as I climbed back into bed. "I've had two weeks of practice putting Alphas in their place."

"Oh, is that what we've been practicing?" Rosie giggled in that vulnerable way that was just for me.

"I'm up for a bit of practice now," I said, sliding between her legs so my face was in line with the most delicious part of her. "Scream for me, baby," I demanded, before diving in for my first and most important meal of the day.

91

— ⋅ —

EPILOGUE

Rian

"Hey, Rian. Do you think you could take this next meeting for me?" Lilly, the gamma's mate, asked me as I was sitting across the desk from her, going through her list of contacts for pack events.

Rosie and I just got back from a short two-day trip to Alfheimr, which was the equivalent of two and a half weeks here in the human world. Since summer break is over soon, Parker is having Rosie and I get a taste for our leadership training before we leave to spend the rest of summer vacation in Blue Cliff, visiting the rest of my family before college starts. I'm shadowing Lilly as Rosie shadows her father.

"I just got a mind link from the hospital. Julia is being released from rehabilitation earlier than expected by request, but her parents are an hour away, stuck in traffic. I need to go sort her discharge paperwork in her parents' place."

"Yeah, I'm sure I can handle it," I smiled, happy to hear that Rosie's friend was finally getting free. She completely healed, except for her leg. The infection from the siren bite was so bad they ended up having to amputate her legs after weeks of trying to save it.

Rosie and her dad kept the demented siren who kidnapped Julia alive until the fate of Julia's leg was decided. The day Julia's leg was amputated, Rosie had me force the siren to shift into his fins and tail, and then she slowly sliced off each individual scale, one by one, not letting him ever recover from the pain.

In our siren bodies, our scales are what helps us sense the magic in the waters, so they are really sensitive, unlike in fish. He was in agony. When every scale was gone and he was hanging like a limp fish, barely hanging on to his life, Rosie shifted and tore off the rest of his tail, then left him to bleed out all over the cell room floor. He was dead by the time Julia woke up from surgery.

It was vicious and a little unnerving seeing her do that, but when it was all over, and we were alone in our room, Rosie broke down crying in my arms, mourning for her friend's lost limb, blaming herself for not saving her faster.

My love for my adorable Alpha mate grows day by day. That was when I asked her if she was ready to go visit my parents and take a break from the stress of the pack. It took about a week to convince her father, but now we are back and she looked so relieved seeing how quickly Julia recovered from the amputation, and how high Julia's spirits were.

"This isn't a very important meeting. It was really just set up to tell this person face to face that we weren't a resort and didn't do events. She and her friends have been calling nonstop over the last few weeks trying to book an event. They're human, so you really just need to welcome them at the visitors' center and let them down so it sticks."

"They wouldn't take a 'no' over the phone?"

Lily sighed and rolled her eyes, gathering her purse to head out. "They wouldn't take a 'fuck off and quit calling' over the phone. They had been driving the secretaries crazy and Trevor had to schedule a formal meeting when one secretary gave the person a piece of their mind and it resulted in them asking for Parker. Say whatever you have to say to just get it through that this isn't a resort and we won't host a stinking event for anyone."

Jeez. I wonder what kind of even this person is trying to hold that they would get so aggressive with getting on pack lands. The pack is beautiful, but there seem to be many other beautiful places in Miami as well, and many event centers.

I hopped in Rosie's Tacoma. We're flying up to Blue Cliff next week and then driving my car back down so I can have it, but until then, I have been using Rosie's truck or one of the pack vehicles. She's riding around with her father, so she won't miss it.

The welcome center is the checkpoint to make sure all who are entering the pack are either members or allowed, like delivery drivers and the occasional taxi. It was a quick two-minute drive before I pulled into the parking lot, parking in the spot designated for 'PARKER SNIDER'.

I waved at the guards on the way inside, growing more familiar with them from mealtimes in the dining room and hanging out with Rosie. Just being her mate made the pack open up to me. I thought I would get some discrimination, but I haven't faced any.

"What can I do for you, Prince Rian?" Daryl, the lead guard, asked with a friendly smile.

"I'm here to fill in for an appointment for Lilly?" I looked around the waiting room, not seeing anyone there.

Daryl's smile turned into a sneer. "Good luck. The wench and her posy are in the meeting room at the end of the hall. I had to escort them back because they wouldn't stop taking pictures of our guards. If they were men, it would have been considered sexual assault, the way they were behaving."

"Yikes." I could feel his frustration. "Are they all women?"

"Every last thirsty one of them. I was actually hoping Luna Carli would be the one to handle this. You should probably give her a call. I wouldn't go in there alone."

I grimaced, knowing what he meant. Rosie wouldn't want me walking into a room full of flirty women on my own. No Alpha or she-wolf anywhere would be okay with their mate doing that.

I sent Carli a quick mind link, asking if she was busy.

"I'm two delicious bites into a jar full of pickles that I plan on chasing down with a bucket of fried chicken. Why? What do you need? I hope it's not one of my pickles, because I'm not sharing."

"No, I don't need pickles. I have a meeting at the visitor's center with a group of human women that have been persistently causing problems for the pack, including harassing the guards here. I don't want to walk into this room alone. Do you think you can come help me, so Rosie doesn't-"

"So Rosie doesn't break necks later?" Carli giggled. *"Don't hold me back from a good time. I'll be right there."*

There was something about her tone that set warning bells off in my head, but she closed the mind link before I could ask her what she was planning. My mother-in-law was always planning something, and it usually had to do with my 'groin gravy', as she calls it, impregnating her daughter. She is determined to have a grandchild. Her determination is impressive. I'll give her that.

"What is taking so long!" I turned at the sound of a bleached human woman with orange skin and eyelashes that curled to touch her eyebrows coming out of the meeting room down the hall storming towards the welcome desk. A few other women followed leisurely behind, giggling at one another as they gazed around at all the warriors standing guard. Most of the warriors turned their backs in annoyance, not wanting to give the humans the time of day.

"We have been waiting forever! When will we get to speak to a manager or someone?! I have an appointment."

"Ma'am," Daryl gave her a cold stare, "It has not even been five minutes. I asked you to wait patiently in that room and someone would be here soon. If you don't like that, you are welcome to leave."

"I don't know how you stay open with that rude attitude of yours," the girl crossed her arms, not giving in or turning to go back like she was asked.

"Like we told you several times already, this is not a resort. We are not open to the public and the only reason you are getting this meeting today is because you made a secretary have a nervous breakdown last week. Either get your asses back in that room and wait for someone else to give you the same speech, or fucking leave."

The woman scoffed, holding her hands to her chest in offense as the others gawked at Daryl for his frank speech.

"If you or anyone else could just tell me what this place is and let me talk to someone who is actually in charge, I'm sure we could get this all worked out. I can not wait to speak to your manager and let them know how you have spoken to me. You all should feel grateful that I even want to hold my wedding here."

Ah. It is a wedding she is trying to hold. Talk about a bridezilla.

Daryl looked ready to have an aneurysm. He was turning the same shade of red dad turns before he started bellowing loud enough to shake a building. I held my hand out to stop him, sending a current of magic through him to help him relax.

"Ladies," I put on my most charming smile, knowing that if Rosie saw me, she would have my ass later, but these women were going to cause one of the guards to turn if someone didn't deal with them. "I was actually sent from headquarters to speak with you. My name is Rian. I am one of the leading supervisors of Crystal Moon Enterprises. If you could all head on back to the meeting room, we can get started."

The blonde woman eyed me in a way that would make Rosie snarl, twirling her fried bleached hair around a finger while loudly smacking her chewing gum. I think she was trying to make herself look flirty and attractive, but she looked revolting. I was having a hard time not showing my revolution on my face.

"I'd follow you anywhere, big boy."

"Oh, goddess," Daryl muttered.

"Carli's on her way," I whispered to him.

"Let's hope she gets here fast."

I was barely in the room when the blonde woman decided to press her body up against mine from behind, muttering an "oops" as she slid past me and took the seat near the head of the table. She patted the seat next to hers like she wanted me to take it, but I pretended I didn't see her and stood back, waiting for the other women to file in. She pouted her plastic lips, but said nothing more.

There was a stool at one end of the room with a whiteboard behind it. I sat there instead of chancing being near any of the women and sitting at the table. I hope Carli drives like she usually does. I'm surprised she isn't here yet.

"So, ladies, like my friend out there was explaining to you all, we are not a resort and we do not lease any of our land or locations for any sorts of events. Never in our history have we done that and we are not about to do it now. I'm so sorry about your wedding planning, whoever the bride-to-be is." I looked around the room, surprised to see the brazen blonde woman shyly raising her hand. I instantly felt bad for her future husband. I coughed to hide my surprise. "Like I said, I'm sorry if you had your heart set on any of our lands for your wedding, but we are not in that business. You will have to search elsewhere."

"Um, that's not true!" the woman sitting next to the bride raised her hand. "I know for a fact that there are events here all the time. A friend of mine had a friend who attended a wedding here once, and she said it was the best wedding her friend had ever been to. I've also seen articles in the papers about the Mayor attending a meet and greet here a few months ago, and on my social feed, I found pictures of birthday parties and all kinds of social events taking place at some mansion you have on this property. I know our rights as consumers. I want the same opportunity as anyone else to have my friend host her wedding here. We already lost one reservation because of jealous bitches somewhere else. You have to let us at least look around your grounds so we can make a decision if this place will suit our needs."

I let out a huff of annoyance. I couldn't help it. The entitlement was strong with this group.

"Those events you are speaking of were done for people who work or live here. We have a, uh, community center of sorts that is only available to our workers and their families." I smiled tightly. "Since not one of you has family working for Crystal Moon Enterprises, I am going to have to ask you to leave and to quit harassing our staff. No matter what you do, the answer will not change."

The blonde woman and her friend exchanged a glance, then stood up from their chairs at almost the same time. They prowled towards me, batting their huge eyelashes.

"Are you sure there is nothing we can do?" The blonde ran her finger up my arm.

"We will do anything," the other said, pressing her spilling chest against my side.

I looked up towards the ceiling, praying that Carli would be here any second.

A ferocious snarl, poorly hidden by a loud cough, was the answer to that prayer. I looked over towards the door with a smile, expecting to see my mother-in-law, but instead, I saw my mother-in-law with my mate. My very pissed mate. My smile dropped at the look on Rosie's face.

"Look who we have here," Carli said, striding into the room with a cat-ate-the-canary grin. She had a jar of pickles tucked in one arm, and she was eating a pickle with her free hand. She looked way too amused by this situation. "Don't I know you from somewhere?" She pointed her pickle at the two women pressed up against me.

Both of them gasped, taking steps back and hurrying to grab their purses. "No. No. You don't know us. We have never seen you before. We were just leaving."

"I do know you!" Carli grinned, her mouth full of pickle. "You're that bridezilla bitch from the club. Oh wow. Small world. How's the wedding planning coming? I heard there was an issue with your reservation at the resort you had booked." Carli made a show of pouting her lips mockingly.

"Just our fucking luck," the friend said to the blonde.

The other girls that came with them looked frightened and started to file out of the room, giving my murderous mate a wide breadth. When the last two women, the bride and her friend, tried to leave, Rosie blocked their path, shouldering the friend who was pushing her chest up against me to the ground.

"If either of you ever touch my fucking fiance again, I'll help your fiance get out of the biggest mistake of his life."

Both girls whimpered, running on their clunky heels to follow their friends.

"Oh, that was fun," Carli laughed, taking another bite of her pickle. "It was so lucky that Rosie just happened to be at the warrior center with her father. My hands were so full with this pickle jar, I would have had a hard time driving. They gave me a ride." She smiled at me like she did me a favor. "I'll leave Rosie with you. I saw you had her car out front. Parker is probably still ranting about you taking his spot. I'm going to go cool my Alpha off. Good luck doing the same."

I should have known she was up to something. I was too stunned to even move off the stool. Carli was the answer to one problem, but then she just caused an even bigger one between me and my very possessive Alpha mate.

"Rosie, I was just-"

"Take it off," she sneered, not letting me finish what I was about to say.

"What?"

"Take it off," she nodded at my shirt. "It reeks of skank. Take. It. Off."

"Okay. Okay," I murmured, hurrying to pull my shirt over my head. "Look. It's off. All better, right?"

"Not even close," she said in a dangerously low voice. "Pants too."

I gaped at her. "Um, how about we go home first?"

"Pants. Too," she said through gritted teeth.

I rolled my eyes but followed what she said, kicking off my sandals and taking off my pants and tossing them on the ground with my shirt. I was left in just my boxers, and she was eyeing me like I was about to get eaten.

She strode towards me like a predator. She hooked her fingers in my boxers and pushed them down my thighs until they fell to the ground. I was now completely nude.

Rosie leaned in and whispered venomously in my ear, making shivers move all through my body. "You are going to fuck me in this room until I can no longer smell the stench of those skanks, and all I can smell is us. Is that clear?"

My dick jerked to life, ready for the challenge. Maybe Carli did me a favor after all. I hope for Daryl and everyone else's sake this room is soundproof. I am going to follow my Alpha's orders thoroughly for as long or as loud as it takes.

"Oh, that's clear as day, my Alpha," I cooed, pulling her towards me and tugging her hair to the side as my fingers skimmed over my imprint on her shoulder, making her cry softly in need.

"Get to it, my prince."

92

— • —

Bonus Chapter One

Rosie

Four Years Later....

"No!" Tammy screamed, clinging to Rian's neck. "Ry-Ry go with me."

My almost four-year-old sister was glaring daggers at me.

"I'm so sorry, guys," Grandma Elena said. "I thought the coast would be clear."

She gave Rian some cryptic look, but he just smiled gently. "We're a bit late. We had a swimsuit malfunction."

I rolled my eyes. We didn't have a swimsuit malfunction until he used his sneaky fairy magic to snap the strings of the bikini mom had just bought for me. When we mentioned our date planned for today at my birthday dinner last night, mom told me that the bikini would be perfect. Her added wink was very telling of what she thought it would be perfect for, but I liked her insinuation so I was set on wearing that swimsuit today.

Rian liked it, thinking it was lingerie, but when he realized I was planning on wearing the thong bikini bottoms out of the packhouse with only a sheer coverup on top of it, he protested like you wouldn't believe.

His possessiveness has only gotten worse over the years. He has no shame in showing it now. Probably because he knows it's such a turn on for me. Usually.

This was not one of those times, though. The magic-wielding punk snapped the sides of my bikini bottoms so I couldn't ever wear them again. When I started to throw my own hissy fit at my ruined bikini, he turned that magic on me, zapping my mark with pleasurable currents until I couldn't fight him anymore. He had me screaming in agreement to everything he said soon after, and now we're here in the lobby, two hours late for what was supposed to be a lunch date on the beach, my sassy and spoiled baby sister trying once again to steal my mate from me.

I couldn't help but laugh at myself. Tammy was adorable, but a handful. She always preferred Rian over almost everyone else, much to my dad's annoyance. When she fully comprehended that he was a prince, she declared him hers and attached herself to him when she could. Her princess complex was strong.

"Tammy princess. I go with Ry-Ry." She nuzzled her pouty face against his chest.

Rian mouthed 'I love her' at me, hugging her back tightly while Grandma Elena and I chuckled.

"Why don't we just take her with us?" I offered. It wasn't like she hadn't tagged along on dates before.

Rian and Grandma's smiles faltered.

"Well, uh, it's nap time and-" Grandma started to say.

"Your dad said he was going to take her to training and-" Rian said at the same time.

I narrowed my eyes suspiciously at their hurried, tangled words. I was about to ask them what was going on and why they both suddenly started acting sketchy, but then Reece jogged down the stairs, looking breathless like he ran as fast as he could from our parent's apartment.

"Tammy-girl! There you are!" he said excitedly, then bent over to catch his breath.

"Jeez, you puss. Are you winded from the stairs?" I asked.

"I was in a rush," he said, straightening back up. He smiled, still a bit breathless, and walked over to take Tammy from Rian. "There's my girl. I was looking for you."

Tammy hesitated to let go of Rian, but Reece was a close second in her book. "Buh-buh look for Tammy? Why?" she wrinkled her little nose untrustingly.

"It's time for our ice cream date!" he said dramatically.

"Ice cream?!" she squealed excitedly. "Tammy gets ice cream?"

"All the ice cream." Reece tickled her sides.

"Funny," I smirked, tossing my bag over my shoulder. "Grandma said it was time for her nap and Rian said she was going to train with dad." I leaned forward and bopped Tammy on the nose. She wrinkled it and puffed out her cheeks angrily. It just made me laugh more. "You're a busy little girl."

"I a princess," she stated grumpily. She then tucked her face into Reece's shoulder, dismissing me.

"Yes, you are," I sighed, feeling tired. I know I was never my sister's favorite, but her growing hostility towards me is starting to really wear me down. I know I'm not exactly nurturing or overly affectionate like Reece, Rian and my dad, but neither are Grandma and mom, but Tammy likes them just fine.

My mood was already a bit sour because of my ruined swimsuit. Now I'm worn out and losing interest in leaving our pack, wanting to go back to our bedroom. I kinda just want to go take a nap now.

"Maybe we should reschedule," I said to Rian, checking my watch. The beach was always busier in the afternoons, and I was not in the mood for people now.

"What?" Rian's expression dropped. "No. I planned.... I mean, we already planned to go."

"Yeah, honey," Grandma stepped in quickly to add. "You two should go."

"I got the little princess," Reece hurriedly said with a forced smile that didn't reach his tense eyes. "Go and have fun. I know Rian was looking forward to having you to himself today."

"He shouldn't have ruined my swimsuit then," I grumbled, smoothing my hand down the old coverup hiding my boring athletic swimwear.

"Baby, come on." Rian pulled my hand to tug me against him. "I really want to go out with you today. I'll stop and get you a new bathing suit. Let's just go."

There was a nervous energy and a type of desperation I had never felt before coming from him. His galaxy eyes were swirling and compelling me to give in. His touch as he strummed his thumb rhythmically over my skin was making me cave.

"Okay," I groaned. Almost unanimously, everyone breathed a sigh of relief. Everyone but Tammy, who was looking around at them like they were crazy. I was too.

"Off you two go," my grandma practically pushed us out the door. "Have fun!" I then heard her whisper in Rian's ear, "Good luck."

Goddess, was she wishing him luck in dealing with my bad mood? I didn't think it showed that bad.

True to his word, Rian stopped at a surf shop on the way to the harbor. I wasn't really in the mood for another bikini, but he was so encouraging that I ended up picking one at random, putting it on after he bought it at his urging. When I came out of the shop's restroom and he saw the cinched butt of the bottoms, he made that face again like he was about to declare that this was another outfit meant for his eyes only. He must have sensed the storm brewing in me because he kept his mouth shut. He couldn't resist walking right on my ass so no other guys could see me, not that anyone was looking, anyway.

The shop was filled with mostly tourist women who were too busy making goo goo eyes at him. I was not crowding him and covering his ass, which looked way too snug in his swim shorts. I swear, one girl even made biting motions with her mouth as Rian walked by, but nothing was said about that. Having a hot mate that doesn't notice how hot he is sometimes is a downer, especially when my ego has already been wounded by my own fun-sized sister and I can't assert my dominance in front of humans.

My mood was pretty foul after that. I stared at the window the rest of the drive, provided one-word responses and bland grunts to his attempts at conversation. He eventually gave up with a sigh and just traced magical patterns on my thigh with his free hand while I tried to ignore the sparks.

"So...." mom decided to randomly mind link me as we searched the packed parking lot for parking. *"How is the date?"*

"Just fucking peachy," I grumbled.

"Wow, what a grump. Did he not.... I mean, did the swimsuit not help?"

"He ruined it. He broke the fucking straps."

"With his teeth?"

I accidentally scoffed out loud, causing Rian to look over at me briefly with concern.

"No, with his magic," I answered my mom, feeling a little bad when I felt Rian's anxiety take a spike. *"I'll talk to you later, mom. We're having trouble finding parking."*

Mom sighed, *"Okay. Be kind, sweetie. There are healthier ways for a couple to handle pent-up aggression."*

"BYE, MOM!" I quickly closed the link before she could tell me to sit on Rian's face or something.

Rian circled the parking lot for the third time and cursed under his breath, still not finding a spot.

I closed my eyes, taking a few calming breaths to collect myself, then turned to finally face him, trying to suppress my sourness. "Rian, we can just try again next weekend. It's really okay. We're at the height of the tourist season. It's going to be a nightmare anywhere we try to go."

"No," he sounded frustrated. He gently threw his head back on the headrest. "I took so long to plan this. It needs to be today."

"What does?" I asked, turning completely and really studying his features. I felt how tense he was, but seeing it in him mixed with this worried anxiousness made all my sourness melt away. "It's okay, Rian. The beach and the ocean aren't going anywhere."

"No, but," he turned those swirling galaxies on me. "Rose, it has to be today. I really wanted to... to go on this date with you."

He held my gaze, imploring me with his eyes. All of the foul emotions inside of me started to ebb away with the power of those eyes the longer we sat in his idle car in the packed parking lot.

Movement caught the corner of my eye.

"Look, a spot," I said with a shy grin, pointing to a diesel truck backing out of a space. Rian quickly hurried to take the spot before someone else could, since we were not the only ones trying to find one. His smile when we beat a Cadillac SRX to it was infectious. "You won," I laughed softly.

He grinned, taking my hand in his and bringing it to his lips. "I win." He kissed my fingers on my left hand one by one, seemingly enamored with the task. His lips lingered on my pinky and ring finger for an extra few seconds before looking back up into my eyes, captivating me again.

"Will you still go on this date with me, Rosie? I won't force you. I know it's been a rough day so far, but I would really like it if you would."

His pleading, magical stare did me in. There was no way I could say no to him.

"It has to be today?" I giggled, repeating his words. I didn't know what he was getting at, but it didn't matter anymore. I just wanted to make him happy. My bad mood was already starting to fade completely.

93

Bonus Chapter Two

"Callum? Soph?" I said in surprise, seeing them at the dock at the end of the beach-side dock on one of Aumt Sim's speed boats. They have been in town all week visiting family and were even at my birthday dinner last night, but I didn't expect to see anyone we knew here.

"Took you long enough!" Sophia yelled, pushing herself off my cousin's lap. Her hair was tied up with her mate mark showing proudly in the sunlight, along with several hickies along her neck and collarbone.

Callum groaned, pushing his large body up from the bathing bed on the front dock. He had to situate himself, letting me know he and Soph were getting a little too carried away while out in public. People were already staring, but Callum and Soph didn't seem to care.

Rian chuckled low under his breath, guiding me along. "They're just our ride."

"Our ride?" I gave him a puzzled look. "I thought we were just having a picnic on the beach?"

"I never said what beach, did I?" he said teasingly.

All the people stared as Callum turned on the engine and meticulously weaved his way through the water around the other boats and then picked up speed in the open ocean when the coast was clear. Sophia sat on his lap as he steered the boat while Rian and I sat behind. The engine roaring and the sound of the water splitting around us defined any attempts at conversation, but I was content just relaxing in the sun while leaning into Rian's side. His fingers were laced in mine, and he kept strumming his pointer finger up and down my ring finger in a calming motion. His lips were teasing the sensitive flesh behind my ear, kissing my neck every once in a while.

I was really enjoying myself. I'm glad we still went out, and I didn't give in to my bad mood in the parking lot. I've been preparing to take over the pack from my dad in the next year or two, and the training has been stressing me out recently. Dad has been giving me more and more responsibility since Tammy was born, but now that I've graduated from university, I'm not just working in my free time. I'm working around the clock.

I knew it was a never-ending job being Alpha, but now that I'm stepping more into the role, it's become more apparent how much sanity my dad actually sacrifices to do his job. Getting calls at three in the morning to deal with heinous crimes that affected members of the pack or other supernaturals, and having to be the one that personally dealt with much of the aftermath, wears on you. Rian could probably see I needed time away. He's really the sweetest and best mate I could ever imagine. I shouldn't have gotten an attitude earlier about something so stupid as a fucking swimsuit.

"We're here," Callum yelled above the roar of the ocean and the engine. I sat up and looked over his shoulder to see a little island coming into view.

"Where is here?" I turned to ask Rian. He had a playful grin and just shrugged. I narrowed my eyes at him. "You planned this and you don't know?"

"I know," he laughed. "It just doesn't have a name. The fairies of Miami use it when they want to escape human eyes and be free."

My eyes lit up, realizing why he brought me here. "Does that mean....?"

He chuckled, kissing his imprint on my scarred shoulder, running his nose over the sensitive markings he left of our butterfly. "You want to go for a swim with me, my princess? A real swim?"

"Yes!" I said excitedly as Callum pulled the boat to the shore.

Rian jumped over first, then reached up and helped me down before I could do it myself. Sophia was jumping back and forth on the balls of her feet, looking at us excitedly. Callum gave her a coded look, then yelled, "We'll be back for you later," before they set off into the open water again. I swore he said 'good luck' to Rian as he revved up the engine.

Good luck with what? I know I wasn't acting grumpy on the boat.

"Ready?" Rian took my hand, pulling me towards the deserted beach.

I looked around, confused. "Ready for... Swimming?" I lifted my brow, wondering what else there was to be ready for.

"That, among other things," he smirked, lifting me by the hips and twirling me around in the water.

I screamed and laughed with him, then he took off running towards the center of the island. I chased him through the trees, until we came out on the other side, and then I froze. My mouth hung open at the things I saw set up on the soft sand. There was a white, two-person tent closer to the treeline, and a large blanket spread out and spiked to stay in place in front of it. Two wooden folding chairs with a table between them were set up to the side, and there was a yeti cooler nearby.

"When did you do all this?" I asked, lifting the lid to the cooler to see drinks and all kinds of different foods. There were even cans of spam and a small carton of eggs. It was way too much food for the both of us for a simple picnic.

"I had help," he grinned.

"Was this why everyone was acting all cryptic?"

His lips quirked up, and he shrugged, then lifted his shirt over his head. "I wanted to celebrate your birthday with just me and you. I know it's a day late, but this is a special day for me, too."

"Why?"

He just smiled, pushing off his shorts and throwing them in my face. "Catch me and I'll tell you."

I gawked at his naked body, then tossed his shorts to the ground and took off after him, pulling my cover-up off as I went. He dove into the waves before I could reach him, and I drove in after, opening my eyes in time to see his magic overcome him and his body shifting into his siren form.

The sunlight beaming through the water illuminated his glittering power wrapping around his muscular body. Seeing his legs take the shape of his tail and the fins protrude on his arms always takes me back. He was as majestic as ever, his scales taking on a gold-ish tint as evidence of his title as heir.

Rian caught me gawking at him, holding my breath as I tried to stay under as long as possible. His grin was sinful. With a powerful thrust of his tail, he was sailing through the water towards me. He circled his arms around my waist and brought me up to the surface so I could get much needed air while clinging to him.

I brushed the wet hair out of my face and smiled lustfully at him. "You're so sexy in the water."

"Uh, I'm so sexy to you all the time," he reminded me, giving my ass a tight squeeze.

"I like you best when you're wet," I said teasingly.

"Oh yeah? Me too." He moved his fingers to the inside of my bottoms and skimmed them over my folds. I bit my lip and hissed, tightening my legs around his waist. "Mmh, you're already wet for me."

"It's just ocean water," I lied.

He grinned, moving his fingers just inside of me before taking them back out and bringing them to his lips. He sucked on his fingertips. "Ocean water isn't this sweet."

"Are you sure?" I leaned forward and sucked his two fingers into my mouth, teasing and twirling my tongue around them. I could still faintly taste myself, but I wasn't giving in just yet. "Maybe you should double check?"

His galaxy eyes started swirling, his lips full and tempting. He held my gaze as he slowly sank back into the water, his hands pulling my bottoms down too. Sparks were shooting all throughout my limbs, concentrating at my center as it was exposed to the elements.

When his mouth connected with my sex, I cried out, my legs squeezing around his neck. His hands were keeping my body upright in the water as my back arched and I flailed about. He was sucking and teasing me, making me scream as my legs shook. When his tongue dove inside of me, curling up and flexing against my walls, I was done for. I was drawing in a powerful orgasm, screaming for the dolphins and fishes, and whatever else might be out here in the void ocean.

Shivers were still traveling down my limp legs as his tongue traced my lips, devouring everything leaking out of me. I eventually went limp, fully trusting my siren prince mate to keep me from drowning.

I could feel his chuckles in my head. The water was moving around me, but I kept my eyes closed, soaking in every lingering sensation while he continued to massage me with his tongue. It wasn't until I felt the soft sand of the beach that I finally opened my eyes. He was staring up at me with a cocky smile on his face.

"I'm still not sure it was ocean water," he said before running his tongue over my clit, making my back arch. "I may need to check one more time."

94

Bonus Chapter Three

After Rian checked one more time, then let me have a taste on his lips as he made love to me in the sand, we were both hungry for more than sex and finally got to that picnic. Rian had chicken caesar wraps in the cooler and cut up fruit. I laid naked in his lap as he fed me pineapple and grapes.

He had planned for us to stay overnight. That's why there was such a large cooler stocked with so much food.

"Did you bring a stove to cook that spam and eggs with?" I asked teasingly, looking around for a place to build a fire pit. "You brought everything else."

"I'm the only fire you need," he smirked, snapping his fingers and making greenish sparks fly.

"Aren't you capable?" I grinned, turning and crawling up to straddle his lap. He leaned back on his hands, welcoming me with one of his panty-dropping cocky smiles and those swirling galaxy eyes.

"I'm very capable," he husked, bucking his hips.

"Show me," I whispered, reaching for a grape and placing it between my lips. He leaned forward and stole it, biting down so the juices burst into my mouth. I watched his mouth as he chewed, then moaned when he licked the juice from his lips.

"Gladly," he whispered.

Eyes shone with his royal magic, the green and gold sparks lighting up his face. I screamed out when my imprint tingled, and I felt the tingles all the way to my core. He didn't lift a finger, still leaning back on his hands, but I could feel him there all the same. It felt like he was touching me, but his magic had me pinned in place, straddling his lap.

His breath caught, and his magic lifted me, just enough to give him enough room and the right angle to thrust into me, not leaving that to his magic. I screamed, feeling so full because of him, and then the kiss of his power brushing all the most sensitive places on the rest of my body. I could do nothing but hang on as he played me, using me and his magic to get us both off. I was just coming down from my fourth orgasm since we arrived when he started to shoot himself deep inside of me.

I collapsed on his chest, worn out and fully satisfied, full in every way.

"How's that for capable?" He chuckled, holding me and brushing the sweaty hair from my face.

"Fuck, you're amazing," I croaked, my voice hoarse and dry. He's had me screaming all stinking day. I think Rian has a slightly sadistic side. He's way more dominant in the bedroom than anywhere else. He's sweet as can be out in public, and the definition of a gentleman, but all gentlemanly behavior goes out the window when we are alone.

"I'm glad you think so," he said roughly, kissing the top of my head. "Because you're mine forever."

"Forever sounds good to me," I said lazily, content and ready for a nap.

After a very short power nap, Rian and I went back into the water, swimming and exploring the most magical parts. He's able to use magic to keep a bubble of air around me, so I rarely have to break the surface. While he is showing me the natural wonders of the ocean world he loves, I'm just watching him, amazed that just an amazing man is my mate. Sometimes it just hits me hard that I have absolutely the luckiest woman alive. I wouldn't trade anything for this man.

After we exhausted the sea with our exploration, we swam back to the island just as the sun was setting. The spam and eggs were our dinner, cooked over a small fire we built in the sand thanks to my capable mate and his magical sparking fingers.

It was the perfect ending to what I thought would be a horrible day. I was so happy that my previous bad mood didn't put a lasting damper on us. I don't think I have ever been on a more perfect date ever, and that is saying a lot considering who my mate is.

Laying naked in the sand, full of spam and my love for him, I relaxed into his arms as he held me, watching the sun setting over the direction Miami must be. The moon was soon the only light in the sky, full and powerful, illuminating the ocean and making it look as magical above as it was below. The glittering waves were gentle, lulling me into a blissful stupor.

"I love you, Rian. Thank you for making this such a perfect day."

He smiled and kissed the tip of my nose. "I love you too, Rose. And the day isn't quite over yet."

"It's not?" I asked, staring up at him with confusion.

His eyes swirled, his royal magic stirring. He lifted a hand, opening a small portal right in front of us, and then suddenly thousands of our magical glowing butterflies filtered through.

I sat up and gasped, laughing as the feather-soft wings tickled my skin. The butterflies were circling around us, landing all over me before taking back off in flight. At one point, I was covered in the beautiful tiny creatures, and then they all lifted in the air, mixing in a dancing circle above our heads, like they were wishing us goodbye before disappearing back into the portal, heading back to the fairy kingdom.

"That was.... That was unbelievable, Rian! How did you get them to come like that?!"

"I may have had some help," he grinned, lifting his hand and closing the portal back up. I swear I saw a glimpse of his mother on the other side, but I couldn't be sure.

My skin still held the sensation of the butterflies' magic. I looked at my right hand, amazed at the glittering residue left by them. I then looked to my left, following their glitter trail on my body, but then my eyes knit in confusion when I saw something else glittering on my left hand. I thought maybe one butterfly, a smaller one that couldn't have been bigger than my pinky nail, was straggling behind its brothers and sisters. I wiggled my fingers and noticed something hard between them. There was something stuck around my ring finger.

Bringing that finger to my face, that's when it hit me what it really was. My eyes went wide, and I gasped in surprise and excitement.

"This is a ring!" I exclaimed, studying the gorgeous butterfly-shaped stone. It was the color of the ocean, maybe a bit lighter. It shone and glittered in the moonlight and the band had diamonds inlaid all around it. "You got me a ring?!"

Rian smiled crookedly, holding my gaze for a few seconds until it clicked in my head what finger it was on, and what that usually meant. Then, my mouth dropped.

"Rian..... Rian, is this....?"

He laughed, then stood up, pulling me up with him. He held both of my hands in his, running his thumb over the ring a few times before he dropped on one knee. That was when I got so excited, I had to press my lips together to keep from screaming from my excitement. My eyes were already filled with happy tears, my heart hammering in my chest. Just when I thought this day couldn't get any better.

"Rosie," Rian husked, his voice thick with emotions. "My Rosie. My princess, my Alpha, my future queen, will you please do me the everlasting honor of taking on one more title and becoming my wife?"

"YES!" I burst out, falling down against him, my tears sticky and flowing from my face. My cheeks were painful from my stretching smile, and I knew without a doubt that this was the best moment of my life. "Yes, Rian! Yes!"

He laughed, holding me close, his arms wrapping around my shoulders and he buried his face in my neck. I could feel his smile against my skin and feel the moisture from his own happy tears.

When he pulled back to stare at me, I grabbed his face and kissed him deeply, my emotions wanting to bleed into him so he could taste how truly happy I was.

"I love my ring!" I said, putting my hand between us to look at it. "The stone looks like the one from my necklace. The one you got me for my eighteenth birthday."

He choked on a laugh, then nodded. "It is that stone," he said. "It was broken, so I had this made from the pieces."

My jaw dropped again. I thought I had lost that necklace forever. I had no idea Rian had kept it all these years.

He laughed at my expression, then crawled two feet to the tent to dig in his bag for something. When he found it, he sat back in front of me and handed me the box.

Inside, there were another two rings. One was a thin silver band with the jewels inlaid all around its center. The large one matched, only it was thick and obviously made for a man.

"The stone broke in two. I tried to have it fixed, but it was impossible. I couldn't throw it away though, so I had these made instead. It had to be fixed in the strongest metal to make sure it wouldn't break again, and now the stones are stronger than anything in this world." He grabbed my left hand and gently kissed the ring. "I thought I lost you forever when I found the necklace and the stone broken in half. Like this stone, I think we both had to break and be tempered to grow stronger together."

A fresh tear slipped from the corner of my eye. I rested my hand on the side of Rian's handsome, perfect face, then kissed him one more time.

"I am so in love with you, my fairy prince."

95

ABOUT THE AUTHOR

C helsie is an author based out of the southern United States. She lives with her two awesome teenagers that refer to her as "bro", her very supportive husband, and enough animals to start a small zoo. She loves the sand and surf. Her passions outside of writing include traveling, fitness and enjoying nature.

To find out more about the author and her other works, visit www.chazlewoodauth or.com

www.ingramcontent.com/pod-product-compliance
Lightning Source LLC
Chambersburg PA
CBHW050914030726
47503CB00007BB/2287